Jax's Dilemma

AN INSURGENTS MC ROMANCE

Chiah Wilder

I love hearing from my readers. You can email me at chiahwilder@gmail.com.

Sign up for my newsletter to receive updates on new books, special sales, free short stories, and ARC opportunities at http://eepurl.com/bACCL1.

Visit me on facebook: facebook.com/Chiah-Wilder-1625397261063989

Description

Jax, Sergeant-At-Arms of the Insurgents Motorcycle Club, likes his women easy.

Raised in the outlaw biker world, Jax has bedded more women than he can count. The only things on his mind are big ass Harleys, scorching whiskey, and pretty women who can spread on command.

Then he meets Cherri—the stripper with ice blue eyes and white-blonde hair.

He wants her in his bed.

She would rather not.

Cherri has complicated stamped all over her. Jax doesn't need a woman like her messing up his life.

Too bad he can't stop thinking about her.

Cherri ran away from a bad situation back home.

She has secrets she hasn't shared with anyone. Stripping is her means of making enough money to start a new life, and nothing's going to screw up her plans.

Then she meets Jax.

He's gorgeous, sexy, and a cocky bastard. His tattooed, ripped chest and biceps make her drool. She knows she should run far away from him, but her body wants him in the worst way.

Just as she begins to relax, her past collides with her new life. Cherri must navigate a deadly obstacle course littered with outlaw motorcycle clubs and a power-hungry politician.

Jax won't stop until he claims Cherri. He vows to protect and love Cherri no matter what. When put to the test, will Jax betray his family—the Insurgents MC—or will he lose the woman he loves forever?

The Insurgents MC series are standalone romance novels. This is Jax and Cherri's love story. This book contains violence, strong language, and steamy sexual scenes. HEA. No cliffhangers! The book is intended for readers over the age of 18.

Titles in the Series:

PROLOGUE

THE SCORCHING SUN bored into Cherri's skin as she lay among the wildflowers. Vibrant blues, purples, yellows, and pinks carpeted the verdant field. Evergreens stood tall on the mountain range as a gurgling creek lulled her to a state of peacefulness. She could almost feel goosebumps on her forearms as a light breeze caressed her.

"Fuck, that feels good, hon."

The raspy, male voice brought Cherri back to reality, and she looked at the thirty-something man grunting and sweating as he thrust his dick in and out of her. She stared at the peeling paint in the corner of the ceiling. If only the jerk wouldn't have opened his mouth, she would've been able to stay in her safe place.

"Fuck, you feel good," he said as he squeezed her small breasts too hard. Putting his mouth over her pink nipples, he sucked them like a vacuum.

Fuck, when is this tool going to come? Cherri tried hard to get back to her safe place, but she couldn't; her valley of wildflowers and sunshine was gone, retreating to the far corners of her mind until the next time she needed a haven.

She had created her safe place when she was fourteen years old and her life had turned to shit. It kept her sane until she split three years later to make her own way.

Finally, at the age of eighteen, her wildflower valley made the sex tolerable, especially with old men like the one who kept pawing her and pushing his lame dick into her. At least she'd get five hundred dollars for this trick. Even though she normally didn't turn tricks, this guy was different—or so Brandon, the bartender at the gentlemen's club where she danced, told her. The guy was rich and someone important. A councilman, she thought. The money was too good to pass up, so she agreed to be with him. She just wished he'd finish already; she wanted to go back to her apartment and take a long shower to wash off his stench.

"Are you getting close to coming?" He squeezed her breasts again.

"Huh…? Oh, yeah, sure, baby. You make me feel real good. I'm coming now." Putting on one of her better performances, Cherri writhed and screamed as she bucked under him.

"I'm coming now, too," he grunted. He stiffened, exhaled, and collapsed beside her.

It's about fuckin' time. Turning her head toward the window, she could see the blue sky. Tightness covered her chest while her throat grew thick. She wondered if being a whore was her destiny. Saltiness stung her eyes as she squeezed them shut, willing herself to be anywhere but in that mediocre motel room with the tobacco-stained curtains and the peeling paint.

A swat on her butt made her turn her head toward her paying lover. He leaned in close; his sweat was pungent. He kissed her deeply, his tongue thick and wet in her mouth, making her want to gag.

"That was awesome, hon. You and I are going to be regulars. I like the way you make me feel. I know you liked it." Running his eyes over her, he lingered on her young breasts. Wiping his brow with his fingers, he said, "I can be a real generous man. You think you'd like to be my permanent girlfriend? I can set you up real good."

Could I stand him pawing at me all the time? "Would we live together?"

"I'd love that, but no, we'd have to be discreet. You know, with my political position and all. I'd set you up in a nice apartment. I'll use untraceable funds. I'd come see you a few times a week. We may be able to sneak away once in a while for a weekend trip or so, but, for now, we'd have to stay in. I'll give you an expense account, of course."

"So, I couldn't see you every day?"

Dragging her closer to him, he smiled. "I know that's a disappointment, hon, but I'll make every minute count when I come over. Oh, I won't be spending the night, either. I have to stay under the radar, you know? Once things calm down after the election, we can see each other more. What do you say?"

Inside, her body sang for joy. Did this two-bit politician think she *wanted* to be with him all the time? *What an ego he must have.*

"Oh, and I have one condition: you have to quit your job at the bar. You won't need to strip anymore. I'll make sure you're well taken care of, if you make sure I am. You know what I mean?" Winking at her, he leered and twisted her breast.

Wincing at the force of his touch, Cherri nodded. What did she have to lose? Not having to strip for a bunch of sweaty, lecherous men was a dream come true. The possibility of moving out of her roach-infested shithole made her giddy. For once, she'd be in a nice, safe place and wouldn't have to worry all the time about being evicted or attacked. Plus, the proposition sounded a hell of a lot better than the shit life she currently had. Maybe she'd finally be able to save enough money so she could get out of Denver and go somewhere quiet and respectable, pretending her past never existed.

"Sure, why not?"

He hugged her while he rubbed her dry slit. "You're making me horny again, hon."

As he groped her body, Cherri sighed, fixing her eyes on the ceiling.

CHAPTER ONE

Three years later
Pinewood Springs, Colorado

"CHERRI, I NEED your ass out there waiting tables. Miranda called in sick and we're short tonight," Emma, the club manager, said.

"What about my dance set?"

"I switched you to the last slot. You'll be on in about two hours. You're the only one who's worth shit around here. You can dance *and* waitress. One of your tables will be the Insurgents."

Cherri's stomach lurched. "Can't Liza take it? She likes catering to them."

"They asked for you, and since they're paying your salary and own the club, you fuckin' do what they ask. Go on, now. Get your ass out there, and be sure to wiggle it so you can get some big tips."

Cherri peeked out from behind the curtains to take in the room. Yep, there he was, sitting at the front table, his jean-clad legs straddling the chair backwards. He wore a black vest with patches all over it; the left top side had a diamond-shaped, 1% er patch, while the right side had one which read Sergeant-At-Arms and underneath it, his name: *Jax.* Tight across his muscular chest, his black t-shirt showed off his well-defined pecs and abs. His sandy brown hair was longer on the top and shorter on the sides, and pierced eyebrows framed his hazel eyes. A full sleeve of tattoos decorated his right arm while his other bore various designs of skulls and daggers. He was handsome in a rugged way, his five o'clock shadow giving his face a hard edge.

Staring intently at one of the dancers spreading her legs and running her red-tipped fingers over her slit, he leaned forward, his bulging biceps moving with him.

"Come on, Cherri. Get a move on! We got a full house," Emma barked from behind her. Shutting the curtains, Cherri ran to her dressing room, threw on a turquoise t-shirt and a short skirt over her thong, and rushed out to the bar area.

Dream House was utter chaos that night, and she knew her feet would be blistered and sore from standing on her four-inch heels for too long. Even though she was aware she should be grateful to be alive and at the strip club, she was sick of everything. When she had learned she was primed to be the Mountainside Strangler's next victim and had narrowly escaped torture and death, she shuddered. If the Insurgents hadn't come to the Deadly Demons' clubhouse a couple of months before rescuing her, she'd be six feet under.

Choosing to work at Dream House hadn't turned out so bad, and it was a lot better than waitressing at one of the Insurgents' restaurants. She knew the MC wanted to keep her close because she knew a bit too much about what happened that early November morning at the Nomads' clubhouse. What the MC didn't get was she was happier than hell they had eliminated the pieces of shit who'd enslaved her. She'd never squeal, not in a hundred years, but these outlaw bikers didn't trust her, so there she was, shaking her ass once again at another strip club.

When she came up to the Insurgents' table, her stomach felt queasy. The guys always made her go into panic mode, never knowing when one of them might touch her or, worse yet, force himself on her. So far, they'd contented themselves with just looking and making lewd comments, but she saw the way they fucked the club whores. It was like the whole club, including the women, just wanted to fuck all the time. It was disgusting.

"Come on over here, sweetness," Jax said, looking at her with lust in his eyes.

She had avoided going over to his side, preferring to stand next to Chas and Axe, who were engrossed in watching the dancer play with her big tits.

"What do you want to drink?" she asked.

"I said to come on over by me. Now," Jax growled, his boyish grin gone.

Cherri walked over to him, and he squeezed her butt through her skirt. She flinched. He laughed. "Why so jumpy, sweetness? You got a soft ass that is way too tempting." He slipped his hand under her skirt, pinching her cheeks.

"Don't do that! You don't have the right to touch me."

Anger flashed in his eyes. "Yeah, I do. Fuck, we own you. You're Insurgents property, and I can do whatever the fuck I want." He pulled her toward him.

"No one owns me. Do you get off on forcing yourself on women?"

Jax clenched his jaw and narrowed his eyes into slits. "Don't *ever* fucking say that to me again. I don't have to force any bitch, got it?"

"Then leave me alone." Cherri knew she should keep her mouth shut, but she couldn't. For the past two months she had been with the Insurgents, Jax had been sniffing around her. She had to admit he was good-looking and sexy, but she had no interest in any man. Men wanted a woman for fucking, nothing more. She was *so* not into that. If she had to fuck, she expected to get paid well for it.

She knew Jax wanted into her pants real bad; he made it clear every time he looked at her with his desire-filled eyes. Whenever she was in the clubhouse or at the strip bar, he'd take every opportunity to brush against her, rubbing his firm chest against her small breasts. She hated the way her body would feel all funny, like a million butterflies were flying around inside her, when their bodies touched in passing. She didn't need the guy complicating her life, needing to stay focused on her goal of leaving the club and making a better life for herself. Jax was turning out to be a distracting nuisance.

Jax raked his gaze over her body, his hands in his lap. He threw her a half-grin. "Bring me a shot of Jack and a Corona, sweetness."

She nodded, took the other members' orders, and went to the bar. Returning with the drinks, she placed them in front of the bikers.

Leaning across the table to give Jax his, she realized too late he had a full-frontal view of her breasts. Hearing his sharp intake of breath, her cheeks flushed as her blue eyes locked with his for a heartbeat. Turning away, she busied herself with the other tables. She didn't like the intensity, the spark of connection that coursed through her body when their eyes met.

For the next hour, Cherri ran her ass off waiting tables, clearing glasses, and fending off advances from many of the patrons while trying her best to avoid getting any closer than necessary to Jax. When she came back to the Insurgents' table to bring more drinks, he didn't call her over to his side anymore. She was grateful, even though his eyes bored a hole into her each and every time she placed drinks in front of the bikers. It was downright unnerving.

As she stood by the bar waiting for her newest drink order, she felt a hand on her shoulder. Glancing sideways, she saw Emma.

"Cherri, go ahead and get ready for your dance set. I can take over from here," Emma said.

Cherri ran to the dressing rooms in the back of the bar, trying not to fall as she dodged the boxes of liquor and napkins littering the floor behind the stage curtains. Freshening her makeup, she teased and sprayed her shoulder-length, white-blonde hair. Her eyeliner and eye shadow made her blue eyes look like two ice cubes surrounded by black smoke. Cursing when her sheer thong sported a run, she replaced it with a silver-colored one, breathing heavily as she tried to get herself together before she was announced. After dusting iridescent glitter over her body, she pulled on a pink, metallic short skirt, her heart-shaped ass peeking out from underneath it. The matching halter top fitted tightly over her small, round breasts. She slipped on her five-inch Lucite pumps, checked herself out in the full-length mirror, and waited for her cue to take the stage.

The stage was a decent size, not as big as some of the other strip clubs she had danced for. There were two poles on each side of the stage and a stainless-steel chair in the middle. Sometimes Cherri would use the pole, sometimes the chair, but mostly she liked to dance the old-fashioned way—no props or gimmicks, just relying on the rhythm of her body.

The lights dimmed, and the mist from the fog machine created a web around her and the stage. Throwing her head back, her long hair touched the top of her skirt. The clear, crystal-jeweled barbell dangling from her belly button caught the light, glimmering like chunks of diamonds. Buckcherry's song, "Crazy Bitch," filled the bar as Cherri moved her hips while licking her full lips. She strutted around the stage, thrusting out her ass and pressing her breasts together. Lowering herself to the floor, she began a series of movements she was sure would make any man's cock hard.

As she rolled her head in circles, her hair brushing against the floor, she saw all eyes on her. Some of the guys in the front row had their hands on their dicks as they watched her crawl forward and, leaning in to them, she almost touched her forehead to some of theirs. As she inched forward, her breasts bounced, spilling out of the confines of her halter. Straightening out, she rocked back on her knees, her glittering thong peeping out as she played with her breasts.

When she threw her head forward, she looked straight at Jax. He stared at her, his face tight, hands on the table. Even from where she was, she saw hunger in his eyes. Placing a finger in her mouth, she sucked it, dragging it out as her other hand grabbed her sex. Smiling seductively at him, she unhooked her halter and let her high, rounded breasts free. She liked teasing him, and on stage she felt safe; he could look, but not touch. From the way he stared at her, his eyes crazed with desire, bulge aching to break free, she knew he wanted her. That was what she loved; the power she held over men with her body. When men were wild with lust, they'd do anything to stick their dick in her. That was where she had the control, and no one could take it from her. Amid all the shit she had in her life, knowing she had *some* power, *some* control, made her feel stronger.

Cherri looped her fingers around the waistband of her skirt, pushing downward as she shimmied out of it. When she stood upright once more, the mist swirled around her, the lights glimmered, covering her like a shroud, and the glitter makeup on her body sparkled. Stroking her covered slit with her pink-tipped nails, she licked her lips as she spread her legs wide. Turning around, she bent over, looking at the entranced spectators between her legs. It was at that moment she watched Jax blow a kiss to her; a simple gesture which made her stomach flip-flop. The stage lights went out, and the audience applauded and cheered.

She exited the stage and went to her dressing room to get her robe. As she massaged her sore feet, she heard a shuffling sound behind her. Turning around, she saw Jax standing in the doorway, his eyes glinting with arousal.

"You outdid yourself tonight, sweetness," he drawled.

"Got to pay the bills, you know?" She didn't like him being there, in her space, so close to her. It made her uncomfortable, causing her heart to race, her temples to throb. She didn't know why she had such a reaction to him; she never felt anything in a man's presence except disgust. It was something about this biker that threw her off-kilter, made her think of her childhood dreams of happily-ever-after before they became distorted. Cherri snorted, shaking her head to dispel her foolish thoughts.

Jax came up to her, his hands on her shoulders, pulling her close to him.

"What the fuck are you doing? I'm wiped out and want to get home. I don't have time to fend you off, got it?"

"Shh, calm down, little one. You're always fighting, trying to be so tough. Just relax and let things take us where they will." He cupped her chin and brought his lips down on hers. It was a gentle kiss, like a brushstroke on canvas, and his tongue skimmed over her mouth. Cherri instinctively leaned in closer to him, her mouth pliant under his. "You've got such kissable lips, sweetness," he murmured against her mouth.

Counter to her reason, her body responded, but when he brought his hand up toward her breast, she shut down. She was no longer Cherri, exotic dancer at Dream House—she was a frightened young teen hiding under the stairs of her home. She jerked away from Jax, pushing him back. "I told you I'm tired. I gotta go. Stop fuckin' groping me."

Looking surprised, he said, "What just happened? A couple of seconds ago, you loved it, and now you turned into a frigid bitch. What the fuck?"

Her ice-blue eyes flashed with anger. "Why don't you leave me alone? What the fuck is your problem? I'm not interested in you or *any* man. I have to do this shit for now, but my job description doesn't include having one of the owners handle me. There are plenty of whores around here who'd love to suck your dick. Go to them and leave me the fuck alone."

"That shit you were doing on stage was meant for me. If you don't want the attention, then don't be such a cock tease. And watch your fuckin' mouth when you talk to me. I don't like bitches thinking they can say whatever the fuck they want."

"Well, I don't like assholes thinking they can paw me whenever the fuck they want, so I guess we're even, aren't we?"

Rage filled his eyes as he pitched toward her. She ducked out of his grasp, scooped up her clothes from the floor, and locked herself in the bathroom. The door vibrated as he slammed his fist on it, making the wood groan under the force of his strength.

"Your ass better *stay* in there. You fuckin' need to learn respect, bitch!"

"Give *me* respect and I'll give it to *you*," she replied as she put on her clothes.

Cherri waited for about twenty minutes, not sure if he was still outside the door. Weary to the bone, she decided she'd have to deal with him if he were still there since she couldn't spend the night in the bathroom. Opening the door, she peered out, seeing no one. Breathing a sigh of relief, she threw on her jacket, slung her tote and purse over her shoulder, and rushed out the back door.

Outside in the parking lot, the frosty air made her feel alive as it stung her cheeks. The haziness of the night transformed the moon into a blurry orb hanging in the dark sky. While driving to the apartment she shared with two of the other dancers, she replayed the encounter with Jax in her mind. His gentle kiss made her feel mushy and funny inside—funny in a good way—but then he had to go and start his grabbing shit, just like all the men she had ever known. It was like they all wanted a piece of her to devour until she had nothing left of herself. *Why do men have to be such assholes all the time?*

Once she entered her apartment, Cherri went straight to her bedroom, threw her purse on the floor, stripped off her clothes, and flopped on her bed, too tired to take off her makeup. A few minutes later, she was sound asleep.

CHAPTER TWO

DECIDING CHERRI WAS going to plant herself all night in the bathroom, Jax bashed his fist against the wall, leaving the club through the back door, all the while cursing under his breath.

The bitch messed with his head *and* his dick. Ever since her ass came to the Insurgents' clubhouse, his cock had been hard, and he couldn't get her out of his mind. She had the most beautiful face he had ever seen, with high cheekbones and porcelain skin framed by her long, layered, white-blonde hair. Her almond-shaped eyes changed between various hues of blue, depending on her mood. Those full, pouty lips were so fucking kissable, and he kept imagining them around his cock, sucking the shit out of it. Most of his biker brothers liked women with big tits, but he loved small, rounded ones, just like Cherri's. He got a hard-on just thinking of sucking and biting her pretty nipples. And damn, her sweet, heart-shaped ass invaded his thoughts way too much. *Fuck, I have it bad for this one.*

He sensed a vulnerability about her. Maybe it was because of her small stature, he wasn't sure, but one thing he was sure of was he needed his cock in her pussy real bad. He couldn't understand why she resisted him so much. Most women came on to him, and the ones *he* came onto always ended up in his bed. This one was not so easy, and it frustrated the hell out of him. He liked easy pussy, and Cherri was driving him crazy.

"Are you heading back?" Chas asked as he took a hit on his roach before offering it to Jax.

Inhaling, Jax nodded.

Walking toward his bike, Chas said, "Then we can ride back together."

They each straddled their Harleys, peeling out of the parking lot and heading toward the Insurgents' clubhouse.

SATURDAY NIGHTS WERE crazy at the compound. The members loved to party, and the booze and pussy flowed freely at the parties all the time. The club whores and hoodrats loved servicing the bikers, and each weekend, women in skimpy outfits lined up to get into the compound, leaving their inhibitions outside the chain-link fence that surrounded the club.

As Jax and Chas walked across the parking lot, the frosty breeze wafted the sweet scent of weed from the clubhouse. Jax, at six foot two, and Chas, at six foot one, made an imposing duo. Sporting tight jeans and black t-shirts with their cuts, they entered the room and headed to the bar to knock down a few shots of Jack.

"Thought you'd be bangin' the shit outta that icy blonde at Dream House," Chas said before throwing his shot down his throat.

"You mean Cherri? Nah, she's a bitch."

"Could've fooled me. Every time you see her, your dick gets hard." Chas chuckled.

"Why the fuck are you looking?" Jax joked as he punched Chas in the arm. "Anyway, she's just another stripper. Who the fuck cares?"

"You haven't missed one of her numbers since she's been at Dream House."

Jax was getting pissed. "When did this become your fuckin' business?"

"Just sayin'. She's got a pretty ass, but her tits are too small."

Jax grunted as the heat from his anger spread throughout his body. If Chas didn't shut the fuck up, he was going to have to kick his ass good. Luckily, a short brunette with big tits came over to Chas and started rubbing his thighs. Turning toward her, Chas pulled her between his legs.

Jax turned around to survey the room and spotted a few members from some of the charter clubs he hadn't seen in a long time. Most of the brothers were either fucking one or two sluts or playing pool. He looked around for his favorite club whore, Rosie. He *so* wanted to get laid. He had hoped his sweet Cherri would have been up to the task, but she was turning out to be a pain in his ass, so he decided he'd fuck his brains out with Rosie instead.

Finding her by the worn-out green couch in the corner of the room, he noticed she had her short skirt hiked high around her waist, her ass in the air, face twisted with desire. One of the brothers, Throttle, had his dick in her pussy as he banged away. A bitter smile whispered across Jax's lips as he shook his head. He liked fucking Rosie—she was a firecracker in bed, and her mouth did amazing things to a man's cock. She used to be a hoodrat who hung around on the weekends before deciding to become a club whore. After making sure she was who she said she was, she became property of the Insurgents and earned the club's protection and a place to sleep upstairs, in the attic. Lola bitched about having another club whore around, but that slut would bitch about anything. Since Rosie was new, she was very popular, and Jax knew that pissed the hell out of Lola.

He wanted her, but she was too busy servicing Throttle and it looked like Axe was next in line. *Fuck, I really need to get laid.* Looking around at the half-naked women in the room, his eyes landed on one of the dancers from Dream House. As a rule, the dancers stripped and nothing more. The women didn't come to the clubhouse or club parties unless they wanted to; then they came as club girls and were available for servicing all the men, all night long. Insurgents never forced women to have sex—that wasn't their style, and they didn't allow any of that shit to happen at their club. Sometimes, when charter clubs or other biker guests came to party, things got out of hand and a few rough and drunk guys would force themselves on the women. If the Insurgents knew about it or found out about it, though, the guy would be banned from coming to any more parties at the clubhouse.

Peaches, a cute blonde with brown eyes, had a firm ass and muscular legs. Her tits were a little too big for Jax's liking, but he was horny as hell and he thought Peaches, in her tight spandex skirt and neon blue tube top, would do nicely.

After pushing himself from the bar, he swaggered over to her. He saw her watch him from the corner of her eye, pretending she didn't see him. Putting his hand on her shoulder, he leaned near her ear and said, "Baby, do you wanna have some fun tonight?"

Turning toward him, the tip of her tongue between her teeth, she looked him up and down. Jax had noticed Peaches checking him out many times at Dream House, and he guessed she wanted to fuck him in the worst way. A few times, she made some moves on him at the club, but he wasn't interested in going out with her. Going out with the dancers could be complicated since they weren't regarded as free-for-all whores like the club sluts and hoodrats. But Peaches was at the club-house, on his turf, and he was ready to shove his thick cock into her wet warmth.

Planting a kiss on her lips, he jerked his head toward the doorway, saying, "Let's go and have a good time."

Peaches molded her body against his as he encircled her waist, walking out of the great room. They climbed the stairs to the third floor where Jax had his own room, since he was a board member. The third floor was reserved just for board members, and each of the six officers and three elected board members had rooms even if they didn't live at the club regularly, like Hawk or Banger. Jax had lived at the clubhouse since his father was killed at Sturgis when he was eighteen years old and a prospect with the Insurgents. Seven years later, he was a fully patched officer and wore his colors proudly.

Kicking open the door of his room, he pulled Peaches in. Pinning her against the wall, he roughly kissed her lips, darting his tongue in and out of her mouth while her groans made his dick grow harder. When he pulled down her tube top, her breasts spilled out and he rubbed them, tweaking her nipples as he kissed her neck. Peaches squirmed against the wall, her knee grinding against his cock. Yanking her skirt up over her hips, he shoved his hand down her panties, squeezing her wet pussy.

"I like that, sexy," she purred.

He threw her one of his boyish grins, the one that melted women's hearts. "Fuck, I like that you're wet for me."

"I've been wet for you since I saw you at Dream House. I've wanted you inside me for a while now," she murmured against his moist lips.

Throwing her on the bed, Jax stripped off his clothes and joined her, his body looming over hers. Using his tongue, he traced from her neck down to her mound. Spreading her legs, he buried his face in her slit, his tongue flicking up and down between her folds. Peaches writhed beneath him as he stuck a couple fingers in her pussy. Not able to hold back any longer, Jax grabbed a condom, encased his dick, and thrust into her inviting wetness. He rode her hard, slamming in and out. Looking down on her as he fucked her, he did a double-take—Peaches had disappeared and Cherri had taken her place, her pouty lips slightly parted, and her mouth quivering with her satisfied moans. Jax felt his cock tighten before he spurted his release.

He pulled off his condom, threw it in the trashcan next to his bed, and rolled over. Peaches snuggled against him, kissing his side. She ran her long nails over his sculpted chest. "Wow, you're built. How do you do it?"

"I work out a lot." It was true; ever since he was thirteen years old, he had been working out like a fiend. It helped control the rage caged between his bones and his flesh. The obsession with pushing himself physically to the max was born the day his mom ditched him and his dad for another biker. His fury was born that day, as well, and grew as his father, too weak to handle his wife's betrayal, gave up on being a father and threw himself into the slippery hands of Jack Daniels. If that wasn't all fucked up, he didn't know what was. A darkness spread over his face as his thoughts took him to places in his past he didn't want to go.

"Whatcha thinkin'?" Peaches asked as she nuzzled deeper into the crook of his arm.

"You're a good fuck. How many brothers you serviced so far tonight?"

"You're my only one. This is the first time I've come to one of the parties. I came hoping you'd be here."

"Is that right?"

"I've seen you looking at me at the strip bar. I have a bit of a crush on you," she whispered.

"Don't be having that shit on me. I don't do this 'one woman' thing. You're a good fuck, and I'd like to have you in my bed again, but don't think I'm gonna be pining for you or bringing you roses, or shit like that. I fuck pussy, and that's about it."

Nodding, she said, "That's fine. I just want to be with you. Is it okay if I don't do any of the other guys?"

"If you come to the parties again, you're considered a club whore for the night and you're open to all the members. If you come with me, then you're with me."

"Can I come with you? I mean, to be with you at the parties and at other times?"

"I'll let you know when I want to fuck you. Remember, you won't be my girlfriend, just my fuck-buddy. If you're cool with that, I'm down for that… for a while."

"I'm down." Peaches kissed Jax's face, her leg rubbing against his thigh. His dick twitched, and immediately her blonde head started its descent toward his hardening shaft. Watching as her thin lips wrapped around his dick, he found himself wishing it were Cherri sucking his hardness.

Fuck it all to Hell.

CHAPTER THREE

"Y OUR ASS IS fuckin' outta here. We don't tolerate drug use, you fuckin' crack head!" Emma was beyond pissed. She ran a clean club, and this sniveling bitch had been given a couple of warnings from her already, yet there she was, flying higher than a damn kite.

"Please, Emma. I swear, I'll never use again. I need this job! I got a kid to support," Mandy said, eyes dilated and nose running, her words rushing out.

"You're toast, bitch. I gave you more than enough chances. I'm done with your shit. Pack up your stuff and get the hell outta here." Emma looked toward Holt, who was wiping down the bar, and yelled out to him, "Make sure this slut's outta here in ten minutes, or throw her ass out, got it?"

Not looking up, he nodded in agreement. Mandy ran out of the room, screaming obscenities. Emma looked at Cherri who sat at the corner of the bar, sipping an iced Coke with lemon. "You'll take Mandy's spot," she said.

Swallowing hard, Cherri wiped her mouth then said, "What, you want me to be the lead dancer?"

"Yep, and I want you to be the one supervising the dancers in the back before the shows."

"I can't do that! I don't know what the hell I'm doing. I've only been here for two months. Give the position to Peaches. She wants it bad, and she's been here longer than me." Cherri stabbed at the ice slivers in her glass, her eyes cast downward.

"You misunderstood. I'm not asking if you want it; I'm *telling* you that's what you're gonna do."

"Peaches is gonna be pissed," Cherri mumbled.

"Why would you think I give a fuck about that?"

Shrugging, Cherri continued playing with her straw.

"Your new position starts today. I'll go over some stuff with you, and then you can get into it tonight." Emma turned on her heel and walked toward her office in the back.

Emma had been in charge of Dream House for the past four years. She loved running the place, and she made it her mission to have a well-organized strip bar. She selected the dancers and the wait staff, and, except for a few minor upsets, Dream House ran well under her strict direction. Each time a dancer fucked up, it pissed her off to no end. Whenever a dancer tested for drugs, she'd go ballistic; she broke her ass for her dancers, and when they screwed up, it was like they betrayed her.

Before she ran the strip bar, she was a club whore. She first came to the Insurgents for a weekend party ten years before, and she never left. Emma loved being a part of the Insurgents' world, and she used to love partying and fucking just as much as all the brothers. She had fucked practically all of them before she met the love of her life, Danny. It took her a while to get him to realize he couldn't live without her, but he came around and they shared a small house together in the outskirts of town. Danny still enjoyed the weekend parties and the raunchy fun they brought, but he only indulged about once a month, and Emma was just fine with that.

A tightness in her chest made her realize how upset she was that Mandy had forced her hand. She trusted Mandy; they were a bit like friends, and she had given Mandy so many chances, way more than she had to any of the other girls she threw out for testing dirty. She couldn't let Mandy slide again, though. If she did, she'd lose the respect and control of the club, and she had no intention of doing that.

She was confident Cherri would do a good job. The girl was an odd mix of toughness, coldness, and vulnerability. Emma suspected she had gone through a lot in her short life. Cherri had a frailty about her that brought out men's caveman instinct to protect. She was one of the most popular dancers in the club, and every guy fantasized about fucking her. As far as Emma knew—although she didn't know much, because Cherri was so private—Cherri hadn't given it up to any of the men in the club, including any of the Insurgents. Cherri was a strange one, all right, but she was smart and level-headed, and that was what Emma needed in a lead dancer and supervisor. Cherri was going to work out just fine.

"WHY SO DOWN?" Lexie sat down next to Cherri at the bar. "Give me a draft, Holt."

"Emma threw Mandy's ass out. She tested dirty."

"I heard. Mandy was cussing up a storm in the back room. I can't feel sorry for her, though; Emma warned her two times before. That slut just can't give up the crank. Don't spend any more time worrying about her."

"But she has a small daughter to support."

"She doesn't give a shit about her. She's always dumping the poor little thing with someone. Fuck, she only wants money for crank. I'm glad she's gone."

Cherri chewed the shards of ice left in her glass. "Emma put me in charge."

"Yeah? That's cool. You're always organizing the back room and stage, so it makes sense. Mandy's been a pain in the ass for the last several months. She screwed things up all the time, and we had no direction. She's an addict."

"So, you think the other dancers will be okay with me taking her place? I don't have a choice, you know."

Lexie laughed. "We all know Emma, and she scares the hell outta us. I'm pretty sure all the girls will be fine with it, except for Peaches. She's wanted to be in charge since she got here."

"I know Peaches won't like it. She hasn't liked me from the start. I don't know why, but she's always been a bitch to me. I don't want Mandy's position…" Cherri chewed on her straw.

Reaching over, Lexie grabbed a Diet Coke from the ice chest on the bar. As she opened her can, she said, "She hates that Jax can't keep his eyes off you."

Cherri looked at Lexie, wide-eyed. "What? I don't have anything with him or any other guy around here."

"I didn't say *you* were into him. I said he's got the hots for you in a major way. All the girls know it, and it kills Peaches, 'cause she's obsessed with being his ol' lady. Like *that* is gonna happen." Lexie rolled her eyes.

"So, that's why she's such a bitch to me? How stupid is that? Anyway, aren't they together? She keeps telling me that every chance she gets, and she's all over him when he comes into the bar. I thought they were dating, or something."

"Damn, girl, you *are* green. First off, Jax isn't the dating type. Hell, most of the bikers aren't—they fuck, but don't date. For now, Peaches is his main fuck, but she's not his only one. He's been fuckin' three other sluts at the clubhouse. My friend Brandi told me. There's no way Peaches is his girlfriend. And *absolutely* no way she'll be his ol' lady."

"Well, if they're fuckin', then what's her problem?"

" 'Cause Jax's got it for you, even though he's bangin' her. He calls here every day to see if you're dancing and what time you go on. He just called now askin' if you were here. I bet his ass will be here in a few. If you were smart, you'd take him up on his offer. It doesn't hurt to make a friend with one of the Insurgents."

"I don't want to start anything with him."

"I'm just telling you to think about it. He's a nice guy, but he *does* fuck too many women. I guess as long as you know that and are cool with it, he'd be a good one to have on your side."

"I don't know."

"Why don't you have a man around?" Lexie asked.

"I just don't need a man in my life complicating things, that's all. There's a guy who comes here a lot, you know, the older guy who sits by himself at the back table?" Cherri said.

"Oh, you mean Gunner? He's cool. He's a big tipper, and underneath all that rough exterior is a total sweetheart."

"He kinda creeps me out. He's always sitting in the back, just staring. He's an Insurgent, right?"

"Yeah. He's a bit of a loner and doesn't hang too much with the young guys like Jax, Axe, and Chas, but he's decent. He comes to see you. He always checks out the new girls."

"Big tipper, you say?"

"*Great* tipper."

"I guess I'll have to be friendlier next time he comes in. I need the money," Cherri said with a sigh.

"Don't we all?"

"I better head to the back and get things in order for tonight's line up. Good talking to you, Lexie."

"Later, girlfriend."

Cherri walked to the back room, hoping her new position would be a smooth transition with the other dancers. She wanted to do a good job since she knew Emma trusted her, which meant a lot to her, especially since she had only been at the club for a short time. The extra money she'd earn in her new position was a godsend. She thought about what Lexie said about Jax and that old guy, Gunner. She needed someone who would pay her well for services rendered. She was too scared of her attraction to Jax. Deep down, she knew if she started something with him, she'd be doomed because he made her feel things she never felt before. No, she didn't want anything to steer her from her goal of getting out of there.

I'll cozy up to Gunner tonight, check it out and let him decide if he wants more.

Peaches' giggles grated her nerves as she walked out to the bar area. Immediately, Cherri spotted Jax on a chair with Peaches straddling him, her breasts smashed against his chest as his hands dove under her skirt, rubbing her ass. Cherri's chest tightened and her stomach gurgled. For a split-second, a deep sense of emptiness consumed her. Shaking her head, as if that would erase the image of Jax and Peaches clutching each other, she dashed for the bar, hoping he wouldn't spot her.

"Hiya, Cherri," Peaches said between her moans.

Cherri tipped her head in response, cursing the bitch under her breath while avoiding any direct eye contact. Over the rock tune playing on the local station, she heard Jax say to Peaches, "Later, babe. I got stuff to do."

"What the hell? We're both getting off. Can't your *stuff* wait?"

"I said off. *Now.*"

Cherri heard a soft thud and the scraping of a chair against the floor. Thinking if she just engrossed herself in the employment ledger, she'd be left alone, she lowered her head, staring at the numbers and words.

"How are things, sweetness?"

She jumped on her bar stool when Jax's breath tickled the back of her neck.

Not looking at him, she shrugged. "Okay, I guess."

"Heard you're the one in charge of the dancers now." His mouth brushed her earlobe, making her skin pebble in anticipation.

"Word travels fast." She kept her eyes focused on the ledger. Cheap perfume invaded her nostrils.

"Whatcha doin', honey?" Peaches smacked a wet kiss on Jax's cheek.

"I'm busy talkin' business. I'll catch you in a few."

"What's the business?" Her voice had an edge to it.

"Not your concern. In a few, okay?" Jax pushed her off him.

From the corner of her eye, Cherri saw Peaches glaring at her. *I so don't need this shit.* "I think we're done here." Sliding off the stool, Cherri turned toward the back room.

"We're not done here, sweets. We haven't even started." As Jax nudged her back toward him with one hand, the hairs on Cherri's arms stood up as shivers coursed through her body. She wheeled around, connecting with his smoldering gaze. Holding his stare, she ran one finger up his arm, feeling the goosebumps pricking his skin.

"Then let's get started," she murmured. Her body shifted to high-alert: blood rushed to her temples, her mouth was dry, and her legs clenched, causing a spasm of pleasure to spread through her core. Peaches' hiss of disgust brought Cherri back to the moment, and her porcelain skin stained red when she saw Jax's knowing grin break out on his face. *He's adorable when he smiles. How can one man have this effect on my body? He's sex in leather, and I have to stay far away from him.*

Peaches stormed out of the bar, her stilettos clacking on the wooden floor. Cherri watched her as she slammed the back door.

"Your girlfriend's pissed."

"She's not my girlfriend." Jax trailed his finger along Cherri's jawline.

"That's not what she says. Anyway, you two looked pretty cozy not too long ago." She shifted from one foot to another.

"You jealous?"

"Nah."

"Or are you wishing it were you straddling me, rubbing your sweet pussy against my cock? I know I'd rather have you, but you're playing hard to get for some reason, and I don't go for that shit, sweet one." Jax bent his head and lightly brushed her throat with his lips.

"I'm not playing anything. I'm just not interested. You got Peaches and plenty of other sluts who'll fuck you, so no need to pursue me." She touched her throat where his lips had been.

"Pinewood Springs can get mighty lonely in the cold, winter nights. An icy one like you is gonna want some heat. When that time comes, I'll be here, waiting for you."

"Oh, I'll manage. I always do." She smiled sweetly at him.

His gaze moved down to her lips then back to her eyes, making her body tingle all over. Tilting his head, he kissed her gently while his hands squeezed the back of her neck. He pulled back, smiling, his eyes twinkling. Cherri, lightheaded, grabbed the back of the stool, steadying herself. No man had ever kissed her like that. The tenderness of it brought tears to her eyes. She had to get away from him before she broke down and sobbed like a blathering idiot.

"Emma has confidence in you. I do, too—I know you'll do a good job with the dancers. Mandy was a fuck-up. You have some work ahead of you, but you're smart, so you'll be able to get things back on track. Just remember to stay on Emma's good side. She can be a bitch. If you ever have a problem, let me know. I can take care of it."

Waving to Holt, Jax threw his leather jacket over his shoulder. Cherri, transfixed by his movements, watched him. He turned around when he was near the door and said, "I'll always be here for you, baby girl, no matter what. You remember that." The metal door clanked shut behind him.

"Are you okay, Cherri?" Holt asked.

Nodding, she struggled to regain her composure. *This is so lame. What the fuck? Why did he have to go and kiss me like that—like he cared and he didn't just want to get in my pants. Why doesn't he leave me the fuck alone? I don't need this shit. Not. At. All.*

Glancing at the clock, she said out loud, "Fuck, it's already three o'clock. I gotta check the line-up and get the dancers ready for tonight. See ya later, Holt." Cherri scurried to the back to make sure all the dancers had arrived and everything was in order for the evening show. Thursday nights were always busy at Dream House, and she wanted to show Emma and Jax—yeah, Jax—that she could do this job and do it well.

In the back room, Peaches greeted her with a dour face. "Fuckin' leave my boyfriend alone, slut!"

"He told me he's not your boyfriend."

"He didn't tell you shit, you jealous bitch. Find your own man, and fuckin' leave mine alone."

"I don't want your man, so don't get in my face about it."

"Bullshit! I see the way you flirt and throw yourself at him. Back the fuck off. I'm gonna be Jax's old lady, and I'll beat your ass if I see you making moves on him again."

"Why don't you tell *your* man to leave *me* the fuck alone? He's the one sniffing around my ass all the time. I can't help it if you're my replacement."

"You slut!" In one swift move, Peaches had Cherri by the hair and shook her like she was a limp doll. Cherri, regaining her balance, hauled off and punched Peaches right in the stomach, eliciting a yelp from the enraged woman. Peaches swung at Cherri, who hit her back as they both screamed and cussed at each other. A few of the other dancers gathered around, some egging Peaches on, others in Cherri's court.

"You fuckin' bitches, break it up! This ain't no fightin' arena." Holt pulled the two women apart. Twisting out of Holt's grasp, Peaches lurched at Cherri, hatred brimming in her eyes.

With a handful of Peaches' hair, Holt yanked her back. "Fuckin' stop, Peaches, or I'm gonna kick your ass outta here for tonight." His harsh voice stopped her in her tracks. She had worked long enough at Dream House to know that when Holt gave a warning, he always acted on it if he was ignored.

"Just tell this slut to stay away from my man. I don't fuckin' want to see her near him, or I'll beat the shit outta her!"

"I'm not tellin' her shit. Anyway, it looked like Jax was the one making all the moves. I've got a bar to stock, and I don't have time to babysit bitches with man problems, got it?"

"What the fuck's goin' on 'round here? Why are you all standing here not even lookin' ready? Cherri, what the fuck?" Emma's scowl sent the dancers dashing to their dressing tables to put on their makeup for the night's performances.

Cherri, pissed for succumbing to a rumble with Peaches over Jax, said in a small voice, "Sorry, Emma; it was my fault. I'm in charge, and I shouldn't have let things get out of hand."

"You're fuckin' right 'bout that. Don't let it happen again. I won't tolerate this shit. And Peaches, you better fuckin' fix your attitude, or your ass is outta here for good. And newsflash—I don't care that you're fuckin' the Sergeant-At-Arms. I'll throw your ass out, and the Insurgents, including Jax, will back me. Do I make myself clear?"

Peaches looked at Emma, defiance in her eyes. "Whatever."

"No, not 'whatever,' bitch. You give respect, you get it back; you don't, then your ass is history. No more warnings. Cherri is now your supervisor, so you show her respect. If not, you'll have to answer to me and I promise you, it ain't gonna be pretty."

"Why did you give *her* the position? You know I was next in line."

"I do what I think is best for the club, and I don't need to explain myself to you. Get your ass washed up and start prepping for tonight."

Once Peaches stomped off, Emma turned to Cherri. "I'll chalk up what happened as inexperience, but don't ever let shit get outta hand like this again."

"I won't. I better get going. I have to get ready for my dance set."

"Oh, yeah, you're not lead dancer anymore."

"Why, because of this? Am I being punished?"

"No. You won't be dancing at all. You'll be in charge back here with the dancers and help in the front with tables and whatever else comes up."

"What? Not dancing? But I need to dance. I need the money, and that's where I make it. I make more in tips for one hour of dancing than I do waiting tables for a full shift. I need the money, Emma." Cherri's voice cracked.

Emma threw her a sympathetic look. "I understand where you're comin' from, I really do, but this isn't my decision. There's nothing I can do. I'm sorry."

"Whose decision is it?"

"It comes from the Insurgents. I can't go over their heads. What they say goes—no arguments."

"The Insurgents? You mean the club doesn't want me to dance? Why do they care? I bring them a lot of money. You'd think they'd want me to strip."

Emma whispered, "The order came from Jax. The Insurgents back him. I'm sorry, but there's nothing I can do. I'll give you the big-tipping tables."

"Jax…? By waiting tables, you know I'll never be able to match what

I get from stripping." Cherri's eyes searched Emma's face for answers.

Shrugging, she said, "All I can do is give you the best tables. I can't defy the Insurgents. That's just the way it is. Go on. Make sure everyone's moving their butts."

Cherri stood in the hallway for a long time trying to grasp the enormity of the situation. She knew without stripping, her wages had been cut in half. *That bastard! He's getting back at me because I don't want to fuck him. How could he punish me by cutting my earnings? Now I'll never get out of this shitty life. I have to find another way to get money to make up for my lost wages.*

Knowing Emma depended on her to make sure everything was on schedule, she put her anger aside until later then entered the dressing area.

CHAPTER FOUR

CHERRI STOMPED HER feet to get the feeling back into them. She breathed in the chilly air—it crackled as it slid down her lungs. It was cold out, especially since she stormed outside without her jacket. She was so fucking pissed, the night's frigid air felt good as it cooled her down. How could he take away her dancing, her livelihood? Men were such treacherous assholes. They acted like they cared, then when they sucked a woman in, they reverted to their true selves. She let her guard down with Jax—she was beginning to relax a bit around him. The gentleness of his kisses, the way he looked at her, and the way he tucked her hair behind her ears made her fall prey to his deception. She stupidly thought he cared, so she let go of her distrust a bit, but then Jax did this shit to her. His true nature shone through. *What a bastard.*

"You coming in?" Holt asked. "Fuck, it's cold out here." He lit a cigarette.

"I just needed some air, you know?" Cherri said. "I'll see you inside." Holt jerked his chin at her.

When she entered the backroom, the blast of heat hit Cherri like a wall. Dancers ran all around: hopping on one leg while putting their heels on, dusting glitter over their bodies, and adjusting their costumes. It was like an off-kilter circus.

"Cherri, my fuckin' boob keeps hanging out 'cause this strap isn't staying up," Liza, one of the dancers, complained.

Motioning her to come over, Cherri took out the needle and thread and tightened up the strap. Liza stuffed her breast in the top, smiled at Cherri, and said, "Thanks. If you weren't here, I wouldn't know what to do."

"No worries, that's why I'm here." Cherri couldn't believe how helpless these dancers were. She rushed around, making sure the line-up was complete. As she came back from the DJ booth, she spied Jax leaning against the bar, his arms crossed, looking at her. Chas was next to him, slugging a beer and talking to him. Jax tilted his chin at her while he threw her one of his smiles. Fuming, she wasn't in the mood for his boyish charms. Turning her back to him, she jumped up on the stool at the far end of the bar and looked over the inventory list.

She was so absorbed in her task she didn't hear Jax's black leather boots click on the floor as he approached her. She smelled his earthy pine scent before she saw him—his fragrance was enticing, calming, and deceptive. She quickly reminded herself this guy with the sexy scent was the one who set back her get-the-hell-out-of-here plan.

"Whatcha doin', sweetness?" Heated air tickled her ear as his hand caressed her back.

Stiffening, Cherri said, "Working."

"Hey, what's up?"

"Nothing, just busy."

"Why're you being so cool, sweetheart?"

Glancing at him sideways, her blue eyes glinted with anger. "Why did you take dancing away from me?"

Jax blinked several times as if he were trying to put his mind around the shift in the conversation. After a long pause, he shrugged, saying, "I don't want men looking at you naked."

"What the fuck does that mean? I'm a stripper. I need the money. What are you, some possessive, macho asshole?"

Jax bristled. "Watch your mouth, sugar." Grasping her shoulder, he turned her so she faced him. "You don't need to worry about money, I'll help you out. I don't want any guys jerking off to my sweetness dancing. Not anymore."

"I'm not your sweetness, your sugar, or your baby girl—I'm not anything to you. I'm just another dancer trying to make a living in this shitty place." Her blue eyes glistened.

"Oh, you're something to me, sweet one—you just don't realize it yet. I have plans for us, and the fucking will be sweet like you."

"So, you did all this just to fuck me?"

"I don't need the brothers seeing your naked ass anymore. You're not dancing, and that's final."

"You asshole!"

Jax clasped Cherri by the shoulders and yanked her toward him, their faces almost touching. She could see his nostrils flaring, his eyes glinting like knives, and his mouth twisted in rage as his hands held her tight, his muscular arms bulging. She knew he was trying to control himself. Instead of backing down, she glowered at him, insolence in her eyes. "Let me go. *Now.*"

"You're a hot piece of ass, sweetness, and I'm very fond of you, but you don't fuckin' tell me what to do. Nobody tells me what to do. You're not in charge; I am. You better learn that, or I can make your life miserable. Do you understand that, *baby girl?*" He gritted his teeth, tightening his grip even more.

Throwing her head back, Cherri laughed dryly. "Do you think I give a shit? My life is already miserable as hell. I don't give a damn what you do. You've taken away my dancing and any chances of earning decent money, so fuck, go ahead and make my life miserable, if that's what gets you off."

"Don't tempt me. You've got a mouth on you that needs to know when to shut the fuck up." He glared at her.

Cherri knew she was pushing him too far; this scary biker was pissed way off. She didn't want him to see she was scared, nor did she want him to think she was weak. He thought all he had to do was puff out his chest and she'd acquiesce with the "yes, Master" shit all these bikers wanted from the women around them. Fuck, she'd had it worse back home. She didn't have time for this.

"You get what I'm saying, sweet one?" Jax's voice was a tad softer.

Cherri pushed against his chest. Not expecting it, he stumbled and released her arms. She stormed away, turned her head around, and said,

"Stay the fuck away from me. Now, you got *that*, macho man?"

She stepped up her pace and scooted behind the black curtain. Her pulse raced as she waited for Jax to come barreling through, ripping the curtain out of his way. She didn't dare breathe. She waited. Nothing. Peeking out from behind the curtain, she saw Jax at the Insurgents table with Chas, Ruben, Banger, and a few guys she didn't recognize. By his clenched jaw, Cherri knew Jax was mad as hell, but he left her alone. Sighing in relief, she took a breath, happy she had averted an unpleasant scene. *Who the fuck does he think he is? I'll be damned if I take orders from him, or any man, ever again.*

Looking around the club from behind the curtain, Cherri saw Gunner, all by himself at a table, taking long draws from his beer. For a split second, she wondered why he wasn't at the table with the other Insurgents.

"Cherri, we have a problem. Patty called in sick."

"Oh, shit, I'll have to get a replacement. Liza, you're going on first, then go in the order on the sheet until the replacement comes in." Cherri grabbed her cell phone and dialed numbers as the music grew louder and the whistles and hoots began. She couldn't wait for the night to be over.

A COUPLE OF hours had passed and Cherri had everything in control. Simba came in to take Patty's place, the place was crowded, no undue rowdiness, and all the waitresses showed up for their shifts. Things were going along just fine.

Deciding to play the good hostess, Cherri went up to each table to check how everything was. When she came to the Insurgents' table, she saw two of the dancers, Crystal and Angel, sitting on Chas and Banger's laps, and Peaches and Jax lip-locked and tangled in each other. Peaches ground and wiggled against Jax, his raging hard-on not difficult to miss. Cherri's insides twisted and her eyes dampened when she looked at them. She'd never been jealous of any woman, but for an instant, she

32

wished she were the one on Jax's lap.

I can't believe I feel hurt that he's with Peaches. I despise him. Damn body—don't betray me. I loathe him, and I shouldn't care he's with this pumped-up bitch. I should be glad he has someone else to focus on, but... I'm... not. Fuck.

Peaches, boobs in Jax's face, gazed over his head and threw Cherri a smug look, hatred glinting in her eyes. Cherri turned away and asked Banger if everything was fine. He nodded and said, "Yeah, I think we're being taken care of real good."

Chas and Jax laughed, agreeing with Banger. Jax held Cherri's look for a heartbeat then, stone-faced, he yanked Peaches' head back and kissed her deeply. Tears formed in the back of Cherri's eyes, and she rushed off before they spilled down her face. She'd be mortified if Jax thought she was crying over him. God, no, she couldn't let him know how her insides ached and her gut felt like it had just been sucker-punched.

After checking on most of the tables, she headed toward the one where the lone Insurgent sat. When she came up to Gunner, he looked at her with surprise and delight. He had friendly eyes, and they made her feel welcomed. As she came closer, she had a good look at the rugged biker. She had never seen him full-on, only in the shadows surrounding him at his favorite corner table in the back.

He wasn't a bad-looking man. Cherri guessed him to be around forty years old. He had a full head of shoulder-length brown hair pulled back in a ponytail; single strands of white wove through it. His rough face had some lines from too much riding in the sun, and a large scar from his left temple down past his ear marked his face. He had a neatly trimmed brown beard, and his dark eyes twinkled as they gazed at Cherri. Each arm held two full sleeves of colorful work, and a tattoo of a gun peeked out from the top of the black Metallica t-shirt he wore under his aged cut.

Cherri guessed him to be about six-feet, and his shoulders were broad like a football player's. Gunner didn't suffer from a soft belly like several of the older Insurgents members: pure muscle molded his body without one ounce of fat on him. Intrigued by him, she wanted to know his backstory. To Cherri, he seemed like a contradiction—he appeared to be a loner, yet was in an outlaw MC.

"Hello, are you enjoying yourself? Is there anything I can get you?" she asked the biker.

"I'm all right, just happy you came by. Will you sit?" His voice was deep and tinged with a rasp that came from smoking too much.

"I'd love to. I'm Cherri," she said as she sat down.

"I know—I've had my eye on you since you first hit the stage. I'm Gunner."

"You're an Insurgent, right?"

"Yep."

"I see your vest, but wasn't a hundred percent sure, since you aren't with the others at their table."

"Yeah, been an Insurgent for 'bout twenty-four years. I don't sit with the young guys—I prefer to be alone or with the older brothers. Banger'll join me after he's done with his whore."

"You don't have a woman? I always see you alone."

"I have pussy like all the guys, but an ol' lady, nope. Done that… twice. I got sick of 'em and threw 'em both out. My first ol' lady liked fuckin' all the brothers too much, and the second one was just a pain in the ass. No, darlin', I like comin' here alone and watchin' you dance."

Cherri, scooting her chair closer to his, said, "I notice you watching me all the time. When I dance, I dance for you."

"Really? It looks like you're dancing for Jax. I can see that, though; he's young, and he's got all the bitches hot for him."

"I'm not hot for him."

Gunner looked at Cherri, a big smile breaking out over his face, the skin around his eyes crinkling. "I'll tell ya somethin', darlin'. You've caught my eye, and I can't get enough of you. The way you dance and shake your ass, well, that's the sexiest thing I've seen in a long while."

Cherri tilted her head back and laughed, reaching out and lightly touching Gunner's forearm. "Now, aren't you sweet?" She licked her lips with her tongue as she glanced up at him with a doe-eyed look.

Gunner leaned forward and whispered in her ear, "I'd like to get to know you a whole lot better."

Coyly, she said, "I'm sure we'll get to know each other."

"When are you gonna dance tonight, darlin'? You're my favorite."

"Never. The Insurgents won't let me dance anymore." She pushed out her lower lip.

A dark shadow passed over his face as his eyebrows contracted and his forehead wrinkled. "Really? Why does the MC care? I don't remember discussing that."

"Well, it was Jax who nixed my dancing."

"That's stupid. What did he do that for?"

Cherri shrugged.

"I need to talk with that asshole. You not being able to dance is stupid as fuck!"

"And a hardship, because I made a ton of money in tips."

"Yeah, I bet you did, darlin'; you're a lot of the guys' favorite. What about a lap dance? Would you do a lap dance for me?"

Cherri's eyes lit up. "Sure, why not? I was told I couldn't dance on stage. I'll give you a good lap dance. I'll treat you right." She placed her hand over his, rubbing it.

"Hey, buddy, how's it going?"

Spinning around, Cherri saw Jax pull out the chair next to her. He sat down and started talking with Gunner about motorcycles. Cherri stared at him, but Jax, acting as though she wasn't at the table, continued to talk with Gunner, laughing too loud at things Gunner said that weren't all that funny. *You want to play games with me, Jax? Go on—I'm a great player. I've had a lot of practice, especially with men. Bring it on, asshole.*

With sparkling eyes, she leaned close to Gunner, her hand on his shoulder, and said, "I gotta get back to work. Come find me later." She felt Jax's glare on her. Ignoring him, she stood up from the table and walked away.

Standing against the bar, Cherri watched as Peaches took the stage. She turned toward Gunner's table and saw Jax was still with him, talking his ear off. The whole time she had been at Dream House, she had never seen Jax speak with Gunner, yet the jerk acted like he was Gunner's best friend. She hoped he wasn't telling Gunner shit about her, trying to scare him off, although Gunner didn't look like he intimidated easily.

Glancing back at the stage, she noticed Peaches looked at Jax, but he had his back to her as he spoke with Gunner. Cherri couldn't help the surge of satisfaction rising in her. Whenever she danced, Jax couldn't keep his eyes off her. A deep ache pulsed through her as she thought about her stripping and Jax's lust-filled eyes watching her. When she danced, she'd catch his eye, and they would be connected through the music, the dance, and *their* desire. She yearned for that connection right then, but he took it away from her.

On the stage, a frowning Peaches stared at Jax's back. Cherri was glad Jax couldn't care less that Peaches was working extra hard to shake her ass and boobs—he just kept talking to Gunner.

Serves you right bitch.

A couple of hours later, while busy moving boxes of supplies to the storage area, Emma came over to Cherri. "Gunner's waiting for his lap dance in the red room. How did that come about?"

"I got talking to him and he asked when I was gonna dance. I told him the deal, and he said he wanted a lap dance. He seems like a nice guy, by the way."

"Really? I don't know him too well. He hangs with the older bikers. He always seems gruff to me." Emma shrugged.

"I think he's probably a big teddy bear."

"I don't think I'd describe him like that, but whatever."

"I gotta change. Tell him I'll be there in ten minutes." Cherri raced to her dressing room and pulled out different outfits from her closet. Finally settling on a skimpy leopard print skirt with a pink thong, along with a black lace and leopard print push-up top, she hurriedly dressed.

The guys loved this outfit because it always made her boobs look bigger than they were. Stiletto black pumps completed the ensemble.

Throwing on a cover-up, she headed toward the red room where Gunner waited. She glanced into the bar area and saw Peaches and Jax practically doing it. It was late and most of the patrons had gone, leaving a few guys and several Insurgents inside the club. Swallowing the lump in her throat, she walked to the lap dance rooms.

Cherri closed the door behind her when she entered the red room. It was swathed in variations of old-west saloon reds: deep red velvet walls with mirrors, a plush Persian carpet on the dark wood floors, an over-sized wraparound maroon leather couch hugging the walls. Erotic art dotted the mirrors while the shimmering light from two floor lamps draped in rosy chiffon lent a sultry ambience to the space.

Gunner, reclining on the couch with his arms resting on the top of it, smiled, his eyes smoldered with heat. "Don't you look delicious, darlin'. Come on over and make me feel good."

Cherri held his blazing look and swayed her hips as she neared him. "Do you have a couple of favorite songs you'd like me to dance to?" She placed her hands on his jean-covered knees and bent over, her face close to his.

Swallowing hard, he nodded. " 'Pour Some Sugar On Me' by Def Leppard and 'Cherry Pie' by Warrant are good."

"Nice choices." Cherri walked over to an elaborately carved wood cabinet, opened the doors, and pressed some buttons. Wiggling her shoulders and tossing her hair back, she said, "The rules are no touching. I can touch you, but you can't touch me. Got it?"

Gunner nodded while he sucked in his breath.

She came back over to him and waited for the music to start. On the first beat, Cherri moved her hip to one side, then another. She strutted around, ran her fingers through her hair then down her neck, her chest, then to her hips and around her butt. Tossing her hair, she looked at herself in the mirror behind the couch, then shifted her gaze to Gunner as she drew his eyes to hers. Gunner stared at her, transfixed; lust filled his black eyes as her head slowly fell forward then rolled back up, her hair draping around her like a shroud. Keeping her hands in contact with her body, she let them ride up her sides and back toward the nape of her neck.

Cherri came up to Gunner and placed her body between his legs as she swayed to the music, her ass bumping and grinding his crotch. Turning her head to look over her shoulder, her eyes never left his as she dry-humped him. Slowly leaning back, her shoulders pressed into his hard chest as she wrapped her arm around his neck—giving him a perfect view of her supple breasts—while she rubbed her ass on his hard shaft. She heard Gunner's guttural moans.

Swinging around, she faced him, her eyes locked with his once again. A sweet, subtle grin whispered across her face as she straddled his lap. As she bent forward, her orange blossom-sugared scent caressed Gunner's nostrils, and Cherri pushed her breasts toward his face. Arching her back, she unhooked her bikini top, releasing her boobs while she moved her butt against Gunner's massive hard-on. His breathing was fast and shallow as he shifted under Cherri's gyrations.

"You're fuckin' killin' me, darlin'," he said huskily.

Still holding his gaze, Cherri licked her lips as she nestled Gunner's face into her breasts, squeezing them around his face with her hand while grinding on his hardness. Not able to control himself any longer, Gunner's arms circled her petite waist and crushed her glistening body against him. The song ended, but Gunner didn't release her.

"The songs are over. I'm finished," she said into his ear while gently pulling away.

"That was a fuckin' hot dance. Way better than you on stage." He reached in his pocket and took out his wallet. "Here you go, darlin'." He handed her three one hundred dollar bills.

With wide eyes, Cherri said, "The dance is thirty dollars. This is way too much."

"That's your tip, darlin'. You deserve every bit of it and more. There's somethin' 'bout you makes me wanna take care of you. Can I give you another hug?"

As his warm smile caressed her, Cherri's eyes misted and she nodded. He squeezed her in his large arms, making her feel appreciated and protected. From behind her, she heard the door open and slam against the wall. Peeking over her shoulder, Jax emerged from the doorway—red-faced, eyes blazing, and fists clenched.

"What the fuck is going on here?" he demanded.

CHAPTER FIVE

"**H**OW IN THE fuck is this your business?" Gunner growled back, his arms still clasped around Cherri.

Seeing her practically nude in Gunner's arms made Jax's hazel eyes darken like angry thunderclouds. He wanted to pound the old man to a bloody pulp. He picked up one of the iron chairs and chucked it across the room, its impact shattering the mirror on the side wall. Gunner sprung off the couch and grabbed Jax. "What the fuck is your god-damned problem?"

"Don't you fuckin' touch her. Stay away from her."

Gunner threw a confused look at Cherri. "You his property? He claim you?"

Looking down, face turned away, she shook her head.

Directing his attention back to Jax, he said, "Seems like you got no say in this, so get the fuck outta here." He shoved Jax backward.

"Don't mess with me, old man." Jax's muscles twitched and bulged from the tension.

"I don't wanna mess with you. If you get the fuck out now, every-thing is cool."

Jax glanced at Cherri. Biting her nail, she avoided him.

"She's not supposed to be dancing." Jax stared hard at Gunner.

"She's not on stage, and what two adults have goin' on in here is none of your fuckin' business. For the last time, take your fuckin' ass outta here." Gunner took a couple of steps toward Jax.

Jax lunged for Gunner, whose fist smashed against Jax's jaw. Stum-bling for a moment, he pitched forward and punched back. The two of them hammered and knocked each other senseless. Cherri screamed,

"Stop, now! Stop!"

Ignoring Emma as she burst into the room, the two men kept bashing each other even as the blood spurted from their faces. Rushing into the hallway, Emma cried for help.

Banger, Chas, and Ruben raced in with Holt on their heels. They pulled the guys apart.

"What the fuck's goin' on?" Banger roared.

Wiping the blood from his nose with the back of his hand, Gunner replied, "This fuckin' punk is abusing his position as Sergeant-at-Arms. He's got a thing for Cherri, but she ain't been claimed. He needs to back the fuck off right now, or I'll do somethin' that's gonna land me in the pen." Gunner's body shook with fury, his nostrils flaring.

"What the fuck, Jax?" Banger's eyes bored straight into his, waiting for a response.

Jax, rubbing his swelling jaw, said, "The fuckin' old man needs to learn she's off-limits to the brothers." He wrapped his arms around Cherri's trembling shoulders.

"Have you claimed her?"

Jax flung a defiant glare at Banger and tugged Cherri closer to him.

"Well, have you?" Banger swung around and faced Cherri. "Are you Jax's woman?"

Shifting from one foot to the other, eyes cast downward, Cherri's white-blonde head shook as she said in a half-whisper, "No."

With fury in his eyes, Banger yelled at Jax, "Get the hell outta here! You've no stake in her. She and Gunner can do what the fuck they want. You're outta fuckin' line on this one."

Without saying a word, Jax tossed Cherri away from him. She stumbled and fell, landing on the couch. He stormed out of the room into the bar area. "That fuckin' old man better watch out, 'cause I'm not done with him yet. Asshole!" he yelled. He slammed his fist on the bar, pain ripping through his hand. Feeling a cool rag on his face, he whipped around and saw Peaches standing next to him, wiping away the drying blood.

"What happened, baby?" she cooed. "I'm here now, and I'm gonna take care of my best guy. I love you, baby. I love everything about you. I'd never pick some old fart over you. You're so sexy and lovable." Peaches put her arms around Jax's neck and planted a wet, soft kiss on his bruised cheek.

Jax turned toward her and kissed her.

"Don't ever try that shit again with another brother, you got that?" Banger yelled as he approached Jax. "Gunner is cool to let this go, but if you do this shit again, your ass is gonna get a beating from me. All this shit over a bitch. You had your chance and you didn't go for it, and now Gunner's got her."

"He doesn't have shit. A lap dance doesn't mean he's *got* her." Jax spat.

Eyeing him, Banger warned, "Back the fuck off. The bitch has picked Gunner, so be a man and deal with it. I don't want any more trouble from you on this. Got it?"

"I'm fuckin' outta here!" Jax yanked Peaches' arm, dragging her behind him as he left the bar. He jumped on his Harley and motioned Peaches to get on. He needed a back warmer, and later, he'd want a cock warmer. Peaches was eager, and he liked her well enough. If Cherri wanted to suck old cock, then let her do it. He was beyond pissed at her. He needed a pint of Jack and Peaches' pussy to erase that cold bitch with the glacier blue eyes out of his mind. He left the parking lot and sped toward the clubhouse.

The wind rushed around their ears like a wind chamber. Evergreens, aspens, and pine trees blurred as Jax rode hard and fast, taking the curves at dangerous speeds. With every bend in the road he leaned the bike further, and he felt Peaches wrap her arms tighter around him. He knew she was terrified, but he didn't care. The inky blackness, the wind around him, and the ride blocked out the fury which radiated from him. *How the fuck could she pick Gunner over me? I know she's got issues, but this is just fucked.*

Images of Cherri invaded his mind the whole ride to the clubhouse.

He had never been so pissed at a woman in his whole life. He fucked women, stayed with them for a while, then left them for another. Usually, he was getting pussy from two or sometimes three women at the same time. Rarely did he settle for one, and when he did, it was short-lived. The last thing he wanted was to settle down or have a permanent girlfriend—he wasn't ready for that shit, so he couldn't figure out why he cared so much about Cherri. He hated pain-in-the-ass women, and when it got too hard or complicated, he'd bail. So why was he still sniffing around the frigid bitch's ass? She was more than difficult, and he still wanted to get her in his life and him in hers. *Fuck!*

Jax screeched to a stop and waited for the prospect to open the chain-link fence to let him into the clubhouse parking lot. Lights from inside the compound cast an eerie glow on the asphalt where numerous Harleys were parked. Laughter, heavy bass, and breaking glass emanated from the club. It was Thursday night, and the brothers began their weekend early.

Inside the great room, several brothers sat drinking beer and whiskey while watching car racing on the big-screen TV mounted on the back wall. A few brothers played pool while some others were busy with the club whores and mamas on the couches that circled the room. There weren't any hoodrats since the party girls usually came around the club on Friday and Saturday nights to have free booze, drugs, and sex.

The club whores hung around every night, making themselves sexually available to the brothers. Lola and Brandi were the more popular ones, but Rosie, the newest addition, was all the rage since she came on board a few months back. Kristy was one of the favorite mamas since she knew how to suck some good dick. Unlike the club whores, the mamas wore the property patch of the club, and they were the lowest members in the club hierarchy. In exchange for being the Insurgents' public well and grunt workers around the club, the mamas lived upstairs in the attic of the schoolhouse-turned-clubhouse. They also had the protection of the Insurgents: if anyone messed with their mamas, the brothers would come down hard on the offenders. In exchange, the mamas were expected to service the brothers and other bikers who visited the club; they had to be available twenty-four-seven to please a member. It was a grueling position, but a voluntary one.

Jax entered the clubhouse hauling Peaches behind him, not even stopping to say anything to the brothers. Peaches, tripping over her feet as she tried to keep up with Jax, heard the members' hoots and whistles as Jax dragged her upstairs. Jax opened his room's door and pushed Peaches inside. It was a simple room with a king-sized bed, two reading chairs, a nightstand, a floor lamp, and a small TV. Pin-up posters of half-naked women posed on Harleys decorated his walls. A small en-suite bathroom completed his living quarters. A large picture window overlooked the back of the clubhouse and the forest of Aspen trees in the distance.

"Fuck!" Jax said as he threw his leather jacket on one of the chairs. He kicked off his boots, shed his jeans and t-shirt, and jerked Peaches to him. He kissed her fiercely, biting her shiny-red lips.

"Ow, Jax, that hurt," she said, turning her face away and rubbing her bottom lip with her finger. "What's wrong, baby?"

"Nothin', just wanna fuck."

"Okay, but play nice."

"Take your clothes off and join me on the bed."

Peaches peeled off her short denim skirt, her purple top, and lacy bra, but kept on her thong. She eased herself on the bed and snuggled up to Jax.

"Get rid of your g-string."

Peaches slid off her thong. Jax smiled. *Yeah, that's what I like—no arguments, just an easy woman who wants to please me. Nothing complicated like Cherri.*

"Baby, you seem so upset. What's wrong? What happened at the club?" Peaches asked, rubbing Jax's back.

Flinging her hands off him, he said gruffly, "I'm not looking for nice tonight. I wanna fuck hard and rough. You down?"

"Anything you want, baby. I love you, and you know there isn't nothing I wouldn't do for ya." Shoving her down on the bed, he kissed her roughly while he tweaked her nipples. She cried out, and he flipped her over. "On your knees. Now."

Peaches did as ordered. After putting on a condom, Jax rubbed her clit, making her moan. As her moaning rose to a high-pitched whine, he rammed into her, fucking her hard. When she reached her peak, she screamed out while Jax growled. He rolled on his back and covered his eyes with his arm. Peaches rested her head in the crook of his arm. "That was awesome, baby. Did you like it?" she asked.

He snorted his response. The truth was their fucking did nothing for him. His hunger was still there—he wasn't satiated at all. All he saw when he was fucking Peaches was Cherri's firm ass wiggling and his cock slamming into *her* sweet pussy. After he banged Peaches, all he could think of was Cherri stroking Gunner's dick with her butt. He knew sleep would not come easily that night.

Peaches' even breaths told him she had fallen asleep. Why couldn't he forget about Cherri and embrace Peaches? Peaches was in love with him. She was pretty, good in bed, and would do anything for him. If he made Peaches his permanent girlfriend, his life would be easy. He knew she was the type who would forgive his extra pussy on the side. Why the fuck did he have the hots for a troublesome ice bitch? He didn't want that shit in his life, but, for unknown reasons, he was drawn to her—needing and craving her. He was pissed as hell at himself for allowing a woman to do that to him. *Fuck!*

A FEW HOURS later, sunlight filled the room through the curtainless window. Cussing under his breath as the light pierced his eyes, he looked down at Peaches' curly hair. She hugged him in her sleep. *Maybe if I spend more time with her, the less I'll think of Cherri.* He wanted to get the white-blonde with the sexy strut out of his mind. Seeing her with Gunner made him attack another brother. He knew he overstepped the line, knew he was out of control while he was punching Gunner's face, but he didn't give a shit; he wanted to hurt Gunner for having his hands on Cherri. Not only was he beyond fucking perplexed that she picked an old brother over him, he was hurt as shit, but that was somewhere he didn't want to go. The problem with Cherri was she stirred up bullshit deep inside him he didn't want to think about.

He looked down at Peaches again. *Fuck, why can't I crave her the way I do Cherri? She's crazy about me.* He knew Cherri was pissed at him for not letting her strip on stage anymore, but to hook up with Gunner to spite him? That wasn't okay. It was true Gunner was a generous tipper, which made him more desirable to the dancers, but Jax had told Cherri he'd take care of her and give her money to make up the lost wages. She wouldn't go for it, though. *So she takes the old man's money, but not mine? She's all kinds of fucked-up.*

The whole turn of events pissed him off to no end. He suspected Cherri had some issues from her past; her eyes told him she was hiding secrets. Ever since he first saw her—after the raid on the Deadly Demons Nomads' clubhouse and the Insurgents rescued her—he was drawn to her. It was more than her hot body and pretty face—it was an aura of vulnerability and determination which excited the fuck out of him. He guessed her life hadn't been easy, but that's why he was there—to take care of her.

How in the fuck did she choose Gunner over me? Fuck! Jax had to be with her. He had to forget her. His cock needed her and only her. His life was suddenly a whirlwind of conflicting emotions. Why the hell did she have to come into his world and fuck it up?

"Whatcha thinking about?" Peaches asked as she squeezed his waist.

"Huh? I thought you were sleeping."

"I was, but your heavy breathing woke me up. Do you want something, baby?" She smiled while she ran her hand over his dick.

Shifting his weight, Jax brushed her hand away. "Not now. I got stuff to do." He sat up, his back to her.

"What went on between you and Gunner last night?"

Pausing, Jax debated about telling her the truth. He decided Peaches wasn't to blame for his weakness, so there was no reason to hurt her. "Club business."

Anyone who hung out with outlaw bikers knew when one of the guys said something was *club business*, it meant no more questions, end of discussion, nothing revealed. The Insurgents were protective of their club and its goings-on. The brothers would rather die than reveal anything of the club's activities. The weekly meetings, called church, were for full-patched members, and no one else was allowed to hear what was talked about at church—not the Prospects, the hang-arounds, and, most certainly, not the women. The deep loyalty and fierce protection of all that was Insurgents was not unique to them, it was the code, the way of life for all outlaw motorcycle clubs.

Peaches didn't ask any more questions about the fight. She placed her hands on Jax's tense neck muscles and massaged them while she whispered in his ear. "Why didn't you watch me dance last night, babe? I was looking at you, and each time I shook my titties, it was for you. It always is, you know?"

"I was talking club business with Gunner. Something had come up. You know how that goes," he lied. He didn't want to hurt Peaches—it wasn't her fault she couldn't hold a candle to Cherri. This was *his* deal, not hers.

"Oh, that's good. I thought maybe it was because of that bitch Cherri. I saw her chatting up Gunner then you going over there. I dunno… I thought maybe all the shit last night was because of her."

"Nah, just club business."

Peaches kissed his neck while she ran her hands down his chest, landing on and grabbing hold of his hardening cock. Jax groaned. She swung around, straddling herself on his lap, kissing him while caressing his chest with her breasts. She pushed him back down on the bed and rested her knees on either side of him, his length ready for some relief. He threw his head back, letting Peaches take him on a ride while he fantasized about his sweet Cherri.

WHEN THEY ENTERED the great room an hour later, Jax, with his arm around Peaches' waist, spotted Gunner at the bar having a drink with Ruben. Gunner tilted his chin when he saw Jax, who nodded back with a clenched jaw. He thought the anger would have dissipated by that point, but he was still pissed as hell at Gunner and it took everything he had to hold back. He so fucking wanted to finish what he started the night before at Dream House with the old brother. Even though his body was ready to pounce, his mind told him he'd acted stupid, fighting a brother over a woman who wasn't claimed. He was losing his grip with this one, and he knew Banger wasn't going to put up with his shit at all.

"I'd like some orange juice," Peaches said.

"Go into the kitchen and get it in the fridge. The bar doesn't have any."

"Okay, be back in a minute." She placed a kiss on Jax's cheek and headed toward the kitchen.

"Gimme a beer," Jax said to the prospect who tended the bar. The prospect put a Coors in front of Jax. All the prospects were expected to know what each of the members drank—it was one of their duties. Jax lifted his chin at the prospect.

"Heard there was some trouble at Dream House last night," Hawk said as he clasped Jax on the shoulder.

Jax shrugged as he took a big gulp from his beer bottle.

"You need to back way the fuck off on this one. You starting shit like this with a brother over a stripper who isn't interested in you is disrespectful and… pathetic. I'm giving you the benefit of the doubt, and I know you were thinking with your dick instead of your head, but the shit that happened last night can't happen again. You got that?"

Jax hung his head. He'd always looked up to Hawk; ever since Hawk joined the Insurgents eleven years before, he treated Jax like a little brother. Hawk was a good ten years older than Jax, and when his father was murdered when Jax was eighteen years old, Hawk and the club were the stable force that helped him through the dark moments. Ever since, he could count on Hawk to be there for him when the demons started to creep in again.

"Yeah, you're right. I was outta line. I dunno, that bitch just has a hold of my cock." Jax stared at his beer bottle.

"Yeah, bitches can do that shit to us. Stick with Peaches. She hasn't fucked any of the brothers but you, seems friendly, has a hot body, and she fuckin' wants to be with you. Leave the other one alone—she's messed up and seems like she has too much baggage she's pulling along."

"Yeah, like Cara was so easy." Jax stared at Hawk.

Shaking his head, he said, "You got me there. Fuck, I'm the last one to give advice. Cara had me so mixed up I couldn't think about anything but her. Hell, I still can't get enough of her, and she's my old lady now. But I never went against a brother for an unclaimed woman. Seems like this bitch wants Gunner. It sucks, but you gotta let it go."

Jax felt like Hawk just kicked him in the gut when he said Cherri wanted Gunner. He knew Hawk was right, but there was no fucking way he was giving up. He couldn't forget about Cherri's dainty body, her full lips, and her small tits. Knowing he couldn't fight a brother on it again, he was still more determined than ever to make Cherri his.

CHAPTER SIX

"**F**UCK! LIKE I need this shit," Cherri said as she stepped on the wet kitchen floor. Looking at the overflowing sink, she groaned. "I'm so sick of *everything* right now."

"Sorry I can't help you, but I gotta go to Dream House. I have a double-shift today," said Amy, one of the two women with whom she shared the townhouse. Grabbing a power bar, Amy flew out the door, leaving Cherri alone to deal with the clogged sink.

"Just great!" Cherri yelled out to no one. Her other roommate, Ginger, also had a double at Dream House. Cherri, on her only day off in eight days, was left to plunge the sink and clean up the mess.

After the plunger did nothing, Cherri, exasperated, called Emma. "Em, we've got a backed-up kitchen sink and nothing I'm doing is helping. I don't want the water to go into the living room and ruin the carpet. What am I supposed to do? Do I call a plumber or do you take care of it? Not sure."

"I'll call the Insurgents; they take care of all that with the properties they own. Sit tight, and someone will be over to fix the problem."

"Thanks." Cherri, pissed that her day off was ruined, climbed the stairs to her bedroom.

The Insurgents provided housing for the dancers. They owned several townhomes for the women—three to each unit—and paid for all expenses except groceries, cell phones, and personal incidentals. The houses were comfortable and convenient, close to the club and downtown area, but they lacked the coziness of a home. Each unit had a small living room, a kitchen with an island, a half-bath on the main floor, and three bedrooms upstairs with two bathrooms. Off the kitchen there was a small laundry room, and the back yard had a postage stamp-sized patch of grass and a small deck for a Smoky Joe grill and a bistro table with two chairs.

The color scheme in the townhome was neutral. The couches were various shades of brown and the walls were white with nothing on them—very blah. Most of the women didn't care about decorating the unit; they used it to sleep in since most of them only planned on staying short-term. The majority of the dancers dreamed about meeting a rich man at the strip bar or hooking up with one of the bikers and being his old lady. Cherri dreamed about being on her own in a respectable job. She hated stripping and it made her feel dirty, but without much education, it was the one job that paid well and gave her a chance at a better life.

Cherri went into her bedroom—her home, her refuge. Unlike her other roommates' bedrooms, which were just beige and brown, Cherri painted the walls of her room a pale yellow to reflect the light. Having a corner room gave Cherri the light and brightness she loved. A pretty quilted comforter with over-sized pillows covered a double bed. Two white nightstands held wicker-shaded lamps while an overstuffed chair, covered in a floral and striped pattern, nestled in the corner of the room. Two white chests of drawers and a hand-painted trunk held most of her belongings. Next to the bathroom, a small closet overflowed with her clothes and shoes. Cherri's most recent purchase, a small TV, sat on the corner of a compact writing desk against the wall, facing one of the windows.

On the walls, she hung antique prints of flowers and a few reproduction prints from American artists; her two favorite ones were *Nighthawks* by Edward Hopper and Norman Rockwell's 1942 *Freedom From Want*. Cherri often looked at the two replicas whenever her life seemed overwhelming or the despair threatened to suffocate her.

She could identify with *Nighthawks* because it dripped with loneliness and estrangement, two things she experienced frequently. Her Norman Rockwell reproduction was her fantasy—a smiling family gathered around the table for Thanksgiving. She knew it was corny—her roommates just shook their heads and whispered about how strange she was for having it—but it was her image of what a happy family was. An image she kept in her heart and what drove her toward her goal of changing her current life to a better one.

As she picked up her hamper of dirty clothes and made her way to the washing machine, she regretted her day off was blown and she couldn't go to the library as she had planned. She loved going to the library because it was quiet and safe. Always having enjoyed reading, she spent many hours browsing through the book aisles. When she was a child, going to the library was one of her favorite things to do. When she was in high school, it was her hiding place from *him*. *Cherri, don't go there. Don't let the images of the past invade your mind. Don't let them.* She squeezed her eyes shut as if to block off the shadows which always lurked in the dark corners of her mind.

When she heard the doorbell, she jumped, her heart pounding. For a split-second, she didn't know where she was, imagining she was back in her room at home, terrified that he'd open the door and come in. The bell rang again, snapping Cherri back to reality. Shaking her head, she rushed down the stairs to open the door.

She saw the surprise reflected in Jax's eyes when he saw her at the door. *What the hell is he doing here? I didn't expect him to be at the door.* It had been two weeks since Jax and Gunner beat each other up over her—not one of her proudest moments.

"What are you doing here?" she said.

"Emma said there was a backed-up sink that needed fixin'?"

"You're the plumber?"

Chuckling, he said, "Yeah, I do most of the plumbing for the businesses. I got a knack for it—go figure." He threw her a wide smile that lit up his face. She felt a twinge of warmth from it.

"Okay, then, come on in." Cherri stepped aside. The narrow foyer made it awkward for him to pass with his tool box, so he brushed past her, his hard chest skimming her breasts. She held her breath as his touch made her nipples harden, spreading a throb of sweet desire between her legs. His pine and earthy scent wafted around her. She loved his scent—it was a combination of the beginning of spring and the freedom of riding. She heard his sharp intake of breath when he touched her. He looked at her, lust glittering in his eyes. They stood there, the moment suspended like a small piece of eternity. He leaned in to her as she tilted her face upward, but then his phone rang and the moment flitted away from them before they could hold onto it.

"Yo, talk to me," Jax said in his phone as he moved away from Cherri and went to the kitchen.

Cherri flushed and smoothed her hair down. She despised the way her body reacted to him. She had fucked her share of men, but she always felt detached, like she was above herself looking down at a girl who was doing nasty things. She never had a boyfriend, didn't even go to her junior prom—her stepfather had made sure of that. She had cried over it, pleaded with her mom to convince him to let her go. But, being the constant money-obsessed bitch, she played dumb and deferred all decisions to her husband.

The money her stepfather brought home made her mother ecstatic; she loved the trips, the jewelry, and the fancy cars. Born on the other side of the tracks, she got pregnant, married at sixteen years old, and became a widow at the age of twenty-six after Cherri's dad slammed his pickup into the side of the mountain after a hard night of drinking. For two years, she and her mom were dirt-poor until her mother, an attractive, petite blonde, caught the eye of a successful businessman. They married when Cherri was thirteen years old, and her new stepfather gave them all the material possessions they never had.

Cherri's mother was beside herself with her new status in life. She told Cherri on numerous occasions she was never going to be poor again and she'd do anything to keep the life she had. Her mother lived up to her promise: she never stood up for Cherri, and she deferred all discipline and decisions to her husband. She even gave her daughter to her husband in exchange for a pampered, luxurious life. Cherri's stepfather started taking an un-fatherly interest in her when she turned fourteen.

"What shit do you women put down the garbage disposal?" Jax snatched Cherri out of her memories as he came out of the kitchen, his shirt off, muscles rippling.

She took a step backward as her eyes slid up and down Jax's fine physique. She had never seen a man who had such a well-defined body. His abs and pecs were perfectly sculpted, and his hard, bulging biceps made her drool. She wanted to wrap her hands around them and lick them. She was a sucker for ripped arms, and standing before her was a man who oozed sex from every pore of his body.

Clearing his throat, Jax smiled and said, "Well?"

Red streaks glowed on her pale skin when she realized Jax knew she was checking him out and loving what she saw. "Uh… I don't know, the usual, I guess. I don't use it that much. I don't cook very often."

"I gotta talk to the other two. This is, like, the third time I've been out here in six months. They keep pouring grease down it."

"Oh?" Cherri couldn't take her eyes off Jax's body—it was magnificent. Skull tattoos, Gothic designs, daggers, and Insurgents' sayings wove around his chest and arms, creating an eclectic tapestry. His snug jeans showed off his firm ass and a dick that she imagined would feel real good inside her. *Damn, this guy is sexy.*

"Like what you see, sugar?" Jax, voice husky, approached her.

Wide-eyed, Cherri shook her head, backed up, and fell down on the sofa. Jax bent down, put his face close to hers, and said, "No need to be scared, sweetness. It makes me fuckin' horny to see you lookin' at me like you wanna fuck me." He licked his finger then gently traced her full lips with it.

She knew he felt her shiver under his touch. Turning her head away, she mumbled, "I wasn't checking you out, not really. It's just that it looks like you work out a lot." Who the hell was she kidding? She was almost salivating, her breasts ached to be touched, spasms built in her core, and her panties were damp. What was the matter with her? She didn't want a boyfriend in her life; she had no time for that type of problem.

"I do work out, sugar. A lot. Glad you like it. Why don't you explore with those pretty hands of yours?"

Snapping out of her desire-filled fog, Cherri pushed Jax back a little then stood up. "Can't. Today's my only day off this week, so I have a ton of shit to do."

She moved out of his reach, sprinted up the stairs, and ran to her room, the sound of Jax's chuckles echoing in her ears. She closed the door, breathing deeply. Why did he have such an effect on her? It wasn't like she'd never seen a good-looking man before. When she used to strip in gentlemen's clubs in Denver, she'd seen several nice-looking guys from all walks of life. She'd do lap dances for them, take their phone numbers, and move on. She never got involved with any of the customers outside of the club; she kept her private life separate. But this deal with Jax blew her mind and pissed her off. She had to keep her body in check. She had to keep reminding herself he was a controlling bastard and heartbreaker... but his touch was so gentle, and his eyes sparkled whenever his smile lit up his face. *Damn, girl—stop it!*

Noticing clothes strewn over her chair and several pairs of unboxed shoes on the floor, Cherri busied herself by straightening out her room. Turning up the music, her body moved to the songs of Green Day. When she finished, she bent down to pick up the last pair of shoes, her butt hitting something behind her. Spinning around, she fell into Jax's arms.

"What the hell? Don't you know you're supposed to knock?" She brushed the hair off her face.

Jax, hunger in his eyes, tightened his grip on her. "I did knock, but you didn't hear over the music. Sink's good to go. And... nice ass."

Tugging away, she said, "You're finished already? Whoa, you're fast."

"Well..."

Blushing, Cherri shifted in place, occupying herself with a pair of shoes in her hands. Out of the corner of her eye, she saw Jax look her over before she went to her closet and put the shoes in a box on the floor.

"Do I need to pay you, or something?" she asked.

Throwing his head back, he laughed. "You're too precious, sweetness. You don't owe anything. We take care of our properties *and* our tenants, if you know what I mean." He winked at her.

Ignoring the double entendre, Cherri leaned against the door. "Well, then, thank you."

Smiling at her, Jax looked around her room. "You've done a nice job putting this all together. I like your prints." Pointing at the *Nighthawks*, he commented, "This one's interesting."

Nodding, Cherri said, "That's one of my favorite paintings. I guess it's because I can understand the feelings of isolation, separation, and loneliness. I feel like that, you know?"

"Yeah, I get it. Sometimes, I feel that way, too. I still miss my dad."

"Did he die?"

"Yeah."

"When?"

"It's been about seven years. It's weird, 'cause some days, it's like a long time ago, and other days, it's too fresh. Fuck, I don't know... It sucks."

"It does. I lost my dad when I was ten years old. For me, it seems like a long time ago. I'm scared to death I'll totally forget what he looked like or sounded like." Her voice grew tinny.

"Was your dad sick?"

"No, just drunk. He ran off the road."

"Fuck, that must've been tough."

"Yeah. Was your dad sick?"

"Nah. He got himself killed by hitting on a biker's old lady at Sturgis. He was shit-faced; he never had a chance against the fucker's gun."

"That's awful. Were you close?"

"As close as we could've been, considering the Hell my mom put us in. She ran off with a rival club's president when I was thirteen years old—just killed my old man. He took to drinkin' to get rid of the pain and humiliation. When he wasn't drunk, we had some good times." Jax smiled. "Yeah, he was okay, you know. He got dealt a shitty hand, that's all. The Insurgents were my main family. Hawk was there for me all the time. I'll never forget that. What kills me is seeing my fuckin' mom at bike rallies. I can't stand her. She treated my dad like pure shit."

"Does your mom talk to you when she sees you?"

Jax gritted, "Fuck no. She's a bitch. She's also Reaper's old lady."

"Who's Reaper?"

"The asshole president of the Deadly Demons MC. Insurgents and Deadly Demons are rivals—we've hated each other since the clubs started. That's what killed my dad the most—she fucked his arch enemy and threw it in his face. The bitterness ate away at him until there was nothing left of his old self. It was hard enough she slutted around, but hooking up with Reaper? It's something I'll never forgive her for." Jax stared at the floor then combed his fingers through his hair. "Fuck, I can't believe I'm telling you all this shit."

Cherri shrugged, a warmness spreading through her. She hoped she was the only woman he had told his feelings to. *Stop being stupid, Cherri. Why does that matter? You're just biding time; you'll be leaving all this behind soon enough. Don't get emotionally involved with this one.*

"So, your mom raised you?" His voice sliced through her thoughts, startling her.

"Sorta. I mean, she remarried so I had a... you know... a stepfather."

"And how was that?"

The minutes ticked by as the sun streamed into the quiet room, casting bright, rectangular patterns on the floor as a tree branch, swaying in the light breeze, scraped against the window. Jax watched Cherri; her eyes were flat, and her body was stiff. Recoiling from the present, she stood still as images from her past assaulted her mind: dark shadows approaching, locked doors pried open, hands touching her, thin lips crushing her mouth. The blood began to pound in her ears, the room seemed hotter, smaller, and Jax's presence was suffocating…

I have to get out, get away before I lose it, before—

"Cherri, you okay? What's going on?" Jax's voice brought her back.

Willing herself not to fall apart, she sat on the edge of the bed and filled her lungs with air. "Sorry. Shit from the past creeps in sometimes, you know?"

"Like what?"

She looked off to the side, a wry smile painted on her face. *Damn, he's good. He acts like he really cares.* "Like my mom gave more of a shit about the money my fuckin' stepdad brought in than she did about me. Like he was a bastard, and my mom didn't do shit to back me up. I split at seventeen, and I've never gone back. Nothing to talk about. We all have some stuff we don't want to remember, you know?"

"You got that right, sugar. How'd you end up with the fuckin' Deadly Demons Nomads?"

"I stripped for a while in Denver then got into a messy situation, so I left. I wanted to go to a place where no one knew about me, where I could get a new start for me and…" Her voice trailed off.

"For you and who?"

"Just me," she said tersely. "Anyway, I ran out of money and wanted to get here, so I hitched. Then the asshole Nomads picked me up and my nightmare began. Glad your club got me outta there. Those guys were evil, violent assholes."

Jax looked at her intently, his body stiff. "Did the fuckers mess with you?"

"I told 'em I was a virgin." She laughed dryly. "They believed me, so they left me alone, except for that asshole Viper. He made me suck him." She grimaced at the memory.

"That fuck! Hawk should've killed his ass. At least Hawk made sure he'd be singing in the boys' choir for the rest of his life." Jax kicked the side of the bed then sat down next to her.

"I haven't said this, but thank you for getting me outta that shit. I do appreciate it." She placed her hand on his forearm. In a barely audible voice, she said, "You know, I may do dirty things but inside, I'm good." Pointing at the Rockwell reproduction print on her wall, she continued, "I'm that girl in the poster, the one in a loving house with parents who love her and each other." Her voice cracked.

Wrapping his arms around her, Jax pulled her flush against him. "We are two of a kind. We're both carrying shit from our past and were damaged by our parents."

"I have this empty spot inside me I can't fill no matter what." Tears burned behind Cherri's eyes, and her voice was tight as she tried to keep the sobs from escaping.

Jax placed her head on his chest. His kisses against her head were like feathers in the wind. "I can fill your emptiness, sweetness. I think it's time you let me in."

With glistening eyes, she and Jax locked gazes, both of them lost and craving each other. His eyes shone with empathy. Moved by his compassion and the knowledge they were broken in some way by their pasts, she needed his touch. After sharing some of her story with him and listening to him confide his feelings to her, she desired some intimacy with him. Still keeping his gaze, she lightly trailed her fingers over his forearm; his blond hairs stood up after her fingertips passed. He licked his lips and kept his eyes on her.

Bringing his face closer to her, she sought his. As she brushed her lips over his, his sharp, indrawn breath made her insides quiver. Pulling back, she smiled at him, his eyes misted in a fierce desire. He put his hand behind her head and guided her back toward his mouth. Leaning into him, she tilted her head as Jax pressed his soft lips against hers. His tongue swept over her mouth, probing the seam to allow entry. Parting her lips, he eagerly slipped into the minty recesses of her mouth. When her tongue met his in a swirling dance, his breathing turned into short pants. Tugging her closer to him, her breasts pressed against his hard chest, and his earthy scent enveloped her. As his fingers dug into her hair, goosebumps shimmered across her skin.

"Sweetness, I want to taste every inch of your body," he murmured against her lips, pushing her down on the bed. He searched her face and asked, "You want me to stop?"

Shaking her head, Cherri tightened her arms around his neck and covered his mouth with hers. He lay down on the bed by her side, still holding their kiss as he slowly trailed his fingers down her neck to her t-shirt and slipped his hand under it. She shuddered under his light touch and arched her back, jutting her breasts out in the air. He cupped one of her tits, rubbing his finger against the lace of her bra.

Her body tingling with anticipation and excitement, Cherri lifted the bottom of her shirt upward. Looking at Jax's eyes, she saw tenderness and lust reflected in them.

"You sure you want me to do this?" he asked in a husky voice.

"Yes," she whispered against his neck as her tongue explored his Adam's apple. His low groan told her she hit a tender, sexy spot on him. She tasted the saltiness of his skin as she trailed her tongue down his neck. Pulling his shirt up over his head, she then continued trailing her tongue over his skull tattoo, the one with the smoking pistols and the flames. His breathing was short as he pushed her down on the bed and undressed her. She lay there, bared to him, a light breeze from the open window caressing her naked body while his smoldering eyes made her insides melt.

"Fuck, you're beautiful, sweet one," Jax gasped as his eyes took in her delicate form. Her skin was white, almost translucent; the only color on her was her taut pink nipples and the rosiness of her folds peeking out from her shaved pussy.

He ran his fingertips over her nipples, softly pinching them. Cherri moaned, "That feels so good."

"I bet it does, sweet one. I'm gonna make you feel a whole lot better. You're beautiful, and your sweet tits were made for sucking, sugar."

When his hand cupped her naked breast, squeezing it tenderly, she stiffened. He moved his finger to the underside of her tit then hesitated, her reaction stopping him. Looking down at her face, he raised his eyebrows in surprise.

Covering her face with her hands, she avoided his look as she flinched away from his touch. All at once, her face, neck, and ears felt impossibly hot. Gently removing her hands from her flushed face, Jax held her chin so she couldn't turn her head to avoid his gaze.

Pulling up her breast, he sucked in his breath and said, "Shit, what happened?"

Angry white lines zigzagged underneath; small scars, close to the breast bone. Cherri was an expert with concealing makeup, so no one ever noticed them. Cursing herself for forgetting to cover them up, she caught his concerned look and lied, "I had to remove some stuff on my skin when I was younger. They look worse than what you're imagining. I'm so used to them that it's no big deal for me." Pausing for a few seconds, she asked, "Is it for you?"

A grin broke out on his face. Lowering his mouth, he kissed her hot and deep. When he came up for air, he ran his tongue down her chin to the underside of her tit and licked her scars. "No, sweetness. Every inch of your body is beautiful, even your scars. Hell, I got a nasty one on my side thanks to the fuckin' Nomads."

As he covered them with light kisses, a few tears escaped from the corners of Cherri's eyes, running sideways into her hair. Jax scrunched her tits together then laved his tongue over them until he caught her nipple between his teeth, grazing each hardened tip as he massage her tits.

Bolts of pure, intense desire coursed through her as he sucked her nipple and his hand played with her tits. The desire started at her core and worked its way upward until she thought she would explode. Squirming, she clenched her thighs together, trying to rub them to gain some relief.

Chuckling, Jax pulled her legs apart. "No way am I gonna let you come before I get down there. I just bet you're wet as fuck."

He was so right; she was dripping. She couldn't understand why she had this reaction to him. Hell, she'd fucked men before, but nothing felt like this. This was the first time she'd *enjoyed* being with a man. Jax had done exactly what she didn't want him to do: he invaded her world—her mind, her body, and her heart. Cherri wanted him inside her so much, but he was taking his time with her. He was going slowly, even though she suspected he wanted to ram his cock into her and fuck her hard. His sweetness and consideration touched her.

She reached down to grab his crotch and realized he had half-unzipped his jeans, his dick peeking out. As she rubbed his silky head, a few drops of pre-come dampened her fingers. He groaned when she circled his head with her hand. "Take these off," she whispered into his chest as she tugged at his jeans.

Jax grinned and twisted his jeans off then moved on top of her, his hardness pressing against her stomach. "Do you feel how hard I am? You're makin' my dick like this, sweetie." Lowering his head, he kissed her deeply. Relishing the feel of his muscled body on hers, she closed her eyes as she ran her hands up his arms.

"Open your eyes, sugar. I want to see you while I touch you."

Eyes wide, Cherri watched as he left her prickling breasts and kissed his way down her stomach to her thighs. He ran his tongue over the inside of each, causing her to moan and writhe. He threw her a sexy smile and, on his knees, he lowered his mouth to her aching pussy. With one sweep, his tongue stroked from the bottom of her entrance to her hardening nub. She wanted to jump out of her skin.

"I knew you'd taste sweet." He stroked her bud to firmness with the tip of his tongue. "How does that feel, sweet lips?"

Cherri whimpered, since she couldn't talk. Her mouth was dry, like it was filled with cotton, and her insides jumped. She had never felt this alive; it blew her mind. Her body was like a ball of excitement, throbbing and tingling.

"You feel good inside your silky pussy, sugar," Jax said as he inserted two fingers while he continued stroking her clit. When he spoke, his breath tickled her mound, making her giggle. She looked down at him as he licked and sucked her nub, his digits moving in and out of her wetness. She ran her fingers through his hair—it was soft, like plush velvet.

When the deep spasms began to grow within her depths, she pulled his hair and bucked her hips, arching herself closer to his mouth and the wonderful things he was doing to her. If she could help it, she never allowed a man's tongue near her pussy, but with Jax it was different. Jax licking her wetness didn't make her feel dirty—it was awesome. She didn't feel guilty, only happy and connected to another human being—something she had rarely felt in the last several years.

"I'm going to get inside your warm pussy, sugar. You're good with this, right?"

"Yeah," she said breathlessly.

Stretching an arm behind him, Jax grabbed his jeans and took out a condom. After she watched him put it on his long, thick cock, her fingers curled around it, stroking up and down. Before she could explore further, he pushed her hand away then leaned over and rubbed his cock in her wetness. Spreading her legs further apart, he guided his dick to her entrance.

"Fuck, you're soaking wet. I like that. Yeah, I like that a lot." Covering his cock with her juices, his broad head parted her lips as he pushed in.

"Ah! So good," Cherri gasped.

Pushing more, he buried his hard length inside her. He rolled back and forth, grunting and sweating, while she wrapped her legs around him. Her fingernails dug into his shoulders while she moaned loudly.

"You like having my cock in you? You like the way my big cock feels in your tight, sweet pussy?"

"Oh, yeah. Fuck me hard and fast, Jax. Go on, do it. I won't break." She dug her fingernails deeper into his flesh, and sweat shone on her face.

Holding her look, he asked, "You sure?"

"That's what I want."

"Okay, sweetness. Hold on."

Jax pulled out and slammed back in to her, knocking her breath away. With each thrust, heat spread through her, and she bucked her hips to meet his relentless plunges. His feral grunts filled her ears and competed with her groans of pleasure. As he rammed his thick cock inside her, her sex squeezed and covered it like a glove.

"Damn, sugar, my cock feels so good in your hot pussy. This is where I'm supposed to be. Only me; no other brother, got it?" He bent down and crushed his mouth against hers, kissing her wet and deep. Lifting back up, he gripped her legs and pushed them back further until her feet were resting on his shoulders.

She was spread wide, her glistening pussy with its pink, swollen lips splayed out. Jax's eyes lingered on her sweetness before he flicked his finger over her rigid bud. Sliding out of her, he pounded back in then rode her fast and hard, his balls slapping against her ass.

Biting down on her lower lip, her pussy clenched as the waves of bliss began to roll. The pleasure kept rising, and she didn't dare exhale. His pants became labored as his legs tightened. When the ecstasy burst inside her, spreading throughout her body, she screamed out like an animal in heat. Jax grunted, his face burrowed in her neck as he shoved in and out a few more times before she felt his cock swell and his body stiffen.

"Fuck, yeah, fuck!" he cried as he shot his load into her warmth.

Shaking with delight, Cherri encircled him tighter. He kept ramming her, milking himself dry until they were both utterly sated.

She stroked his back until his breathing came back to normal before he kissed her, rolled off, and nestled her against his side. Lying with her leg flung over his, her arm around his waist and her head on his chest, she heard his heart beat. Sunlight bathed them as Jax ran his fingers through Cherri's tousled hair. In the distance, the sound of a freight train's whistle echoed.

"That was fuckin' awesome, sweetness," Jax said as he lifted her chin up toward his face. He bent down, and with a tenderness she had never experienced from a man, he kissed her; first on her eyes, her cheeks then her mouth—soft, gentle kissing that made her toes curl and her stomach coil. Affection spread through her, and she realized that, for the first time in a very long time, she felt safe, cherished, and happy.

"You're mine now, sweetness. You belong to me, understand?"

"I don't know what to say."

"Nothing to say; I'm just telling you like it is. You're mine. I'm claiming you. No more of that Gunner bullshit, got it? You're mine."

"Gunner…? I never had anything with him. I just did a dance for him."

"No more dances for any of the brothers—or any guy, for that matter. I'll take care of you now."

"What about Peaches? I thought you guys were together."

"Don't worry about her. She's a nice bitch and all, but sugar, my eyes have been on you since I first saw you. You pushed me away, but it's always been you I've wanted. You do something to me."

A flush of adrenaline tingled through her body as giddiness built inside her. Cherri nuzzled into the crook of his arm and said against his skin, "Right now, everything seems so simple when yesterday it seemed so complicated."

"Yesterday is gone. Today is the beginning for us." He squeezed her closer to him.

The minutes ticked away and Cherri felt her eyelids grow heavy. She loved being in Jax's strong arms. Why had she wasted so much time fighting him? Being with him in that moment seemed perfect, like she had found someone she could begin to trust with her secrets. She was falling for this rough biker who had an unexpected gentle side to him—one she was sure few people ever saw.

His phone startled her out of her reverie. Jax grabbed it from the nightstand. "Hey, what's up?" His body tensed as he listened to the caller on the other end of the receiver. He sat up and ran his hand through his hair, his face paling. "Don't do anything stupid. Calm down. I'm coming over now. Just calm down and wait for me."

He rolled out of bed and grabbed his jeans from the floor, pulling them up as he searched for his boots. Throwing his cut on over his t-shirt, he glanced at Cherri as he walked toward the door. "Gotta go."

"What? Where? What's going on?"

"This doesn't concern you, Cherri. I'll call you later."

"Are you fuckin' serious?" Her eyes searched his face.

"Like I said, I gotta go. Later."

After he walked out of the room, he left the door open and headed for the stairway. Cherri sat dumbfounded as she watched him descend the stairs. The front door slammed shut, and the rumble of his bike vibrated in her ears. She lay in bed listening to his engine until she couldn't hear it anymore. *What the fuck just happened? We just made awesome love, he told me I was his, he got a phone call, and he abandoned me without even a goodbye kiss or any goddamned explanation?* The rush of blood to her head made her dizzy as the fire from her building anger began to consume her. Behind her eyelids, hot tears formed. *That fucker!*

Her breathing became shallow as she grew rigid. She forced herself to calm down, to think rationally. There had to be a reason for him taking off with only a glance at her. *It's probably club business. I know they're all psycho about telling anyone who's not in the club what's going on. Maybe I'm just overreacting.*

Cherri curled up on the bed as an empty darkness weaved its way inside her. A dull ache replaced the anger; she had a sick feeling. She wanted to go away, far away. She wanted to be the girl in the Norman Rockwell print, the one who was always smiling.

Nothing bad ever happens to her.

CHAPTER SEVEN

A S THE TIME faded away, Cherri noticed the stillness of the room—it was stifling. She wanted to get out of the house, go somewhere. Since the Insurgents had brought her to Pinewood Springs a few months before, she had only danced and slept. She kept to herself a lot, and she hadn't made friends with any of the other dancers. She didn't know anyone outside of Dream House or the Insurgents; her life revolved around the club's world. The only place she could think of going was Dream House. She had a ton of paperwork to catch up on, so even though it was her day off, she decided to do some work at the strip club. Keeping the club's books and being in charge of the dancers was more than a full-time job. She freshened up and headed to Dream House.

"Hey, Cherri, I thought it was your day off," Holt said as she entered the club.

"Supposed to be, but the ton of paperwork on my desk was eating at me, so I decided to do some catch-up. How's business?"

"Slow, but Wednesday afternoons are always the slowest for the club. Want a drink?"

"No, I'm good." She watched the stripper on stage. "Chloe looks like she's sleepwalking up there."

"She's got the flu, or something." Seeing Cherri's eyebrows go up, Holt continued, "She needs the money real bad, so she dragged her ass in here."

"With that dancing, she's not gonna get shit for tips. She should've just stayed home. Gotta get crackin'," she said as she walked toward the office behind the stage.

Looking at the stack of receipts, invoices, time sheets, and inventory lists, Cherri pulled her hair back into a messy bun then sat behind the desk, determined to make some headway in catching up. She was glad it was a slow, quiet day. As she started to work, she heard indistinguishable voices, then soft moaning coming from the backstage area. She strained to hear, to make sure it wasn't her mind playing tricks on her. No, definite moans were coming from the dressing room area.

I hope one of the dancers isn't turning a trick. Fuck, can't anything be smooth? From time to time, some of the dancers would turn tricks in their dressing rooms to make some extra money on slow shifts, but it wasn't allowed on Insurgents' time. The MC turned a blind eye if a dancer was tricking in her spare time, but during work hours, it was reason for termination. Cherri hoped she didn't have to can someone.

She approached the closed dressing room door, pausing to listen. She heard high-pitched groans; it was a woman moaning. Placing her hand on the doorknob, she turned it as she heard a low, male voice. Something rang familiar in the man's hushed tones. Opening the door, she saw Peaches straddling Jax who was seated on the leather couch. Peaches' tits bounced while her ass wiggled on Jax's hardened cock.

Bolts of shock shot through her body as dampness covered her cheeks. Her mouth hung open and she gasped.

Peaches turned around, her tits smooshed against Jax's face. She smiled wickedly.

Jax stared at Cherri, panic etched on his face, and said, "No, Cherri, this isn't what you think." He peeled Peaches off him. Cherri whipped around and ran out of the room with Jax at her heels. He grabbed her arm, swinging her around.

"Stop! Let me explain. This isn't what you think."

"It is *exactly* what I think. I was a fucking fool to let you into my heart. You're worse than *any* of the other guys because you pretend to care. All that gentle shit you fed me was just a trick to get into my pants, you sonofabitch! You're the worst! I hate you! Get the fuck outta my life and *stay out*. Fuck you, asshole!"

Cherri, breaking away from his grasp, ran out of the bar into the bright sunlight. Bleary-eyed from unshed tears, she managed to get in the car she borrowed from her roommate. Jax rushed over toward her, screaming, "Dammit, Cherri, just stop! I have to talk to you. Stop!"

She threw the car in drive and screeched out of the parking lot. She had no intention of speaking with him ever again. There was nothing to explain; he'd used her and treated her just like a hoodrat or a club mama. He didn't care shit for her; he just wanted to fuck her. *How could I have been so stupid? I will never forgive him. Ever. I will make him pay for what he did to me.*

The whole drive home, her phone rang and pinged. When she got to her place, Cherri sprinted up the stairs, closed her bedroom door, and flopped on her bed. Looking at the ringing phone, Jax's number blinked. *It's a little too late, asshole.* She turned off her phone and buried her head in her pillow as sobs overtook her body, tears streaming down her face. She hated the way men used women, and she swore she'd go back to not letting any man mean anything to her ever again.

JAX, FACE TIGHT, eyes burning, went back into Dream House. "Gimme a shot," he said to Holt.

Holt placed a shot of whiskey in front of Jax, a knowing look on his face.

"Why the fuck are you lookin' at me like that, asshole?" Jax growled.

"Hey, man, your fight ain't with me. I'm just mindin' my own business." Holt wiped the bar with his rag.

"Just don't fuckin' look at me and I won't have to beat your ass, got it? Gimme another."

Holt nodded and placed another shot in front of Jax, who was radiating anger. Peaches, finally dressed, came up to him and wound her arms around him. She kissed him on the neck, murmuring, "How come you didn't come back?"

He pushed her away. "You fuckin' set me up, you dirty slut!"

Peaches, wide-eyed, protested, "I didn't do that. I needed you here—

I was desperate. I was gonna kill myself."

"Like hell you were. You called me and said you and Emma had a fight and she was throwing you out. You fuckin' told me you had a gun to your head and you were gonna off yourself. You cried on the phone, made me think if I didn't come, your suicide would be my fault somehow. You lying cunt!"

"I didn't lie."

"Where's Emma, then?"

"She left right before you came."

Turning his head sideways, he said, "Is that right, Holt?"

Holt shook his head. Peaches glared at him.

"Has Emma been here today, Holt?" Jax asked.

"She came for an hour, but had to do something with her old man. She left me in charge for a few hours."

Jax gripped Peaches' arm roughly, his fingers turning white from his grasp. "Listen to me, bitch. You fuckin' set me up, and I wanna know why."

"I love you; that's why. I'm the one who's here for you any time. I want to be your old lady. I've been good to you." Hardness laced her blue eyes.

Jax relaxed his grip on her arm and ran his hand through his hair. "Peaches, you've been good to me. You're a great fuck, and you're always available when I need you, but I'm not looking for an old lady. I'm sorry you fell in love with me. I made it clear to you we were just fuckin' and nothing more." He paused and looked her straight in the eyes. "There's only one woman who has my heart, and that's Cherri. I was gonna tell you later tonight that our fuckin' has to stop 'cause I'm with her. I wanted to—"

"She certainly didn't look or sound like she wanted to be with you, Jax. How could you want that icy bitch over me?"

"You made a fuckin' mess with me and Cherri, something I gotta fix, but don't be sticking your nose into my business anymore. You got that?"

"If you think I'm just gonna let some skank take my man, you're crazy. I'm gonna fight for you, honey, all the way." She clasped her hand on his denim-covered thigh and stroked it.

"It's over, Peaches. That's the way it is." Jax moved her hand off him then pushed her back a little. "I'm outta here." He turned to leave.

"Waiting for that icy bitch to melt is gonna take time. I'll be here when you get lonely and tired of waiting."

Jax snorted, turned his back on Peaches, and walked out of the strip bar with his phone to his ear, hoping Cherri would pick up. Swinging his leg over his Harley, he revved it up and took off, his heart heavy.

Fifteen minutes later, he was at her front door. "Cherri, I know you're in there," he said as he pounded on the door. "Open the fuck up!"

Silence. He pounded again, this time kicking the door. He heard the crackle of splintered wood. "Fuck, do I have to break down the god-damned door?"

Silence. Pissed as hell, he called her again. *Hi, this is Cherri. Leave a message.*

He growled in frustration then threw his phone against the front door, broken pieces exploding around him. He stomped on the broken phone until it was a pile of parts. "Fuck!" He jumped off the porch and onto his bike, riding away as his exhausts ripped through the quietness of the neighborhood.

Walking into the clubhouse, he motioned to Johnnie to give him a shot. Sitting at the bar, Jax downed the whiskey, enjoying the way it burned and warmed his throat at the same time.

Hawk came over and clasped his hand on Jax's shoulder. "I tried calling you."

"My phone broke." Jax poured another shot down his throat.

"How'd that happen?"

"I threw it against a door."

"Yeah, that'll do it. What's up?"

"Fuckin' bitches. They're a pain in the ass. I'm going back to fucking multiple pussies without any faces."

"Problem is once one of them gets into your system, you're fuckin' screwed—you don't want anyone else but her. That's how it was for me with Cara."

"Yeah, but Cara wanted you, too."

"It was a struggle, but the best ones always are. You'll figure it out."

"You like challenges, but I like easy pussy."

"If your cock is aimed at that stripper, then easy is not what you're gonna get." Hawk laughed, downed his beer, and turned to leave. "And yeah, get a new phone. Club business requires you have one at all times."

Jax grunted as he played the events over in his mind. What the fuck was Cherri doing at Dream House anyway? Wasn't it supposed to be her day off? He knew it looked bad when she came into the room, but she wouldn't fucking let him explain. He wasn't doing shit with Peaches. He had got to the club, worried Peaches was going to hurt herself, and when he went into her dressing room and saw her in her stripper outfit, sitting on the couch, she didn't look all that upset to him. After they talked for a bit and he realized she had exaggerated so he'd come to the club, he started to get up to leave when Peaches pushed him back and started pushing her tits in his face and rubbing her barely covered pussy over his dick.

He tried shoving her away, but she kept moving all around him, and his dick got harder. He was peeling her off him when Cherri opened the door and got a full view of a half-naked Peaches and his hard-on. He didn't blame her for being pissed. She probably thought he used her. And, of course, he had a hard-on—he was a man, and any soft ass grinding against his cock would wake it up. But it didn't mean he wanted Peaches or was going to fuck her. Since he'd tasted Cherri, he craved only her. He had to make things right with her. He just *had* to.

SLIVERS OF MOONLIGHT pierce through the shutter slats. Quiet stillness lends an eeriness to the night. Several high howls and low barks from the

neighborhood punctuate the blackness.

It is a hot, thick night. The oscillating fan in the corner of the bedroom blows streams of hot air in Cherri's face. She hears the floorboards creak outside her door. Her heart beats faster, her chest heaving, and she fears it will burst out of her. Silence. She knows he's out there, can almost hear his short breaths. Dampness forms under her breasts and upper lip. She pulls the sheet up above her chin, encasing it around her like a cocoon. Under the sheet, the oppressive heat surrounds her.

The doorknob clicks and turns slowly. She holds her breath, waiting—waiting for the door to open and the man to enter. Click. It opens, a shadowy figure looming in the doorway. He comes closer. Cherri, covering her head with her sheet, hopes it'll make her invisible. The mattress depresses as he sits down next to her. She hears him panting, his excitement palpable. She shivers despite the temperature. His chuckles come from deep within his chest, and his drumming fingers against the mattress sound like a metronome. She wants to scream. He's playing with her.

He tugs the sheet away from her grip, sliding it out of her clammy hands. She opens her eyes and sees his lust-filled ones shining as they fix on her ripe, young breasts. He leans toward her, and his mouth silences her small, "No." Kneading her breasts with his hand, he pushes her down on her back as he lifts up her cotton nightshirt. She whimpers. He presses his lips against her mouth as his hand rubs her hips.

"No," she snivels.

"Shh, honey. I'm not gonna hurt you. Daddies never hurt their special girls." His mouth starts its descent toward her breasts. Something hard, like a wrench, rubs against her private parts.

No... no...

Cherri woke up gasping for air, sweat pouring down her neck and under her arms. She rubbed her forehead, trying to dispel the ghosts of her past. Getting up, she put a cold washcloth against her hot face, the coolness giving her some relief. She looked at her phone; it read seven-thirty in the evening and twenty-five missed calls—all of them from Jax.

"Are you okay, Cherri?" her roommate, Ginger, asked as she softly knocked on the door. Cherri sat mutely on her bed, looking at the door.

"Cherri?" Ginger's voice was louder that time as she came into the room, gazing at Cherri. "I heard you yelling; is anything wrong?"

Sighing, Cherri shook her head. "No. Just a bad dream, that's all."

"Must've been some dream. You were screaming."

Cherri shrugged. "Sorry."

"You sure you're okay? You look real sad."

"All men are assholes."

Ginger laughed. "You just figuring this out now? Don't be sad over that, 'cause it ain't gonna change them. I've known men are assholes for a long time, but they fuck good and they can be a helluva lot of fun." Ginger brushed her curly auburn bangs to the side.

Cherri sat and watched Ginger. A few minutes of awkward silence passed. Ginger, backing out of the room, said, "I gotta get going. I got another shift at the strip club. Just wanted to make sure you were all right."

"Thanks," Cherri called out after her.

Standing up, Cherri went over to the picture-sized window and looked out. Cars drove by, people walked around, and children played in the street. She wondered what each of their lives was like—were they happy, lonely, or in love. Her mind drifted to Jax and their lovemaking earlier that afternoon. She was so happy, but then he had to go and spoil it all. Anger emanated from her when she thought about the way he used her for fucking then ran back to Peaches for loving. He was the worst asshole she had ever met. At least with the other jerks in her life, she had known what the score was, but with Jax, he hid what a fucker he really was. He had hurt her. She thought she was immune to a man hurting her, but she let her guard down, let this one sneak into her life and heart.

Her phone pinged. She picked it up and saw it was a text message from Gunner:

Gunner: *How are you? I'm at the club but don't see you. Are you here?*

Cherri: *It's my day off. You missing me? :)*

Gunner: *Always.*

Cherri: *I'll be there tomorrow.*

Gunner: *You doing anything now?*

Cherri: *Not really.*

Gunner: *Want to get some barbecue with me?*

Cherri read the text a couple of times. Gunner was a nice guy, and she knew he wanted something with her. He was generous, and she knew there wouldn't be any chance of her falling in love with him. Plus, Jax was history, and she was done with him. Gunner could give her the money she needed to leave Pinewood Springs and start a new life. Gunner wouldn't be a bad sugar daddy.

Gunner: *You there?*

Cherri: *Yeah, sorry, doing something at the same time. Dinner sounds good.*

Gunner: *I'll pick you up in thirty minutes?*

Cherri: *Yeah.*

Gunner: *Ok. Don't need to give me your address. Know where u live. See you soon.*

Cherri: *:))*

She stared at the phone, a calm caressing her. If Jax could grope Peaches, she could cozy up to Gunner. She might even go to a clubhouse party and hang all over him. She'd show Jax two could play at his game. A sneer broke out over her face as her heart turned to ice.

CHAPTER EIGHT

THERE WAS AN excited tremor in the air at the Insurgents' clubhouse. It was Saturday night, and that meant it was party time. Parties at the clubhouse were always wild. Since several chapters were coming that night to party, the members told Emma and Cherri they needed several dancers to entertain the men, along with a few who wanted to dance and fuck afterwards.

The only drug the Insurgents tolerated at their compound was weed, but at big parties, crank and crystal flowed. The basement of the clubhouse had many rooms that could accommodate the various brothers if they passed out or wanted to crash. The old ladies had been cooking since the morning to prepare the food for the party; platters of ribs, beef brisket, and hot sausage links, along with mountains of mashed potatoes, corn, and coleslaw, would soon be laid out on the long wooden tables in the great room. It was too cold to put them outside—spring in Colorado was a mixture of pleasant days and frigid nights.

The old ladies, after setting up the food, would leave. Sometimes, they would go over to each other's houses and drink. They rarely went to the weekend parties; the family parties that usually happened on Sundays were cool, but most of the old ladies hated the weekend ones because of all the sluts who spread their legs for the brothers.

There was a definite hierarchy among the Insurgent women, and the old ladies were at the top and garnered the full respect from the other women and the brothers. The lowest rungs were the club whores and mamas—they were nothing more than public holes to satiate the brothers and their guests at any time. The hoodrats were the weekend sluts who came to party, drink, and fuck. They may come to one party or to many parties, but they came and went as they pleased. Before they entered, they were patted down, checked out via an elaborate ID system Hawk had set up, and photographed. The Insurgents didn't need any undercover badge or any infiltrator from a rival club on their property.

The women, who lined up outside the chain-link fence for hours before entering the hallowed doors of the clubhouse, dressed in tight-fitting, barely there outfits. To a passerby, it would seem like the women were planning to audition for a porn movie. Overdone makeup and heels made for sitting rather than walking adorned most of the women. It amazed many of the bikers that so many women would spread their legs for them each and every weekend, just to have biker sex, but there was never a shortage of women.

Cherri and Emma hurriedly put the last trunk in the van. The dancers would change into their outfits at the clubhouse, since some of them were elaborate and ran the risk of tearing a strap or losing a few buttons if they were worn before the show as the dancers mingled with the brothers. Cherri had agreed to be Gunner's date at the party. The big, mean-looking guy had turned out to be a sweet teddy bear, and he treated her like a goddess.

"Jax is gonna be there tonight. He always is on Saturdays," Emma said as she steered the van toward the clubhouse, which was about twenty-five miles outside of Pinewood Springs.

"So? I don't give a shit what he does."

"I'm just sayin'. We don't want a repeat of what happened between Gunner and Jax at Dream House a few weeks back. It's not smart to play one brother off the other."

"I'm not doing that at all. I'm finished with Jax. I was never really with him, anyway. Gunner and I have been hangin' out for the last couple of weeks. He's a sweetie to me, and I'm with him. I'm not playing games here." Cherri turned her head and watched the trees and wildflowers rush by as Emma took the curves at a higher speed than Cherri would have if she were driving.

"Okay, but I didn't realize you and Gunner were going out. He's a quiet guy, but he's solid—no bullshit or game-playing with him."

Smiling, Cherri said, "I do like him. I like him a lot. I've never had someone so nice to me. He cares for me."

"If Gunner cares about you, he'll give you the world. If someone crosses him, he'll give them a knife to the throat. Just be careful."

Gunner did care about Cherri, and he proved it in the way he treated her: buying her anything she wanted, helping her pay her bills, holding her while she slept, and not pressuring her for sex when she told him she wasn't ready. Oh, sure, they kissed and touched each other, and she gave him blowjobs, which he seemed to love, but she didn't want him inside her. She couldn't figure it out, but she just didn't want it. Sometimes, it was like if she did let him put his dick inside her, she'd be cheating on Jax. Ludicrous thinking on her part, but that was the way she felt. *Go figure.* She was glad Gunner had been so patient, but she couldn't tell him the truth—it would hurt him too much, and the last thing she wanted to do was hurt him.

Turning into the parking lot, Emma tooted the horn. Roach, the newest prospect, waved and opened the electric gate. Cherri saw Gunner standing by his Harley, arms crossed, nodding at her as Emma pulled into a space.

"Hey," Cherri said as she ran up to him and kissed him on his cheek. He pulled her into his massive arms and kissed her hard on the lips.

"Hey, woman," he said. "You look fuckin' hot." His eyes roamed over her body, taking in her micro mini-skirt, her cropped, lavender crochet top with a lacy black bra underneath, and her thigh-high, black leather boots.

She giggled as his beard tickled her face. Looking over her shoulder, she asked Emma, "Do you want me to help with the boxes?"

"Nope, I got a couple of prospects unloading the van. Go on in. Make sure the dancers are straight about when they go on and what the rules are."

The rules were the dancers were off-limits to the guys except for lap dances. If a dancer wanted to share in the fucking sessions then she was a free agent, but once she crossed the line from dancer to slut, she was open game for any of the brothers. Emma and Cherri wanted the women to be crystal-clear about that.

"Gotcha. See you inside."

Snuggled in the crook of Gunner's arm, Cherri entered the club-house. As she came into the big room, crowds of people bumped into her, and sweet smoke, sweat, and motor oil invaded her nostrils. It took a few minutes for her eyes to adjust to the low lighting. Suffocating body heat wrapped around her as Gunner tugged her along to get some drinks. As she approached the bar, brothers in leather jackets talked to each other, a few of them checking her out. She was glad Gunner had his arm around her so protectively; otherwise, she would've been like a deer in a lion's den.

She shivered in spite of the heat emanating off the throngs of bodies. Several topless women glared at her as the men raked over her body with their lustful eyes. She diverted her glance toward the bar and saw Jax sitting at it with Chas and Jerry, holding a beer. Jax turned around, staring wide-eyed at Gunner's arm around her. Red blotches surfaced on his cheeks and chin as his nostrils flared. He stood up and leaned against the bar, his arms crossed.

Glaring at her, his knuckles turning white, his jaw tightening, he slammed his steel-toed boots against his barstool. Their gazes locked with one another; his were shards of glass reflecting anger, while hers were hard, glinting with hate. She tossed her head and leaned further into Gunner, who, oblivious to the tension between Cherri and Jax, ordered two beers. He grabbed the two bottles in his large hand and turned around toward the center of the room, taking Cherri with him as he spotted two buddies from Wyoming he hadn't seen in a long time.

All around her, people drank, smoked, or fucked. The room was packed, and classic rock blasted from the speakers. The heat was unbearable, and the sweet smell of weed made her sick. Cherri needed some fresh air.

"I gotta make sure the dancers are ready for tonight. Emma wanted me to go over some stuff with them. I'll be back soon," she yelled in Gunner's ear.

"I'll walk you to where you need to go. Not safe for you to go alone since you ain't patched." He took hold of her and walked her to another room down a long hallway.

It wasn't as large as the great room, but was still big enough to fit two stripper poles on two small stages. The linoleum floor was a colorful checkerboard pattern, a remnant from the past when the clubhouse was a school. A few saggy couches around the back wall and four low tables, some of them with cut-out circles on the top—Cherri could imagine what *they* were used for—completed the room's décor.

"I'm good now. Thanks, Gunner." Cherri smiled at him.

"If you need to leave, call me and I'll come get you. Don't walk around here unaccompanied, got it?" He leaned down and kissed her, rubbing his hand up and down her back.

She nodded, watching his imposing figure leave the room. Then she went to work to make sure everything and everyone were in order for the show that would start in about thirty minutes. Head down, clipboard in hand, Cherri moved toward the door when she smashed into a muscular wall. Looking up, she stared into Jax's hazel eyes.

"Oh, sorry," she said.

Jax wound his arms around her waist. "No worries, sweetness. You're where you need to be."

Cherri struggled to break away, but his arms were too strong.

"Stop that. What the fuck's your problem? Why haven't you returned any of my phone calls or texts?" Jax demanded.

"Because I don't waste my time with assholes. You're the worst kind, you know that? You pretended to care. I'll take an honest asshole every time; at least I know what I'm getting." Her eyes flashed.

"Fuck, you're difficult! It isn't at all what you think. What we had was real. It wasn't a come-on, and you fuckin' know it. You won't let me fuckin' explain. Damn, you piss me off!"

"I don't believe a damn thing you say. You're a liar, and I don't want to hear your damn excuses." She tried pushing him away, but Jax squeezed her tighter. "Let me go!"

"I won't. I'm never letting you go. Fuck, you don't know shit. You're beautiful, sexy, and the only fuckin' thing I can think of since you first came to the clubhouse."

He hugged her and stroked her back tenderly. Her knees became rubber with each stroke and caress. *What the fuck? I hate my body for responding to him. I can't get sucked into this again. I can't.* When Jax relaxed his hold on her, Cherri yanked away from him.

"Don't you get it? I don't want to be with you. Stay the fuck away from me."

Anger oozed from Jax as he jerked Cherri back into his embrace. "You come here with Gunner? What's up with that shit?"

"It's none of your business who I come with. You can fuck whoever you want and so can I. We don't have a claim on each other. Just fuckin' deal with it." Her voice was cold and her eyes were steel.

Tilting his face down to hers, he kissed her hard. She kissed him back then twisted her head away as his mouth sought her lips again.

"Brother, I don't think we want things to get messy here tonight," Gunner's low voice said. "Leave her alone. She's with me."

Jax glared at Gunner, saying, "To spite me, *brother.*"

"Don't matter the reason. Point is she's with me, and you know the boundaries here."

Jax knew the boundaries all right. All Insurgents knew you didn't mess with another brother's woman—old ladies, girlfriends, and dates were always off-limits. It all came down to respect; members had to give respect to each other in order to be in the club. It was simple, and respect meant everything in the Insurgents' world.

Jax raised his arms in surrender, backed off, and motioned Cherri to go to Gunner. Cherri, embracing Gunner, glared at Jax, but she was really pissed at herself for enjoying being in his arms again. Gunner hugged her, and she kissed his cheek, smiling. Gunner was a decent man. He had been so good and generous to her that he didn't deserve to find her in Jax's arms. Just the week before, she had mentioned she wanted to take an online class in graphic art since she'd always loved art, and he paid for it, not even expecting her to fuck him for it. Sweet man. He was rough and would kill a man in a blink of an eye if the circumstances called for it—she was certain of that—but with her, he was gentle and adoring. He made her feel like she was a goddess on a pedestal. He couldn't do enough for her. She didn't want to hurt him.

"Come on, baby, let's go. I gotta make sure the dancers are ready," she said.

He laughed. "You lead, I'll follow."

They left the room, but not before Cherri looked over her shoulder and saw Jax leaning against the doorway, his eyes full of regret.

An hour later, the strip show was well underway. Several of the dancers swung around the poles and writhed on the stage floor as the men crowded around, hooting and leering at them while they gyrated to the overhead music. Cherri stood to the side of the stage, making sure none of the guys got too crazy with the dancers. Gunner acted like her bodyguard, his scowl a mask of intimidation.

Each of the rooms was packed. The smaller ones had couples fucking, while the larger rooms had music and sexual entertainment. One of the dancers, Dakota, came up to Cherri, a worried look on her face. "I think India may be in trouble. There's a woman in one of the rooms who looks like her from behind, and there're all these men around her."

"Do you know if it *is* India, for sure?" Cherri asked. India was one of her top dancers, and Cherri didn't see her in the strip room.

"No, but I haven't seen her and it looks like her. I don't know…"

"I'll check it out." Cherri turned to Gunner. "Watch the stage; I'll be right back." Before Gunner could protest, she was gone.

In a smaller room down the hall, Cherri saw a young woman who looked like India: long, straight black hair, firm butt, and heavy breasts. The woman turned her head, catching Cherri's eye. Relief spread over her—it wasn't India. Cherri started to leave when she heard the woman scream. She looked back and saw her moaning and squirming on her hands and knees. She was riding one of the brother's cocks, another member had his dick up her ass, and yet another had his in her mouth while her head bounced like she was bobbing for apples. Someone said, "Fuckin' hot, the slut's got three cocks in her. What a fuckin' horny bitch." About fifteen men stood around as they waited their turn. Several of them had their hard dicks out, stroking them.

Cherri stared in horror at the sight. "Is this turning you on, sweetness?" Jax's voice whispered in her ear, and his heated breath sent chills down her back to the pit of her stomach.

Mutely, she shook her head, her eyes transfixed on the sex act before her. Her arms prickled as Jax ran his fingers over the back of them. He was right behind her, his hardness pressing between her butt cheeks. Cherri was more than aware of his presence and a cold sweat slid over her, making her tremble. She could hardly breathe in the small, crowded room, thick with smoke. The room grew smaller and blood rushed to her temples as black spots floated in front of her eyes. *Fuck, I've gotta get outta here. I'm gonna pass out. I can't breathe. I can't—*

Cherri crumpled to the floor.

WHERE AM I? Cherri looked around the darkened room, trying to make out the contents. A shadowy figure hunched in a chair, and the full moon's light looked like gnarled fingers as it filtered in through the window blinds. Every inch of her skin pebbled in goosebumps. Her muscles stiffened while her breathing strained; she was on high-alert. The figure rose from the chair and made his way toward her on the bed Tremors made her whine—her chest heaved as she gasped for air.

"No, no, stay away from me. Leave me alone! I'm gonna tell Mom! Leave me the fuck alone. Oh, please, leave me alone." She was a tight ball of nerves smashed against the headboard, her nails clawing at it as she sobbed.

"Shh, I'm not gonna hurt you, sweetness. You're having a bad dream, or something."

What, who is that? It isn't my stepdad. Where the fuck am I?

Jax approached her carefully. He switched on the lamp and released a warm glow which filled the room. Cherri, hair plastered to her wet forehead and curled up in a ball, relaxed when she saw Jax. *That's right; now I remember. I'm at the Insurgents' clubhouse.* She was safe.

"You're shaking like a leaf, sweet one. What's the matter?" Prying her hands off the headboard, Jax held her close to him. "You fainted, so I brought you up here. You were out for a while, and I was beginning to freak out." Wiping away her hair from her face, he placed a gentle kiss on her forehead. "Everything's okay. I'm here—you're okay."

Letting out a long breath, Cherri allowed Jax to hold her. Her trembles began to subside with every gentle stroke of her hair. Jax's strong arms gave her the much needed comfort she sought. She wished she could rid her mind of her past demons. She wanted safety and peace. She wanted to rest.

Jax held Cherri for a long while. Neither of them spoke, both of them taking comfort in being with each other. Cherri, wrapped in Jax's arms, felt like she was insulated from everything bad and scary. Wishing she could stay like that forever, but knowing she couldn't, she cleared her throat.

"Um... I gotta go. Uh... thanks for... like... helping me out, you know?"

"I'm real sorry for all the shit that went down with Peaches. I swear it wasn't anything. She made up some bullshit—"

"Jax, I don't want to hear it. You helped me out and I'm tired, so let's not go into all of it. Not now," she whispered, her voice strained.

"Okay, I know you're not in a good place right now. I get that." He got up from the bed, pulling her with him. Crushing her to him, he kissed her softly on her head; her body twitched, and her stomach fluttered. *How can he give such tenderness and be such a selfish sonofabitch?*

While opening the door, Jax asked, "Who did you think I was? What'd you mean when you said you were gonna tell your mom? Tell your mom what?"

"Nothing. I was dreaming."

"You were awake when I came to you. You were freaked out. Why were you so scared? Did someone do something to you?" Concerned eyes searched her face.

"No, just shit from my past. Let's go." Hurriedly, she went out into the hallway to stop the questions and the memories.

When they came downstairs, Gunner rushed up to her. He circled her shoulders and mashed her to him. He glowered at Jax, giving him the evil eye.

"This is the last time I'm gonna tell you to stay the fuck away from my woman," Gunner grunted.

His words made Jax's face screw up, a grimace replacing his usual stoic look as his eyes narrowed with a hint of sadness brimming in them. Cherri felt his pain as it emanated from him, causing her insides to lurch. She closed her eyes to block out the hurt stamped on his face.

"Come on, baby," Gunner said.

"Jax helped me. He wasn't doing anything else except helping me. I fainted and he was there."

Gunner looked at Jax and nodded his thanks to him. "What do you want to do, baby?" he asked Cherri, his breath smelling of whiskey.

"I want to go home," she whispered in his ear.

Gunner kissed her deeply, swung her around, and walked out of the clubhouse. The night chill invigorated Cherri. She hopped on the back of Gunner's Harley and held on to his waist. The bike's engine ripped through the quiet of the parking lot as he headed out toward the open road. Cherri turned around and saw Jax standing in the cold, watching her leave. Her eyes stung with the wind against her tears as she rode off into the blackness.

Chapter Nine

"WE'VE GOT A real fuckin' problem with our charter in Kilson, Nebraska. Fuck, it pisses me the hell off." Banger pounded his fist on the table during the emergency church he had called.

"If you ask me, those fuckers have been given too many warnings. It's time for us to go up there and tell them how it is. If Dustin can't get his shit together and run a proper club, then we need to cut them from the Insurgents family. I'm sick of their bullshit," Hawk said.

"Yeah, I agree. And I think we all know we can't have that kind of shit associated with us. What's the latest fuck-up?" Banger looked at his vice president.

Clearing his throat, Hawk said, "Word is they're fuckin' underage girls and whoring them out, and that can't be tolerated."

Outraged shouts bounced off the plastered walls. Banger slammed the gavel down on the table. "Okay, keep it down. We know that shit is sick and no Insurgents club is gonna do it. A bigger problem we have is this arms deal Hawk and Jax set up for the assholes in Kilson. As you know, we're not doin' that shit no more thanks to the Colorado voters who made weed legal. We get so much fuckin' money from our dispensaries we can make money legally now. Fuckin' sweet." Banger laughed, then taking a sip of his beer, he continued. "The thing is, we threw the fuckers a bonus by setting up an arms deal with Dustin and Liam. I just know they're gonna screw this up, and that puts shit on us we don't need."

The grumblings and nods in agreement reinforced that the club was on the same page with Banger and the other officers. Dustin, the president of the troubled Nebraska club, had been running it into the garbage for a while. The Kilson club had ignored the national rules each charter had to abide by if it wanted to display Insurgents colors. The Nebraska club was rife with alcohol abuse, use of hard drugs, and underage girls.

"These members are so fuckin' outta control. We need to go down there and beat their asses." Jax echoed the sentiment of the brothers. "Now they fuckin' screwed up the gun deal because they didn't deliver when they said. This makes us all look like a bunch of weak, two-faced pussies. Fuck that shit!" Jax's face contorted with rage.

Many of the brothers yelled, pounded the table, and demanded to know what their president was going to do. To lose face was the worst thing for an outlaw biker club—respect and honor were everything. The Insurgents set up the gun deal with their charter club and Liam, an Irish smuggler they had worked with many times in the past. Hawk had been reluctant to help the troubled club in the arms deal, but Banger, as national president, always lent a hand to help the charters. But the dirt bags were fuckin' things up by not delivering the guns, and the Insurgents' reputation was in jeopardy.

Banger was especially pissed since he went out on a limb for Dustin. They used to be buddies back in the day when Dustin was a member in the national club. After he proved to be a straight-up brother, Dustin asked Banger if he could set up a charter in Kilson, Nebraska, his hometown. Banger agreed, and for years things had run smoothly. It had just been in the last couple of years that things in the club started to veer off course. Banger knew he should have taken control right when it started going sour, but he let his friendship and affection for his fellow brother override his instinct to lay down the law. The Insurgents had a real mess on their hands.

"I've been in contact with Liam. I told him we're voting on whether to send a few of our brothers to Nebraska to finish up the deal. He's pretty pissed, but our prior transactions give him assurance that we'll get the job done. I'm fuckin' pissed we have to get involved. This shit shoulda been done by now. It was a small operation. That club is fucked.

Let's take a vote on whether we should send some brothers down there to kick some ass." Banger surveyed the sea of faces; all thirty members raised their hands and shouted out their support for their president.

Banger nodded. "Then it's a go. Hawk, Jax, Chas, PJ, Axe, and Throttle will go to make sure the deal goes down. They'll also see what the fuck is goin' on with Dustin's club. If those fuckers don't follow Insurgents code, then we're gonna cut 'em out. No more fuckin' chances."

"When do we take off?" Jax asked Hawk.

"In about an hour."

SUNSHINE BEAT DOWN on the riders as they rode two by two on the highway toward Nebraska. A cool breeze made the journey pleasant, but the darkened skies to the east didn't bode well. It was a bitch traveling in a thunderstorm with raindrops pelting down like bullets, but inclement weather was a small price to pay for the freedom and thrill of the ride.

Jax, as the Sergeant-At-Arms, roared behind the other motorcycles. Doing ninety-five on his maroon Harley CVO Road Glide was intoxicating and invigorating. He had worked two and sometimes three jobs to save enough money to afford his baby. After Hawk customized it, it was one badass bike. He loved how she handled. *If only women handled as smoothly and reliably as my bike—my life would be complete.*

The one he wanted to handle with the same deft precision as his Harley was Cherri. What the fuck was her problem anyway? As he blasted by the acres of cornfields, images of Cherri in her skin-tight skirt on Saturday night made him shift in his seat. He'd bet anything she was commando that night; he hadn't seen a panty line. She was definitely sexy. It made him madder than hell to think about Gunner enjoying her. He knew Cherri was punishing him by hanging with Gunner, but this shit was getting old.

Pursing his lips, he was mad at himself for wasting his time thinking about her. She wasn't the only bitch around. There was plenty of good pussy—always a steady stream of it at the clubhouse. And there were a hell of a lot of bitches who weren't as messed-up and would be more than happy to be in his bed, riding his cock. *Why the fuck don't I just move on?*

As Jax pressed down on the gas pedal, his Harley picked up speed, its exhaust pipes thundering. Slight gasoline fumes tinged the air while waves of heat from the engine and the rush of the wind all about exhilarated him. *Damn, why am I kidding myself? I feel something for this girl—she gets to me.* He shook his head as if by doing so, he'd rid his brain of her image.

Every time he saw her, he wanted her even more. What was up with that shit? He had fucked a lot of women, and he wasn't a one-woman man, but he never had feelings for the women he banged like he did for Cherri. Hell, Peaches was good pussy, nice and all that, but she didn't have the pull on his heart like Cherri did. He didn't have a clue how he could make it right with her. He wanted Cherri to be all his. He claimed her the day they fucked in her room, but she went ballistic when she saw him with Peaches. She didn't even let him explain. He told her he was sorry, but she threw his words in the garbage by hooking up with Gunner.

She could be such a bitch. He suspected her coolness was a protection from the fear she held inside her—something was behind those cold and panicked eyes. He wished she'd let him know what the fuck went on inside her head. When she freaked out on him in his room the past Saturday, her nonchalance attitude about it didn't convince him at all. She tried to act tough, but he knew she was a scared little girl in a grown-up body. He had a hunch she had some serious shit from her past, and he wanted to help her deal with it. The problem was she wouldn't let him in. She pretended she had no feelings for him, but her moans of pleasure as he screwed her told him otherwise.

There's no way she faked her screams when we fucked. Her blue eyes turned from ice to flame when she writhed beneath me. Damn, I need to get back into her silkiness and feel her pussy tightening around my dick. I've got a damn hard-on just thinking of her, like I'm in junior high. Fuck!

He saw Hawk's turn signal blink, and all riders took the next exit and pulled into the gas and convenience store off the freeway. Jax, nursing a raging hard-on, sat on his seat and pretended to be engrossed in reading his text messages.

"You don't need any gas?" Chas asked as he came over to Jax.

"Doing somethin' right now," Jax replied.

Chas looked at Jax and laughed, clapping him on the back. "Fuck, you got it bad for her, don't you?"

Glaring at him, Jax said, "I don't know what you're talkin' about."

Chas's laughter brought the other brothers over, who guffawed when they noticed Jax's erection.

"What the fuck were you doin' on your bike?" Hawk teased as he winked at the others.

"You fantasizing 'bout your little stripper?" PJ joked.

With arms crossed, Jax sneered, "Fuck off."

"I think that's what you're aiming to do, brother," Axe said, while he filled his gas tank.

Brooding, Jax placed his sunglasses back on his eyes and stared straight ahead, his mouth forming a tight line.

"Okay, let's leave horny boy alone with his thoughts. We'll take fifteen minutes to fuel and piss, then we're back on the road. I want to reach Kilson before dark," Hawk said.

Jax slinked off his bike; he still stung from the embarrassment of having a hard-on with no chick in sight. He was a wuss, but he didn't care. He'd do anything to get Cherri back into his life.

THE BIKERS APPROACHED the charter clubhouse as the sun began its descent, the western sky painted in hues of purple-tinged grey, orange and pinkish rose. A couple of prospects came up to the bikers, quickly wiping down the grime from the road trip off their motorcycles. Taking off their sunglasses, the men sauntered inside the clubhouse. Once their eyes adjusted to the dim lights, they noticed several members smoking crack and snorting coke. Women, stoned and naked, lay on the floor next to passed-out brothers. A few of the more alert women, covering their nakedness with their hands, scurried out of the room when they saw the Insurgents' members walk in. The skittish girls looked about fifteen or sixteen years old. Chas muttered, "Fuckin' perverts," under his breath.

A charter member came up to them. "Hey, welcome," he said as he stretched out his arms and looked at them through red, wavering eyes.

"Get your fuckin' president. Now," Hawk growled.

CHAPTER TEN

"HEY, BROTHER, HOW'S it goin'? Didn't know you guys were coming. You shoulda told me; I'd have made sure we got the finest whores and whiskey for you all." Dustin clasped Hawk's shoulder while a wide grin spread across his face. He nodded his chin at the other guys in the group.

A brick wall met Dustin's friendly gesture. Hawk, staring Dustin in the eye, said, "Get your members together. We're calling an emergency church."

"Oh, sure, sure, but we got time for that. How 'bout a few shots?"

"Now." Hawk's voice had a steel edge to it.

Dustin glared at them, turned around, and gathered up the twelve charter members. They all went into a large room which housed a wooden square table and folding chairs along the walls. The Insurgents emblem, carved in 3D, hung on the wall. Dustin slammed the gavel on the table and immediately, the room fell quiet.

"Our brothers from the mother club are here for a visit. We welcome them," he said as he gestured toward the out-of-state bikers.

The charter members cheered and nodded toward the visiting brothers. Several of the members cried out, "Let's party like fuck tonight." Hoots and hollers ensued.

Hawk, standing up, slammed his fist on the table. Surprised, they all quieted down.

"We're not here to party. We're here to find out what the fuck is goin' on with this club," he said.

Angry voices replaced the excited ones from a few moments earlier. Jax went on high-alert. His job as a Sergeant-at-Arms was to keep his club and his brothers safe from harm. He had to be focused and aware of everything going around him at all times. He scrutinized the faces and body language of the irate members in the room.

"Why the fuck didn't Banger pay me the respect to come himself if he had a problem with the way I'm runnin' things?" Dustin demanded.

"I don't owe you an explanation about shit. The point is this shithole club is outta control and things have got to change ASAP. Got it?" Hawk bored a hole in Dustin.

"Change what?"

"For starters, all underage girls have to go. Now. No minors stripping or prostituting, and no minors fuckin' any of the brothers. Next, all hard drugs are out since you fuckers don't know how to use without losing. Your drug use is making your brains mush, which means bad decisions on your part. We're fuckin' tired of bailing your asses out all the time." Hawk paused, his words hanging over the room's stunned silence.

"Fuck you, asshole!" Shack, the charter's vice president, yelled, breaking the silence.

Several charter members cussed and pounded their fists on the table. One burly man with a long, unkempt beard approached Hawk, hand reaching inside his cut. Before Hawk could react, Jax had the big man face-down on the floor. The man grunted and flailed like a harpooned fish out of water.

"Don't try anything stupid or I'll gut you right here and now," Jax hissed in the man's ear. "Got it, asshole?" The man growled his response.

Shack, red-faced with fury, said, "Let our brother go."

"Not until he shows some respect. I'd advise you to do the same. Hawk represents our president and our club. You don't respect that, I'll fuckin' stomp each and every one of you," Jax said in a deadly calm voice.

He nodded at Hawk to continue, who said, "And one last thing. We're taking over the gun deal. You've fucked it up enough."

Dustin clenched his jaw, his eyes narrowing while he rubbed his face.

"That's our deal, and you fuckin' know that."

"*Was* your deal. We fixed it up for you morons, and you fuckin' blew it. We're taking it over. This isn't open for discussion." Hawk crossed his arms over his chest.

"Fuck, we need the money. Banger can't do this." Dustin paced back and forth in front of the table.

"Banger can and did. You'll get your money. It's just that we're orchestrating this operation now. We'll show you fuckers how it's supposed to be done." Hawk sank back down into the black leather chair.

Jax slowly let the large man up from the floor, his face covered in blood from the force in which Jax slammed him to the ground. He kept his eye on the charter member until the man went to the back of the room, took out a large rag, and wiped his face.

"If we get the money, then do what you need to do. I can't say I'm happy with this, but I'll take it up with Banger, president to president." The jab Dustin made on Hawk's second-in-command status was not lost on the Colorado members. Dustin picked up the gavel and pounded it on the table, saying, "Church is adjourned. Let's show our national members a good time tonight.

Jerking his chin to his brothers, Hawk said, "Let's get our shit outta our bikes."

Outside, the Colorado brothers huddled near their Harleys. The lights from the clubhouse illuminated the parking lot. Jax, still pissed from church, said, "These fuckers should be nixed out of the Insurgents family. They don't have respect, and they don't know what the hell Insurgents stand for." He jumped up and down in place so he could burn off some excess energy. If he didn't, he was afraid he was going to hurt someone; his anger was palatable.

"Steady, man. We can't have you blowing your fuse. Let it ride; we've more important things to do," Hawk said.

Jax grunted as he continued to jump up and down.

"Things could get a bit sticky because Banger and I believe there's a double-crosser in the charter club, and that's why the deal didn't go down. We got a scout who's been keeping track of the comings and goings of these assholes. I'm meeting up with him later. We gotta find out who it is if we're going to be successful in delivering the guns and not getting our asses wasted." Hawk looked at each of them.

"Jax, I need you to pass bullshit to these sorry-ass members that we're moving the guns tomorrow afternoon to the red barn by Jackson Road and the deal is going down on Friday night. We're actually gonna meet with the Irishman on Thursday night. Let's see who shows up at the red barn tomorrow night. No one knows what's going on but us, understood?"

They all nodded in agreement. After they took their clothes and toiletries out of their saddlebags, they headed back to the clubhouse.

Two hours later, Chas and Jax sat on barstools downing their shots of Jack. The clubhouse party was in full swing. The coke flowed freely, and the club sluts swayed their scantily clad bodies to the beat of "Cherry Pie" by Warrant. Dustin came up to them, a slut on each arm, and said in a thick voice, "Hey, here's a welcoming present for each of you. The blonde can suck like a pro and the brunette loves it in the ass. You guys decide who gets who." He shoved the women toward Chas and Jax.

A stunning redhead walked by, her ass cheeks exposed. Dustin grabbed her and slammed her against Hawk. "Oh, fuck," she said as her head collided with his jaw. Rubbing her head, she looked up at Hawk and smiled. "Hey, you're good-looking." Chas and Jax laughed while Hawk lightly pushed her away.

"What the fuck, man? You don't like red pussy?" Dustin asked.

"Nah, just not interested." Hawk replied.

Jax, his arm around the blonde, shook his head and said, "He's got an old lady. He's off the market."

"Really? I never figured you'd get an old lady."

"Well, I did." Hawk threw back his Jack, gave a knowing look at Chas and Jax, and said, "Gonna get some fresh air then call it a night."

He walked out of the clubhouse.

"Fuck, never thought I'd see the day Hawk would turn down some prime pussy. Never thought I'd see him leave a party, either," Dustin said as he scratched his head.

"He's taken now, but I'm not and I love all colors of pussy," Jax said as he pulled the redhead into his hard chest. The blonde was stroking his cock while he played with her tits, and the redhead kissed him deeply, rubbing her big tits against his chest. He looked over to Chas who was busy licking the brunette's mound.

"Let's get more comfortable on the couches," Jax said to the two club sluts. They jumped up, each taking one of his hands, and led their man to a tattered blue couch in the corner of the room. Blocking out images of Cherri, Jax took a deep gulp of whiskey, pulled the women down with him on the couch, and let the fun begin.

JAX WOKE UP to a pounding headache. He looked around the unfamiliar room then noticed a warm body next to his back and another against his chest. He looked down and saw the blonde who'd sucked his dick dry earlier.

He wasn't sure how he ended up in this room, but he remembered fucking the two women every way possible. The blonde sighed and pressed her ass harder into his cock. The redhead bumped against his ass with hers as she turned in her sleep. Jax looked at both women and a sense of emptiness filled him. *What the fuck? I just had amazing sex with two beautiful women and I'm… what? Depressed? What the fuck?*

Jax glanced at the glowing red numbers on the clock beside the bed; they read two-fifteen in the morning. He reached over the blonde—he couldn't remember either woman's name—and retrieved his phone. Without thinking, he dialed Cherri's number.

"Hello?" Her lilting voice lifted his spirits.

"Hey, sweetness, how've you been? Still at Dream House?"

"Hi, Jax. I'm okay. Yeah, I'm still here. I'm finishing up some paperwork then I'm going home. You've been keeping a low profile."

"Yeah, it's been, like, two weeks since I saw you at the club party. I'm in Nebraska right now."

"Really? Whatcha doin' there?"

"Club business."

A long silence ensued.

"Well, I guess, I… um… I better get goin', you know? It's late and I'm tired… okay? Yeah, right."

"Sweetness… I miss you," he whispered.

More silence.

"Sweetness?"

"Yes?" Her voice was so low he barely heard her.

"Did you hear me? I miss you."

"I heard you. I don't know what to say."

"You don't have to say anything. Just wanted to tell you."

"Thanks. I've been missing—"

"Hey, sexy, ready for another round?" The blonde had woken up and began stroking Jax's dick.

Jax froze in place. Cherri's gritted sigh grumbled in his ears.

"*Really*, Jax? You called to tell me you miss me while you're fuckin' a whore? Fuck off, and don't call me again!"

The phone went dead. Jax stared at it. *How do I keep fuckin' up things with Cherri?* The redhead, finally awake, rubbed Jax's back while kissing his shoulders. Nothing stirred in him except for the sinking pit in his stomach. He wanted Cherri in his bed. Pushing the women away, he said, "Not now. I gotta sleep. Go on and find another brother. I'm done."

Shrugging, the two nude women jumped up and walked out of the room in search of another pair of arms to hold them. Jax groaned and fell back on the pillow, his arm over his eyes. He let his mind drift back to the afternoon when he and Cherri fucked. After so many months, he finally had her trust, and then he fucked the whole damn thing up. All he could think about was her and how he wanted his Cherri back in his arms. *Fuck Gunner. Cherri is mine, and I'll have her, no matter what the consequences are.*

After much tossing and turning, he fell asleep with Cherri's sultry smile on his mind.

CHAPTER ELEVEN

E ARLY THE NEXT morning, Jax and the others met at the diner on Elm Street. Kilson was a small town, and the diner seemed to be the hot spot for the locals. Thankfully, the charter members were still passed out when the Colorado Insurgents left the clubhouse.

"So, what's the news?" Jax asked as he sipped his coffee.

PJ lowered his voice and said, "Hawk and I went out last night to meet up with the scout. He's been tailing the charter members for a while. He said Shack's been leaving the clubhouse late at night and meeting up with some bikers far out of town. He told us the bikers have leather jackets with the colors green and purple. He made out an emblem on the back of one guy's jacket—the grim reaper on a Harley."

"The Demon Riders? What the fuck are they doing in Insurgents territory? And what the fuck is the VP doing hangin' with them?" Jax scanned the faces of his brothers.

"It's what you think—Shack is double-dealing. He's working with the Irishman *and* the Demon Riders. I knew he was a piece of shit, but now he's a traitorous piece of shit." Hawk clenched his fists.

"Do you think Dustin is in on this?" Jax asked.

"It seems Shack is acting alone. Hell, the others are too busy getting high and fucked to know what the shit's goin' on," PJ said.

"The Demon Riders have an affiliation with the Deadly Demons. Is Reaper involved in this?" Chas asked as he winked at a waitress who was checking him out.

"Not sure. That's something we're gonna have to find out when we get back to Pinewood Springs. Right now, we have to make sure the Irishman gets his weapons, the Demon Riders get squat, and Shack is taught a lesson for betraying the Insurgents." Hawk paused as he drained his coffee cup.

"More coffee for you good-looking men?" The cutesy waitress with ample cleavage bent down low to give the brothers a view of her assets. She smiled broadly and licked her lips as her eyes settled on Chas' face.

"Come back in about fifteen minutes. We don't want to be disturbed. Got it?" Axe snarled.

Flustered, her cheeks reddened and she turned around, scuttling back to the counter.

"Why'd you do that, Axe? She was sorta hot." Chas smirked.

"She's a bitch who wants some biker cock. We can find that shit anywhere. We gotta finish up here so we can head back home."

"Axe is right. The way I'm figuring it is the Demon Riders are paying Shack big money to sell the guns to them. The fucker's gonna let the assholes know when and where the deal is going down. Shack will meet with the Irishman, get the money, then give him the guns. The Irishman and his henchmen will probably be ambushed at some point by the Demon Riders. They'll be history, and the Demon Riders will get some fuckin' heavy-duty artillery." Hawk's jaw tightened.

"No wonder Shack was so fuckin' pissed when you told him we're taking over the deal. The asshole is screwing his own club brothers and bringing all this shit down on the Insurgents. Let me take care of him." Jax narrowed his eyes into slits.

"Oh, yeah, you can take care of him tonight when his ass shows up at the barn. You guys spread the word we moved the weapons to the barn, yeah?" Hawk asked.

Chas, Jax, PJ, and Axe nodded. Each of them had anger mixed with excitement etched on their faces.

"Now, I'd like some more coffee." Chas grinned as he waved the waitress over to the table.

FORTY MILES OUTSIDE of Kilson in an abandoned grain tower, the

Insurgents observed two SUVs kicking up dust on the back road. The sun had just set and the full moon shone brightly in the eastern sky.

Exiting the SUVs were six men. The Insurgents recognized all but one of them. Liam—a short, round man with reddish-blond hair and blotchy skin—smiled wide when he recognized his old friends.

"Good to see you again," he said in a thick, Irish brogue.

Hawk nodded. "Likewise. We're here to fix what the Kilson club fucked up."

"Appreciate it. Your club has always been top-notch, and I hoped you'd step in. This club here is fucked up. They don't know a damn thing, and that's what makes them dangerous," Liam said.

Jax eyed each of the men who fanned around the Irishman. He kept his eyes on their hands—he didn't want any surprises. If something went wrong, he knew the Insurgents were prepared. His job was to make sure nothing went wrong.

A sweaty man with a pock-marked face stood to the right of the Irishman. His suit was crumpled by the night's humid air, and his slight pot belly strained against his shirt. He chewed gum, and his constant jaw movement jarred on Jax's nerves in the worst way.

"Who's this?" Hawk pointed to the sweating man.

"This is a colleague of mine, McFahey."

"What the fuck is he doing here, Liam? That wasn't the deal. We don't know him," Jax said, his tone harsh and chilling.

"He's cool. He's been on several transactions with me, and he's funding this one. McFahey is a councilman from your neck of the woods," Liam replied.

"Pinewood Springs? Well, fuck, imagine that, a crooked politician." Jax laughed dryly.

"Why the fuck are you funding this?" Hawk asked. Under his breath he said to Jax, "I don't like this."

Jax moved closer to McFahey. The rotund man shifted in place.

"As I said, he's funding—"

"Let him talk for his fuckin' self," Hawk ordered, cutting Liam off.

McFahey wiped his forehead with a white handkerchief then threw a politician's smile at the Insurgents. "I've worked with Liam on several arms deals. I'm trustworthy."

"What's in it for you?" Hawk glared at him.

"Favors. In the political arena, favors are worth more than cold cash. Liam provides me with favors, and I wanted to ask a favor of your club. I can help you and you can help me. I need bodyguards for some of my, shall we say, not politically correct activities. You get my drift?"

"We're not here for that. This deal is between Insurgents and Liam. All the other shit you take up with our president, Banger. For now, keep the fuck outta the way. You get *my* drift?" Hawk gave McFahey a steely stare.

Jax moved in closer to McFahey who took a few steps back, threw up his hands and said, "I'm not here to make trouble. I'm totally in the background."

"Fuckin' stay there," Jax said through gritted teeth.

After the air cleared, the deal went down without a hitch. The Irishman and his guys inspected the weapons to make sure they all checked out while Chas, PJ, and Axe counted the money. Jax, Throttle, and Hawk stood watch.

Shaking Hawk's hand, Liam said, "It's always a pleasure doing business with you. Today seemed like old times."

"Yeah. See you," Hawk said.

Liam, the politician, and the bodyguards drove off in their SUVs. The Insurgents waited until they couldn't see the vehicles any longer. The deal had taken less than thirty minutes.

"Let's get down to the barn and wait for the back-stabber to show up so I can kick some traitor ass," Jax said.

They all laughed. Night had crept in, and it was imperative they reach the barn before it became too dark. Darkness shadowed all levels of evil, and both the traitor and the Insurgents needed the cover of nighttime to hide their grim secrets. They kick-started their bikes and sped toward the red barn.

An hour later, the rumble of a Harley alerted the Insurgents some-one was approaching the barn. Taking up their positions, they crouched down. The door creaked open and a tall figure walked in, a high-beam flashlight in his hand scanning the barn's interior. With his boot, he swept away the dust and hay on top of the floor. Once cleared off, he kneeled down and knocked on the wooden floorboards as if to see if there were any spaces beneath them.

"Looking for somethin'?" Jax said as he stepped out of the shadows.

The man jumped up and wiped his hands on his dirty jeans.

"Maybe I can help you." Jax smiled menacingly.

"Wh-what are you doing here?" Shack's gaze flitted around the room.

"The more important question is, what the fuck are *you* doing here?"

He shrugged. "I was here the other day looking for old parts, scrap metal and such, and I lost my blade. Came back to look for it, that's all." His eyebrows drew together.

"That's the lamest shit I've ever heard. The problem with you is you can't think so good on your feet, Shack." Jax took a few steps toward him.

Shack started to move toward the barn door when Hawk and Chas appeared out of the shadows. Axe, Throttle, and PJ stood watch outside in case Shack brought anyone along. Hawk and Chas blocked Shack's way, and Jax walked over until he stood in front of Shack. Jax was so close he could smell the fear on Shack's skin.

"What the fuck are you doin'?" Shack said. "You're in my territory, and I don't like or put up with this shit."

Jax smiled and turned sideways, looking at Hawk and Chas. "Do you believe this asshole? *You* don't like what *we're* doing?" Jax kicked one of Shack's legs, making him crumple to the floor. "*We* don't like what *you're* doin', you traitorous piece of shit." Jax punched him in the stomach.

Shack groaned and looked up at Hawk. "Are you gonna let him treat me like this?"

A small smirk tugged at Hawk's upper lip. "Nah, I'm gonna let him treat you worse. This is your lucky day. We're in a good mood 'cause we just made a shitload of money in a smooth-as-silk deal. So because we're all good, we're not gonna gut you. We'll let you decide your form of punishment. Aren't you lucky today?" Hawk slammed his fist in Shack's face, and blood spurted out of his nose.

Jax, pushing Shack down on his ass, said, "Your choices for being a fuckin' back-stabber—to not just your club, but to all Insurgents—are: having your right hand maimed, having your legs broken, or crushing your balls so you can join the boys' choir."

"See, we can be generous—we're letting you choose." Chas laughed.

"You think I'm scared of you fuckers? You come here thinkin' your shit don't stink. You're a bunch of assholes." Shack struggled to stand up.

"Now that's not the right attitude to have 'cause our good mood may turn bad, and we may decide not to give you any choices and just do whatever the hell we want to." Jax crossed his arms; he was itching to beat the shit out of this back-stabber. If Shack were one of the brothers of the national club, he'd already have been tortured and killed, but since he was a member of a charter club, they decided to teach him a lesson and let Shack's own club burn him.

"What's your decision? We're done with this shit. My boys and I gotta grab some dinner and whiskey, so let's get this over with," Hawk said.

"You think I'm gonna make this easy for you motherfuckers? You think I'm scared of a bunch of pussies? I faced a helluva lot worse over in Iraq."

Jax looked over to Hawk who nodded in response. Reaching for the sledgehammer, Jax grabbed it, motioned for Chas to hold Shack still then slammed it down on Shack's hand, crushing it. Shack screamed before Jax brought the hammer down again, breaking more bones in the traitor's hand. Shack grunted as he curled up in a ball on the wooden floor. After a couple of blows to his ribs, Jax stepped away from Shack, who had passed out from the pain. Chas stood up and kicked him in his side. Shack emitted a low moan.

"Fuckin' double-crosser. He's goddamn lucky we didn't cut his throat," Jax fumed.

"We'll let Dustin know what a fucker his VP is and where to find him. Let him deal with the asshole the way he and his club see fit. Let's grab some dinner," Hawk said.

The five of them recovered their bikes from the thicket behind the barn. Revving up the motorcycles, they headed toward the diner in Kilson.

After dinner, as the Colorado Insurgents milled around the clubhouse, Jax overheard Dustin ask where Shack was as his arm draped around a young-looking girl. Jax couldn't believe the charter club was part of the Insurgents family. He took pride in his brotherhood, and all these jerks wanted to do was fuck underage girls, snort and smoke crank and coke, and back-stab. If it were up to him, he'd throw their asses out of the Insurgents family. He turned away in disgust and threw back his shot of whiskey. They were going to leave the next day, and for Jax, it couldn't come soon enough.

Gazing around the room, Jax spotted the blonde and redhead from the previous night heading his way. With their long hair swinging, their tits hanging out, and their short skirts revealing no panties, his dick should've been hard as hell as they approached him. It wasn't. He didn't want those women; all he wanted was to put his arms around Cherri and show her how good he could make her feel.

As the two women came closer, Jax made his way down a hallway and ducked into a small closet. He dialed Cherri's number. No answer. *She's probably working.* He wondered if she were giving any lap dances. The image of her grinding her ass on a man's dick made his skin prick from stabs of anger. He didn't want to think about whether Gunner was at Dream House, waiting for Cherri to finish her shift so he could take her home with him and fuck her. *That* thought made the anger rush to his temples and throb painfully. He slammed his fist into the door over and over, ignoring the pain and the dripping blood. The door opened, and the blonde and the redhead stared at him, wide-eyed.

"Whatcha doin' in there, sweetie?" The blonde took his aching hand in hers and wiped off the blood with a Kleenex.

"Let's go to your room and fix you all up. We'll make you forget whatever's bothering you. We'll give you a real good time." The redhead winked at him as she placed a wet kiss on his cheek.

Fuck, this is what I need to get my mind straight. I'm tired of thinking about that ice princess. She set all this shit in motion. Fuck her—two can play at her game.

Snaking his arms around both women, Jax squeezed them close to him as they made their way to his room.

"WHAT THE FUCK? The deal was done yesterday? Why wasn't I informed?" Dustin stomped his feet on the parking lot gravel as he stared at Hawk, who packed up his saddlebags on his Harley. The other bikers, finished packing, sat on their hogs, waiting for Hawk's signal to pull out.

"No reason to tell you. You fucked-up big time, and Banger didn't want our reputation ruined by a bunch of flunky morons," Hawk said.

"You disrespected me, brother."

"*Disrespected?* You don't know what the fuck the word means. You're lucky we came down and saved your sorry ass on the arms deal. No more chances, Dustin. The next fuck-up your club does, Insurgents will throw you out. Your club will be done. Got it?"

Dustin glared at Hawk, his lips pursed.

"Oh, and we're taking seventy-five percent of the money for all our trouble. We had to haul our asses over here to save yours. That's bullshit, and you know it."

"Seventy-five percent? That's fuckin' stealing." Dustin moved toward Hawk.

Hawk clenched his hands into fists and gritted through his teeth, "Don't take another step. I don't wanna hurt you, but I will. The money is not open for discussion. We didn't have to give you anything since all you did was fuck things up."

Dustin stood in place, hatred radiating from him.

Jax laughed. "Smart move, Dustin. You better not move your old ass."

Hawk swung his leg over his Harley, put on his sunglasses, and took a long look at Dustin. He said, "We found out the double-crosser is your fuckin' VP. You can find him on the floor of the barn off Highway 287. We taught him a lesson, but we left the rest of him for you. Clean up your club, or it's history."

Hawk signaled for the bikers to pull out, and the Colorado Insurgents peeled out of the parking lot without a backward glance. The sun reflected off their sunglasses as they rode in formation, the wind whipping around them, the thrill of freedom pulsing through them. Jax breathed in deeply. This was what he loved—the freedom of the ride. When he was out on the open road doing ninety-five, his body was suspended in the air, like he was flying—like nothing mattered anymore. There was nothing better than hauling ass on his Harley with his brothers around him. He wanted to keep riding and not go back to Pinewood Springs where he was forced to see Cherri with Gunner. Increasing his speed, he hit one hundred and ten miles an hour. Blasting down the freeway was the only way he knew how to get Cherri out of his mind.

CHAPTER TWELVE

C LOSING THE BRIEFCASE full of money, Banger said, "This is a good chunk of change to add to the club's reserves. Your tires weren't even cooled before Dustin called me up talkin' shit 'bout you all." Banger's face broke into a wide grin. He was enjoying this. "Told him he's run outta time. Any shit I hear 'bout his club, they're outta the Insurgents. Told him our history is what let him get any money from the deal they fucked up big-time. What a fuckwad he turned out to be. Too much shit up his nose, clouds his judgment."

"We shoulda beat his ass for being so stupid and letting his club get so fucked up." Jax pushed back his chair, his body jerking forward, his nostrils flaring.

"It's done now. Next fuck-up, they're out. Now we gotta decide on providing incognito security for this councilman, McFahey." Banger looked at each of the thirty members crowded in the meeting room.

"He was at the arms deal with the Irishman. Think they've got somethin' going. Not too sure 'bout him. Rubbed me the wrong way. What did you guys think?" Hawk looked at the brothers who were with him in Nebraska. They all nodded in agreement.

"We're gonna need him to get some of the licenses and zoning shit through for that strip mall we're doing in West Pinewood Springs. Normally, this isn't shit I'd consider, especially with politicians, but we're gonna need some favors." Banger stood at the head of the table, his arms crossed, waiting for the discussion to begin.

Jax puffed his chest out a bit, his heart beating faster. This is what he loved about being in the Insurgents—they were together on everything. They were his family. They always had each other's back. It was a great feeling.

At the end of all the discussions, the yelling, and the uneasiness, the club voted they would provide clandestine security for McFahey, and he, in turn, would provide all necessary permits for the Insurgents' construction project and make sure all inspections were passed. McFahey was dirty, but as long as he delivered on his end of the bargain, the MC didn't give a shit about what he was doing.

During church, Jax tried not to picture Gunner and Cherri together, but he couldn't help it. Every time Gunner glanced at him, Jax narrowed his eyes and his face would tighten. If Gunner noticed, he didn't act any differently, making Jax even more enraged. As the brothers milled about in the great room, downing beers and shots the prospects had ready for them, Jax walked over to Gunner and seethed, "You know, I had somethin' with Cherri before you started sniffing around her."

Gunner scratched his beard, took a swig of his cold beer, and said, "That don't mean shit to me. I don't give a fuck what my baby had before or with who. Don't matter." He took another gulp of beer before he leaned toward Jax. "Get used to it, man. Cherri is with me and she wants to be with me. She chose me. Fuck off." He swallowed the rest of his beer, belched, and picked up another.

"She chose you to get back at me. Are you so thick that you can't see that?" Jax, face reddening, clenched his fists.

Gunner turned his back and started talking to another member. Jax, breathing heavily, pushed Gunner forward, who then whirled around, swinging his fist at Jax's jaw. He missed, but before either of the men could react, several members pulled them apart.

"He's fuckin' crazy. I'm tired of his shit, the whiny pussy." Gunner slicked back his hair and rubbed his beard, chest heaving.

"Asshole knows she's mine, and he's fuckin' throwin' it in my face." Jax struggled to break free from the hands that held him. "Let me at him."

"Cool the fuck down. Right. Now." Hawk's calm voice had a sharp-as-a-knife edge to it.

Jax, still struggling, glared at Gunner, who waved his hands toward Jax and muttered, "I'm done with this childish shit. Stay the fuck away from Cherri *and* from me." He turned around and clasped his hand on his buddy's shoulder. "Let's get a drink." They made their way to the bar.

"Dude, you gotta get a grip. You're acting like a twelve-year-old pussy, not like a man. Fuck, this bitch ain't worth your pride." Chas put his arm around his friend and shook Jax a little as if to shake some sense into him.

Jax shrugged Chas off. He pulled down his black t-shirt, adjusted his cut, and left the clubhouse, well aware that every single brother's eyes were on him. He knew they sided with Gunner. If he weren't involved in this situation, he'd side with Gunner, too. He *was* acting like a weak excuse for a man. He needed to clear his head and get some fresh air.

Jax jumped on his Harley and gunned the motor. The cams exploded. He loved the roar and power of his Harley. Needing to get away, he rode out of the parking lot and hit the road in the direction of the town.

THE AFTERNOON SUN warmed Cherri as she walked back from the drugstore. The plastic bags she carried were heavy, so she shifted them from hand to hand. She had to get a car, but they were so expensive and she didn't think she'd be able to save enough to pay for it. Gunner told her he'd help her buy one, but she couldn't let him even though she hated always borrowing Ginger or Emma's car.

Gunner was such a sweet man. Cherri wished he was a prick so she could take advantage of him without any guilt, but he was a teddy bear, and she didn't want to take him for a ride. He was nothing like the sweaty sugar daddy she'd had in Denver. The only good thing about that asshole was he'd been busy climbing up the political ladder, so he'd left her alone most of the time. And because he'd had a wife and kids, overnight stays were rare. The rest of the time, she'd been on her own in a nice apartment.

When she'd walked around the neighborhood, she'd pretended she was respectable and like everyone else. She'd carry on conversations with the neighbors and they'd all treated her like she was one of them. They hadn't known she was dirty—a kept woman who'd been soiled long before the sweaty sugar daddy came into the picture.

No, they didn't know she was no good. Her family knew because they used to tell her all the time. The whole situation in Denver seemed like eons ago, but it'd been only three years. She ran away because she had to. She knew her lover was madder than hell at her, and he probably believed she set him up. The whole situation had just become too sticky, so she'd lied to him and took off.

In Pinewood Springs, the lifestyle was slower, and Cherri liked it. She was making small steps toward her dream of living a respectable life. Even though she'd been pissed at Jax for taking away her dancing, she was happy she didn't have to take her clothes off to earn a living anymore. Being the second in charge at Dream House filled her with pride, and it was a legitimate job. Some of the white-trash stench was beginning to wash off her.

Thinking of Jax always made her heart skip a beat and her stomach lurch. He was dangerously sexy. She wished Gunner made her feel the way Jax did. She wanted Jax in the worst way, but she needed the easiness, the comfort, of Gunner. He was solid, and she knew he adored her. He also knew she was not in love with him, but she treated him with respect and kindness and loved him as a good friend. He seemed fine with the relationship, so they spent their time together in a stagnant kind of bliss while her mind repeatedly replayed the afternoon she and Jax spent together.

Cherri didn't want a complication like Jax to interfere with her life's goals. He was heartache on two legs, and she was sure if she let herself fall for him, she would fall too hard and he would trample on her love. No, he was best left to memories.

She stopped to rest, setting the heavy bags on the sidewalk. She tilted her face up toward the sun, and, with closed eyes, welcomed the warming rays.

"Whoa! Aren't you a hot one?" a deep voice said.

Cherri jumped, eyes flying open. A brown minivan had pulled over to the curb. Three guys in their mid-twenties gawked at her. One of them had his head out the window. Cherri tugged her jean shorts down and pulled her top more firmly into place. Picking up her sacks, she walked away.

"Hey, beautiful, need a ride?" the man hanging out of the window said as the van rolled beside her. The other two laughed.

Ignoring them, she walked and focused on reaching the main road where there'd be traffic and people. She was on a residential street, and no one was around.

"You aren't being so friendly, are you?" the guy with a red t-shirt said.

"But you're friendly when you take off your clothes so you can get our tips, bitch," said the man in the backseat as he hung his head out the back window.

Turning her head sideways, Cherri said, "Please, leave me alone. I have no problems with you. I need to get home."

"But we wanna talk to you, baby." The exhaust from the van hung in the air, its dusty, gritty scent suffocating in the summer heat.

Ignoring them, Cherri picked up her pace, but the damn plastic bags cut off the circulation to her fingers so she had to shift them. She stopped in front of the alley to rearrange the sacks and the van turned in, blocking her way. She darted her eyes all around; she had to get away from these guys. The bile rose in her throat and she willed it back down. Her insides quivered as her nerves tightened.

The three men jumped out of the van. Two of them were medium height with brown hair. One of the two had a lanky build and wore a red t-shirt while the other had a black t-shirt over his medium build. The third man was broad, muscular, and sported a blond buzz cut. Their eyes brimmed with lust and anger.

"Please, get out of my way."

"We're not stopping you. Go around," the broad guy said.

Cherri started to walk around when the man with the buzz cut grabbed her arm.

"Don't!" Cherri yelled.

"You're not being too chummy. Aren't you the hot stripper from Dream House?" He raked his eyes over her body with a fierce hunger.

She wished she would have worn her jeans instead of shorts. As the three men stood around her in the alley, her lips trembled while her face lost its color. Her voice pounded in her head. *Damn, why isn't anyone around? If I scream, will anyone hear me? Will anyone help me?*

"We've given you enough tips, so it's your turn to be friendly, you know?" he said.

"I don't know any of you. Leave me alone."

"I don't think we're gonna do that. Now, be a good slut and show us how good you are at pleasing your fans," ordered Buzz Cut as the other two guys moved toward Cherri.

"Show us your tits, babe," the lanky guy said as he reached for Cherri and jerked her closer to him.

The three men formed a close circle around her. She tried to break free, but she was like a captured bird in a cage, beating its wings against the metal bars. She swung her arms and pushed against them but was no match to their strength. The one with the medium build grabbed her from behind and held her arms back. The men shoved and dragged her further down the alley. With her heart racing and her legs weak, Cherri opened her mouth but nothing came out. Holding her breath, beads of sweat broke out on her forehead.

The jerk wearing the black t-shirt held her arms in his vise-like grip. Gaining some strength, she kicked at her attackers. Buzz Cut punched her full-on in the stomach. She bent over and gasped for air as the pain tore through her body, tears rolling down her cheeks. One of the men, she wasn't sure which one, pulled her hair, making her stand upright while Buzz Cut kissed her and squeezed her breasts.

Her breaths became short, stilted, like she was starving for air. Everything stopped. Darkness surrounded her. The three men were no longer there, only the looming shadow of a man creeping toward her.

She is hiding under the bed and can see his white tennis shoes gleam in the dimly lit room. The shoes stop right where she's hiding. She holds her breath, lest he hears her panting and finds her. The shoes move away, and a small feeling of relief washes over her. He's leaving and she's safe for now. Breathing quietly, she relaxes a little…then whoosh, *her body's pulled from behind.* No, no, no! *her brain shouts. He's going to do horrible things to her. She screams. A dry hand covers her mouth.*

"Shut the fuck up," the lanky man said, slicing into her memories.

As the men began to drag a kicking Cherri behind a garage, the low rumble of a motorcycle vibrated in the distance. Cherri, her heart jumping, turned her head toward the street, hoping the cycle would pass then she could cry out for help. It was a long shot, but it was all she had. She couldn't let these fucking assholes rape her without doing everything she could to stop it.

The motorcycle came closer as its engine pierced the silence of the neighborhood. The three men turned her head toward them, each of them kissing her, pinching her nipples, and running their hands under her shorts and squeezing her butt.

"What the fuck's going on?"

Looking through bleary eyes, Cherri saw Jax's tall, ripped body. An enormous relief washed over her, making her cry.

"This isn't your business. Move on," Buzz Cut said.

"Fuck, is that you, Cherri?" Jax's quizzical look transformed into a dark, angry one. "The hell it isn't my business! She's with the Insurgents. By messing with her, you're fuckin' messin' with me."

The lanky guy released Cherri's arms as he turned toward Jax, saying, "Figures this trash belongs to your club."

In one swift move, Jax's fist laid the guy out. The other men went after Jax, but he threw a high kick, his steel-toed boot hitting Buzz Cut in the face. Cherri heard the crunch of bones as his nose broke. The medium-build guy threw up his hands, saying, "I was just out for a ride.

I didn't mean for any of this shit to happen."

Jax gripped him by the shirt, glaring at him. "Well, fuckwad, it *did* happen." He slammed the guy's face against the garage's brick wall. Blood gushed from the man's head as Jax kicked him in the lower back. The man groaned as he slid down, crumpling in a heap on the concrete.

Jax picked Cherri up and cradled her in his arms as he walked toward his Harley. Cherri buried her head in his chest. Tenderly, he placed her on his bike, placed her sacks in the saddlebags, then seated himself.

"Hang on, sweetness, or you may fall off once I start this baby up." The bike lurched into motion, and Cherri wrapped her arms around Jax's waist as the bike roared away. Thinking Jax would hang a right on Orchard Way, she was surprised when he kept going straight.

"You missed my street," she said.

He glanced back at her. "Not going there yet."

Cherri didn't ask where they were going because she didn't care; she loved being on the back of his bike. She had ridden a few times on Gunner's bike, but it didn't feel the same as it did with Jax. Her arms around Gunner were so she wouldn't fall off, but with her chest pressed against Jax's back, the warm wind stroking her face, she felt safe and complete. Loving the feeling, she squeezed her arms tighter around Jax, leaning her head against his back.

He veered onto a back road which took them out of Pinewood Springs. They went down country roads, leaving a trail of dust behind them. The hum of the motor and Jax's nearness relaxed her. His scent of motor oil and sweat tinged the air, and she breathed it in deeply. On each side of them, carpets of wildflowers beckoned and the rush of the Colorado River bounced off the chiseled mountains.

After twenty minutes, Jax turned off the road and stopped the bike in an alcove surrounded by evergreen trees. He cut the motor and before he could help Cherri, she jumped off the Harley, her wobbly legs giving out. Jax caught her before she hit the ground. He chuckled and each note of his low voice skimmed across her skin making her shiver.

He held her close. "You're safe now, sweetness."

"I was so afraid. I don't know what I would've done if you hadn't come by. They wanted to hurt me..." Her chest heaved and wet streaks stained her cheeks. She pushed her head harder against his chest.

"It's all over now. Don't think about it. You never have to worry with me around. I'll always be there for you. You don't know how precious you are to me, sugar."

Cherri bent her head back, holding Jax's gaze. He leaned down and kissed her softly then stepped back, his eyes flitting over her face while a half-grin played around his lips. Tugging him toward her, with her hand behind his head, her mouth sought his. She crushed her lips against his and heard him groan. Leaning closer to Jax, she ran her hands under his leather jacket so she could feel his sculpted back better.

"You are beautiful," she said against his mouth.

Jax laughed. "Never had a chick call me beautiful before." He wrapped his arms tighter around her waist.

Cherri smiled. "You're beautiful like a Greek statue."

She kissed him again then slowly drew her lips away. His hard dick pressing against her, told her he was just as turned-on as she. She lingered for a few seconds then kissed him again while her tongue brushed his mouth. Parting her lips, Jax slipped his tongue into her warm cavern. She moaned. Their tongues danced together as she pushed a little deeper into him then withdrew, pulling back a little. She looked at him, eyes flaming with desire as she brushed her finger over her swollen lips. Jax pulled her close then gently bit her lower lip. Cherri bit back, her teeth grazing his lips as she moved away.

"You're killing me with your kisses, sweetness."

She kissed him again as she threaded her fingers through his hair. His hair was soft, and the short strands tickled her as she played with them. He stroked her back, cupping her ass. Cherri jerked a little as his touch lit a fire in the pit of her stomach. Her legs clamped together as she felt a slight dampness. When she arched her back into him, his mouth nibbled her earlobes then her neck.

"I want you so bad, sweet one. Let's stop playing games and be together."

She stiffened as she pushed back. Clearing her throat, she said, "I'm sorry. I didn't mean to do all this. I was so scared and then relieved... I don't know, but we gotta stop. Like, now."

"What the fuck?"

Cherri twisted out of Jax's embrace and stood in front of him, looking down at the ground. She bit her lower lip and fiddled with a few strands of her hair.

"Nothing. We have to stop before it goes too far, that's all."

"We've already gone too far." He paused, looking at her as though he were trying to get into her head to see what made her tick. "Why have you been ignoring me?"

"You know why. You and Peaches were pretty cozy."

"You never let me explain that to you."

"Nothing to explain. You're just that type of man. You could've waited until the sheets had dried, at least." She drew small designs in the dirt with her shoe.

"It wasn't what you thought. I wasn't—"

"You don't owe me anything. I thought—"

"Will you shut the fuck up, woman? Damn, you piss me off sometimes. I'm gonna tell you how it was, and you'll fuckin' keep your mouth shut. Got it?"

Cherri, seeing the anger in his eyes, nodded.

After Jax explained to her how Peaches had tricked him into going to Dream House the afternoon he and Cherri spent together, and what she saw was not him groping Peaches, but rather him trying to get Peaches off him, Cherri hung her head.

"I'm so sorry I misjudged you. If I had known, things may have been different."

"I tried to talk to you, but you never fuckin' gave me a chance to explain. It's like you didn't want to hear what I had to say, like you'd already made up your mind I was a piece of shit."

"Yeah, I do that, especially where men are concerned. I've never had any good dealings with men. It's like they only want to use or abuse women."

"Man, baby, you been hurt so bad in your life. I'd never hurt you. Never."

She smiled at him, but sadness whispered around her mouth.

"You know you torture the fuck outta me by hangin' with Gunner. Now that we're good, you can tell him, 'Adios.' He'll get it." Jax tugged Cherri back into him then kissed her on the lips.

Cherri pushed back. Looking up at Jax, she said, "I can't just leave Gunner. He's been good to me. He's been solid and dependable."

Eyes flashing, anger emanated from Jax. "What the fuck is that supposed to mean? You know goddamned well you only went with Gunner to spite me and make me jealous. Well, it worked. I was jealous as hell every time he touched you or looked at you. Now it's done, and we can pick up where we left off. You don't give a rat's ass about Gunner. You only care about what he can give you."

Cherri narrowed her eyes. "That's not true. I do like Gunner. He is a sweet and kind man. He may not have your good looks, but he sure as hell isn't fuckin' different women every night."

"You started this shit, sugar, not me. What did you think I was gonna do? Sit around until you decided I'd been punished enough? You don't fuckin' call the shots, I do, and you better get that through your pretty head. Sure, I fucked around; what of it? It didn't mean shit, just warm holes to drain my cock. Don't try and lay some guilt shit on me. And what, you weren't fuckin' the old man?"

"It's none of your business what I do with Gunner."

"Get your ass over here and give your man a kiss so we can get us back on track."

Dropping her voice, Cherri said, "There is no *us*. I can't walk out on Gunner just like that. You can't promise me you won't screw around on me, can you?"

"What the fuck does that have to do with this? I fuck pussy, and it's just that—fuckin' pussy. It has nothin' to do with us."

"But it does. I don't want to be waitin' around for you while you're getting off with another woman. I couldn't handle that."

"I can't promise you I won't stray sometimes, especially if I'm on a run and we're outta town. I *can* promise you I won't fuck Peaches anymore."

Cherri smiled wryly. "Thanks, that means so much to me."

Jax fixed his eyes on her. Watching him, she suddenly felt weary. She wanted to go home so she could collect her thoughts. Never had she anticipated her day would include making out with Jax in the woods. Her body ached for him, but she wasn't so eager to jump back into bed with him. Fear of loss and heartbreak clouded her desire for him, and her trust in him wasn't secure. Gunner was stable and, in truth, if Gunner wanted club pussy, she'd be cool with it. However, if she were with Jax, she'd beat the shit out of any slut who came near her man. She was better off with stable, safe Gunner, who made her life less volatile.

"I think it's time we head back. I have to get home," she said.

"I want you as my woman. That's all I know. I'll treat you right and support you. I'll have your back and give you respect. I can't get you outta my mind. The day we fucked is always on my mind, on replay. I want us to be together." Jax looked at her with soulful eyes which melted her heart.

"I have to think about all this. I can't deal with it right now. I wanna go home."

He reached out, gripped her arms, and drew her to him.

"You gonna give me something?" he said while rubbing her back.

Cherri's pussy clenched. She wanted him to fuck her hard, on the ground, but she couldn't face Gunner if she gave in to her body. She had to do the right thing. If she were going to go back with Jax then she would have to tell Gunner. He'd been so good to her she couldn't bang Jax behind his back. She wasn't a bad person—just one who had shitty luck for most of her life.

"It's getting late. I need to go." She glanced at the sky. Hues of gold, orange, and purple cast a warm glow across the approaching twilight.

Rigor replaced the softness on Jax's face. He stormed toward his Harley, yelling over his shoulder, "Okay, let's go. Get the fuck on my bike."

After she climbed on, Jax floored his Harley and it shot forward, kicking up dirt and twigs. They blasted down the empty road toward Pinewood Springs and her home.

As they stood in front of her townhouse, the silence was thick between them.

"Gonna invite me in?" he asked.

Shaking her head, she patted his hand. He placed two hands behind her head and kissed her hard. He released her and swatted her butt. She yanked away.

"I just can't do this. I owe Gunner my respect. He's been good to me, and he was there for me when no one else was. I can't do this to him."

"I wanted to be there for you, but you pushed me away. You fuckin' didn't give me a chance to take care of you. And you let an old man take care of you after you fucked me? You know what, *baby girl?* You're so fucked up by your past. You need a daddy, so you ran to the old man. Well, fuck you. Got that? Fuck you. I don't need your crazy, fucked up shit." Jax swung his leg over his bike and turned on the ignition.

Cherri, stifling her tears, ran up the stairs to her home. She heard Jax peel away, and she turned around and watched his retreating figure. Her heart ached when he rode away without even a backward glance.

CHAPTER THIRTEEN

"**F**UCK! OF ALL nights for the strip club to come down with a flu epidemic. Shit, not only are we down four dancers, but Holt's out sick, too," Emma shouted.

Cherri watched as Emma paced around the office, beads of perspiration forming on her forehead while a deep red flushed her neck and cheeks. She understood Emma's nerves. Hell, her stomach had been fluttering since the second dancer called in sick. The club had been rented out for a bachelor party, but word was it wasn't an ordinary guest list. No, this list had all the Pinewood big-shots like judges, lawyers, politicians, cattle ranchers, and oil men. Cherri's stomach lurched again. *All my stomach action better be from my nerves and not the flu. Shit, I can't afford to be sick.* She shivered as her palms grew sweaty.

"Did you get any dancers to replace the four out sick?" Emma's eyes darted from Cherri to the door and back to Cherri.

"Could only get two, but Crystal said she'd do an extra shift, and I'll dance to replace Ginger. I think we've got it covered. Oh, yeah, I did get two bartenders. We should be good *if* everyone shows up."

"Don't even *think* that," Emma said.

"It'll be fine. I'll make sure it goes smoothly." *I hope I can deliver. Now if my damn stomach would just quit churning, I'd be good.*

"Hey, baby doll, you look pale," Gunner said as he drew Cherri into him, placing a kiss on her forehead.

"Stressed, is more like it." She kissed him on the cheek.

"I'm here officially tonight. Banger wanted a group of us here to make sure everything goes okay with the dancers and all the guys. Are you gonna be busy all night?"

Hugging him, she said, "Most of the night. Too many dancers called in sick, so I'll have to dance. It's gonna be crazy, but everyone's counting on us to give a good party. I'll have some time to sit and have a drink with you later, though."

"That's all I want, baby doll. I gotta go and meet up with the other Insurgents. See ya later."

Gunner walked out of the office and went to the bar. Cherri followed him until she reached the curtain that shut off the backstage area from the bar. She wondered if Jax was going to be one of the Insurgents at the party. It had been two weeks since she'd last seen him, and he'd left madder than hell at her. She couldn't blame him; she'd teased him, which definitely wasn't right. She wished she could've told him he was the one she wanted to be with in a romantic way, not Gunner.

Gunner was a wonderful man, but he was so much older than she was, and she loved him only as a good friend. For her, passion and desire didn't exist in her relationship with Gunner, only with Jax. When she and Gunner were together, his touches were nice, but they didn't ignite the fire as Jax's touches did when they'd consumed each other a couple of months back. Reliving the memory of their time together helped her cope with the loneliness which often crushed her. She wished things could have been different, but they weren't. Anyway, she planned on moving on, and it would be much easier to say goodbye to Gunner than it would've been to Jax.

Peeking out from the curtain, Cherri saw him, and a wide grin spread over her face as her sparkling eyes took in his fantastic body. It had been too long since they had seen each other. He'd stopped coming to Dream House the past couple of weeks and she suspected he was the indirect cause of her irritability. Clasping her hands over her mouth to stifle her giggles, a burst of energy coursed through her.

Dark hazel eyes focused on the curtain. Closing it to a sliver, her heart pounded against her chest as she watched him dart his eyes around the room—she liked thinking he looked for her. Smoothing her hair down, she straightened her shoulders and stepped into the bar area. She made a beeline for Jax—she had to say hi to him and hear his voice.

Peaches bounding over to Jax stopped Cherri in her tracks, though. When Peaches reached him, she circled her arms around his neck and planted a big kiss on his soft lips. His eyes widened and he did a double-take. After realizing Peaches had a hold of him, he untangled her from him and shoved her back, then spotted Cherri. She stared at him, and their eyes locked for a suspended moment in time. She smiled. At that instant, Gunner came over and hugged her to him. Jax, face dark, eyes fastened on Cherri's, yanked Peaches back to him, kissing her deeply as his hands ran over her body.

An overwhelming need to flee attacked Cherri as her eyes grew hot and her body felt broken. It sickened her to see Peaches touch Jax's arms, chest, and lips. Cherri knew too well how good he felt; her fingers had crawled over his taut skin many times. Gunner took Cherri's hand and led her to his table in the corner, and after sitting down, he dragged her down on his lap. She snuggled her face in his neck, yearning to block out Peaches and Jax.

Emma tapped Cherri on the shoulder. "I need you in the back." She walked away, disappearing in a crowd of people.

"I have to get backstage to make sure everything's good," Cherri said.

"Go on back, baby doll. I'll be waitin' here for you when you get a break." Gunner chugged his beer and ordered another.

"Whoa, honey, don't you think you should take it easy with the drinking? The night is long, and you don't want to get wasted. Slow down a bit." Cherri wrinkled her brow as she fought to suppress her over-protectiveness.

Gunner flushed her closer to him. "Now aren't you sweet, worrying about your ol' man like that? Fuck, I haven't had no one care 'bout me in years. Don't worry your pretty little head off. I can handle my drinking. Nothin' new—been doin' it for years."

"I know. I'm just saying to slow down a bit, that's all. Don't you have to keep an eye out on things tonight? Can't do it if you're shit-faced." She gave him a quick kiss on the lips. "Gotta run." She dashed off.

Backstage, some of the dancers lined up for their upcoming dances while others wiped off their drenched bodies as they exited the stage.

"The guys tonight are generous. We should have private parties with them all the time," Tiffany, one of the strippers, said.

"Make sure you circulate for lap dances. You can make two weeks' salary just by doing lap dances. The house makes money, and so do you," Cherri said as she went into her dressing room to get changed for her dance number.

Looking at herself in the mirror, Cherri applied the concealer under her breast to cover the scars. Thankful for the dim lights and the illusions of the night, she doubted anyone could see any hint of deformity on her body. After the makeup dried, she pulled her peach, metallic, one-piece outfit over her body. It had a very low-cut scoop neck that pushed up her breasts, and the middle and side cut-outs showed off her firm body. The outfit narrowed at the crotch, barely covering her mound while a string of fabric fit snugly at her crack, exposing her firm, heart-shaped ass.

It was not an outfit for a public outing, but was perfect for entertaining a bunch of horny men. The entire spandex piece had a silver sheen which made her blue eyes shimmer like lightning bolts. Crystal charms dangled from her pierced belly button and shone like twinkling stars when they caught the light. She finished her look with large crystal hoop earrings and a three-strand crystal collar necklace.

Standing by the stage, Cherri waited for her cue. Her hands shook, her mouth was dry, and a dull ache throbbed behind her eyes. Chiding herself for being silly, she wasn't sure why she had butterflies twirling around in her stomach since she had danced so many times before. Maybe it was because Jax was in the audience with his penetrating eyes. Bending over, she gulped in deep breaths to calm herself. She wanted to dance for him; it would be her gift to him.

More deep breaths.

He made her crazy. He invaded her thoughts when she went to bed, when she awoke, and several times during the day. As much as she tried to rid her mind of him, he clung to her, almost mocking her. Her attraction to Jax wasn't fair to Gunner. The last thing she wanted to do was hurt him, but it didn't seem right for him to be tied to a woman whose thoughts, desires, and heart pined for another man. She had to do the grown-up thing and talk to Gunner about it later that night, after all the festivities died down. She owed him as much.

The stage went black, Cherri's cue to go on. The song she picked— "Whore" by In This Moment—blasted out of the speakers. The lights went on and Cherri twirled her body around the pole, her strong, long legs wrapping around it as she hung down. Her hair, streaked red by the stage lights, brushed the floor. Her body glimmered from the metallic threads and crystal jewels, which picked up different lights surrounding the stage. As she twisted around on the pole, high above the audience, she saw Gunner transfixed, his red face plastered with a grin as his eyes glowed with affection. Cherri nodded in his direction.

Hanging upside-down, her hair cascading like a waterfall, she searched for Jax. He leaned against a tall wooden island, his arms crossed and his sexy biceps bulging. Peaches hung onto his arm, but he didn't pay any attention to her—the only thing he looked at was Cherri.

Through the low, red lights and the fog machine, she detected the hunger burning in his hazel eyes as they bored into her. After bending her torso back up, she swung around and faced the audience, her eyes locked on his. Together they held each other's gaze as if no one else was in the room. For Cherri, no one else in the room mattered—she danced only for him.

Flipping backwards, she landed on stage with her back to the spectators. She bent over, her ass cheeks opening, and placed her head between her legs as her hair touched the stage. Still locked on Jax's eyes, she noticed he nursed a hard-on while lust and raw desire radiated from him. Spinning back around, she laid on her stomach and wiggled around on the floor, her tits almost popping out of their metallic harness. She puckered her lips and blew a kiss to the hooting and whistling men. *Let each of them think it's for them, but I'm dancing for Jax.* From the way he seized her eyes, shifted his weight, and adjusted his denim-covered dick, he knew her dance was for him. She threw him a smoldering, come-fuck-me look. A half-grin softened his face.

Twirling, swinging, and bending around the pole during her next dance to the music of My Darkest Days' song, "Porn Star Dancing," Cherri felt someone watching her. Not Gunner or Jax, but someone else, someone who made her skin crawl. As she slid down the pole, swinging her head around, she scanned the sea of faces. Near the front, he stood there, arms crossed, licking his lips—his beady eyes glued to her.

Someone from her past.

Someone she never wanted to see again.

No, it couldn't be him.

He lived in Denver.

It can't be him.

Her heart thumped against her rib cage like it would break through. She held her breath.

The crowd went wild when she ended her routine with the splits. Running off-stage before the lights went off, she had to have some air—she had to breathe.

Cherri locked the door to her dressing room and went to the bathroom to wipe her sweaty body with a washcloth. The coolness of the rag against the heat of her skin made all her nerves jerk to attention. Her muscles screamed from soreness, and her head throbbed from all the smoke and noise during her dance set. Walking back into her dressing room, she sat on the edge of her loveseat, kicking off her five-inch metallic pumps. Curling her toes, she massaged the balls of her feet.

She lay back and closed her eyes as her mind drifted to a different time and place. It was three years before and she'd agreed to be a low-level politician's mistress. She'd been down on her luck and hadn't given a shit about anyone for quite a while. Having someone pay for a nice apartment and giving her a car, an expense account, and nice clothes was like she'd won the lottery. For a twenty-year-old used ex-stripper, it'd been a dream come true. It all seemed like a lifetime ago…

He's coming through the door. Is it Wednesday already? Cherri's gut twitches. The days go by too fast. Her days without him speed by, but the days he spends with her seem like they drag on. Shit, he'll want to paw her and stick his puny thing in her, taking forever to come.

Looking out over the twinkling city lights and the snow-capped Rocky Mountains silhouetted against the darkening sky, Cherri knows she could've never afforded an apartment like this luxurious one. The grunting, pawing, and insufferable attempts to get her lover to orgasm are worth this view. It isn't all bad—it's like holding someone for a dance three days a week.

"Hey, honey. We got to talk." The medium-sized man with the pock-marked face comes over to her and draws her close to him, kissing her neck. She turns her face, squeezing his arm lightly then pulling away.

"What's up?"

"I found you a good doctor, and I have the money to give you so you can take care of your problem. Just wanted to make sure you don't think I'm dropping the ball here."

"I've changed my mind. I don't wanna go through with it. I wanna keep the baby. I'll take care of it. I won't bother you." She stops talking, noticing her lover's face is beet red—he's livid.

"Listen, bitch, you're getting rid of it like we agreed, and that's final. I don't need this complication. I'm not even so sure it's mine."

She looks out of the floor-to-ceiling windows, noticing the stream of headlights looks like an electric snake curving around the tree-lined boulevard below.

"It's yours," she whispers.

"Get rid of it. I'm vying for councilman in Adams County. I don't need this shit to ruin my chances. It's hard enough to keep you undercover. Oh, yeah, you're going to have to do without me for a bit, honey. Not too long, just until the campaign and elections are over. I know it'll be hard, but it'll give you a chance to recuperate after your procedure."

The thrill of not seeing her pompous lover makes her body sing for joy.

Damn, I wish the election would go on forever.

"That's too bad, but of course, I understand. I want to make things easy for you, not hard."

"I know you'll miss my loving, but when everything's done, we'll go on a nice trip together and you can have all of me for two weeks. Remember to keep your doctor's appointment; it's in a couple of weeks. I don't want you thinking about any of this. We've got plenty of time to start a family. Just make sure you do the right thing. I'm leaving the money here on the table so you're covered."

He puts his arm around her waist. She stiffens, not meaning to. He leans in to her and says in her ear, "You're going to do the right thing, aren't you, honey? You don't want me pissed. I can be sweet or a bastard... it's really your choice." He nibbles her earlobe.

Cherri cringes, remembering his anger when she threatened to tell his wife about them. She had bruises for weeks, and her ribs took a while to heal. She can't risk that, not with a baby growing inside her.

"I'll see the doctor. I don't wanna cause you any trouble. Thanks for paying." She stares out the window at the city below.

"Good. Since we've straightened it out, let's get naked and have some fun. I gotta be home in a couple of hours. Sorry I can't stay later, but one of the kids has something going on at school, and I promised my family I'd be there, even though I'd rather be here with you." He grabs her breasts and massages them, tweaking her nipples roughly.

"You gotta go—that stuff's important to a kid. It's the kind of thing that stays with kids their whole life."

"Let's get screwing, honey. It's been a long day, and I need your young, soft body to relax me."

Cherri walks into the bedroom, grateful he'll only bother her for two hours.

Thump. Thump. Cherri sat up with a start. For a minute, she didn't know where she was. Shaking the fogginess from her brain, she said, "Wait a sec."

Thump. Thump.

"I said to wait a sec."

Not wanting to answer the door in her stripper outfit, she grabbed her floral silk robe and tied it around her waist. Maybe it was Jax at the door. Bubbles of joy rose in her. She hoped it was him so she could nestle in his protective arms and breathe in his scent. It was probably Gunner; he always came by to tell her what a great job she did after she danced.

Thump. Cherri opened the door, her smile fading as all the color left her face. "It *was* you," she said. Black floaters swam in front of her eyes, and her breathing became shallow pants while clamminess covered her body.

"You're not going to invite me in? Long time, no see, hon." McFahey pushed past Cherri who stood like a marble statue. He glanced around her dressing room then plopped down on the loveseat and patted the space next to him. "Come on over here. We've got some catching up to do."

Cherri closed the door and sat down on her vanity chair, opposite McFahey.

"What're you doing here? I mean, in Pinewood Springs."

"I moved my family up here a while ago. In Denver, I was just a small fish in a big pond, but here I'm a big-ass fish in a tiny pond. Works better for me. I'm a councilman here. I didn't know you lived here. When did you move? Right after you left me without even a note?" He bent forward and gripped her cold hand.

"No, just been here a few months. Doesn't life like to play fuckin' games with us?" She slipped her hand out of his fingers.

He ran his eyes over her body, his stare lingering on her breasts. He sucked in his breath.

"You looked real good up on stage. I about shot my load seeing your tits bouncing and your ass wiggling. It reminded me of old times, honey. Now that we're living in the same place, we can start where we left off. I'd like that. I'd like that a lot." Staring at her, he stood up and came next to her. His fingers kneaded her neck, and he kissed her on the side of her mouth. "I've missed you, honey. I've missed our time together. I've missed the sex. You're a great lay. Why did you run out on me?"

Cherri shrugged his hands off her, shaking her head while she kept her eyes glued to the floor.

"Didn't I treat you right? Didn't I give you nice things, like that killer apartment? Fuck, the apartment set me back at least two grand a month. Glad I had other… uh… business deals going on. You were an expensive piece of ass, honey, but I loved our time together. Didn't you?"

"It was what it was for that time in my life. I had to move on, that's all," Cherri said.

He fixed his eyes on her as if he were certain her face held all the answers to his questions.

"Why you so cold to me, honey? I'm the one who should be madder than hell at you. I should punish you for what you did to me, but I'm so glad to see you, I'm going to forget what a fucking bitch tramp you were, and open my heart and my wallet to you instead. I want to set you up with something nice here in Pinewood. I know you're hurting for money. There's no way taking off your clothes for men every night pays big every time. You won't have to do that dirty shit anymore. I'm here to take care of you, hon." He ran his fingers up her arms, making her cringe.

"Thanks for the offer, but I'm not that girl anymore. I've moved on. I like being on my own. Anyway, I'm with someone." She darted her glacial eyes around the room. "I have to change and get back to work. You'll have to leave." Standing up, she moved away from him then waved her hand, palm up, toward the door.

As he squinted at her, his face grew a shade darker. "Did you take care of that mess you got yourself into?" he asked.

Nodding, she said, "I took care of everything."

"The doctor said you never showed up for the appointment I made for you."

"I wanted to go to a female doctor, so I found someone and took care of things."

"You better not be lying to me because this time, I won't be so forgiving." He stood there, eyeing her. "Come on over here, honey."

"No," she said.

In two long strides, he had her struggling in his arms. Like a Jack-in-the-Box, she bobbed her head, turning it from right to left while she pushed his approaching lips away from her face.

"Stop it," she hissed.

"I've missed you honey. I've missed *this*." He rubbed his hardness against her. "I want you back in my life. I'll set you up real good here. I can be very generous; you know you won't want for anything."

"No, I don't want your money. Stop it. Leave me alone." Cherri kicked him in the shin, but he didn't relent.

"Come on, honey, you know you want it. We had some good times. We can have better—"

"Take your fuckin' hands off her before I break them." Jax's voice bounced off the walls.

McFahey jumped and whirled around, scowling when he saw Jax. Cherri sprinted away from him, and, looking downward, she massaged her sore arms.

"Come to me, sweetness," Jax said, his hand extended out to her.

Cherri took his hand and in one movement, he pressed her close to him, his delicious scent enveloping her. She was safe—*for now*.

"This isn't your fuckin' business. Get out." McFahey's scrunched face made him look like a caricature.

"It is when you're forcing some shit on a woman who doesn't want anything from you." Jax's eyes bored into McFahey, and his chest rose and fell as his body became more rigid.

"You work for me; don't forget that."

"I don't give a damn. You're messin' with my woman. We're together."

McFahey, wide-eyed, peered at Cherri's face. Trying to make herself invisible, she squeezed tighter under the crook of Jax's arm. Staring at

McFahey, she nodded as she ran her fingernails down Jax's back.

"Now get the fuck out, asshole." He opened his cut, displaying a knife at his waistband. Jax placed his hand on it. "Any questions?"

McFahey, locking on to the knife at Jax's side, said, "You'll be sorry you messed with me." He glanced at Cherri as he retreated. "I'll be in touch."

Then he was gone.

Taking in a few deep breaths, Cherri ran her fingers through her hair. "Thanks for helping me out."

"How do you know that ass-wipe?"

She shrugged. "Met him through some people in Denver a few years ago."

"Did you have somethin' with him?"

"This was a long time ago."

"You didn't answer my question. This jerk is bad news. He doesn't play nice or fair."

"No shit."

"Did you have somethin' with him?" Jax swung her around so she faced him.

"I told you, this is part of my past and I want to forget about it. Leave it alone, please, Jax."

"I'm gonna ask you one more time if you had somethin' with this fuck, then I'm gonna get real pissed. I hate repeating myself, sweetness."

"I don't have to tell you anything. This isn't your business. We aren't together. Why can't you leave me alone?" The anger in her blue eyes made them flash like a match striking against its box.

"I'm never leaving you alone, baby. We belong together, and you know it. You want *us* just as much as I do, so can the drama."

She twisted away from his grasp and before he could reach her, she bolted out the door, almost crashing into Peaches who stood half-hidden by Cherri's dressing room. When Cherri looked at her, Peaches had a funny expression on her face. In that moment, Cherri knew Peaches heard everything and would delight in betraying Cherri. Shrugging off her paranoia, she rushed out to the bar area.

Cherri heard Jax's boots clack on the floor as he rushed after her. She saw Gunner by the bar with Banger and ran up to him, looping her arm around his. Turning around, he smiled and drew her into him, kissing her deeply. She hugged him and from the corner of her eye, she saw Jax's glare as he stood by the stage.

Her heart raced and her head pounded. She couldn't believe McFahey was there in Pinewood Springs. Her brain hadn't yet assimilated everything he said to her. Just when she seemed to be back on track, shit from her past came to fuck her over. Wasn't that the way it always was, though? If she was a quitter, she'd have given up a long time before, but she wasn't. She'd have to think things through. There was no way she could stay in the same town as her ex-lover; she'd have to move out of Pinewood Springs sooner than she planned.

"Hey, babe, have a shot," Gunner said, his words slurred.

"No, I'm good. Don't you think you should slow down? You're past tipsy."

Gunner bent down and placed a wet kiss on her lips. He tasted like smoky oak. "You're so cute, baby doll. You worry 'bout me. That's nice, but you don't need to. I'm good." He slid a shot of Jack to her.

Shaking her head, she slid her shot over to Banger. "You take this."

Banger, nodding at her, threw back the whiskey.

Cherri scanned the room for Jax and McFahey. She spotted Jax, his back to her, his arm around Peaches as he spoke with other Insurgents. Her heart broke a little. Earlier, before McFahey came into her room and crushed her dreams, she'd decided she couldn't be without Jax—she yearned to explore a relationship with him. But how could she tell him that since she had to leave him and her life in Pinewood Springs? It'd be hard enough to leave, but if they reconciled and gave each other their hearts, she'd never be able to do it. And she *had* to go. Tears burned behind her eyes for the life she could've had.

"You look exhausted," Emma said as she came up to the bar.

"I am tired," Cherri admitted.

"Why don't you take off? You've been working too hard, and I don't need you coming down with the flu, too. Go on, get outta here. I can handle closing up."

Cherri hugged Emma. "Thanks. I'll take you up on that."

She leaned into Gunner and said, "I'm going home. I'm so tired I could fall asleep right here. Let me take you to my apartment. You can leave your bike here and I'll drive you back in the morning to pick it up."

"You do look tired, baby doll. We'll catch up tomorrow."

"Come with me to my place. You've drunk too much. I can drive you."

He kissed her on the forehead. Shaking his head, he said, "Baby girl, I never had any woman give a shit about me the way you do, but you don't need to worry 'cause I'm just fine. I can handle my liquor. I've been livin' this way longer than you been alive, so don't worry your pretty head over me. I'll see ya tomorrow."

Cherri, ready to argue with Gunner, saw McFahey headed her way. Not wanting another confrontation with him, she looped her arm in Gunner's and said, "Okay, babe, let's go." She steered him toward the door as he leaned a little too much on her.

Outside, the night sky was inky black, and dark clouds covered the normal carpet of twinkling lights. A faint glow from the moon pierced the darkness, casting a dim light in the sky. Cherri shuddered as a cold chill ran through her, a nagging feeling of doom weighing heavily on her. She chided herself for being so silly; her nerves were on edge after seeing her ex-lover. She just needed a good night's sleep and she would think more clearly.

Gunner swayed a bit as he threw his leg over his bike. He pulled Cherri close to him and kissed her. She kissed him back.

"I wish you would let me drive you home."

Smiling, he wiggled her nose between his fingers, saying, "I love you, baby doll."

"Don't love me. I'm no good," she said under her breath.

"I'll be by tomorrow. We'll go for a ride."

"Drive carefully," she said.

His Harley's engine grumbled as he took off, his hair blowing around his shoulders. She watched him until the night's darkness consumed him and she couldn't see him anymore.

CHERRI'S PHONE VIBRATING on her nightstand woke her up. Dazed, she looked at the screen, seeing Emma's name flashing on it. Rubbing the sleep out of her eyes, she answered the phone. Emma was crying. *Wait, why is Emma crying? What the fuck? Am I dreaming?*

"What's wrong, Emma?"

"I'm so sorry, Cherri. I can come over if you need me. Cherri? Are you there?"

"I'm here. Why're you calling me so early? It's four o'clock in the morning."

"Didn't you hear what I said?"

"No."

"Gunner had an accident. A semi hit him as he sped around Bend's Curve. The truck driver fell asleep at the wheel and when he woke up, it was too late to avoid hitting Gunner. I'm sorry." Emma's voice cracked.

"Is he in the hospital?"

"No. He's... well, he's—"

"Where the fuck is he?" Cherri's voice was strained.

"At the county morgue. I'm sorry, Cherri, but Gunner didn't make it."

"Make what? Why don't you just say he's dead? He is, isn't he? Gunner's dead. He's dead, he's dead—"

A high-pitched wail interrupted Cherri's words. She pounded the bed over and over as her body heaved and shuddered, wetness coating her face. She threw her phone across the room. Everything she touched turned to shit. Wrapping her arms around her knees, she rocked back and forth on the bed, listening to her gasps, to her breaking heart. The moonlight, breaking through the dark clouds, covered her with its cold, white light.

CHAPTER FOURTEEN

THE HOT, BRIGHT morning seemed like a cruel joke to Cherri. The day should've been rainy with the sun hiding behind the gray clouds. Instead, the day the brothers laid Gunner in his grave was a clear, bright day without a cloud in the big, blue sky. Birds soared high, purple, white, and pink flowers dotted the blooming trees, and the low whir of lawnmowers echoed in distant neighborhoods.

Cherri sat in the front row of Calvary Christian Church. The simple, stained-glass windows cast rectangular patterns of red, blue, and green on the church's beige carpet. A large wood cross hung down in front of the altar, the colored patterns on the white wall behind it looked like a rainbow after a rainstorm. The church, packed with Gunner's home club and fellow bikers from both charter and affiliate clubs, was unusually somber. They were all there to pay their tribute to Gunner. The crowd was so large not everyone fit in the church, so many spilled out to the parking lot surrounding it.

Five hundred Harleys shone like beacons in the morning rays. All the bikers wore black bandannas and armbands. Their colors, proudly displayed out of respect for a fallen brother, created a kaleidoscope against the black leather jackets. Gunner, who lay in a black and silver casket, wore his colors.

At the pulpit, Reverend Jake looked at the sea of leather and denim, pointed to the coffin in front of the altar, and said, "Gunner was a fearsome man, but underneath all the muscle and tattoos beat the heart of a generous man, the heart of a brother." Murmurs whispered in agreement. Men raised their arms, hands in fists, paying homage to a man who was taken from them too soon.

Cherri stared at the coffin, wet lines running down her pale face. It had been a week since the semi-truck mangled Gunner and his bike, and she still couldn't believe her gentle giant was dead—that he was no more. Why hadn't she insisted he come home with her that night? She blamed herself for letting him ride when she knew he'd had too much to drink. The heat in the crowded church suffocated her. She wanted this to be over so she could throw herself on her bed and cry until she fell asleep. However, the day seemed like it was going to last forever. After the services, there would be the cemetery procession, and then the party—a massive send-off to Gunner. She didn't think she could make it through all that.

The mourners filed out of the church, their heads down, arms around each other, faces dark and somber. They glanced at the heavy police presence. Some cursed under their breaths, but most of them ignored the cops and went over to their bikes. The police ensured there wouldn't be any trouble at the outlaw funeral. They stood respectfully at a distance, giving the bikers some space in mourning their comrade's death.

Cherri climbed into a black limousine, scrunching herself as far against the door as she could. Gunner's mother and sister followed her into the limo. They smiled at her and she half-smiled back. She'd never met them before, and she remembered Gunner had wanted her to, but she always came up with an excuse why she couldn't go with him to his mom's house. The truth was she didn't want their relationship to move to the next level. It seemed that if she met his family, it would mean they were serious—really together. However, she wished she would've met them if for no other reason than to make Gunner happy. God, she was so fucked-up.

The roar of all the Harleys starting up was deafening. Cherri turned to look out the back window and gasped when she saw the wave of motorcycles lined up behind the limo. The hearse pulled out, the pall bearers rode behind the hearse, and the limousine followed. The club officers rode on their Harleys behind the family, the members of

Gunner's club behind them, and the rest of the chapters and affiliates behind that, a two-abreast bike procession. Cars took their second-class position behind the bikes. Along the street, citizens took pictures of the droves of motorcycles in perfect formation, cars stopped on the road, and people in stores and buildings watched as the bikers rode by, their colors bright, their hearts heavy, and their "Ride to Live, Live to Ride" patches displayed on their jackets.

At the cemetery, Reverend Jake said a few words about Gunner's freedom ride. Banger stepped toward the open grave, dropped a devil's skull motorcycle ornament into it, cleared his voice, and said, "We lost a great brother; one we're gonna fuckin' miss, that's for sure. He's lookin' at us now, and he's in a place where citizens and cops can't hassle him. He's riding his Harley with the angels."

The crowd clapped as Banger, in Insurgents tradition, threw a shovel of dirt into the grave. Hawk walked up to the grave and followed suit. He looked at the others and said, "In losing a brother, we have revitalized our biker spirit. May Gunner rest in peace."

Each officer stepped up, said a few words, shared a few stories then shoveled dirt into the grave.

Eventually, Jax came up. Cherri saw the tautness in his face, his neck flushed red. Some of the bikers turned away when he took the shovel. Others, knowing the bad blood between Gunner and him, chose not to pay him any attention and started talking among themselves.

Jax cleared his voice and said, "It's always sad when a brother falls. As many of you know, we had some problems between us, but he was a brother and he'll be missed." Jax tossed dirt in the grave and moved to the side.

Lines of bikers came up to the grave, many of them wearing t-shirts depicting a Harley soaring over a tombstone with the caption, "Death Ride." Several of them muttered, "If you gotta go, a spectacular motorcycle crash is the best way to do it."

The bikers threw beer cans, bandannas, and motorcycle parts into the grave before placing dirt on Gunner's casket. From a player, the notes and lyrics of "Free Bird" hung over the gathering at the gravesite. Cherri was happy Gunner's brothers gave him such an awesome send-off. He was loved by so many of them. She could see his twinkling eyes with the lines around them smiling from above, and her heart lurched. She glanced at Jax, but he avoided her look. He'd been dodging her since the night of the accident. Maybe he felt guilty—she knew she did.

Fuck, it's gonna be a long day...

THE SUN WAS high in the sky when everyone converged on the Insurgents' clubhouse. In the parking lot, brothers hugged each other as they milled into the great room. The tangy, smoky deliciousness of roast pig tantalized the men as they came into the clubhouse. The old ladies had come to the compound right after Gunner's church services, setting the tables and warming up the food they'd prepared for the last few days. They knew the brothers were going to give Gunner the send-off he would've wanted: beer, barbecue, and stories of him and other fallen brothers. It was times like these when the harmony and oneness of the Insurgents clubs made the old ladies proud their men belonged to the outlaw community.

Beer and whiskey flowed as the men laughed, slapped each other on their backs, and reminisced about Gunner. Many of the men at the funeral were older and remembered Gunner from back in the day when he first joined the Insurgents. Old ladies, girlfriends, and female relatives were the only women present at the party; club whores, mamas, and hoodrats were not welcomed, as this was a day of respect. Gunner's mother and sister were there, so the women Gunner had enjoyed for years were relegated to the dark corners of the club only to be brought out the following night at the club's party, to which old ladies, girl-friends, and female relatives were not privy. It was the way the Insurgents' world worked.

Music from overhead speakers played tunes which had undertones of freedom and defiance. The lyrics and musical strains from Lynyrd

Skynyrd's "Free Bird" and Led Zeppelin's "Stairway to Heaven" lent a somber note to the gathering, while Steppenwolf's "Born to Be Wild" and Iron Maiden's "Run for the Hills" picked up the crowd and reminded them why Gunner's life and the life they all chose mattered. When Manowar's "The Fight for Freedom" played, all the veterans sang along, arms in the air, hands fisted while tears streamed down their tanned faces.

Cherri sat alone on an overstuffed brown chair and watched the men pay homage to Gunner, the man who loved her and accepted her the way she was. The one thing he wanted from her was the only thing she couldn't give him: love. Gunner was a good person, but he was dead. She was a bad person, but she was alive. Wasn't life fucked up?

"Here, eat some food, Cherri." Cara bent down, holding a plate of ribs, potato salad, and corn.

Cherri thought she was going to throw up. "Thanks, Cara, but I'm not hungry. I couldn't eat a bite."

Cara put her hand on Cherri's hand. "Are you sure? Do you want me to bring you anything?"

"No, I'm okay. Thanks, though."

"I'm so sorry for your loss, Cherri. I know you must hurt. If you need anything, please let me know. I mean it."

"I will, thanks."

Cherri watched as Cara walked away. She was one of the nicest old ladies she had met, and she knew Cara meant what she said. If things had been different, she might have been friends with Cara, but that would never be. She wanted to leave and lie down on her bed. *Would it be in bad taste if I leave right now? Is it too soon? Probably no one would even know I'm gone. I should just go and forget about—*

"He talked about you every time he came by to see me. You made my son very happy." A white-haired woman with wrinkled skin interrupted Cherri's thoughts.

When Gunner's mother hugged her, Cherri grimaced as bitter bile rose up her throat. She forced a smile when she looked into the old woman's sad, brown eyes.

"Your son was a wonderful man. I was lucky to know him." Cherri placed her two fingers on her trembling, paled lips. She meant what she said. Gunner was a piece of luck that was placed in her life, and he was gone. That was the way it went with her; good things came and then they were taken away.

"You'll have to come by and see me sometime. We can get to know each other better. I know Gunner wanted that." She stroked Cherri's arm.

"Yes, I'd like that. I'll come by," Cherri lied, having no intention of ever seeing Gunner's mother again. *Fuck, I can't take much more. I have to get outta here. I wish I could run out and keep running until I drop dead from exhaustion. I need to get away from everything. Especially Jax.*

How messed up was she? Even at her lover's funeral, she thought of Jax and how wonderful his lips felt on hers, how she loved the way his calloused hands scratched across her skin, and how her body ignited when he sucked her nipples. She squirmed in her chair and looked around to see if any of the badasses had a fucking clue as to what she was thinking. She was bad. Her mom and stepfather were right—she was no good.

Cherri caught Jax staring at her from the corner of the bar. There were throngs of men in black leather, but she spotted his beautiful eyes fixed on her. Her heart beat faster. Since the accident, it was the first time he'd looked at her. He stood there with his lips parted, shifting back and forth while they held each other's gaze. Though Cherri was certain he wanted to come over to her, she knew he wouldn't out of respect for Gunner. She noticed some of the other brothers frowned as they darted their eyes from Jax to her, and she turned away. She knew the brothers had to deal with the tension between Jax and Gunner, and she also knew they blamed her. Hell, she blamed herself for it.

Once more, she thought about her mom telling her she was bad because she let bad things happen to her. Her mom told her that no matter how hard Cherri tried to break the mold, she wouldn't be able to because she was "just plain no good."

Except for Gunner's mother and Cara, no one approached her. It was like she was encased in an invisible shield and no one could see her. All around, men and women talked, laughed, shed a few tears, but not one Insurgent came up to her and told her they were sorry for her loss. Not one of them. It didn't matter to them that she was sad and missed Gunner—she was nothing.

Cherri stood and went to the bathroom. After locking the door, she splashed cold water over her face. She looked at her reflection, noting her face was pale, she had dark circles under her eyes from lack of sleep, and her lips were colorless. She stared for a long while at herself then crumpled on the floor, sobbing.

CHAPTER FIFTEEN

One month later

"YOU'RE HITTING THOSE pretty hard, aren't you?" Chas asked as Jax threw down his fourth shot.

"What the fuck? Are you my dad?" Jax slammed his shot glass on the bar, his eyes darting around the strip club, looking for Cherri.

"Why the fuck don't you just talk to her, man? It's better than getting yourself wasted every day and looking like a pussy-whipped sap." Chas pushed himself back from the bar with his boot.

"When I want your fuckin' advice, I'll ask for it. Right now, I don't fuckin' want it. Got it?" Jax's face reddened and his biceps twitched. He glared at Chas.

"Fuck, this blows. You've wanted her in the worst way. It's been enough time since Gunner's death. Go on and make your move. Your lovesick shit is annoying more than me, brother. Man up." Chas drained the last of his beer, clapped Jax on the shoulder, and sauntered out of the club.

Heat coursed through Jax's body. He was pissed. He should have clobbered Chas, but he knew the real reason he was pissed was because the brother was fucking spot-on.

Jax ran his hand through the top of his hair. He couldn't get the moody, fucked-up vixen out of his mind no matter how many bitches he banged. Chas was right—a respectable amount of time had gone by and he needed to claim Cherri. And if anyone started sniffing around her, he'd beat the shit out of the guy, brother or no brother. Even though Gunner was dead, he was still jealous and pissed that he'd had his cock in *his* Cherri. He tried to push it out of his mind, but he just couldn't.

He had a tightness in his chest most days since Gunner's accident. What the fuck was wrong with him that all he thought about since he found out Gunner died was how he could get back between Cherri's legs? He was too fucked up over her.

The problem was Cherri was special, and he'd never felt that way with any of the women he banged. Ever since they fucked, he couldn't forget about her soft, supple skin, her tasty pussy, and her beautiful ass. He'd explored every inch of her as she writhed and begged for more; her soft groans still echoed in his head. Every time he fucked, he was fucking Cherri—he didn't even know what most of the sluts he bedded looked like. The woman had him all in knots, and he needed her in the worst way.

"Do you want another shot?" Holt said.

"I'm good. Isn't Cherri supposed to be here?"

"Yeah, but she called in about fifteen minutes ago and said she had something to do so she'd be by tonight."

"What did she have to do?"

"I dunno, man. It's not for me to question. I only take the messages." Holt wiped off the bar.

A tingling on his skin crept up the back of Jax's neck and across his face. His ears burned hot as he gritted his teeth and pressed his lips tight. Shit, this woman made him ask pathetic questions to the bartender.

He already knew she was supposed to be at the club later because he'd checked her schedule. He also had one of the prospects tailing her to make sure she wasn't fucking around. Keeping tabs on her, asking Holt stupid as fuck questions, and ignoring the heaviness in his heart were things he wasn't proud of. He hated all this shit, and he wished he could tell her to fuck off and move on. Hell, he'd never chased a woman in his life; if she was a pain in the ass then she'd be history and he'd move on to another one. He liked easy, not all this complicated bullshit he'd had since he first saw Cherri's blue eyes.

The prospect had told him Cherri wasn't seeing any man in Pinewood Springs. It appeared she went home alone every night, but almost every day she left town, returning three hours later. The prospect wasn't able to follow her too far out because he had to be available at all times to all members. When Jax found out about her comings and goings, he imagined all kinds of shit and none of it was good. Convinced she had a man away from Pinewood Springs, he made it his mission to find out.

"Hiya, Holt." Cherri's voice barged in on Jax's musings.

Her heels clacked as she walked past Jax. He reached out and grabbed her, dragging her toward him.

"Oh. Jax, I didn't see you. I'm kinda in a hurry."

"How're you doing? It's been a while since we've seen each other." He bent his head and gave her a kiss on her cheek.

Flushed, Cherri said, "I've been good. You've been a stranger. I'm sorry, but I can't talk. I've gotta go. We can catch up another time." She twisted out of his hold and sprinted toward her office.

"Where're you goin'?"

"I have a bunch of errands to do," she said over her shoulder as she kept walking.

Before she opened her office door, Jax was behind her, rubbing against her. "I'll go with you, sweetness," he whispered in her ear.

She pushed open the door. "No. Absolutely not. I have to go alone. I gotta go. I'm already late. Don't make this hard for me." Her face paled and her features were taut, her lips trembling slightly.

Jax's eyes grew cold. "Where're you really going?" His voice was hard like steel.

Swallowing and looking at the floor, Cherri said, "I have errands to do. I told you that. Don't make a big deal over this. I have to go. I only came here because I forgot something." She motioned to a green tote on her desk. "I have to go. Now."

Jax took her in: the red streaks across her cheeks, her full lips, and her sad eyes. She'd lost some weight since Gunner's funeral and appeared too thin and frail. She rubbed her arms and looked everywhere but at him. Something was up with her, and he had a sneaking feeling this wasn't all about Gunner.

"You okay?" he said in a low, caressing voice.

She glanced at him for a second then down again. Exhaling, she said, "Yeah. Just gotta go. Bye."

He lifted her chin up, making her look into his eyes, their gazes locking together before she moved to pass him. As Cherri walked away, he snagged her by the waist and crushed her into him, kissing her fiercely. Balking, she twisted and pushed as she tried to break free of his arms. Holding her tighter, he rubbed his hands up and down her back in an attempt to calm her. When she stopped twisting, he seized her lips again, and that time, she gave in to his kiss. Their tongues intertwined as she moaned into his mouth and arched her back. In his hands, her hair was like cashmere, and her lavender-vanilla scent was intoxicating. Jax pushed in deeper with his tongue, yearning for more of her sweet minty taste, her warm mouth, and her soft lips. His desire for her was so extreme, he wanted to crawl inside of her to have his fill.

Pressing closer to her, he knew she felt his cock against her—nice and firm, the way she liked it. As one hand cupped her breast over her t-shirt, the other gripped her pert, denim-clad ass. Sliding his hand over her butt, he kneaded and pinched her cheeks. She stiffened, and he knew their shared moment was lost.

When she shoved him back, it caught him off-guard, making him stumble. Before he could recover, she dashed out the door and said, "Gotta go. Later."

Then she was gone.

His instincts told him she was hiding something, and he'd be damned if he'd let another man have her. Not for one minute did he buy her "doing errands" bullshit. His face grew hot as he imagined her running off to meet a secret lover. He hoped it wasn't that because he didn't want to kill a man in front of her. *Fuck, she's complicated.*

After the low lights in Dream House, the brightness of the day pierced Jax's eyes. He squinted and blocked the sun with his hand as he perused the street and spied Cherri waiting at the bus stop. When it came, she went inside as Jax jumped on his bike, switching on the ignition when the bus doors closed. Keeping his distance, he followed the bus as it snaked its way around Pinewood Springs.

After two stops along Main Street and County Line Road, the bus squeaked past emerald-green forests, fields of kaleidoscopic wildflowers, and the glittering waters of Grizzly Creek. Jax, eyes fixed on the bus, curved around the road carved out of the Rocky Mountains which rose high above, punching the sky. After thirty minutes of climbing, the road began its descent, and a grassy valley blanketed with brick and wood houses emerged. As the bus entered Dexter, Jax hung back.

Turning down what appeared to be the main street in the small town, the bus stopped. Several passengers alighted, Cherri among them. Jax parked his Harley on the street in front of the diner then followed an unaware Cherri at a safe distance. She walked with purpose past a mom-and-pop grocery store, a bakery, and several clothing and notion stores until she turned down a small street lined with birch trees and well-kept brick houses. The whir of lawnmowers punctuated the neighborhood while rainbows danced among the sprinklers of several front yards.

At the end of the street, Cherri turned left, where most of the neighborhood houses had fenced yards and metals swings on the large front porches. Stopping in front of a modest, two-story wood-framed house, she opened the gate and went up the front porch's wooden steps. From her pocket, she took out a key, turned the lock, and let herself in.

What the fuck is she doing here? And she has a key? What the fuck? Knowing her family lived in Denver, Jax's pulse raced. Hell, people didn't have keys to houses unless there was some relationship to whoever lived there. *Fuck, she better not be with a man.* With a clenched jaw, he ran up the steps two at a time, the wood creaking under his weight. He knocked on the front door.

No answer.

He knocked harder.

No answer.

A cold sweat crept up the back of his neck to his forehead. He wiped his brow, pursed his lips, and banged on the door.

No answer.

"Fuck this," he said under his breath. "Cherri, I know you're in there."

Still no answer.

"Open the door, Cherri. Now. If you don't, I'm comin' in. I'm not even fuckin' kidding."

Nothing.

The doorknob was cool in his hot palm as he turned it, opening the door. A small foyer greeted him, and a few pictures hung on the wall in front of him, like the photos people had on their wall calendars—these were scenes from different islands. He walked forward. His breath was shallow, and his eyes darted around; he was on high-alert. Putting his hand inside his cut, his fingers landed on his 9mm revolver.

He turned to the left and entered a living room decorated like something out of a 1970s catalog: orange couches with a bold brown and yellow geometric pattern, lacquered coffee table and end tables, brown shag-pile carpet, and pine wood-paneled walls. In the middle of the room, Cherri sat looking at him, her eyes misty. She was on the carpet, cross-legged, with a girl of about eight months on her lap, holding the child close to her. The little girl had on a yellow onesie with a pink gingham giraffe on the front. The girl's white-blonde hair and blue eyes were miniatures of Cherri's. A medium-sized yellow gingham bow covered half of the baby's hair.

Jax glanced around the room as if looking for answers to his unasked questions. He blew out his cheeks then released them. Squeezing the baby closer to her, Cherri stared at Jax. Breaking the silence, she said, "This is my baby, and no one's gonna take her away from me."

CHAPTER SIXTEEN

JAX OPENED HIS mouth, but nothing came out. He just stood there, staring at her as she held the little one. Cherri brushed her lips against her daughter's hair and turned away.

Exhaling, Jax said, "This is your baby? Why didn't you tell me?"

Cherri's chin quivered. "I don't want anyone to take her from me. I don't care what happens to me, but I want her to be safe and loved."

"Why would I take her away from you? What's going on, sweetness?"

"I come here about five or six times a week to see her. I pay Sarah to take care of her until I can get a place of my own and afford daycare. She's all mine, and I love her." Her voice broke and her eyes glistened as a lone tear glided down her face.

In a flash, Jax knelt beside her and circled his arm around her trembling shoulders. He nestled her close to him, kissing her forehead. With a calloused finger, he wiped away her tear then softly caressed her baby's hair.

"What's her name?" he said in a low voice.

"Paisley. Paisley Benoit."

"She has your last name?"

"Yes." Defiance shone in her eyes.

"Nice to meet you, Paisley." Jax took the baby's soft, chubby hand and shook it.

Paisley gurgled and grasped his finger. He smiled then looked at Cherri who also had a smile playing around her lips. He tilted her head toward him and kissed her warmly on her lips. "She looks like her mama."

Cherri stifled a sob as she wrapped an arm around Jax's neck, drawing his face closer to hers. She covered his mouth with hers, and they sat on the floor kissing; Cherri had one arm around her daughter, and Jax had both of his around mother and daughter.

Pulling away, Jax said, "Why are you afraid someone will take Paisley?"

Cherri brought her fingers to her mouth and chewed her nails. She sighed. "Her father is a rich and powerful man. He was so angry when I got pregnant, and he told me I had to get rid of Paisley. He gave me money, set up an appointment with a doctor, and, well... he ordered me to get an abortion. I didn't want to do it. I couldn't. I wanted my baby so bad. I lied to him and said I'd do it, but I didn't. He wanted me to get rid of her because he thought I'd use her to blackmail him. I didn't give a shit about his money—I just wanted to have my baby. I wanted something of my own to love."

Cherri ripped the nail on her index finger and winced when it drew blood. She put her finger in her mouth and sucked it to stop the blood. After a few minutes, she said, "I love Paisley more than anything and she loves me. She loves me unconditionally, and she doesn't care that I'm bad and dirty." She buried her face in Paisley's downy hair.

Jax stroked Cherri's back, wishing he could alleviate her pain. "Sweet one, you're not bad or dirty. Why do you say those things about yourself? You're so precious, and what you did to keep your daughter, that's good, not bad."

"I took the bastard's money, then I split."

"You needed the money to help you through your pregnancy. That's not so bad."

Tugging at the shag carpet, she said, "You don't know me. You don't know my whole story."

Jax scooted closer to her and stroked her forearm. "Then let me in so I can know you better. I want to. You have to trust me."

She blew out a breath. "All I know is I want to keep my daughter safe. I want her to have a better life than I did. I love her, and all I want is for her to be happy and safe. I miss her when I'm not with her, and my heart just aches when I have to leave her."

Jax placed her head on his shoulder. "Let me take care of you, sweetness. I'll make everything right for you."

"If only you could," she said in a half-whisper.

"Who's the father?"

She stiffened. "Please don't ask me. I can't tell you. Please respect that and don't ask me anymore."

"Does anyone know about Paisley at Dream House?"

"You're the only one who knows."

"Gunner didn't know?"

"No, I never told him anything about my life. I didn't have that kind of relationship with him." She held his gaze. "You're the only one who knows. I'm glad to share her with you."

He kissed her and his teeth grazed over her lower lip as her lavender scent, mixed with the freshness of baby powder, wafted around him. His heart surged as he hugged her. Paisley's wet hands tapped against his tanned forearm, and her bright blue eyes sparkled. He laughed.

"What's so funny?" Cherri said.

"Your daughter's just like you—a real cutie." He pinched the tip of her nose as he kissed her head. "Let's take Paisley and go for a walk. I bet she'd like some ice cream."

Cherri smiled widely at him. "She'd *love* some ice cream, and I would, too."

Less than ten minutes later, they strolled down the main street in Dexter. The downtown area consisted of two blocks on each side of the street. They spied a homemade ice cream parlor, ordered their treats, and took off for the nearby park, which was replete with playground equipment, gazebo, and paved trails which circled around lush shrubbery and colorful flowers.

As they walked around the park, Paisley in her stroller and white bonnet and Cherri licking her chocolate chip ice cream cone, the heaviness Jax felt in his body earlier in the day dissipated. The only tightness he felt was in his dick. For reasons he couldn't explain, Cherri being a mother turned him on. The way she loved her daughter and made so many sacrifices for her caused a funny sensation in the pit of his stomach and in his cock. What the fuck was up with that? Brushing against her as they walked made his skin tingle and his pulse surge. It was like he was a young boy on a first date with his crush, but the urges in his dick were all grown-up. If he could get away with it, he'd have her bent over the jungle gym, banging the hell out of her silky pussy. He readjusted his jeans as they continued on their stroll.

A couple of hours later, Cherri kissed her daughter goodbye while Jax stood in the doorway of the living room and Sarah, the woman who took care of Paisley, sat on the couch.

"I'll see you tomorrow, angel. I love you." Cherri kissed Paisley's chubby red cheeks. "Thanks, Sarah. Do you need anything more?" Cherri asked as she handed a wad of bills to Paisley's caregiver.

"No, that should be okay. I'll see ya tomorrow. You going back with him?" She jerked her head toward Jax.

"Yeah. I've known him for a while." She whispered in Sarah's ear, "He's a good one. A keeper."

Warmth surrounded Jax's heart when he overheard what Cherri said to Sarah. Maybe she'd ease up and let him in her life.

Sarah pointed at Jax. "You take care of her. She's been through enough bullshit with men. Don't you act like no jerk with her. Got it?"

His eyes twinkling, Jax smiled. "Yes, ma'am."

Cherri laughed and they walked out, heading to where Jax parked his bike.

"She doesn't take any bullshit, does she?" Jax said as they walked out of Sarah's earshot.

"Nope. She's been through two husbands and raised five kids. She's a tough cookie with a soft center. I lucked out; she loves Paisley and treats her like one of her own."

"I'm glad to hear it, sweetie." Holding her hand, he brought it to his lips and kissed it tenderly.

Smiling, Cherrie leaned against him.

A few minutes later, they glided down the road. The western sky housed pink and gold hues as the sun began to nestle behind the mountain peaks. The eastern sky darkened, allowing a few shimmering lights to come out to play. Jax, with Cherri flattened against his back, decided this was one of the best days he'd had in a long time. He loved the feel of Cherri's arms around him, her head on his shoulder, and her tits on his back. He never thought spending the afternoon with Cherri clothed and maternal would touch him the way it did. He was hooked, no doubt about that. The guys at the club would have his balls if he told them he had a great time with a woman and they didn't even fuck, didn't get anywhere *near* fucking her.

Yeah… he was hooked.

CHAPTER SEVENTEEN

THE NEXT NIGHT, Jax was seated at his usual table near the stage, ignoring the dancer gyrating on the stage and focusing his full attention on Cherri as she bustled around the bar area, making sure the crowded room was well taken care of. He couldn't keep his eyes off her, loving the way her ass moved in her black spandex skirt and how her snug crop-top clung to her tits, exposing a strip of creamy skin. Jax breathed in sharply; a peek of her skin teased the fuck out of him. And her legs looked beyond sexy in her four-inch heels.

As she sashayed from table to table, wiping down the bar stools where too many drunks spilled their drinks, she exuded sex, and he had to keep shifting in his chair to accommodate his raging hard-on. He knew she saw him because he caught her darting side glances at him every now and then, checking him out. He noticed the way her eyes lingered on his bulging biceps and his corded chest muscles, which were defined through his black, skin-tight t-shirt. Each time she feasted her eyes on his chest, she licked her lips. Oh, yeah, she probably didn't have a clue she was doing that, but fuck, he could think of a hundred places her pink tongue could lick on him. She drove him wild.

Ever since he spent the day with her and Paisley, he couldn't get her out of his mind. Not. At. All. The previous night, during church, images of Cherri played out in his mind's theater. He couldn't even remember a damn thing the members talked about at the meeting. He knew that wasn't a good sign since he was the club's enforcer, and his job was to make sure no one messed with the club or any of its members or loved ones. Being distracted could mean his cut, or worse, a brother's life. He had to stop this pussy-ass daydreaming and claim Cherri. It was time.

From her warm gazes, he sensed she cared about him and wanted it, too.

Cherri came up to his table. "Hi, Jax. Do you want another beer?" She smiled affectionately at him.

His cock twitched. "Sure. How're you tonight?"

"Busy. I've been running like this since about six o'clock this evening. Good for business, but bad for my feet." She shifted her weight on one foot while she relieved some pressure off the other by suspending it in the air for a few seconds.

"Take a break and have a beer with me." He grasped her wrist and pulled her between his legs, his dick pressing against her thighs.

Their eyes connecting, Cherri bent down and whispered in his ear, "I'd love to do that, but it's so noisy. Maybe we can take a break in my dressing room." Her breath stroked his earlobe.

He clasped her nearer to his crotch, his hands resting on her pert ass cheeks. "That sounds real good, sweetness. Lead the way."

Hands on his shoulders, she said, "Let me go first, then you come on back in about five minutes, okay?"

Jax nodded as she eased herself away from him. Gulping down his beer, he watched her swaying hips disappear behind the curtain.

There was no way he could wait five minutes; he could barely wait five seconds. He stood up, wiped his hands on his jeans, and glanced at the stage. Peaches threw him a kiss as she shimmed out of her boy shorts. Turning away, he headed to Cherri's dressing room.

When he opened the door, Cherri sat on her vanity chair with her shoes off, rubbing the balls of her feet. He laughed.

"Don't laugh unless you've spent five hours in four-inch heels. I couldn't wait to get my shoes off. Man, rubbing my feet like this feels way better than sex."

Jax lifted up an eyebrow. "Really? Sounds like you've been dry too long, sugar. I'll rub you all over so your whole body will feel real good, not just your feet." He came up to her, moved her hands away, and began massaging her feet.

She threw her head back and groaned. "Shit, it feels so good. You've got quite the touch."

He bent down and kissed the top of her feet lightly—her red-polished toes drove him crazy. He lightly kissed each toe while he massaged her sore feet, her "ahs" and "ohs" telling him he was giving her what she needed. He moved his hands up her calves and then toward her thighs. As he kneaded her skin, he followed it with a trail of kisses and soft bites. When he reached her thighs, she parted her legs as she grabbed his hair. She threaded her fingers through it while she threw her head back, the veins in her throat quivering under the vibrations of her groans. He parted her legs more and revealed a tiny metallic thong. The shiny patch barely covered her smooth pussy lips. He licked his lips as he ran his finger over her glistening slit.

"Fuck, sweetie. I love how I make you so wet."

Cherri moaned her response as she squirmed under his caressing finger, fixing her gaze on him when he smiled and put his finger in his mouth, tasting her. With her fist in his hair, she pulled his head back then bent over, running her lips and tongue over his face—light, feathery strokes on his forehead, eyes, cheeks, and everywhere else *except* his mouth. He stood up, pulling her with him, and crushed her to his chest. Hearing her gasp—one, single gasp—set his body on fire, and he had to possess all of her, even if it meant he'd lose his soul to her.

Jax yanked her hair back and she cried out, but he cut off the sound with his mouth on hers, devouring her lips as his tongue darted in and plunged deep inside, pushing further until she placed her small hands on his shoulders to ease him away. Unable to let her go, he tasted her mouth, danced with her tongue, licked her teeth, and sucked her bottom lip. As Jax released her, they embraced each other as they caught their breaths.

Covering her mouth with his again, he guided Cherri over to the sofa against the wall, never breaking their kiss. Her arms snaked around his neck, and she held him tightly as he lay her on the couch. Kneeling next to her, their lips still clung together, tasting and consuming each other like it was the end of the world and this was their one chance at pleasure.

He moved his hands around the curves of her body until he reached her ass then slipped them under her skirt, her rounded globes greeting him. As he squeezed and pinched them, he stroked her crack, the metallic fabric scratching his finger.

He tore his mouth away from hers, leaving her gasping for air as he murmured into her neck, "I fuckin' love your body. You make me hard like no other woman."

She snorted. "Sorry, but I find that a little hard to believe. You do have a rep of being a bit of a man-whore. I'm sure I'm not the only woman who makes you hard, but it was a sweet effort on your part to tell me that."

He brought his hand up to cup her breast, squeezing it and loving the way she hitched her breath and tightened her jaw. "Yeah, other women give me a hard-on, but that's not what I meant. With other chicks, it's a way to get pleasure and release. I don't know...it's like I want it, I get it then it's over until the next time. But with you? Oh, fuck, with you, I want, need, and desire it all at once. It's like it'll kill me if I don't get it *with you* and only *you*. I want and need all of you. I crave you. It's more than just havin' pussy. You know?"

Cherri buried her head in his neck and stayed there, quiet, for several minutes.

"What's wrong, sweetie? Did I say somethin' to make you mad? Did I fuck up again?" Jax put his hands on each side of her face and pushed it up; her cheeks were wet and her bottom lip trembled. "Why're you crying?"

She tried to bury her head again, but his hands were like clamps against her face. She locked her eyes on his. "When you say shit like that, you make me feel special," she whispered. "I dunno... you don't make me feel like just another slut."

Jax's eyebrows drew together. "You *are* special. You're very special to me. Don't ever forget how special you are." He kissed away the damp-ness on her face. The sweet saltiness of her tears pricked Jax's tongue.

Cherri crushed her mouth against his, grazing his bottom lip with her teeth. She slid her tongue over his lips, his chin, his Adam's apple, and the base of his neck, until she reached his pecs. She ran her fingernails over his stacked muscles and tweaked his erect nipples, taking each one between her teeth as she flicked her tongue over them. Low growls emitted from deep in Jax's throat and he buried his hands in her hair, grabbing clumps of it. After teasing his nipples, she ran her tongue and nails downward toward the V that dipped under his tight jeans toward his prominent hard-on.

"Fuck, woman, you're busting my balls here."

"I love the way you taste. It's sweet, like a liqueur with a hint of salt. Mmmm." Cherri gave him a big, wet kiss on his belly button, her tongue darting in and out.

"Fuck, woman… fuck…"

She unzipped his jeans and put her hand on his throbbing dick. Jumping out, Jax's hardness hit her against her cheek. Rubbing her finger over its glistening top, she licked his cock on the underside before Jax yanked her up.

Eyes wide, she said, "You don't want a blowjob? I thought it was the one thing all men loved."

"Fuck yeah, I want one, but if you give me one, I'm gonna blow real fast 'cause I've been hard for you for too long. I don't want to ruin this. I want to play with you, give you something to scream about. Then I'll blow inside your warm pussy."

Redness began to color Cherri's cheeks as she shied from his heated gaze.

Jax sat on the edge of the couch and hugged her, pulling her into the crook of his arm. She was stiff as a board. "No reason to be shy around me, sweetness. We can go slow and real gentle. This is the real thing, not some shadow from your past or some jerk you fucked. Don't close down on me now. Trust me." He tilted her chin up, looked at her mouth, and pressed his lips on hers, kissing her softly. Slackness began to replace her rigidity as she took long, deep breaths. When she was soft and pliant,

Jax, ever so slowly, guided her down on the couch, his mouth next to her ear, whispering, "That's it, sweet one. That's it."

He nuzzled his face against hers, the softness of her skin electrifying him. A small moan escaped from her throat and she tangled her fingers in his hair, wrapping her leg around his as she grasped him closer to her.

"I'm sorry; it's just sometimes past phantoms get in the way. I do want to be with you and feel every part of you on and in me." She nestled her face in his neck.

"No need to apologize. I get it. And sweetie, I want to be with you. I can't wait to be inside you. You make me so fuckin' horny, you don't even know. You're the real thing, sweet one. You're special to me; you know that, right?"

Cherri didn't answer, just kept playing with his hair.

"Sweetness?" Jax lifted her face toward his. "You know you're special to me, don't you?"

She nodded then pulled him close as he saw uncertainty lacing her eyes. He wanted to fuck her too much to talk about it right then, but he made a mental note to do so later. It was important that he made her realize she meant the world to him. His face darkened and his brow constricted. Whatever or whoever fucked her up, he had to find out, and when he did, he would exact vengeance.

Cherri, clenching her thighs together, brought him out of his dark transgression. He brushed her cheek with his hand and she opened her eyes. "Sweetie, I want your eyes open so you can watch what I do to you. I want to see the desire and pleasure in your beautiful blue eyes."

"I'll try and keep my eyes open. Whenever I'm tense, I close my eyes during sex so I can go to my safe place if I have to."

"What? What the fuck does that mean?"

Cherri's fingers touched her parted lips as she shook her head. "Uh... I don't know why the hell I said that. It's nothing, just a stupid game I play with myself sometimes..." Her voice trailed off.

"You know you're safe with me, right? I'm not gonna hurt you. When we were together that one time in your bedroom, you were cool.

Why're you so jumpy now?"

"I'm nervous about not being on the floor. I know it's silly, but I should be out there."

"Are you sure that's all that's going on?"

Nodding, Cherri squirmed again under Jax, arching her back while rubbing her wet pussy against his thigh. Lust replaced concern and Jax cupped her breasts in his hands, squeezing them. After he left a path of nips and licks from her face to her cleavage, he bit at the soft flesh of her rounded tits and sucked in his breath when he saw her pink areolas pucker around her stiff nipples. While his mouth latched on to her nipple, sucking it, his teeth grazed over its tautness as his other hand caressed her ass. Cherri gasped and writhed as he sucked her tits, looking at his bent head. Jax glanced up and locked a heated stare with the woman who had entered his heart.

"You like that, sweetness? I love your tits."

In a breathy voice, she said, "They're not too small for you? I thought all bikers loved big tits."

"Not me, sugar. You've got the perfect size for me. I love your tits. Hell, I just fuckin' love your body."

As he licked her breasts, he twisted her nipples, running his tongue over the scars on the underside of her breasts. Shifting under him, he felt her muscles tense.

"N-n-not there," she whispered.

"I love your whole body, sweetie. These scars are a part of you, and they're beautiful, too." He didn't stop licking; he wanted her to trust him and love the beauty of her body. As he licked her scars, the uncertainty and shame slowly melted into desire and lust. He continued his mouth's descent over her stomach and down between her inner thighs where he softly bit the fleshy part, making her groan as she tried to close her legs.

"No way, sweetness. All those juices are for me. I plan to lick you dry."

Spreading her legs even further, he moved his gaze from her smoldering eyes to the loveliness of her pink, glistening pussy. The swollen lips were slightly parted, revealing her shiny, rosy folds that looked so tempting his mouth was watering. He *had* to taste her honeyed slit.

When he slid his finger between her folds, opening her engorged lips, she yelled out, arching her back to bring her pussy closer to his face.

"I can't wait to taste you," he said.

"I feel like I'm going to explode," Cherri panted.

"Not yet, sweet one. I got some plans for your pussy before I take you over the edge." Placing his full mouth on her quivering sex, he ran his tongue up and down, flicking her hardening nub. Sucking her clit, he inserted two fingers into her.

"Fuck that feels so good. So good. Oh, my God," she said.

"You taste like honey and vanilla, and it's become my favorite flavor. You are so sweet. Fuck, I could stay buried in your pussy all day. Fuck, sweetness." His voice vibrated against her sensitive clit, and he saw her skin pebble as he spoke.

Jax's blood heated and his cock throbbed painfully. Slipping a condom from his jeans' pocket, he rolled it on. Taking the tip of his dick, he rubbed it back and forth over her hard bud while he jammed his fingers in and out of her slippery pussy. Her walls tightened around his fingers and he knew she was ready to erupt.

"Jax, it feels too good. Oh, my God. Oh, oh, oh…" Convulsing from hundreds of pleasure spasms, she closed her eyes and moved her head from side to side. She placed one hand on her mouth to stifle her screams and her other hand jerked Jax's hair, making him wince. As her body relaxed, Jax took her legs and thrust them over his shoulders. He massaged her tits and flicked her still-erect nipples, and she panted, still coming down from her orgasm but already aching for more. Bending down, he licked up her juices then leaned over and kissed her, deep and wet.

"You taste good, don't you, sweetie? Have you ever tasted yourself?"

Shaking her head, she licked the taste off her lips and looked into his liquid-hazel eyes. Smiling, he dipped his dick in her wetness and pushed her back further into the couch while his hardness pressed against her entrance. Watching her thrash under him with her tits bouncing, he rammed his cock into her slick pussy. He had planned to be gentle and slow, but his urge was too great, so he banged her hard and with each thrust, he went in deeper. Cherri's panting breaths punctuated with yelps of pleasure drove him harder and deeper. He tensed at the same time her walls closed in around him. With a resounding, "Oh, fuck!" in unison, they both climaxed, each of their orgasms releasing pent-up desires they'd been suppressing for so long.

Jax laid on top of Cherri, stroking her hair as his body cooled down. He rolled off her then placed her on top of him as he wrapped his arms around her. For a long while, they held each other in silence. Stirring, she kissed his chest then pulled herself up. "I better get back to work. I've been gone too long."

"Let Emma handle things for the rest of the night. I want to spend more time with you. Let's go back to your place."

"I can't do that. Emma would be pissed."

"What the hell is she gonna do? Fire you for fuckin' the boss? I don't think so, sweet one." Jax sat up and kissed her shoulders, which were soft like velvet. *What the hell does she do to have such soft skin?*

"I know, but Emma depends on me, and I don't wanna let her down, you know?"

"What about me, sweetness? I want more time with you. You gonna let me down?"

Placing her hand on his, she smiled. "No, I'm not gonna do that. You can come to my place when I get off. I'll be home at three o'clock. You can stay with me."

He hugged her, bringing her flush against his hard chest. Kissing her neck, he said against her skin, "Three o'clock seems like a long time."

"It's only a few hours from now. I really gotta go. Be good and let me get dressed." She gave him a quick kiss on his lips and jumped away from him, avoiding his reach.

Jax watched as she bent over, her ass open, begging for him to come in. He never thought it could be so sexy to watch a woman put *on* her clothes, but the way Cherri poured her body into her outfit made his dick hard as hell. *Oh, yeah.*

She blew him a kiss and walked out the door, her heels clacking on the floor as he watched her until she disappeared. Sighing loudly, he thought about the posers who never rode their motorcycles past their driveways. It pissed him off, and it was exactly what he needed to get rid of his hard-on. Cherri did something to him, and all he wanted was to be back in her pussy, crawling all over her small, sexy body.

Fuck. Remember the posers, the assholes who think they're bikers. I bet fucking Cherri on my Harley would rock. Damn, think about the posers. Fuck!

Thirty minutes later, Jax zipped up his jeans and walked out of Cherri's dressing room. He slammed right into Peaches.

"Damn. Sorry, I didn't see you. You okay?"

Peaches, jabbing a finger in Jax's chest, said, "No, I'm not okay. What the fuck were you doing in the bitch's dressing room?" Her face flushed and spittle formed in the corners of her mouth.

"None of your fuckin' business."

As Jax went to maneuver around her, Peaches blocked his way. "I need to talk to you."

"We don't have anything to talk about," Jax said.

"Yeah, we do. I've missed you, babe. I know you're busy with club business and all, and I understand all that. I'm just glad to see you." Her words rushed out, and her hands kept clenching and unclenching. "I just need to know we're okay. I'm cool with everything. I'll be yours on *your* terms. I won't bug you about being your ol' lady, even though it's something I hope will happen. I'm not gonna pressure you, baby. I'm cool with whatever space you need. I just need for us to be back on track. You know—"

"There is no *us*, Peaches. We had a good time, and you were a good fuck. You should do fine finding another brother to be with. Hell, you'll probably end up *someone's* old lady, but you'll never be mine."

"What're you talking about? We're together. We're in a relation-ship." Peaches frowned.

"*We* aren't in anything. We just aren't. Seems pretty simple to me."

Peaches stood silent, her eyes flashing. Jax, tired of the scene, brushed past her. As he walked toward the bar room, he heard a piercing cry full of hate and frustration. When he spun around, an enraged Peaches barreled toward him: her face beet red, arms flayed, screams deafening. Before she threw herself at him, he caught her by the arms, trying to calm her down as she kicked at him. Narrowing her eyes, she said, "You bastard! You think you can fuck me and leave me just like that? And for some icy cunt? No fuckin' way."

Jax, holding her away from him as she twisted and jerked, said, "Calm down, Peaches. I never promised you shit, and you know it. I told you right from the start it was for fuckin' and if we had fun along the way, great. You told me you were cool with it, and now you're going all fuckin' crazy on me. Fuck that. And don't ever call my woman a cunt again or I'll cut your tongue outta that dirty mouth of yours. Now do you got that? *Cunt?*"

Peaches went limp, slumping down to the floor, her legs spread open as the blood drained from her face. She whispered, "Your woman?"

Jax stared at her with flinty eyes. "Yeah, my woman. I'm with Cherri now, and I'm gonna claim her." His features softened a bit. "You're a lot of fun, and you won't have trouble finding a man. For me, it's always been Cherri. You knew that. You knew you and I were just having fun and passing the time. You gotta move on."

Raising herself up, Peaches threw back her shoulders and looked Jax right in the eyes. "I will never forgive you for humiliating me like this. You're gonna find out what happens to people who mess with me, and so is that little bitch you just fucked. You'll both be sorry." She spun around and ran out the backdoor into the night.

Jax held himself back from running after her and laying into her. No one ever threatened him. Afraid he'd do something real bad to her, like fucking end her life, he stood there, nostrils flaring, hands in fists, and forced himself to chill. Concentrating on the fact that he'd be together with Cherri in less than three hours helped to ease his anger. Calmer, he walked up to the bar, ordered a beer, and watched the dancer stripping on stage.

CHAPTER EIGHTEEN

JAX TOOK A hit on his joint as he waited for Cherri to come home. The neighborhood was dark and quiet, and a freight train's whistle, wailing in the distance, was the only sound penetrating the night's solitude. Many times a night, freight trains clanked their wheels on the steel tracks which ran through the heart of Pinewood Springs. As a child, Jax would hang out by the tracks which curled through the valley, and he'd often daydream of riding the rails and seeing the country. He thought standing on top of one of the boxcars with the wind whipping around him would be the closest feeling to absolute freedom he could find. He never did ride the rails, but he found something better—a lightning-speed Harley with cams that could out-scream any freight train's whistle. His first ride on a motorcycle gave him the freedom he dreamed about as he lay on his stomach in the grassy field, watching the trains speed by. Once the wind slapped his face, he was hooked, and he never looked back.

A resident's car door jarred his nostalgic musings, and he saw Cherri ambling on the sidewalk, her smile infectious and her body luscious. He leaned against his bike with his ankles crossed and his arms resting on the leather seat. Cherri came up to him, snaked her arms around his neck, and said, "Damn, you look sexy on your Harley."

His dick jumped when he breathed in her lavender scent. Tracing the bottom of her lip with his thumb, his gaze lingered on her mouth. Darting her tongue out to lick his finger, he caught it between his teeth and sucked it into his mouth. With the streetlight casting a halo around them, they kissed.

"Let's go inside. It's chilly out here." Cherri shivered and he tugged her close to the heat of his body.

They entered the townhouse, warm air surrounding them. There weren't any lights on, and it was quiet like a tomb.

"Are we alone?" Jax said.

"I think so. Lately, my roommates have been crashing at their boyfriends' pads. It's been nice to have the place to myself."

Jax followed her upstairs to her bedroom, remembering the last time he was there. They'd fucked, and he was on top of the world until that bitch Peaches called and his stupidity made him lose Cherri. But he was back, having been given a second chance with her, and he had no intention of blowing it. He wanted her in his life, and he didn't care why he did or whether he should—all he knew was that was what he wanted.

While Cherri undressed in the shadows, he sat on the bed. When she came toward him, he leaned over and switched on the lamp.

"No, turn off the light." A hint of panic laced her voice.

"I want to see you when I fuck you, sweetness."

"Someone will see us. Turn off the light."

"So what if someone sees us? Could be kinda kinky, you know?" he joked.

A grimace broke out over her face, and she looked like she was in pain. Rising up, he shuffled to the window and closed the shutters. "Better? Now no one can see us. The light stays on. I want us to see each other while we fuck."

Cherri, more relaxed, nodded and lay down on the bed, her silver, lacy bra and metallic thong shining under the lights. Her underwear's brightness made her white skin appear even creamier. Jax bent over and kissed her stomach, his hand sliding under her ass. She moaned in pleasure.

As he kissed Cherri, Jax claimed her. "No other man will ever touch you. You're mine. Your mouth, your tits, your pussy, your ass—all of it is mine." For emphasis, he squeezed each part he claimed. "You belong to me, sweetness. You always have, ever since I laid eyes on you. We lost our way for a while, but we're back, and I'm never letting you go. Got that? Never. Letting. You. Go." Taking out a condom, he slid it over his thick, pulsing cock.

Cherri scratched his back and wrapped her legs around his waist as he entered her. Thrusting in and out of her, her juices slurped around his dick while his balls slammed against her.

"This is what I'm fuckin' talking about. All this is mine. You're mine, sweet one. I'm claiming you." Jax grunted as he continued to push in and out of her perfect pussy, stroking her sensitive part as he fucked her. She scratched the hell out of his back as she climaxed, but he didn't have time to react as his orgasm was right behind hers. He collapsed on top of her, breathing heavily while she moaned softly. Still inside her, he rolled over on his side and drew her into him, her head snug under his chin, her tits against his chest, and her legs entwined with his. He tickled her back lightly as the coolness of the night dried their sweaty bodies.

"I want to be like this with you. I lost you once, and I'll never lose you again," he said.

"Don't make promises to me then screw another woman like I'm easily thrown away. I need you to be there for me one hundred percent. I don't think you can do it."

"I know I've never been true to any one girl, but with you, it's different. I dunno, but you make me want to do shit I've never done. I want to get to know you better. I want to get to know Paisley and be a strong figure in her life. I'm gonna try and be a good boyfriend to you."

"And can you give up the other women? I won't be with a man who cheats on me. I don't have time for that shit. I've proven to myself I can make it on my own, so I don't need to put up with bullshit from any man. Can you give up the variety pack?"

Jax blew out a long breath. "I'm not gonna lie. It'll be hard not being with other women, but I haven't *been* with another woman since I met you." He held up his hand, silencing her when she rolled her eyes. "Let me finish. Yeah, I've fucked other women, and you know I fucked Peaches, but you were the woman I was fuckin' in my mind. I only wanted you. I have you in my heart now, sweet one. No bitch has ever owned my heart, and there's no way in fuckin' hell I want to destroy it."

"I don't know. This is all new and hard for me. You say all the right words, but actions mean more, and you haven't shown me much change."

"You gotta give me a chance. You gotta trust me."

In a low voice, she said, "It's hard for me to trust anyone, especially men. It seems like everyone I've ever trusted has either died on me or betrayed me. No, the only one who is there for me and loves me no matter what is Paisley. I want so badly to make sure she has the love and feeling of safety I never had growing up."

After they lay there in silence for a while, Jax said, "I want you to bring Paisley to Pinewood Springs. She needs to be with her mother, and you need to be with her."

"I'd love it and that's what I've been saving money for, but right now, I can't afford it. I have to work, and I can't afford daycare. I'm doing the best I can."

"No worries. I'm gonna help out with all that." He placed a finger on her lips as she started to reply. "Shh... I don't wanna hear you tellin' me why I can't help. Paisley needs to be with you. You need to raise her, not some stranger."

After a long pause, Cherri said, "I appreciate the offer, but I can't let you take on my responsibility. This is on me, and I own it. I'll make it work."

"What the fuck? What don't you get about being my woman? You are now *my* responsibility, and what bothers you, bothers me. This isn't about you wanting to do this on your own because you're no longer on your own. I'm your man, and I'll take care of you. That's my way. That's the Insurgents' way." He sat up, his back against the headboard.

Cherri, raising herself up and resting on her elbow, looked at him. "Again, I appreciate the offer, but I *need* to do this by myself."

Jax's eyes glowered and his face turned dark as he kneaded his scalp and looked at Cherri. "What the fuck are you talkin' about?" He gritted his teeth and said, "You didn't seem to have any trouble takin' Gunner's money. Why the fuck was that okay, but my money's shit?"

There, he'd said it. He didn't want to throw Gunner in her face, never wanted to mention the whole mistake, but she forced his hand. She was pissing him off, and he'd retaliated.

Cherri balked and her eyes burned, making them bluer in the room's soft light. "How dare you bring that up to me? What I had with Gunner was different from what we have. It was different because I didn't have feelings for him the way I do for you. Gunner was like a very good friend." She shook her head. "Fuck, I dunno. I'm so damn confused. You should stay away from me, because I'm no good. I turn everything that's good into shit. You don't want me. I'm just a girl who's bad and does dirty things. I'm no good." She buried her face in the sheets, her shoulders moving up and down.

Jax stared at her body as sobs overcame it. A dazed look replaced the angered one of a few minutes before, and a heaviness surrounded his heart. He patted her back over and over as her quaking dissipated. Looking at her, face buried in the mattress as her sobs played out, he chewed on his inner cheek. He had suspected for a long time something terrible had happened to her when she was young, something that messed her up and made her feel like she was nothing. He wasn't sure who fucked her over like this, but he was damn well going to find out.

"Sweetness, tell me where you got the crazy-ass idea you aren't good or lovable," he said in a low voice.

Talking into the mattress, she said, "I've known that since I was young."

"Did your parents tell you that?"

Lifting herself up a little, she said, "Not my father—*never* my father. I loved him. I loved him so much. When he died, I died with him."

A small sob from the back of her throat confirmed what he had suspected: her mother didn't cherish her or make her feel loved and wanted. *What a fuckin' cunt.*

"Look at me, sweetness. Come on, look at me." His gaze settled on her moist eyes. Placing his hands on either side of her head, he said,

"You have to trust me. I'll keep you safe. With me around, sweetie, you never need to worry." He pulled her up close to him and folded her trembling body into his arms.

"I want to trust you. I do." Her voice broke, and she clung to him like a drowning person hanging onto a flotation ring.

"Then tell me what haunts your eyes and your dreams. Trust me enough to tell me what's destroying your life."

Drawing away from him, he saw her usual rosy face turn ashen and tight. Her eyes fixed on the yellow, floral sheets. In a voice barely above a whisper, she said, "There's something you don't know about me."

Chapter Nineteen

"I WAS IN my mother's wedding. She wore a silk and lace pink suit, and I wore a beautiful rose dress with spaghetti straps. I felt so grown up because my mother let me wear heels and took me to have my hair and makeup done. My mother was happy—she had finally climbed out of the darkness she'd been in since my dad's death two years before. I was still sad, but I was glad my mom found a nice man to make her smile again. My stepfather came into my life that day…" Cherri pulled at the loose threads in the sheet as she said, through clenched teeth, "It started when *he* moved in. I turned twelve a few months before…" Her breath hitched, and she squeezed her eyes shut.

Jax stroked her cheek and said, "It's okay, sweet one; I'm here. Go on, get it out. You've been keeping this shit in you for too long. Lean on me if you have to, but get it out. Take your time, but get it out. I hate seeing you in all this pain."

She opened her eyes and looked at the moonlight filtering in through the shuttered window. "At first, he just touched me quickly. He'd made it seem like no big deal, and even though it felt weird, it happened so fast I thought I'd imagined it or overreacted to it. He'd slap my butt in passing and say, 'Nice ass,' or he'd put his hands on my hips and squeeze them as he passed behind me. You know, shit like that. Sometimes, my mom was there, but she never said anything. She acted like it was normal, so I thought 'this is what some dads do, and it's cool 'cause my mom wouldn't let someone do something to me that was wrong or bad,' so I went with it.

"When the touching became more frequent and more involved, I didn't know what to think. He'd often take me into their bedroom when my mom was shopping or at a volunteer meeting, and he'd lay me on top of him and sort of rub my body against his so our private parts would touch."

Cherri got up and walked to the bathroom to get a glass of water. Looking at herself in the mirror, she saw a frightened, blonde-haired girl of thirteen staring back at her; fear and sadness reflected in her blue eyes. Cherri closed her eyes and rubbed her temples. *I can do this. I can share the secret that's been ravaging me for all this time.*

"You okay, babe?"

She jumped when she heard Jax's voice. "Yeah, just getting some water." She came back to the bed, glass of water in hand, and took a big gulp. Sitting down cross-legged on the bed, she tied her hair back in a ponytail.

Jax kissed her gently on her jaw and squeezed her hand.

"My stepfather told me it was natural for a father to show his daughter what sex was all about, so she'd be prepared for sexual encounters when she grew up. He said that since my dad had died, it was his job as my substitute father to show me. I lost my virginity to him when I was fourteen years old." She heard Jax's growl, and the bed shook when he slammed his fist on the mattress. "The pain was excruciating. It seared through me as he grunted and slammed in me over, and over, and over. It seemed like it went on for hours. When it was done, he got up and left me bleeding in my bed. I wished I were free of him. I wished I were dead."

"Come here," Jax whispered as he scooted nearer to her. He crushed her against him as he nuzzled his mouth against her ear while he stroked her back.

"After the rape, he'd come several times a week to my room. He mostly came hidden in the shadows of the night. I always cringed when I'd hear the floorboards creak outside my door. My heart would pound as the blood rushed to my head and a cold, icy fear would seize me because I knew what was coming and, worst of all, I knew I couldn't stop it. And he *always* came. His breath stunk of cigarettes and bourbon, and to this day, the smell of cigarettes makes me gag. After a year of fucking me in my mouth, my ass, and my pussy, he must've gotten bored 'cause that's when he started taking pictures and videos of me touching and pleasing myself." Her voice cracked and tears rolled down her face; she wiped her runny nose with the palm of her hand. Clutching herself, her shivering escalated, and as her stomach twisted and turned, she bolted to the bathroom, throwing up in the toilet.

Jax followed her into the bathroom, and his warm hands massaging her shoulders calmed her shivers. Taking the tissues he handed her, she wiped the spittle from her lips as she leaned on her elbow which was propped on the toilet bowl rim. The scream started deep in the pit of her stomach and traveled up through the nausea, the tenseness, and the chills then exploded from her throat. Once it broke free, she couldn't stop screaming. It was like she was watching herself from above: head over the toilet bowl, beads of sweat pouring down her face, Jax's chest covering her back, and her screams, coming one after another, slamming against the pristine white tiles.

Goddamn, I'm fucked-up. Why is this darkness always at my back? Why won't it go away? Fuck, I'm tired of all this shit.

"Cherri, please stop. Please, sweetie. Hang onto me. It's okay. The motherfucker can't hurt you anymore. It's over. You've proven you're okay." Jax kissed her neck while he pushed her stuck hair away from her damp face.

"I'm okay? No, I'm *not* okay. I'm fucked-up. I'm so fucked-up that I can only have sex if I get something in return for it. Usually, it's money. That's why I don't want your money. You're the first guy in my life who I want to try and have something normal with, but I know it won't work because everything I touch goes to shit. I'm no good. I'm dirty and bad." She pushed Jax away and went over to the sink to rinse off her face. After she brushed her teeth, she went back into the bedroom.

"Is that what *he* told you? That you were no good?" Jax asked in a low voice as he followed behind her.

"His pet name for me was 'sweet slut.' He told me I loved what he was doing to me. He said it was my fault 'cause I was so damn sexy and had such a tempting, young body…"

"Sweetie, none of it was your fault. You were taken advantage of by a perv, a fuckin' pedophile. The bastard shifted blame from him onto you. You were the innocent one."

"No, no, I wasn't the innocent one," she said, so softly that Jax had to put his ear to her mouth to hear her. "You see, when he touched me and played with me, sometimes I liked it. It made me feel good. I *liked* the way he made my body explode. I told you I'm dirty. I'm so ashamed. I'm so ashamed. Fuck." She put her face in her hands, her insides churning. She didn't want to lose it again. *Fuck, when will this madness end?*

Taking her hands in his, Jax said, "Sweetie, you were a young girl. You can't blame yourself for the way your body reacted. It's normal. Certain parts of our body are made for pleasure, and it's okay if you felt aroused. It wasn't your fault, and you're not dirty. The fuckwad is the dirty perv, not you."

The round alarm clock on her nightstand ticked away the minutes. Cherri liked a real clock. She hated the digital clocks with their glowing red numbers. She'd had one in her room during the dark years, and she'd look at the red numbers during the nasty things her stepfather did to her, praying the time would fly and he'd be finished. Ever since her stepfather started his shit, her stomach would gurgle when she saw red numbers.

"Did you ever tell your mom?" Jax said, breaking the silence.

"Yeah, and she told me I wore skimpy clothes, and he wasn't my *real* dad, and he *was* a man, so what did I expect? She reminded me what a good provider he was, and how hard we had it after Daddy died. After she warned me not to blow our good life, she suggested I keep my door locked more often. Fuck, she was my mother—she was *supposed* to make sure I was safe no matter what." She looked straight at Jax, her eyes flashing. "You know what I can't even fuckin' believe? She's still with him. She still cooks his dinner, fucks him, goes on trips with him. It makes me wanna puke! I feel like an emotional cripple most of the time, and she's playing housewife to a man who raped her daughter for three years. I'll never be able to forgive her. I blame her more than I do him. She was supposed to protect me."

"Have you had any contact with your mom since you ran away?"

"No, I never want to see her again. I know she's still with him 'cause a friend of mine is their neighbor. I don't care if I ever see her again. That's why I'm determined to give Paisley a life full of love and happiness. I *have* to keep her safe. I remember how life could be good 'cause my dad was wonderful and I have those memories. I'm grateful for that."

Squeezing her hands, Jax said, "Don't freak on me, but you know you gotta get some therapy, right? You can't handle it all on your own. You want to be all good for Paisley. I know you're gonna say you can't afford it, but I can, and you're gonna accept my gift. I won't hear you argue about it. Okay?"

Looking at Jax's half-smile, his warm eyes, and his soft hands holding hers, Cherri's heart melted. Could she fix herself? For so long, she felt broken, but could Jax help her heal? She grazed her teeth over her bottom lip and nodded. Jax brought his thumb up and ran it under her lip, his eyes watching her mouth. He bent down and kissed her, and she leaned in to him and kissed him back. He drew her flush against him and lay down with her by his side. He stretched over her and turned off the light.

In his strong arms, Cherri's muscles slacked, and her breathing was slow and easy. For the first time in years, she had no desire to be anywhere else but right there, in Jax's embrace. The steady beating of his heart against her ear lulled her to sleep.

CHAPTER TWENTY

T HE NEXT MORNING, Jax stood at the stove, cracking eggs and laying raw bacon on the hot griddle. The coffee was made, the table was set, and he had even poured orange juice in the glasses. He knew if his brothers could see him, they'd give him shit and accuse him of being pussy-whipped, but he didn't care what the hell they or anyone thought—he was making breakfast for his woman. He hoped the mouth-watering scent of bacon sizzling and crisping in the pan and the rich aroma of toasted coffee beans would puncture the bleary veil of sleep and bring Cherri downstairs. Hearing her padded feet as she entered the kitchen, he smiled, happy his enticements worked.

Her lavender lotion touched his nostrils as she kissed the back of his neck. He flipped over the bacon then swung around, pulling her into him. "Morning, sweetness." He kissed her deeply.

"Morning," she said when their lips parted. Her voice still had the remnants of sleep in it. "How're you?"

"Great. You?" As he scanned her face, relief washed over him when her twinkling eyes and crooked smile met his gaze.

"Great, too." She stole a slice of bacon and put it in her mouth. "Mmm, that's yummy." Looking at the place setting at the breakfast bar, she said, "Did you do all this?"

He nodded.

"Wow, I hit the jackpot—a hot guy who can also cook?" She laughed. "I've never had a guy cook for me. You're sweet." She kissed him and rubbed herself against him.

"Yeah, you *are* lucky, 'cause I've never done this for any woman. This is between us; no need to be blabbing it around Dream House."

"Ah, now I have something on you. I like that," she teased.

Pretending to be angry, he scowled and drew her flush to him. He kissed her, savoring her minty taste. Swatting her butt, he said, "Let's eat before everything gets cold."

He watched her as she ate her food, making small noises of delight with each bite. She was downright giddy this morning. A wide grin spread over his face as he watched her dance on the stool while she buttered her toast. He was glad he had urged her to open up the previous night; she seemed almost calmer like she had a sense of freedom this morning. However, he had a fire burning inside him. When Cherri recounted her stories of the abuse she suffered at the hands of her stepfuck, Jax pretended to be calm, but the rage in him built with each word she uttered, each image she painted, and each tear she shed. He wanted to kill the bastard for what he did to his woman, and he planned on paying the fuckin' pervert a visit. When he confronted the fucker, Jax would see if the asshole was as brazen with a man as he was with girls. If he were taking bets, he'd say the pervert would crumple into a sniveling wimp after Jax's hand did some damage to the jerk's face. Yeah, he'd make sure Cherri's stepfather paid for every second of pain and terror he caused her.

"Whatcha doin' today? Maybe we can go for a ride on your Harley?" She threw him the sweetest smile.

"Fuck, you're cute, sugar. Sure, we can head over to Crystal Lake. I have an errand I have to run first, then I'll be back to pick you up."

"Okay, what do you have to do?"

"Club business."

Nodding, she put the last forkful of food in her mouth.

STRINGING UP AND torturing the sonofabitch who hurt his sweet babe was all Jax could think of as he sat in Hawk's office at the bike shop, waiting for him to finish with a customer. Blood rushed to Jax's head as he visualized the serious harm he planned to do to Cherri's fucking stepfather. By killing the sick bastard, he could assure Cherri she'd never have to worry about him hurting her again. Even if Cherri didn't realize it, killing the bastard would bring her the peace of mind she'd been craving ever since her abuse; it'd put closure on the horrible years of her life.

If he could manage it, he'd love to do away with her mother, as well. Not protecting her daughter was unforgiveable, and just thinking about it made the back of Jax's neck prick in heat and anger. Since his mother cut out on him and his dad years ago, Jax wasn't quick in forgiving errant mothers. Cherri's mom should've dropped the scum and taken her daughter away from the abuse and shame. Instead, she chose big-screen televisions, new cars, and a nice house over her own flesh and blood. *Fuck, sitting and thinking about all this shit makes me want to break something.*

The door opened and Hawk walked in just as Jax hurled a glass ashtray against the wall. Observing the shards of glass scattered on the floor, Hawk said, "What's going on with you?"

"Just fuckin' pissed, that's all." Jax tipped his chair back while clenched fists tapped against his denim-clad thighs.

"About what?"

"I found out Cherri's stepfather violated her over and over for about three years. He fucked her up something bad, and I can't let it pass. I can't let a perv like him not pay for what he did to her. Fuck, he's made her all messed up about sex, men, and life. I gotta find him and teach him shit like that doesn't go unpunished." Beads of sweat ran down his face as he jumped up, pacing around the small office.

Staring into Jax's rage-filled eyes, Hawk, nodding, said, "You want me to find out where he lives?"

"Yeah, I want to pay him an unofficial visit. This is my deal, not the club's, so I go alone. I own this."

"Okay, I get that. I'd be doing the exact same thing you are if I found out someone had hurt Cara. I have to tell Banger what's up, but I know he'll support you. Fuck, he's got a daughter, so shit like this pisses him way the hell off. If you need my help, just let me know."

Jax pulled Hawk in a bear hug, his hand clasping Hawk's shoulder. "Thanks, man. I appreciate it, but this is something I have to do alone. I do need your help in locating this fuck, but then I'll take it from there."

"Okay, I'll see what I can do. When I get an address on him, I'll let you know."

"Sounds good, brother. Thanks."

As he left the shop, Jax's muscles slackened a bit, and his body was more relaxed. He squinted against the summer sun. Swinging his leg over his bike, he straddled it then revved the engine and headed toward Cherri's place. Having her on the back of his bike was all he could think about as he rode past the tree-lined streets. At the stoplight, he took out his cell and texted Cherri that he'd be at her place in ten minutes.

When he rounded the corner of her street, he saw her waiting on the sidewalk dressed in denim shorts and a green checked crop-top, her blue eyes shielded by sunglasses, and her blonde hair half-covered by a blue bandanna—she looked young, fresh, and fucking hot. Shifting on his seat, he cruised up to the curb and flashed a smile. "Climb on, sweetness." He motioned to the place behind him.

Cherri swung her leg over the bike, circled her arms around him, and leaned in to him, brushing her lips against his cheek. Winking at her, Jax shifted and the Harley lunged forward, making its way into traffic.

Within fifteen minutes, they left the town's noise behind them and rode on one-lane backroads toward Crystal Lake. The sun burned brightly overhead, and the fleecy clouds seemed bolted in the large expanse of sky. Veering to the left, the Harley entered a lush valley carpeted by pink, purple, and periwinkle wildflowers whose sweet perfumes drifted and swirled in the warm, summer breeze.

Jax parked the Harley next to the banks of the lake. He helped Cherri off the bike and crushed her small frame into his powerful chest as his hands cupped her ass. Bending low, he closed his mouth over hers as she circled her arms around his neck, pushing herself even closer to his body.

His hardness rubbed against her as she moaned into his mouth.

"Oh, sugar, you taste sweet," he said against her lips. He moved away, took out a blue blanket from his saddlebag, and led her over to a grassy area next to the lake. After spreading out the blanket, he took her in his arms and eased her down on it. Sitting on the cover, side by side, Jax held her so her head fit comfortably into the crook of his arm.

"It's so beautiful and peaceful here. I never knew this place existed," Cherri said as her eyes scanned the natural surroundings.

"I love it here. I come to the lake often when I need to think or decompress. I've been coming here for years. My dad and I used to fish for trout when I was young. We had some good times. In high school, my buddies and I would drink beer and target shoot. This place holds a lot of memories for me. I wanted to share it with you." Jax kissed the top of Cherri's head, and she snuggled deeper in to him.

They sat in silence as they looked at the mountains' reflection tattooed onto the placid and crystalline lake. Every so often, speckled trout slapped the surface, hoping to catch one of the army of flies which buzzed slightly above the water. Behind them, humming bees flitted from flower to flower, and a feathered medley of birds echoed through the ponderosa pine trees lining the valley.

Cherri tilted her head up and met Jax's intense stare. Cupping her chin in his hand, he brought her face toward his and brushed his tongue over her full lips. His gaze lingered on her mouth as his thumb caressed her bottom lip. As she licked his thumb with the tip of her tongue, he moved it in her mouth, and her lips captured it, sucking and biting it. Burying his face into her hair, a deep heat built up in his body which made his blood pump and his heart race. Cherri's heady lavender scent, her feminine curves, and her hot mouth on his thumb heightened all of his nerves. With his craving for her consuming him, he pushed her down on the blanket, his digit still in her mouth.

"Fuck, baby, I'm so damn horny for you," he rasped. He brushed away some stray hairs from her flushed face.

"Me, too," she said in a low voice as she rubbed her thigh against his shaft.

Unzipping and shrugging off his jeans, he kicked off his boots then stretched out beside her, his toes sinking into the silky soft grass.

"You're so beautiful." He stroked her soft cheek.

Sliding her hand down past his chest, her fingertips slipped under the waistband of his boxers until they grasped his hardness. A strangled moan came from deep in his throat. Cherri pulled his boxers down, exposing his thick, long shaft whose top glistened with pre-come. Wiping away the small beads of come on his dick's head, Cherri put her finger in her mouth and licked it off her with her pink tongue. Watching the act drove Jax wild, and he pulled Cherri up with him as he started to rise. Sitting with open thighs, he nudged his sweet one's head between his legs.

"Look at me when you lick my cock," he said in a low, hoarse voice.

Under half-lidded eyes, Cherri locked her stare with Jax's as she ran the tip of her rigid tongue up and down his cock. Jax bent down, raising Cherri's arms up, and took off her crop-top and bra, exposing her perky tits. Cupping them in his hands, he kneaded them, running his fingers over their stiffening nipples.

"It feels real good when you touch me like that," Cherri murmured.

"I love your tits, baby. They're perfect. I could suck on them all day."

Pushing herself up, she slid her breasts over his chest. Leaning back, she whispered, "I love it when you suck on me."

Bending his head way down, he took a rigid nipple in his mouth and sucked hard on it, making Cherri throw her head back and whimper. As he sucked each of her tits, his hands ran down the sides of her body; tiny bumps popped up under his touch. After he tugged down her shorts and panties, she spread her legs open, and his calloused palm covered her smooth pussy. As he ran his finger between her folds, her wetness glistened around it. "Fuck, you're so wet for me, sweetness. I can't wait to lick you dry."

"I want to taste you, too. Give me your cock so I can suck it."

Tangling a handful of her hair in his hand, he guided her mouth to his dick, relishing in the feel of her warm mouth sucking him. As she sucked, licked, squeezed, and massaged his dick and balls, her eyes never left his. When she had the full length of him in her mouth, he fucked the back of her throat until his body tightened and he exploded, his come spurting down her throat, filling her. Still looking at him, she held his dick in her mouth until it softened. Then, pulling it out, she licked off the rest of his seed, shimmed up his chest and kissed him on the mouth, making him taste his own salty tang.

"How do you like the way you taste?" A wicked smile crossed her lips.

His tongue skimmed over her mouth. "Love the way I taste on your lips, sweetness."

Clasping her against him with his muscled arms, he eased her down on the blanket, nestling her against his side as he caressed her back.

"You okay?" Jax broke the silence.

"Yeah, why?"

"You're so quiet. I wanna make sure you're with me and not with a memory from your past."

"I'm listening to you breathe. It's a lovely sound."

Weightlessness spread over him and he felt like he was on a roller coaster, free-falling from the top of the track. Raising her chin, he said, "You're something real special. You make me feel things no woman ever has. Are you comfortable with me?"

Biting her lip, she looked away. "I'm getting there. You're the first man I've had sex with just for pleasure. I guess that means something. I know I really like being with you and talking to you. You're the only one I've let into my personal life."

Wanting her to say he was everything to her would have to wait for another time. The important thing was she was beginning to trust him and let him into her life. Cherri did something to him no other woman had done: she made him want to think about settling down. He couldn't get enough of her.

Rolling on top of her, Jax nibbled her lips, and penetrated her mouth with one deep thrust of his tongue. Cherri's pleased moan flooded Jax with heat. Leaving her delectable mouth, he took her earlobe between his teeth and bit it gently. He heard her sharp intake of breath as he lavished small kisses from her jaw down to her chest. Instinctively, her body arched toward him, bringing her tits closer to his mouth so he could suck them more deeply while his tongue explored her rosy peaks, bringing them to pebbled hardness. A moan of ecstasy slipped through her lips.

"Fuck, you're so soft and sexy. I want to be inside you, to feel your pussy around my cock, tight and wet." Jax's breathing was ragged, and his hands explored the gentle lines of her waist and hips. Leaving her tits, he trailed his tongue down to her belly button, flicking her crystal piercing. Grasping it with his teeth, he tugged it as his hand squeezed her inner thigh, making her writhe under him, trembling at his touch.

"That makes you feel good, doesn't it, sugar?" he said as he felt her flesh quiver.

"It feels real good. Oh, so good," she gasped in short breaths.

"Wait 'til I lick your sweet pussy."

A small whimper caught in her throat, making the need to fuck her, to possess her, surge through Jax like a deluge. He couldn't have enough of her. Ever. Lowering his head past her thighs, he licked her in one hard swipe, from the opening of her sweet heat to the tip of her sensitive bud. Burying his mouth in her folds, his tongue expertly tapped and circled it while his fingers slid into her heat. Cherri bucked under his plunging fingers and tongue, whispering, "I want you in me. Oh, please, I want you in me."

"Fuck, sweetness, I love it when you beg, but I want to taste you some more. Then I'm gonna fuck you real good." Nibbling her swollen pussy, he slid his tongue between her folds while the tip of his index finger rapidly stroked her clit. As her body tensed and her cries mounted, Jax knew she was close to peaking so he grabbed his jeans, took out a condom, and rolled it over his hardness. On his knees, he glided his palms under Cherri's thighs, hoisting them up so her legs rested on his shoulders.

Teasing her with the tip of his cock poised at her hot opening, Jax stroked her clit until she screamed out, "Fuck me, dammit!"

Slowly sliding his cock inside her, he stretched and filled her as he watched her sweet face contort in desire and pleasure. As soon as his dick was inside, her silky walls tightened, grasping him while she gasped, lifting her hips up to meet his thrust. Bowing his head, he swallowed her cry with his mouth as he kissed her deeply then gripped her hips while he sunk into her again. Wet heat clutched him as he moved in and out, reveling in the friction of her tightness encasing his cock.

Knotting the blanket in her fists, she screamed out as her climax burst into a million pieces of pleasure. As she convulsed, Jax grunted as her spasms pumped his dick.

"Fuck, sugar. I'm on fire, and I wanna fuck your sweet pussy deep and hard," he rasped as he flipped her over, placing her on her knees.

"I don't want to do it that way. I can't do it from behind. No, no, no! Not that. Never that," Cherri cried as she twisted and scrambled away, cowering on the blanket with her arms crossed around her raised knees.

Startled, Jax reached out to her, putting his hand on her knee. "What's going on, sweetness?" He brushed the damp wisps of hair from her face.

Rocking back and forth, she said in a barely audible voice, "I just can't. I'm sorry. I really am. I just can't. *He* always took me from behind. I can't." Breaking into sobs, Cherri buried her head in her chest.

Enveloping her in his protective arms, he said, "Shh, don't cry. It's okay. I'm gonna make sure he never hurts you again." Stroking her hair and cradling her in his embrace, Jax's jaw hardened. The bastard was going to pay for messing up his woman.

It took a long time for the darkness to leave Cherri's mind, but Jax held her close as she pushed the memories away.

She stared out at the lake. "I'm sorry I ruined our outing."

"You didn't ruin anything, sugar. I wanted you to see the lake and spend time with you. Don't beat yourself up over it. It's all good."

"Yeah, I suppose." She kissed him lightly on the chin. "Thanks for sharing this with me. We should probably go."

Standing up, Jax helped Cherri to her feet. After dressing, they walked hand-in-hand to his motorcycle. As the summer twilight brought magenta-purple skies, Jax rode the Harley back to Pinewood Springs with his special woman pressed against his back.

CHAPTER TWENTY-ONE

S ITTING IN A borrowed SUV, taking a hit from a joint, Jax watched as Cherri's stepfather exited the pool hall on Colfax Ave. For the past week, Jax had been in Denver trailing the bastard, learning his routine so he would know when he could exact his vengeance on the piece of shit. When Hawk gave him the slip of paper with all of the fucker's information, Jax couldn't wait to confront Scott Dyer—his woman's fucking boogeyman.

In his mid-forties, Scott played pool two nights a week. He was a small-time hustler and usually pulled in a couple hundred dollars on a good night. Standing on the sidewalk, cigarette dangling from his mouth, he spoke with a few guys before they all scattered to their own lives.

Jax watched the bastard throw his cigarette down on the pavement and stub it out with his foot before he trudged down the street. The asshole parked in a lot around the corner, which was a good thing because there were no street lights. Turning the SUV down the dark street, Jax parked, quietly shut the door, and in four long strides, he was behind the man who caused so much pain in his woman's life. Startled from the crunch under Jax's foot, the stepfather whirled around, fear etched on his face.

"Got a light?" Jax's voice was hard as steel.

"Sure."

Jax sneered as he heard the forced gaiety in the dumb fuck's voice, but his trembling fingers as he handed Jax the lighter gave him away. *Asshole thinks I'm gonna mug him. After I'm done with him, he's gonna wish that's all I had in mind.* Ice flowed through Jax's veins as he took in the slump-shouldered man: about five foot nine; dark hair, which was graying at the temples; small, beady eyes; and a slight belly. The stench of cigarettes and beer wafted from him, and Jax couldn't help but wonder if that was how he smelled when he was raping a young Cherri. A seething rage consumed Jax, but he knew he had to stay cool to make sure everything went as he planned.

"Did you do pretty good shooting pool?" Jax asked calmly as he lit up another joint.

Darting his eyes back and forth, Cherri's stepfather placed his hand on his car door. "Not so good."

When the fuck opened the door, Jax struck, placing a chokehold on him and dragging him to the SUV.

"What the fuck is going on?" the stepfather choked out.

"I'm taking you on a ride to Hell, asshole." A single, vicious punch ended the struggle as Cherri's stepfather slumped on the passenger's seat. Picking up his cell phone, Jax dialed then said into the mouthpiece, "It's in a parking lot on Fourteenth and Lafayette, right off Colfax. You got the car description and plates, right?" Looking over his shoulder, Jax changed lanes as he headed for the freeway. "Yeah, that's it. I'll call you later. Thanks, man. I owe you." Merging onto the interstate, Jax, jaw jutted out and eyes narrowed, turned on the radio to his favorite metal station as he made the trip back to Pinewood Springs.

THROWING A BUCKET of cold water in Scott Dyer's face elicited an enormous surge of pleasure from Jax. He'd been watching the tied-up fuck-face for the last hour, and the jerk was still out of it. Sometimes, Jax didn't realize his own strength. Years of weight lifting and martial arts training turned him into a lethal weapon, a good asset to have as the club's enforcer. One time, after a disrespectful jerk had tried to take his colors, Jax killed him with one punch. He hadn't meant to kill him; he'd wanted to teach him a little respect. It'd been a nasty situation since the jerk had been a citizen, and the badges would've been buzzing around.

His club had stood strongly behind him by making sure there hadn't been any witnesses or evidence. Banger had been pissed as hell over the whole incident, but he'd had Jax's back—all the brothers did—and life went on as though nothing had happened.

Jax was glad his punch didn't kill the piece of shit in front of him, because he wanted to make sure he suffered before he died. Before the night was over, Scott Dyer would beg for death.

Shaking his head, Scott's eyes opened slowly as he struggled against the ropes which secured him to the hard, steel folding chair. "Where am I? Who the hell are you?" he spat.

"I'm the enforcer."

"What the fuck are you talking about?" As he shifted in his chair, a grimace of pain spread over his face.

Taking out a long, thin-bladed knife, Jax walked over to the restrained man, placed the sharp tip against his throat, bent down, and said in a low and cruel voice, "I'm seeing justice is served for all the fucked-up shit you did to my woman, you bastard."

Blinking rapidly, he replied, "Your woman? I don't even know you. I think you got the wrong guy. I don't know your woman."

"Yeah, that's right. I forgot, you don't go in for *women*—only young girls, right? Sick fuck. My woman's Cherri, and I hate your fuckin' wimp ass for what you did to her."

When he heard her name, his face blanched. With trembling lips, he hung his head.

"Let's see how strong you are with a man, you piece of shit." Kicking his prey over with his steel-toed boot, Jax kneeled on the ground next to the whimpering man. "You're gonna pay for every sick thing you did to Cherri. You screwed her up, you made her cry, you made her not believe in herself, and I'm gonna make sure you understand that before I stick my blade in you and hear you squeal like a gutted pig."

"I'll die knowing her sweet piece of ass belonged to me. I was her first. You'll always know it. She was young and pure, the perfect combination for fu—"

Cracking bone from Jax's full-on punch to Scott Dyer's face interrupted him. Yanking him by the hair, Jax sat the scum upright. Blood oozed from his nose and soaked the front of his shirt. Scott laughed dryly then spit out a couple of teeth which had come loose from the punch.

Leaning in close, Jax snarled, "The fun is just beginning, asshole."

IN THE EARLY morning hours of the next day, Jax entered the clubhouse, his t-shirt and jeans stained in blood, and motioned to the prospect to pour him a shot of whiskey. Throwing back the warm liquid, his throat scorched and his insides warmed.

"So, it's finished?" Chas asked.

"Yep, but it ended too soon for me. I could kill that bastard over and over for what he did to Cherri." Jax threw back another shot; the inside of his mouth burned from the whiskey. "Gotta go clean up." Raising his chin at Chas, Jax walked up the stairs toward his room and bumped into Banger.

Moving his eyes over Jax, Banger said, "Didya make sure nothing can trace back to the Insurgents?"

Nodding, Jax leaned against the wall. "Not a trace."

Clapping a hand on Jax's shoulder, Banger walked away without a word while Jax opened the door and retreated into his room.

LATER THAT AFTERNOON, when Cherri opened the front door, Jax smiled as he stepped in and hugged her closely, breathing in her scent. Tipping her chin up, he dipped down and kissed her tenderly. Looking intently at her, he said in a hushed tone, "He's gone and you're safe. It's over, sweetness."

"What?" she said as her eyes widened and her eyebrows lifted.

"I took care of everything. I made sure the bastard paid for what he did to you. He pissed his pants like I knew he would. Your monster was a coward. The nightmare's over." Kissing the top of her vanilla-scented hair, Jax felt Cherri shiver in his arms.

"You killed him?" she whispered into his chest.

"I made sure he paid for what he did."

"What does that mean? Did you kill him?"

Tilting her head up, he locked his eyes on hers and saw relief replacing the fear behind her artic blue eyes. "I made him suffer for what he did to you; let's leave it at that."

Swallowing hard, Cherri nodded. "Thank you," she said in a small voice.

"You never have to thank me. You're my woman, and I have your back. My job is to make sure you're safe and no one hurts you."

"Safe? I haven't felt safe in years. Maybe I can relax again." Gazing at him, she smiled sweetly.

Jax lowered his mouth and kissed her hard, and she melted into him. Need swept over him and every fiber in his body craved her taste, her softness, and her touch. He wanted to possess every part of her and lose himself in her. Cherri met the thrust of his tongue eagerly, rubbing her hands over the expanse of his chest. Creating an inch of space between them, he perused her arousal-tinted cheeks and her lips, red and swollen from his kiss.

"Fuck, I want you."

"I want you, too."

Crashing his mouth on hers again, Jax swooped her up in his tatted arms and carried her upstairs to her room while she trailed her kisses down his jaw to his collarbone. Laying her on the bed, he covered her with his raw power and heat, slipping his fingers under her t-shirt until he cupped her breast. Pushing her t-shirt up over her chest, he licked the hollow space in the middle as his fingers unhooked her bra's front clasp, revealing two pale tits with pink-tipped nipples. She cried out when he took her nipple into his mouth, lightly grazing it with his teeth then sucking it hard as he kneaded her other breast with his hand. Tangling her fingers in his sandy brown hair, she pushed her hips upward, pressing against his cock.

"You're so fuckin' precious, and you're all mine." Jax said against her tits.

Jax pulled away and took off his t-shirt and jeans, then unzipped Cherri's white shorts, sliding them off along with her white lace thong. Desire and lust brimmed in Cherri's eyes, and the heat of her look practically sent Jax over the edge. Fire consumed him and drove him on to give his woman immense pleasure—his release could wait. He snatched Cherri into his arms again and buried his head in her soft flesh, inhaling her scents of vanilla, lavender, and Cherri. Closing her fingers around his dick, she stroked it, her thumb brushing across his smooth tip. He moaned helplessly as his cock throbbed under her touch.

"Damn, sweetie, that's what I like. You holding my cock makes me want to explode."

"I love your cock," she said in a low voice.

"It's all yours, sweetness. It's only for you." Lifting her head up, she pressed her lips to his chest and flicked her tongue over his nipple. Jax let out a primal growl.

Afraid he was going to lose total control before he satisfied her, he grasped Cherri's hands and traced her palms with his tongue, easing her head back on the pillow. Scooting down, he ran his closed mouth over her inner thighs and her engorged pussy lips. She writhed beneath him as his tongue laved her folds, making her spread her legs wider and giving him better access to her delicious mound. Taking in the scent of her arousal, Jax moved his tongue to her heated opening and entered. Small whimpers came in succession as Cherri squirmed under Jax's penetrating tongue.

"God, that's too good. You're gonna make me come. I want to feel you inside me, and I want it raw. I'm on the pill and clean. Just did my monthly test at Dream House."

Tilting his head up, he smiled, her wetness glistening around his mouth. "I'm clean, too. Always use a condom. Can't wait to *really* feel your sweet pussy clenching my cock."

Inserting his tongue back into her hotness, he moved it in and out while she moaned and pulled his hair.

"You taste good. You ready for some good fuckin'?"

"Oh yeah. Oh, oh—" Cherri put her hand over her mouth as her body stiffened.

Placing the tip of his dick inside her, he bent over, kneading her tits and sucking her nipples.

"It's too much, Jax. Fuck me."

Thrusting the length of him inside, he said, "Take it all, sweetness. All of me." Grunting, he plunged deeper and harder, her pussy surrounding him like a cocoon. Their harsh breathing and muffled moans filled the bedroom as he rode her hard; the slapping sound of skin on skin surrounded them. His balls slammed into the crevice of her ass each time he pounded into her, lifting her hips off the bed. Boosting her ass off the bed, he spit on his finger and massaged her puckered opening. She tensed.

"Relax, sweetie, relax. It's me, Jax, and I'm not gonna hurt you. I'm just gonna bring you pleasure. Shh… relax, for me. Do it for me. It's gonna be real good." He brushed his lips against her belly. "I won't let anything bad happen to you. I'll make it so good for you." Her muscles slackened a small bit "That's it. Just relax." His voice was seductive as he put his finger in a little deeper in her ass while in his head, he cursed the dead sonofabitch for making his woman afraid.

Still sensing her nervousness, he withdrew his finger. "You did good, sugar."

As he looked down while he withdrew, he saw Cherri's heat open around his glistening cock, releasing it for re-entry. When he pushed back inside her, her hotness stretched then clutched his length hungrily. "Fucking shit, that's hot," he rasped under his breath. Cherri clung to him as he slammed in and out, her hips surging in rhythm to his motion.

After he crushed his mouth on hers, kissing her roughly, he sped up his pace. As heat rose from their intertwined bodies, sweat shone on

Cherri's face while beads of perspiration pricked Jax's hairline. Bringing her legs up and back toward her shoulders, Jax, in a crouching position, rammed his cock in her pussy, his pleasure intensifying. His balls tightened and, with head thrown backward, Jax surrendered to the pleasure of Cherri's spasms squeezing him as she came. With a few final thrusts, his whole body erupted with an intensity he'd never experienced. "Holy fuck!" His words came from deep in his throat. "Fuck, fuck, fuck…."

His spilled seed filled Cherri's convulsing pussy as her body contorted underneath him. "Oh, my God, that is sooo good," she cried out as she raked her fingernails over his back muscles.

Looking down at her, Jax noticed she had her head turned into the pillow, teardrops spilling from her eyes. His heart dropped; he had been too rough and scared her. He wanted to create good memories for her, not rough, barbaric ones. *Fuck, my need was so great I lost control and fucked her too hard.* "Cherri?" Still in her warm pussy, he lowered his face to hers. "What's wrong? Did I hurt you?"

Shaking her head, she said, "I've never had those before."

Quirking his eyebrows questioningly, he searched her face. "Had what?"

"Intense orgasms, like I have with you. I never knew sex could be so wonderful. I always thought it was dirty. After I left home, I thought sex was the only thing I could use to get what I wanted. I never knew it could be like it is with you."

Laying on his side, Jax tugged Cherri next to him, his arms tightly around her waist and her head snug on his chest. "Sweetness, the times we've fucked may be your first trips to ecstasy, but they sure won't be your last."

Shimmying up to his mouth, she kissed him deeply. His body stirred as he looked into her eyes brightened with pleasure. "Looks like we gotta make up for some lost time, sweetie." Shifting her on top of him, he kissed her.

Throwing her head back, her lips parted, the tip of her tongue under her white teeth. Her gentle laugh hugged him. Pulling in a breath, Jax's gaze was tender. She was beautiful, and she was all his. Bringing her close to him, they kissed.

CHAPTER TWENTY-TWO

One month later

WALKING INTO THE small, intimate restaurant, Cherri scanned the room, looking for McFahey. Spotting him at the booth in the corner, she swallowed, straightened her shoulders, and strode over to his table. McFahey, a scotch on the rocks in his hand, smiled broadly when she stood by his table. His lewd gaze moved over her, lingering on her breasts. The familiar sense of revulsion twisted her insides as she looked into his blue, flat eyes.

"Have a seat," he said as he scooted over on the leather banquette.

Cherri slipped into the seat across from him, crossed her hands on the table, and looked him in the eyes. "So, why did you want to meet me?"

McFahey put his fingers on the top of her hands and caressed them lightly. "Doesn't this seem like old times? I want to talk to you about something." As he stared at her bust, he took a gulp of his scotch. "You look as tempting as ever."

Slipping her hands away from his, she tapped the wood table with her finger. "Denver was a long time ago, and I have a new life in Pinewood Springs. When you knew me, I was desperate and trying to find my way. I'm more grounded now. I wish you the best in your life, but what we had is over. A new chapter has started for me, and you aren't in it."

"Would you like something to drink?" A woman in a short black skirt and white top asked Cherri.

"No, thank you. I'm not staying."

"The lady will have a rum and Coke, light on the ice, with a twist of lime and orange." McFahey smiled at Cherri. "You see, I remembered. I remember everything about you, about us." The waitress left to retrieve the drink, and Cherri sighed as she leaned back in the booth.

"I just can't get over how wonderful you look. Your job at the strip bar agrees with you." He gave her a lecherous grin.

"I enjoy being assistant manager at the bar. Pinewood Springs is a beautiful town, and I like the simple feel of it. It's not a madhouse like Denver. I'm good here. Oh, how are the kids and your wife?"

His eyes narrowed as his finger found a pimple to pick on his face. "They're fine, but you know that's for show. I mean the wife, not the kids. She is a frigid bitch." He popped two pimento-stuffed olives in his mouth and chomped on them.

"You have five kids—she can't be *that* frigid."

"I mean, she doesn't like to do anything but straight sex. She's not adventurous like you were with me. I miss those times. Don't you ever think about how wonderful it was?"

"Uh, no. I was messed-up back then. I got out of a bad situation at home. I'm thankful you helped me with an apartment, food, and clothes, but I like being on my own and earning my own money."

"How much can you possibly make? I can give you a very lucrative allowance."

The waitress slid Cherri's rum and Coke over to her and took their early dinner orders: taco salad for Cherri, steak sandwich with all the fixings and fries for McFahey. Cherri, nervous McFahey found out about Paisley, decided to stay and see what he wanted to talk to her about.

They talked about everything but why he asked her to come by. Cherri sensed McFahey was making time until he brought up the real reason he requested they meet that day.

The food arrived, and the aroma of the spiced taco meat reminded Cherri she hadn't eaten since the morning before. She always did shit like that, forgetting to eat when she was too stressed or busy. When she was pregnant with Paisley, she'd set the alarm on her phone for breakfast, lunch, dinner, and two snacks so she wouldn't forget to eat. Diving in with her fork, the seasoned meat, crunchy lettuce, and sharp cheddar cheese burst in her mouth in an explosion of tastiness. *Yum.*

As the juices of his steak sandwich dripped down his chin then to his wrist, McFahey looked at her intently while licking his lips. "Have your boobs gotten bigger?"

Gritting her teeth, she shook her head.

"I swear they look bigger. After we eat, I got a little room lined up over in the next county. I can test them out and you can test out my dick." He winked and wiped off the grease on his chin.

"I can't go. I have to work tonight."

"Not until eight o'clock. I checked. I can get you to work on time," he said between bites.

"I have a ton of work to do, so I'm going in early. Sorry, it won't work."

He scrutinized her face, put down his sandwich, and asked, "Is the rumor true? Are you some biker's whore?"

She winced.

"You're slumming, aren't you? A *biker's* whore, come on. You know, that's one step below white trash."

Before he could move his head back, she slapped him across his face. He glared at her, his fingers touching the area she smacked. He laughed aloud. "You've forgotten how to be respectful since you've been fucking scum. That's okay because you can make it up to me by fucking me, like old times, and instead of your usual five hundred, I'll give you a thousand, for Auld Lang Syne, you know? Sound good, honey?" He sneered and wiggled his eyebrows.

Her stomach churned, and the room spun. She would still need to leave and go far away from her past. Since she hadn't heard from him in two months, she thought he had moved on. She knew she should've left, but she was crazy about Jax. For once in her life, she was happy, and she selfishly clung onto to it. Smoothing her hair behind her ears, she smiled sweetly. "No way. Not interested."

Laughing, he stuffed another large bite of his sandwich into his mouth. "You'll come around to my way of thinking."

"Don't you have an image to maintain? I mean, you want to run for higher office. You know how the opposition loves to dig up dirt. Do you want to risk it all?"

"That's why I have a PR guy. He's a wiz at making me a role model with my typical American housewife and five children. The guy's a genius." He downed his scotch and motioned the waitress to bring another. "So, why the fuck did you split on me without a word?"

Shrugging, Cherri played with her cocktail napkin. "You keep asking me. I needed a new life. As I said, I wanted to be on my own."

"Listen, Cherri. I didn't have time to talk to you at the strip bar a while back because that muscle head interrupted us, but I want you back in my life. I can give you anything you want. You won't have to work in that crummy strip club and fuck some loser biker. I'll put you up in a nice apartment, and I'll give you a more-than-generous monthly stipend. You won't have to worry about getting pregnant again because I had a vasectomy about two years ago, after my last son was born. It'll be better than old times. What do you say?"

Cherri didn't say a word; she needed to keep the conversation off the child he sired in her womb. Pushing her plate back, she scooted out of the booth, looked at McFahey, and said, "Thank you for the taco salad and the not-so-delightful conversation. I have to go. I'll think about your offer." Of course, she had no intention of ever seeing him again, but she wanted him off her back so she could implement her "blow outta town" plan.

A full smile cracked his rough skin. "That's what I like to hear, honey. I'll give you a couple of days, then I'll look you up." Grabbing her wrist as she turned to leave, he brought her hand to his lips and kissed it, his tongue leaving a wet mark. "We're going to have some good times again, honey. I'll make you happier than that biker asshole. You'll see."

Cold sweat broke out on the back of her neck and trickled down her spine. McFahey could be cruel when things didn't go his way; he'd definitely call her bluff. She had to be out of Pinewood Springs before he had a chance to coerce her into something she didn't want. "Sounds good," she said lightly as her temples drummed. Pulling her hand away, she dashed off and slammed into someone, knocking the woman's purse on the floor. Picking it up, Cherri mumbled, "Sorry."

As she rose from the floor, she handed the purse to the woman then looked at her face. Staring at Cherri, with a smug look and a cruel glint in her eyes, was Peaches. With her hand in front of her mouth, Cherri gasped, and for a split-second, her world stood still as she realized Peaches heard everything she and McFahey said. Cherri had no doubts Peaches would run back to Dream House and tell Jax she was once McFahey's whore. She was sure Peaches was chomping at the bit to do it. Tears pricked the back of her eyes as Peaches shoved her out of her way, snarling, "Slut" as she stormed out the door. With her heart in her throat, Cherri gasped for air—she was fucking suffocating.

"Still here, honey? Waiting for me? Good girl." McFahey pulled Cherri into him and placed his mouth on hers, his pointy tongue pushing to gain access.

Twisting away from him, she said, "I have to go to the bathroom. My stomach is upset. I'll see you around." She wasn't lying; her stomach was queasy and doing the rumba. She rushed into the ladies room and leaned her hot forehead against the cool tile. Not wanting to risk McFahey waiting for her, she pulled herself up on the porcelain sink and climbed out a small window. Taking her heels off, she ran as the autumn wind caressed her cheeks and the rushing river echoed. Heart thumping, temples throbbing, and legs wobbling, she ran and ran as though her life depended on it, which it did. She had to get away from all this, especially McFahey's lust-filled eyes, Peaches' hateful eyes, and Jax's loving eyes. Her carefully painted world smeared around her. She had to leave or be lost forever.

SAFE IN HER room in the townhouse, her heart still tried to beat out of her chest and her body shook so much, she felt like she'd break in a million pieces; she was a spinning top in a distorted world. Pulling down the shades, she sat on her bed for several minutes, willing herself to calm the fuck down. She reached over and opened the top drawer of her nightstand, taking out a black pouch. Standing up, she walked over to the vanity she had bought at the thrift store and opened the pouch, laying out a razor blade, rubbing alcohol, cotton balls, and a washcloth. Her heart raced. Her room, lit only by a single 60-watt bulb, held the heat from the day. It was suffocating. Sweat shined on her forehead, upper lip, and chin. Every nerve in her body tingled, and she was on edge, ready to explode. Part of it was anticipation for what was to come, the other part was fear. Cherri had been on high-alert ever since she saw McFahey a couple of months ago.

Squirming in her chair, her hands trembling, she unscrewed the top of the alcohol. Its familiar, bitter smell burned her nostrils. Her ears were ringing, maybe from the excitement or from the guilt. She wasn't sure. Creeping into her brain were her mother's stifled cries the first time she caught Cherri bleeding. Cherri banished them, refusing to acknowledge their existence.

Don't do it. It's been so long. You've been so good.

It had been three years since she laid out her tools, since the urge took hold of her, refusing to let go. Back in high school, she needed a fix often, but if anyone had to endure what she had to… Cherri let her thoughts dissipate into the night air. She took off her t-shirt then her bra, and saturated a cotton ball in alcohol. *Steady. I have to stop my hand from shaking or I'm gonna fuckin' screw this up.* Taking a deep breath, she lifted her breast, dabbing the cotton underneath it, the cool liquid refreshing her scarred, sticky skin. Breathing slowly, she picked up the gleaming razor blade. She sliced into the skin, drawing blood in a thin trickle. The pain brought calmness, and feelings for Jax, the presence of McFahey, and all the dirty, endless memories went away with just one slice.

CHAPTER TWENTY-THREE

"WHY HAVEN'T YOU returned my calls, sweetness?" Jax, standing in the doorway at Dream House, watched Cherri as she sewed one of the dancer's costumes.

"It was crazy last night. I was so tired after work I crashed when I came home." She averted his gaze.

"What's goin' on? You're not shutting down on me, are you?" From the way her shoulders were drawn tight around her neck and nearly touching her earlobes, Jax surmised Cherri was full of tension. He wasn't sure why, and he gathered he probably wouldn't find out since she was so guarded about sharing her feelings. He walked over to her, placed his hands on her stiff shoulders, and gently massaged them. "Will you tell me what's wrong? I know something is, sweetness."

Cherri putting her sewing aside, brushed her fingertips on top of Jax's hands and leaned her head against him. "I'm okay now that you're here."

"Is work too much?"

"Uh-huh," she fibbed.

"Let me give you a good rubdown to relax you. Come on, lie down on the couch." Pulling her up, Jax guided her to the couch and as she sat down, he closed and locked her dressing room door.

"That's it." Grabbing a blanket, he handed it to Cherri and said, "Take your clothes off and I'll cover you with the blanket. I'll give you a nice rubdown to ease your stress."

Cherri took off her jeans and t-shirt, and wearing a blue plaid bra and matching panties, she laid down on the couch on her stomach, her head turned sideways and her eyes closed. With strong, capable hands,

Jax kneaded her shoulders.

"Fuck, you're full of knots. You need to calm down, sweetie. Nothing's worth getting all knotted up like this."

His fingers, knuckles, and palms kneaded and massaged her neck, shoulder, back, and legs. He removed the blanket and her heart-shaped ass beckoned him to bite her ripe cheeks. The way she moaned and whimpered as he moved his helping hands up and down her body told him she wouldn't complain if he took his massage one step further. "Got any oil in this room?"

From the side of her mouth, she said, "Yeah, in the second drawer of my dressing table. I always keep a bottle on hand for sore muscles from dancing."

Bottle in hand, he poured the amber liquid on her back and legs, rubbing it all over. The oil made her body sleek as his hands glided over her, and Jax felt the tension ease under his fingertips. Tugging her panties down, he squeezed a few drops over her ass and rubbed the oil in, kneading fistfuls of tempting flesh. Cherri squirmed under his touch while she groaned in pleasure and parted her legs slightly. Jax smiled when he saw her open her legs then massaged her ass cheeks harder while he ran his finger up and down her crack.

"Hmmm," she purred.

"Feel good?"

"Oh, yeah," she said in a low voice.

As he rubbed her shiny globes, he parted her cheeks, exposing her pink, puckered opening and her glistening pussy. Moving his finger up and down her wet sex, he stopped at her opening, the tip of his finger pressing against it, and pushed in. Sliding in easily, Jax inserted two more digits and slowly pulled in and out of her as she spread her legs more, her back moving up and down as she breathed. Her moans came out in gritted, ragged pants as his fingers advanced higher in her, twirling around like a corkscrew with her juices covering his digits. As Jax watched Cherri's reaction to his fingers fucking her pussy, warmth flooded his body, and he was aware of his quickening heartbeat. He leaned in closer to her, obsessively craving the scent of her. "You're making me hard, sweetness," he said in a low, husky voice.

"What you're doing feels so damn good," she whispered back.

With his fingers still in her, he flipped her slick body over and, staring into her smoldering eyes, he darted his tongue out to touch her lips. She eagerly strained her neck as her mouth met his. His tongue swirled around in her mouth, and the taste of peppermint cooled his hot tongue as his hand slipped inside her bra and explored her breast. When he cupped her tit, she stiffened and a small cry escaped her throat. He unclasped her bra then lifted her breast up. Looking down, he saw an angry, swollen red line right at her breastbone. "What the fuck happened?" he asked as he ran his index finger under the hot wound.

Apprehension replaced desire in Cherri's eyes as she said lightly, "Those damn underwire bras are lethal if the wire breaks through. They're like razor blades, you know? You don't know how lucky you guys are, not havin' to mess with bras and shit." She moved his hand away quickly and placed it on her other breast.

"Damn, your bra did *that*? In all the years I've been with bitches, I've never seen anything like that. Shit, it must've hurt, huh?"

"It's something I've gotten used to. I've always had super-sensitive skin, so even when I accidentally scratch myself with my nail, I get a nasty cut. My other boob is good and aching for some more of your sweet touch." She circled her arms around his neck, bringing him closer to her. When his mouth crushed on hers, she forced his open then plunged her tongue in deeply.

Jax tangled his fingers in her hair as he returned the kiss while his thumb played with her rigid nipple, making her jerk and groan in pleasure. Moving his mouth from her inflamed lips, Jax trailed his kisses down her slick body until he reached her inner thighs. When his tongue and teeth grazed her soft skin, she bucked under him, her legs wrapping around his waist. As he sucked her flesh, he glanced up, meeting Cherri's eyes which smoldered with intensity and created an electrical current between them. Excitement tingled every nerve in his body, making his dick throb and his breathing shallow as he thought of entering her sweet pussy.

Turning his attention from her soft, inner thighs, his tongue blazed a wet, hot trail to her engorged pussy lips. Her sharp intake of breath when he parted her lips to expose her pink folds, darkened from desire, stiffened his cock even more. With his full tongue, he lapped up her sweetness from the back of her pussy to the tip of it in one long lick. Grabbing the top of his hair with her fists, she pulled hard, making goosebumps appear on his skin from the sweet pain of her force. He played with her folds moving, curling, and flicking his tongue as she writhed and moaned.

"Fuck, I love your taste—you're so sweet. I can't wait to ram my cock in your sugared pussy."

She tugged his hair harder, and Jax, with a wry smile, figured he better fuck her soon or he'd have a helluva bald spot. Spreading her legs wide, her sex was splayed open in all its flush loveliness. Kneeling, Jax touched the opening to her sweetness and rubbed his cock against it. She grunted, and while their eyes locked together, he entered her hard and deep. The warmth of her inside soothed his aching cock as he stayed in her for a few minutes, nothing moving except the twitching of his dick. Then he pulled out and thrust in, that time going deeper.

"Oh, yes!" she shouted.

In and out he went, plunging his dick further each time until all that could be heard in the room were their grunts and the slick whacking of his balls against her. As he banged her fast and hard, he stroked the side of her hard nub while sweat poured down his back, forming pools under his arms. His cock felt her walls tighten then contract as her pussy squeezed and released him over and over while her hand over her mouth muffled her cries of pleasure.

Jax, reaching climax, let go as his pulsing cock released his come into her sweetness. Letting out several guttural pants, the last drop of his seed spilled in her. He collapsed on top of her, nuzzling her damp neck as she stroked his hair. A salty, musky scent drifted in the air.

When his body calmed down a bit, he stood, picked her up, then laid down again with Cherri covering his chest like a blanket. Holding her close, her head nestled against his neck and his arms circled around her. "Fuck, sweetness, I love the scent of me on you. This is the way I want to be with you—naked and close. You're mine, and I don't want any other man near you. You got that?

Pausing, Cherri said, "Let's enjoy what we just shared. Life is so unpredictable—who knows what tomorrow will bring?"

Pulling his head back and tilting her chin up so he could see her, he said, "What the fuck does that mean? You don't want us to be together?"

"I do. I've never felt like this with any other man. I do want us to be together. I'm sayin' everything is different when the glow of sex is gone. Let's talk about all this tomorrow. I want to enjoy being in your arms and being close to you."

He smacked his lips, his hand clenching her soft skin on the side of her body. "Is there another guy?"

"What? No! No, there is no one else. I'm tired and I have to work in a couple of hours, so let's enjoy being together, okay?"

After a long pause, he smoothed down her hair, brushed her cheek with the back of his hand, and whispered, "Okay, sweetness. We'll talk about it tomorrow, but just so you know, you're my woman and there isn't anything to discuss about that."

"Yeah, cool." She turned her eyes away from him.

Jax sensed she was hiding something from him. He'd have to pry it out of her later, though, because if he tried right then, she'd shut down then he'd never learn anything. He wished she would trust him and give herself to him wholeheartedly. Once she started to see a therapist, he was hopeful that a lot of issues would clear up, and she'd be free enough of her baggage to trust him in her life. He wanted to kill her bastard stepfather all over again for doing such a number on his sweet Cherri. He wrapped her tighter and kissed the top of her head as she nuzzled closer until they slipped into sleep.

McFahey's office in downtown Pinewood Springs

PEACHES LOOKED AROUND at Patrick McFahey's office and sneered when her eyes scanned the framed photos of his wife and children, and the placards hanging on the cherry wood-paneled walls denoting McFahey as Citizen and Volunteer of the Year. Dotting the bookcases, photographs of McFahey with senators and the current Colorado governor showed a smiling man with cold eyes. Law books lined the bookcases, and the rich, burgundy leather chairs and couch lent a regal and opulent air to the councilman's office.

Sitting in his swivel chair, gazing out the picture window at the mountains ablaze in gold aspen leaves and green pine needles, he turned around when Peaches cleared her throat. She stared into his cold, flat, blue eyes as they roamed up and down her body, stopping at her breasts shoved into an olive green knit top which revealed a lot of cleavage. When he stopped at her bust, he licked his lips, causing her to shiver— the guy was creeping her out. Without an invitation, she sank down into one of the leather chairs in front of his massive wood desk. Crossing her denim-clad legs, she leaned forward and said, "I have some information I think you'll be very interested in."

McFahey raised his eyebrows. "Is that so?"

"Yep. You know, everything is very expensive nowadays. You'd think living in a smaller town like Pinewood Springs would be cheaper, but it isn't."

"Am I to take it you want to *sell* me the information?"

"Nothing worth anything in life is free." Peaches sat back and rested her hands on her knee.

"Aren't you one of the strippers at Dream House? How do I know you have anything I'd be interested in?"

"Yep, I'm a *dancer* at Dream House, and I think you're interested in *anything* concerning Cherri. Am I right?" As she noticed his eyes come to life at the mention of the bitch's name, Peaches smiled inwardly—she had this creep right where she needed him.

"What about Cherri?"

"I need to see the money first, and then we'll talk."

Hesitating, McFahey stared at Peaches as if he were sizing her up or trying to intimidate her. Maybe he was doing both, but Peaches had a hard edge to her from years of surviving, so she didn't intimidate so easily.

Standing up, she began to walk toward the door, and said over her shoulder, "I can see you aren't interested. I don't want to take any more of your time." Placing her hand on the brass door knob, she pretended to turn it when she heard him push his desk chair back.

"I'll pay you a thousand for the information."

Turning around she laughed at him. "You can't be serious. I can make that on a good night at Dream House. I'm thinking more in the neighborhood of ten thousand."

McFahey's mouth dropped open. "You've got to be insane. I can't give you such a large amount without it being noticed. I can't do it."

"That's too bad. It's even more of a shame your race to the governor's seat in the next election won't make it past you announcing your intent to run." It was her turn to stare him down. "Have a nice day, councilman." She opened the door and as she was about to cross the threshold, a large, frustrated sigh expelled from behind her.

"Fuck! Close the goddamned door and sit your ass back over here. What you have to say better be worth ten thousand, or else I'll make sure you'll regret you ever contacted me."

"It's worth more, but I'm not greedy." She smiled broadly.

"I'll give you five thousand upfront, and when you tell me what you know, you'll get the rest."

"Sorry, councilman, but I'm the one calling the shots, not you. You'll give me ten thousand and then you'll get the information. If you don't agree, I walk."

Red blotches spotted his skin as she saw his eyes narrow in anger. She knew she was pushing it, but this was her one chance to have some real money and screw Cherri at the same time. She was tired of that bitch thinking her shit didn't stink, and she was livid Jax had his cock in

Cherri's pussy and ignored *her*. Peaches had been biding her time, waiting for the right moment to pay Cherri back for stealing Jax. She vowed she'd make the bitch pay, and earning some money in the process was an unexpected bonus.

"Do we have a deal? I don't have all day to waste with this shit."

Nostrils flaring, McFahey nodded, went over to a door, and disappeared through it. Reappearing after fifteen minutes, McFahey laid one hundred crisp one hundred dollar bills on the desk in front of her. "Now, tell me what you know, bitch."

Scooping up the money, Peaches smiled and said, "You're the proud papa of a very much alive and thriving baby girl whose mama is your favorite fuck, Cherri. The money you gave her to get rid of the little one, she used to get rid of you." Peaches laughed. "Your sweet daughter lives in Dexter in a quaint, wooden house with a darling picket fence. You, councilman, are the father of a bastard daughter. Imagine how the media will love it."

Eyes bugging out, face red, and sweat pouring down his face, the good councilman slammed his fist on the desk and yelled, "Are you sure about this? How the fuck do you know?"

"Cherri's a slut who's sleeping with my boyfriend, so I wanted to get something on her. I followed her to Dexter. She goes to see your daughter regularly. She looked downright maternal when I saw her in the park with the brat. It made me sick."

McFahey's face turned from red to white and his hands trembled as he placed them on the desk to steady himself.

"I also know she's planning to blackmail you. She's obsessed with money and she told her friend, 'McFahey is such a buffoon. I can't stand his limp dick in me. He's my meal ticket for a better life. He'll pay handsomely for me to keep my mouth shut about his daughter.' She's been plotting this for a long time, and she came to Pinewood Springs when she found out you were here." By the hatred washing over McFahey's face, Peaches knew he believed her lie. Her hope was to have him get rid of Cherri once and for all, and then Jax would come back to her and she could finally don his "Property of" patch.

"The fucking cunt." The councilman wiped his wet face with a handkerchief. "I'm glad you told me."

"I'm one of your voters. I want to see you as governor come election year." She zipped her purse. "It was nice doin' business with you." She walked toward the door.

"Not so fast. I got a condition attached to the money." He had her wrist in his hand, and the more she tried to pull free, the tighter he gripped it.

"What condition?"

"It involves you on your knees with your mouth wide open."

"You want me to give you a blowjob?" Peaches, incredulous, debated her options.

"If you don't want me to call security and tell them you stole the money. I think they're going to believe a respectable family man before a stripper at a biker bar."

"You'd do that, too, wouldn't you?"

"Great minds think alike, you know. The fucking biker must be hung like a stallion for you bitches to be fighting over him. You can rest easy because you'll have your man back. I'll take care of Cherri."

Joy coursed through Peaches body as her mind exploded with images of Jax kissing her and announcing to his club she was his old lady. Looking at McFahey, she smiled and said, "Ease back on your chair while I unzip your pants."

CHAPTER TWENTY-FOUR

The next day, early evening

SNAKING HIS ARM around Cherri's waist, Jax planted a kiss on the side of her face while she tried to take roll call for the early evening shift. Peaches glared at him when he slid his hand over Cherri's hips as she giggled.

"Cut it out. I'm trying to do my job and look professional doing it." She feigned indignation, but her twinkling eyes told Jax she loved his attention.

"Do any of you ladies mind if I show my woman some love while she works?" He threw a boyish grin at them, making several of them wish they were in Cherri's position. Shaking their heads—except for Peaches, who continued to glare at the couple—Jax grazed Cherri's earlobe with his teeth and breathed in her ear, "The consensus is in, and no one gives a fuck."

Cherri nudged Jax away. "You're so bad." Giving him a quick peck on the cheek, she whispered, "Later tonight, you can show me how bad you can really be." Before he could say anything, she spun out of his arms and marched behind the curtains to make sure everything was set for the evening's rush.

Shaking his head, Jax smiled and sauntered over to the bar to grab a bottle of beer and a shot of Jack. Sitting at his favorite table in the front, he took a long draw of his beer, stretched his legs in front of him, and watched the stage as a cute, short brunette with a generous rack shook and wiggled all her parts to pulsating rock music. As he looked at her, he saw Cherri's face and body. He was hooked on his woman from the beginning and he'd never missed one of her shows, but he hated that the brothers had seen her body. Since she wasn't dancing anymore, he liked it a whole lot better. The members joked and teased him about how crazy he was about Cherri, and he couldn't believe it, either.

When he was at the club the other night, a sexy slut was spread on the pool table with three guys fucking her and a few others waiting their turn. She was a friend of Brandi's, and the slut wanted to be a club whore, so she was going through initiation. The brothers yelled for Jax to come over and get in on the fun, but he didn't want to. It surprised the fuck out of the brothers, and it floored him. He couldn't get Cherri out of his mind, and he didn't want to fuck any of the sluts who hung out at the club—he only wanted to fuck his Cherri. Shaking his head in disbelief, he threw back his Jack and enjoyed the biting sting roll down his throat into his belly, warming it.

As he stared blankly at the stage, a warm, soft pair of arms clung around his neck. At first, he thought it was Cherri, but her lavender scent was missing and a cheap, overpowering floral smell invaded his nose. Turning his head sideways, he noticed Peaches as she planted a hard kiss on his cheek.

"What the fuck are you doing, Peaches? I told you to stop doing this shit." Jax untangled her arms and shoved her away from him.

"I came by to say hi. What's your problem?"

"You don't understand. We're finished. You gotta stop throwing yourself at me all the time. It's pathetic as fuck."

Peaches blinked rapidly as she watched him. "You got some nerve. I was okay to fuck when Miss Bitch was too frigid to take your cock, but now that she's turned into a horny cunt and you've taken your dick to her pussy, I'm history?"

Bristling, Jax clenched his hands into fists. "Stop before I throw your ass outta Dream House for good. And yeah, I decide whose pussy I wanna fuck. You got no say. If you didn't like it, you didn't have to give it up so easily, bitch. Go on, get outta here before I do somethin' I'll regret."

Darkness shrouded Peaches' face as she gazed at Jax. Leaning in close, she said in his ear, "I've something very special to tell you about your favorite stripper."

"I said I'm done with this shit."

"Oh, I think you'll want to hear about your precious fuck."

"You're drunk, Peaches. Go sober up. Don't you dance tonight?"

"I'm tipsy, but what I have to say will come outta my sober mouth."

"I don't do gossip."

"This isn't gossip. What I'm gonna share with you is fact. You know, right from the source."

"Not interested. Move on, Peaches; you've become a pain in my ass."

"Okay, but before I leave, I have one question. Did Cherri tell you who the father of her daughter is?"

His stone face masked the wrestling match his insides were having: tell the slut to fuck off, or find out who fathered Paisley. A thick veil of gloom crept over him, adding to the bad feeling he had about Peaches' information. He should tell the slut he didn't care because it made no difference to him then walk away... but he didn't. "Who is it?"

"Our very own councilman, Patrick McFahey, is the proud daddy."

The words hit Jax full-on in the face like an ice cold bottle of beer. "*Who* the fuck did you say? McFahey? No way. You got some wrong information there, bitch." Jax averted his eyes back to the stage.

"Oh, my information is solid," she said in Jax's ear. "I'm sure you know your *precious* Cherri was McFahey's private whore for six months before she got knocked up. And now he wants her back, you know, to pick up where they left off, and she's more than willing to do it *if* the price is right."

Yanking her arm, his thumb pressed down hard on her skin. Jax growled, "I don't believe any of the shit you just told me. Are you that desperate to trump Cherri you'd resort to spewing this fuckin' bullshit?"

Wincing in pain as Jax's thumb pushed harder against her skin, she said, "I only have your best interests at heart, baby. I love you, and I know the cold bitch has kept the truth from you. If you decide to keep her, then that's fine, but you need to know the truth. Why would I make this up? How the hell would I know about McFahey or that Cherri has a daughter in Dexter? You don't think she'd share with me, do you? I bumped into her when she was with McFahey a few days ago, at an out-of-the-way restaurant. They were in a cozy booth acting very lovey-dovey. I heard her tell him she'd get back with him if he put her up in a nice place and gave her a generous stipend. If you don't believe me, ask Cherri if she was at Le Crystal Restaurant. Ask her if McFahey's the father of her daughter. I think you need to know this, baby." Peaches ran her hand up and down Jax's arm.

He swatted her hand away, his face a distorted mask of hate, anger, and hurt. "Get the fuck away from me."

She brushed a lock of hair from his forehead and said, "Baby, don't be mad at me. I didn't do anything except tell you the truth. You deserve to know the truth."

Through clenched teeth, Jax replied, "Get. The. Fuck. Away. From. Me." Eyes rimmed in sparks of rage and betrayal made his face grue-some. Peaches backed away from Jax stiffly as her knees locked. Leaping out of his chair, Jax loomed over her as she continued backing away from him. He bent down and hissed in her ear, "You disgust me," then stormed away.

Images of McFahey—the fucking, greasy pig—touching Cherri made his stomach lurch as every nerve in his body jumped. He had an edgy, twitchy feeling, and he wanted to break something or punch someone real hard. His muscles and veins strained against his skin. Cherri and McFahey? His mind couldn't process it. Why the fuck didn't Cherri tell him about it?

Standing by the bar, trying to assimilate the information Peaches gave him, he noticed Cherri making her way toward him. An over-whelming urge to dominate overcame him, and he pointed down the hallway where the private lap rooms were. Appearing confused, she shook her head and gestured to the dancers. Rushing up to her, he jerked her arm and dragged her behind him to one of the rooms.

Inside the dimly-lit, mirrored room, the pervasive smell of patchouli filled the space. Shoving Cherri inside, Jax slammed the door. Cherri, tripping over the plush carpet, landed on the velveteen purple couch. Rubbing her elbow, she said, "What's going on?"

"That's what I'd like to know," he said in a low, hard voice.

"What's that supposed to mean?" Cherri gathered her hair in her hand to make a quasi-ponytail.

"Did you meet McFahey at Le Crystal a few days ago?" His words came out in short, staccato clips.

Cherri froze, and but for her eyes widening, her face was devoid of emotion.

"Is McFahey Paisley's dad?" He hoped she'd deny it, but she answered his question with silence. "Were you McFahey's paid whore in Denver? Are you going back to him?"

Cherri sat mutely on the couch, not moving a muscle since his questions started. Taking her silence as affirmations, he clenched his fists as his mouth went dry. Her lies and betrayals were like a sword to his gut, cutting him in two and taking all his blood, passion, and feelings.

"Get your whore ass up. I want a lap dance." Throwing five one hundred dollar bills at her feet, he stood in front of her, glaring.

Staring at the money, Cherri's eyes glistened as she covered her face with shaky hands. She shook her head and said in a barely audible voice, "Please, I don't want to."

In an icy voice, Jax said, "I'm not fuckin' askin' you. I'm fuckin' telling you to get your slut-ass shakin'. Now."

Cherri shrunk against the back of the couch, tears rolling down her face. Yanking her to her feet, Jax jerked her toward him and rubbed his cock against her. "Put the music on and grind your ass, bitch."

While she ground her butt into his crotch, his hands on her thighs, and her tits rubbing against his chest, he swallowed hard as a painful tightness grew in his throat. His thoughts spun and focused inward, and he had a sense of time stopping. Images of Cherri and him with Paisley in the park, eating ice cream, of him and Cherri at the lake making love, filled his brain as the shock and depth of her betrayal rocked his mind.

The music ended long before he even noticed it. Cherri's small voice broke through the haze of memories. "Yes, McFahey is Paisley's father. He wanted me to get rid of her, but I wanted her so bad. He gave me money for the abortion, and I took it and split. A friend of mine helped me through my pregnancy, and she hooked me up with Sarah in Dexter. I had to leave Denver—McFahey was looking for me. I should have told you, but I wanted to pretend none of it happened. I didn't want McFahey spoiling my idea of who I am."

"You were his whore?" Jax's voice had a steel edge.

"I guess I was. I mean, he paid for my apartment, gave me presents, and a monthly allowance. What was I going to do? I had all the shit from my stepfather, I ran away from home, lied about my age so I could strip, and when McFahey offered me the arrangement, I thought I'd hit the lottery. My choice was him, or the streets. Patrick's proposition was a no-brainer." Her voice was flat, and she stared at the lamp on the corner table.

Jax winced when she called McFahey by his first name and a fire burned inside him, making him seethe. "Did you meet with him at Le Crystal a few days ago?"

"Yes."

"Are you going back to him?"

"He wants me to. He made me a very generous offer, and I told him I'd think about it so he'd let me leave, but I didn't agree to it even though I need the money to get out of here. I need to give Paisley a better life than what I had."

Gritting his teeth, Jax said, "I told you I'd help you. Fuck. Fuck!"

"With you, it's different. I have feelings for you. I sure as fuck don't care about McFahey."

Snorting, Jax said, "You have feelings for me? You have a fucked-up way of showing me. You have the goddamned nerve to tell *me* not to fuck other women, and you're entering into a paid whore arrangement? Fuck you, bitch!" The back of his eyes pricked and he trembled inside

Fuck! What the hell is wrong with me? Why is this bitch getting to me? We had some good fucks—move on. Shit!

"I didn't agree to it, and I'm not gonna do it, but if I *had* agreed to it, it wouldn't mean anything to me. No feelings, no emotions, nothing. Anyway, like I said, I didn't say I was going to do it."

"And what the fuck am I supposed to do when that asshole is sticking his cock in you? Go for a ride around the town?"

"I told you I didn't tell him I'd do it. I'm going to tell him no when he contacts me."

"But you fuckin' considered it!"

"No, I didn't."

"Liar! Go on, get out, be a whore! I never should've touched you in the first place." He opened the door, stood aside, and gestured Cherri to leave.

"Jax, please. You don't understand. I have nothing with McFahey. That was a long time ago. I'm with you. What you and I have is real. I care for you. I lo—"

"Correction, bitch—what we *had seemed* real. You're worse than any club whore. Get your ass outta here. I'm done with you."

As Jax saw Cherri's face crumple and her shoulders slump, he wanted to grab her, press her close to him, and stroke her hair. When she looked at him with hurt and disappointment stamped on her face, he returned her gaze with hardness even though his insides were all twisted up. Placing her hand over her mouth as wet streaks painted her face, she ran past Jax; he watched her exit the back door.

From the distance, he spotted Peaches in her skimpy sequined bikini, adjusting her thong before she took the stage. As he looked at her satisfied, smug face, he fought the urge to go over to her, put his hands around her neck, and snap it like a twig. Looking at him, she flashed him a warm smile. The bitch didn't even know he hated the sight of her and despised her for busting open the cocoon he shared with his warm and precious Cherri.

CHAPTER TWENTY-FIVE

CHERRI STUMBLED OUT into the parking lot, looking for Emma's car. She had to get away from Dream House, from Jax's hurt eyes and angry face. How the hell did he find out about McFahey? Was that fucking prick that callous to have told Jax about their past? As the tears blurred her vision, she realized it didn't matter because whatever she and Jax had been building was torn down in a matter of a couple of hours. If she could go back in time, she would've trusted Jax and told him the truth about her connection with McFahey, but it was too late, and she had to live with the fact she lost Jax. She lost the first man who made her feel something. She'd never been in love before, but her feelings for Jax were deep, and it felt like love to her. Wanting to share her and Paisley's life with him told her she loved him. He never gave her a chance to tell him because he was so damn angry, hurt, and disappointed. His disappointment in her crushed her the most.

Unable to find Emma's car, Cherri ran to the bus stop as the Number Fifteen came into view. Boarding the bus, she found a seat. Resting her hot forehead against the cool window, she stared at the trees and houses while they blurred by. How had everything gone so wrong in such a short time? The previous day, she and Jax made incredible love and spent a wonderful morning together, and twenty-four hours later, her life went to shit and he threw her out, making her feel broken inside.

At the curb, in front of her place, Cherri noticed a parked black sedan with tinted windows as she walked up the street. The sourness in her stomach rose into her throat, and she clutched her middle.

She approached her home with heavy footsteps and a bitter taste in her mouth, wishing she could disappear. As she passed the car and fumbled with her keys, a short man with black hair, brown eyes, and a nasty scar from his left temple down to his cheek jumped out from the front seat and blocked her way.

"Someone wants to talk to you," he said.

Before she could answer, the back door opened, and Cherri saw McFahey sitting in the shadows. "Come over here, honey. I want to talk to you."

Cherri supported her weight with both hands on the roof of the car and bent down. "What do you want?"

Patting the empty space next to him, the councilman said, "Come sit by me so I can see you better."

"I'm not getting in. I've had a long day. I'm tired. What do you want?"

"It's fine, honey. I'm not unreasonable. I'll talk to you like this, but next time, I won't indulge you. Where's the kid?"

"What kid?" Cherri stared at him with defiance glowing in her eyes.

"The one you were supposed to have taken care of. I gave you money for that. You lied to me, you bitch. You took my money and took off. Now you want to blackmail me?" He grabbed her arm, tugging her halfway into the sedan. He dug his nails into her skin, making her wince in pain.

"Stop it, you're hurting me. I don't know what you're talking about. I don't wanna blackmail you. If I wanted to do that, I would've contacted you by now. Please, I just want to go away and start a new life."

"I want you and the kid to meet me at our restaurant—you know, the one we met at a few days ago. If you want the brat to keep breathing, you won't tell the biker you fuck about this. Got it?"

She nodded. When he released her arm, she rubbed where he hurt her, and backed away. The car door closed and drove away.

Tearing up the stairs to her bedroom, Cherri's heart pounded as her wobbly legs barely held her weight. *I gotta get out of here. I gotta get Paisley and get outta here.* She kept repeating the words again and again like a mantra.

After slamming her bedroom door, she collapsed on her bed and buried her face in her pillow, bunching up the quilt in her fists as she cried. She cried for the young girl whose mother didn't protect her against her monstrous stepfather, for agreeing to be McFahey's mistress, for her beloved Paisley whom she loved more than life, and for a short-circuited relationship with Jax, Everything turned to shit in her life, but she couldn't stay on the bed crying while Paisley was not with her. She couldn't let McFahey see Paisley because she knew he'd take her daughter away from her forever. She'd rather die than let that happen. *I should've left two months ago. I wanted to spend time with Jax, but my selfishness made Paisley a target. Fuck!*

Wiping away the tears and blowing her nose, Cherri ran to her closet and took out two suitcases. Throwing clothes into them, she scooped up all her makeup, creams, and toiletries. She had to get Paisley and leave town. *Stay focused, Cherri. You need money to get out of town.*

Frantically, she dashed to the closet, pulled out a hamper full of rags and towels, and dug deep down with her shaky hands until she pulled out a metallic bronze makeup bag. Unzipping it, she dumped the contents on the closet floor. Sitting cross-legged, she gathered loose bills—her getaway stash—and counted them aloud, making piles of one hundred, fifty, twenty, ten, and five dollar bills. With a frown on her face, she placed the twenty-two hundred dollars in an envelope, cursing herself for not saving more, and for not taking the five hundred dollars Jax threw at her for the dance.

She'd tried to put away one hundred dollars a week, but with the money she paid Sarah to take care of Paisley, her living expenses and incidentals, and her reduction in salary, thanks to Jax, she was lucky she saved as much as she did in the time she'd been at Dream House. Looking at the stack of green bills again, she shook her head and bounced a curled knuckle against her mouth as her breathing accelerated and her stomach quivered.

Her butt leapt off the floor when a car in the street backfired, sounding like a gunshot. Wringing her hands, she paced the room, prodding herself to concentrate. At one point, Jax would've given her the money, she was certain of that, but not anymore—not after he found out about her past. It didn't matter because she wouldn't have asked him anyway. If he knew the true situation, he'd make matters worse by charging out like a knight in black leather. No, she'd have to figure this out alone—something she was used to doing.

Glancing at her phone clock, she realized Dream House would be closed in about three hours and in four, it would be dark and empty. Dream House was her ticket to taking Paisley and going far away from McFahey. Planning to go as far as she could, she'd make sure he'd never find her by changing both their names. Inhaling a big breath and exhaling it slowly calmed Cherri—she had a plan. Dialing Sarah's phone number, Cherri prayed she was up and would answer the phone. After the sixth ring, Cherri almost clicked off when she heard Sarah's voice.

"Hi, Sarah? I'm sorry I'm calling you so late. Were you sleeping?"

In a strained voice, Sarah answered, "No, not really. Why're you calling so late?"

"I'm coming by to pick Paisley up. Is she okay? Is anything wrong?"

"Everything's fine. I'm just tired, that's all."

"I'll be coming late, like around four in the morning. Sorry, but I want to get an early start. I've decided to move."

"Oh… okay. I'll see you when you come."

"Thanks, Sarah."

A wrinkled brow formed on her face as a knot in her belly pulsed. Sarah sounded odd, and Cherri prayed Paisley wasn't sick or something. Chiding herself for thinking the worst, she went into the hall and tapped on her roommate's door. Ginger, wearing her hearts and rainbows nightshirt, opened the door, yawning. "What's up?"

"Sorry to wake you, but an emergency has come up with my family. Can I borrow your car? Please? I'll owe you big time." Cherri smiled sweetly while her heart thudded against her chest.

"Your family? I didn't know you had any family around here. Is it serious?"

"Yeah, it is. I'll be back before noon tomorrow. Can I?"

"Okay, sure, just make sure you bring it back with the same amount of gas that's in there."

"Thanks. I owe you."

With Ginger's car keys in the palm of her hand, Cherri went back to her room to bide her time until Dream House was empty. Lying on her bed, she closed her eyes, trying to catch some sleep before beginning her new journey. Sleep didn't come, as Jax's hurt eyes filled her mind; beyond his anger, his roughness, and his cruel words, she saw sadness and hurt. For a small slice of time, she thought he may have cared for her, but she'd never know for sure. She didn't want to think about him, to think about what may have been between them; it was over, so there was no point in dreaming about what could have been.

Deep inside her, the pain of never seeing Jax again gripped her with such ferocity it took her breath away. To never again see his boyish grin, run her hands through his soft hair, taste his saltiness in her mouth, or feel his warm lips on hers made her chest ache as an acute stab of emptiness cut through her heart. She turned from side to side, hoping the movement would erase the longing, the pain, and the image of Jax's disappointed eyes. A long, forlorn sob escaped from her.

At three thirty in the morning, Cherri sat upright in her bed, rubbing the sleep out of her eyes. It was eerily quiet, and a cold sweat began its descent from the back of her neck down her spine. Shivering, she pulled her covers around her trembling shoulders as she looked at the time. She had fallen asleep, and even though it was later than she planned, she had to follow through with it; otherwise, she'd be McFahey's whore and Paisley would be lost to her forever. Jumping up, she gathered her suitcases, took one last look at her room, quietly padded down the stairs, and walked out into the chilly early morning air.

As she sat in the parking lot of Dream House, she stared at the dark windows and the security lighting around the building. The strip bar's security wasn't very tight, because the MC figured since the bar was owned by an outlaw biker club, no one was dumb enough to break in. Catching her breath, she knew her stupidity wouldn't sit well with the Insurgents, but she had no choice, and she hoped they'd understand that.

Slowly slipping out of Ginger's car, she walked over to the small back door off the alley, put the key in the lock, and disengaged the alarm when she entered the strip club. Not needing to turn any extra lights on—she knew the club inside and out—she strode over to the office and, once inside, pressed her hand on one of the wall panels which immediately swung open, revealing a safe. Standing in front of the safe, she took a deep, pained breath and closed her eyes as a thickness formed in her throat. The Insurgents—Hawk and Banger, in particular—trusted her to be assistant manager of the club, and she would be betraying that trust. She supposed it was her night of betrayal: Jax, Emma, Hawk, and Banger. Betraying Emma especially pained Cherri because she was the only true friend Cherri had in the town. Emma had believed in her before Cherri believed in herself, and she was slapping Emma in the face with this one action—stealing the day's proceeds.

With shaking fingers, Cherri punched the numbers, entering the safe's combination. The red light flashed and the door swung open. Ignoring her nagging conscience, Cherri focused on what she *had* to do, took out the money, and counted it—sixteen thousand, two hundred and fifty dollars—and closed the door.

As she drove away from Dream House, she made a vow to pay every penny back to the Insurgents, even if it took her a lifetime. She headed toward Sarah's house, muttering, "I'm so sorry, Jax. Please forgive me."

When Cherri arrived, the car's tires crunched over the gravel driveway. Sarah's house was a dark silhouette against the lightening eastern sky. Cherri stepped out on the gravel ground and slowly walked up to the porch, the steps groaning under her weight. Ringing the doorbell, she waited for lights to wink in the windows and Sarah to open the door, but there was only silence. Swallowing hard, Cherri stared at the front door as a thread of foreboding weaved its way around her nerves. With a sweaty hand, her fingers turned the doorknob. The door squeaked open, and she walked into the darkened living room. As her eyes grew accustomed to the darkness, she heard a shuffle off to her right side.

"Sarah?" she whispered.

More shuffling then before Cherri could determine where the noise came from, a strong hand went across her mouth and nose, stifling her startled cry. Shadows flitted to the front and side of her as the room began to shrink and her body floated away, white spots clouding her view. She fell deeper and deeper into the void, and as she slipped away, a low, cruel voice hissed in her ear, "Welcome back, honey."

Everything went black.

CHAPTER TWENTY-SIX

SLEEP EVADED JAX as thoughts of Cherri stuck in his head. A knot in his stomach had been his constant companion since he yelled at Cherri the previous night. Rubbing his eyes with his fingers, Jax sighed loudly. He was so angry at her, but in the first rays of dawn, his fury subsided. Wanting to talk with her and give her the chance to explain things permeated his mind. He grabbed his jeans from the floor, dressed, and left the clubhouse.

The early morning dew misted over the tree branches as Jax revved his Harley. Arriving at Cherri's townhouse, he rang the doorbell. No answer. He rang again while he pounded on the door. From inside, Jax heard a muffled female voice. "Wait a sec. Fuck."

The door swung open and Ginger greeted Jax with a frown. "Who the fuck pounds on doors at the crack of dawn?"

"I came to see Cherri," Jax said brusquely as he pushed past Ginger and started up the stairs.

"She's not home." Covering her mouth, Ginger yawned widely as she leaned against the doorframe.

"She's not home? Where the fuck is she?"

"I dunno. She borrowed my car for some kind of family emergency. I didn't even know she had family in the area."

"When did she leave?"

"Beats me. She came to my room around midnight or a bit later, asking if she could borrow my car. I crashed and didn't hear her go out."

Taking the stairs two steps at a time, Jax burst in Cherri's bedroom and noticed her stripped bed. Opening the closet door, his heart twisted when he saw it was empty. Cherri was gone.

Jax rushed out of the townhouse and jumped on his bike, riding toward Dream House. When he arrived at the darkened strip bar, the knot in his stomach tightened. Scanning the parking lot for Ginger's car, dread slowly spread over him. Racking his brain, Jax decided to pay Sarah a visit. Jax knew Cherri would never split without Paisley in tow.

As he made a half-circle in the lot, he noticed a dim light in the back office. Approaching the back of the building with caution, Jax let himself in. Walking in the office, he sensed something wasn't right. As he looked around, he saw one of the wood panels didn't fit snuggly against the wall. Frozen in his tracks, his heart beating wildly, Jax feared what he may find when he opened the panel and checked in the safe. Taking a deep breath, he punched in the code and the door swung open. Staring into emptiness, Jax exhaled before he slumped down on the leather loveseat next to the wall. *Fuck, Cherri! What the hell have you done?*

Stealing from the Insurgents was a very stupid thing to do. Jax knew what was in store for Cherri once her theft was detected—a severe beating or death. Blowing out a big breath, Jax rubbed his hands on his jeans as he tried to formulate a plan. Knowing his first loyalty was to the MC, pangs of guilt ripped through him. He should call Banger or Hawk and report the theft and his suspicions at once, but he wasn't going to do it. No doubt Cherri needed to be dealt with, but he'd handle it. The tricky part was finding Cherri and replacing the money. Not sure how much was in the safe, Jax hurriedly scouted around the office, trying to find the ledger and any receipts. He found nothing; Emma sometimes took the ledger home with her to finish the paperwork. The money had to be replaced, and he knew the club never kept more than twenty thousand dollars in the safe. He'd have to go back to the clubhouse to get the money.

Jax usually kept a lot of money in his room since he distrusted banks. The MC profited very nicely from the recreational weed dispensaries they owned. Slamming the office door shut, Jax left Dream House quickly. He didn't have a second to waste. The last thing he wanted was for Emma or one of the brothers coming in early and finding out Cherri ripped them off.

As he rode to the clubhouse, he thanked the voters for passing the law legalizing marijuana. Since the Insurgents ran two legal dispensaries and had a grow license through a straw man, the members were reaping in the money. Since all transactions were cash, most of it was not declared to the IRS. From just the dispensaries, the club pulled in over six million dollars a year, and each of the brothers received a share of the proceeds while the rest of the money rolled into other businesses, like strip bars, restaurants, ink shops, and the latest, a construction project in West Pinewood Springs. The Feds left the Insurgents' dispensaries alone because the Insurgents made sure crank and crack stayed out of the county. Even though it was a tenuous line between the Feds and the MC, it worked. And the best part was each member and the MC became richer legally. America *was* home of the free and wealthy.

After Jax took the money out of his safe, he headed back to Dream House. The faster he rode, the more pissed he became. His gut told him Cherri took the money to get away from McFahey, but Jax didn't understand why Cherri was so stubborn and refused to come to him for help. Even though he told her a bunch of things he really didn't mean, he couldn't believe how quickly she forgot their good and intimate times together. It seemed like she was okay with taking money from Gunner and McFahey, but not from him. Her explanation of him being a real relationship and the others weren't didn't make sense to him. Cherri was his woman and she needed help. The way he figured it was he was the only one she *should* go to for help. He had her back, always.

Once the money was back in the safe, Jax turned off the office light, engaged the alarm, and locked the door. Hauling ass on the early morning streets of Pinewood Springs was easy since the town was just waking up. Taking the back roads, he rode to Dexter.

When he turned into Sarah's driveway, he noticed a light in one of the front windows. He crept up the stairs and knocked on the door. No one answered. He knocked harder and said, "Cherri, I know you're in there. Come out. We gotta talk."

Behind the door, he heard padded footsteps approaching. Several seconds passed, and as Jax raised his hand to knock on the door again, it swung open. Sarah greeted Jax with wild eyes, her lips quivering, and a red mark on her cheek. Sensing something was amiss, he said, "Hey, Sarah. I've come for Cherri."

Shaking her head, her hands covered her face, and she said in a broken voice, "She's not here. They took her and the baby. I couldn't stop them. I couldn't do anything. I tried—I really did." Breaking down in tears, Sarah leaned against the wall for support.

Jax's blood went cold. "They? Tell me exactly what happened." He led the crying woman to the couch in the living room.

After she blew her nose and wiped her tears, Sarah said, "I'd just put Paisley to bed when I heard a car in the driveway. I looked out the window and saw a black sedan. Sometimes, Cherri borrows a car and comes over here to tuck Paisley in bed, so I thought it was her. I was putting Paisley's toys away when the doorbell rang. I opened the door but instead of Cherri, there were three men. I about died." Bowing her head, she started crying again.

Jax, anxious to hear the story and find Cherri, forced himself to be patient. "Go on," he prodded.

"The men pushed their way in, demanding me to give them Paisley. I was so scared, but I didn't plan on giving Paisley to them. I told them she was with her mother tonight. One of the men punched me." Sarah touched her bruised cheek lightly. "The other two men ran upstairs, and the one who hit me threw me on the couch, threatening to kill me if I moved. He pulled out a gun to show me he was dead serious."

"Did you know these fucks?"

She shook her head.

"How did they get Cherri?"

"While they were here, she called me to tell me she wanted to pick up Paisley. They were listening in on the call. I hoped she wouldn't come, but I didn't dare warn her because they threatened to kill me and Paisley."

"So, they waited until she came?"

With shaky hands, she smoothed her hair as she nodded.

"What time did Cherri come?"

"Very late. It was around four. I don't know the exact time, but it was something like that."

"What happened?"

"She came into the house. All the lights were off, and when she came into the living room, the ring leader put a rag over her nose and mouth. There must've been something on it 'cause she passed out, then they carried her and Paisley out and put them in the car. After they threatened the shit outta me, they drove off. I'm so sorry."

Nostrils flaring, his hands clenched at his side. A surge of blood rushed to his head as his temples pounded, and an overwhelming urge for vengeance consumed him—he desired to hurt someone and draw blood. "Tell me what the men looked like."

"I didn't see them too well since they kept the lights low. One of the men, shorter than the others, wore a brimmed hat pulled low, obstructing his face. He was the one who put the rag over her mouth and nose. I didn't get a good look at him, but he was the ringleader. He called all the shots."

Jax's gut told him McFahey was mixed up in this, and that the greasy fucker probaby had Cherri and her daughter. Jax made a vow to kill the bastard who dared to mess with his woman. Leaving Sarah motionless on the couch, Jax jumped down the stairs, hopped on his Harley, and raced back to Pinewood Springs.

MOANING SOFTLY, CHERRI opened her heavy eyes, trying to focus. With both hands, she squeezed her temples in a vain attempt to stop her head from pounding. Trying to sit up, Cherri's head spun and everything around her was fuzzy as she looked out of bleary eyes. The room was windowless and simple with only a full-sized bed, two wood chairs, and a small chest of drawers. The small amount of light filtering in the room came from under the door.

Where the hell am I? What happened?

She pressed harder against her temples as if to force the memories. Slowly, the images of shadows coming toward her triggered her memory. Chest lurching, Cherri sat up, choking on shallow breaths as her vision blotched over like a snowstorm. *Paisley! Where is Paisey?* Her mind screamed as her body grew ice-cold. Clutching her stomach, Cherri slumped forward, her head hitting the mattress as a wail broke through her lips. *Paisey! Paisey!* Tears streamed down her face as she howled into the bed.

The lock clicking stopped Cherri. Wiping her wet face, she held her breath and glanced at the doorknob as it turned. A hand switched on the overhead light; the flickering florescent tube hurt her eyes. McFahey closed and locked the door. *McFahey! Fuck, I shoulda known he was behind this shit.* Cherri sat up straight, pretending to be cool and collected.

Throwing a large towel at her, he said in a gruff voice, "Go on and wash up. I want you to be pretty and sweet-smelling for me." He pointed to a closed door next to the chest of drawers then set down a neatly folded stack of clothes. "Put these on when you're finished showering. If you take too long, I'll come in and get you."

"Where's Paisley? I'll do anything you ask, just please, tell me where Paisley is."

"All you can think of is that brat. You didn't even say hi to me when I came in."

"Just tell me where she is. I need to know she's safe."

"Shut the fuck up about the brat." Leaning in close, he roughly turned her head toward him. "You better do as I say or you'll never see your daughter again. Got it?"

Staring blankly, Cherri nodded.

"Good, because we got a lot of time to make up for. I'm going to fuck you, not like the lady I cared about in Denver, but like the whore you've become. Get cleaned up. I got an itch you need to relieve."

After a quick shower, Cherri came out of the bathroom, her hair still damp, dressed in red patent high-heels, fishnet thigh-highs, a very tight and short spandex skirt, and a leopard-print bustier. Pulling down on her skirt, she stood in the middle of the room, watching McFahey as his heated gaze raked over her body.

"Get over here," he said in a thick voice.

As a lump formed in her throat and her eyes welled, Cherri thought of her daughter—her precious daughter whom she would do anything for. She inhaled, stood up straight, and walked over to McFahey.

Grabbing her arms he pulled her down on the bed. Rubbing her bottom with his hand, he hissed in her ear, "That's what I like—you looking like a slut and me touching your ass. Brings back memories, doesn't it, honey?"

Gritting her teeth, Cherri gave a quick nod. The buckle of his belt clanged when it hit the floor, followed by the swish of his pants as they hit the ground. Pulling her up, he flipped her on her back then ran his hands all over her. She twisted under his touch; she wanted so bad to get away. Shoving her top up, he patted her breasts as he whispered against her neck, "We're going to have some fun, honey. Some real fun."

A half-hour later, Cherri held a sheet over her nakedness, her gaze fixed on the floor. Whistling through his teeth, McFahey smiled as he lifted her chin then placed a hard, wet kiss on her mouth.

"You haven't forgotten what I like, honey. That was awesome. Reminded me of the times we used to spend together. I'll let you rest up then we'll kick it up a notch. What do you say?"

"I want to see Paisley. I did what you wanted, so now I want to see her to make sure she's safe."

"Is that all you can fucking say? You're like a broken record. I said you would, but all in good time, *sweetheart.*" Cherri watched him as he walked to the door, dumbfounded.

"Where're you going?" she asked. "Don't go. Please, let me see Paisley. Please." Her voice hitched.

"Not yet."

McFahey slammed the door behind him. Cherri ran to the door and put her ear against it. Hearing muffled voices, she strained to make out some words. Picking up isolated snippets of the conversation—"paid for the brat," "couple coming tomorrow"—Cherri's body went rigid. Dozens of needles danced their way across her skin as the gravity of the situation hit her. Her sweet baby daughter trusted Cherri to keep her safe, and she'd failed her. Pounding on the door, she screamed and begged someone to let her out, let her see Paisley. The muffled voices grew dimmer until silence replaced them. Cherri pounded the door until her red hands began to bleed, screaming until she was hoarse.

Still, no one answered her pleas.

CHAPTER TWENTY-SEVEN

"SIR, I'M SORRY, but you can't go in there. Sir, do you have an appointment with Councilman McFahey? Sir?" The forty-something assistant leaped from her chair, trying to keep up with Jax's long strides. Before she could reach him, Jax kicked the door open to the councilman's office.

McFahey, eyes wide and hand going to the phone, sat behind his large desk.

"Don't even fuckin' think of picking up the phone or I'll break all your goddamn fingers," Jax snarled as he slammed the door shut.

Moving his hand away, McFahey eyed Jax and said, "What do you mean barging in here and throwing your weight around? I'm going to be talking to Banger about this—you can count on that."

Standing next to the councilman's desk, Jax pounded his fist on it. "Where the fuck is Cherri, you piece of shit?"

McFahey licked his lips, his eyes darting around the room. "Who?"

Taking a few steps closer to him, Jax hissed, "You know who she is. Don't fuck around with me. Tell me where the fuck Cherri is, or I'll make sure you regret the day you ever came to Pinewood Springs."

"Now, there's no need for threats or violence. So, your friend is missing? I can see if the cops can find—"

In one swift move, Jax had McFahey up on his feet, his shirt's neck bunched in Jax's steel fist. Leaning his face level with and close to the councilman's, Jax said, "Let's do this again. Where in the fuck is Cherri?"

White-faced, he struggled to swallow. Pointing to his throat, he croaked out a raspy, "I don't know."

Throwing the asshole back in his swivel chair, Jax sat on the desk and placed his steel-toed boot between McFahey's legs. Coughing, the councilman grabbed a crystal glass on his desk and gulped some water. After he set the glass down on the desk, he narrowed his eyes. "I don't know where she is. I haven't seen her since the bachelor party at Dream House."

"Fuckin' liar! I know you had lunch with her, and I also know you snatched her early this morning. I'm giving you a chance to tell me or I'll beat the shit outta you, you crooked motherfucker."

"I told you, I don't know where she is. I also don't appreciate you getting in my face. You know, you work for me. The Insurgents are on *my* payroll, and you are out of line."

"I don't work for any one, and I don't take shit from no kind of man like you. For the last time, where the fuck is Cherri?"

Shrugging, he cried out when the force of Jax's fist crunched against his jaw. McFahey stood up in a feeble attempt to confront Jax, but he fell back in his chair, the wind knocked out of him from Jax's punch to his stomach. Dragging him up on his feet, Jax slammed him against the wall then pushed his full weight in McFahey's chest. "I know you're the fuck involved. I'll find Cherri, and if you touched her in any way, your fuckin' crooked ass is dead. Got it?"

Struggling to catch his breath, the councilman nodded, his eyes bulging. Before Jax could give him a final punch, the door flew open and Peaches walked in. With her mouth flying open, she shuffled back a couple of steps. Jax's eyes bored into her as his posture stiffened, and a sudden coldness ran up his spine.

"What the fuck are you doing here?" Jax's voice dripped ice.

Stammering, Peaches, eyes downward, said, "I... uh... I just came by, you know?"

Tightening his jaw, Jax pursed his lips, his eyes never leaving hers.

Wringing her hands, Peaches backed up further, trying to reach the semi-closed door.

"Why the fuck are you tryin' to leave? Are you fuckin' this scumbag?"

As she nodded, Jax laughed dryly. "It fits, the two of you. You deserve each other." Pulling McFahey away from the wall then slamming him back in it, Jax growled, "For your sake, you better have clean hands in this, 'cause I'm not the forgiving or understanding type." Spinning around, he left without looking back.

When he got outside, Jax's hands jerked as he grabbed hold of his bike's handlebars. Spittle built up in the corners of his mouth as guttural roars shook him. Staring straight ahead, he peeled away from the parking space, his ears pounding and his blood pumping. If it was the last thing he did, he'd make sure McFahey paid for whatever involvement he had in Cherri's disappearance. The first thing he needed to do was to remain calm, even though every nerve and muscle in his body wanted to beat the shit out of McFahey then kill him. Deciding to go to Dream House to see if Emma knew anything, Jax turned his bike in that direction.

When he walked into Dream House, he had calmed down a bit, but his blood still pumped and his muscles were as tight as a virgin's pussy. Spotting Emma and Holt talking, Jax went up to them.

"Hey, what's wrong? You look like shit," Emma said.

"That's about how I'm feeling," Jax replied.

"Too much partying?" A smile crossed her lips. "You know, Cherri didn't show up for her shift. I'm a little worried about her because she's not like that. You know, she's super reliable. I was gonna take a quick drive to her place to make sure she's okay. You wanna do that for me?"

"Cherri and her daughter have been kidnapped, and I'm trying like hell to figure out where they are."

Going pale, her hand over her mouth, Emma asked, "Are you sure?"

Jax nodded, then ran his hand through his hair. "Do you have any idea where she may be?"

"Me? No. Why would someone do that to her? I didn't even know she had a daughter."

"Yeah, she has a little one. I gotta find them both. Fuck, I feel so useless. Each minute I don't find her is another minute wasted. Fuck!" He pounded his fist on the bar.

"I know. You gotta find her. Maybe Chas can help you. He just walked in." Emma nodded her chin in the direction of the front entrance.

Jax turned around and noticed Chas, grim-faced, walking toward him. Jax nodded to him when Chas came next to him. "Hey," Jax said.

"Hey. I need to talk to you."

"Okay, shoot," Jax said.

"Let's go in the office for privacy."

Jax, restless to leave to find Cherri, followed Chas into the back office and said, "What's going on? I've got a situation here, so I don't have much time."

Sighing deeply, Chas replied, "Insurgents know Cherri stole money from Dream House, and we know you're covering for her."

Shaking his head, Jax said in a low voice, "Fuck."

"Hawk came in early to go over the books. He's been doing that ever since one of the Deadly Demons Nomads' old ladies skimmed from the club last year. Anyway, he had the ledger and saw a discrepancy between what was brought in and what was in the safe. He said an extra four thousand dollars was in it. Knowing only three people had access to the safe, it wasn't hard for him to deduce Cherri was missing along with the money. He figured you found out and tried to cover for her, but you put in too much money. Axe saw you earlier this morning rush into the clubhouse and come back out with a money pouch. Fuck, dude. Why the hell didn't you go to the club before you covered for the bitch?"

Looking Chas in the eyes, Jax said, "I thought I could get to her before the club found out about it. She's in some serious trouble. I'm trying to find her and her daughter. I'm sure that pig, McFahey, kidnapped them, and I gotta find out where she is. I'll sort everything else out later. I gotta go, man."

"Sorry, brother, but you gotta come with me. Banger sent me over to drag your ass to the clubhouse for an emergency church. If you know what's good for you, you better come."

"Fuck." Jax pressed his lips together in a slight grimace as he tapped his index finger against his mouth. A heaviness in his body made him wish he could leave and go somewhere quiet to think. He had to find his woman, but he owed his club his loyalty. *Fuck!*

"Let's go," said Chas with determination as he walked toward the office door.

Jax, hesitating, forced himself to follow Chas. "Let's go," Jax replied.

BANGER GLARED AT Jax as the members filed into the meeting room. Jax stared back with defiance until Hawk walked in. Nodding curtly at Jax, Hawk took his seat next to Banger. From his scowling frown and his clenched jaw, Jax knew Hawk was pissed at him. Exchanging looks with Hawk made Jax's breath hitch; instead of anger in his face, Hawk's mouth turned downward and his eyes were bright with pain. Hawk's disappointment in him was the hardest thing for Jax to take. He broke eye contact with Hawk.

The gavel pounding on the table made Jax jump out of his seat. Looking up, he met Banger's cold, bitter stare. Without any preamble, Banger asked Jax, "Did you put twenty thousand dollars in the safe at Dream House this morning?"

"Yeah, I did." Jax heard curses and hisses wrap around the meeting room as the brothers demonstrated their anger and disappointment in Jax's betrayal. "I know what I did was wrong, but I wanted to find Cherri first and let her explain to me what the fuck was going on. She's been a good assistant manager, reliable and all that, so for her to do what she did was out of character, and I wanted her to tell me why."

"Wasn't your first loyalty to the brotherhood and not to some bitch you're fuckin'?"

Jax winced at Banger's words—he knew they were true. His first loyalty was always the club, and he betrayed them all in hiding Cherri's theft.

"Isn't it?" Banger boomed.

"Yeah. I fucked up. I own up to it, but just so everyone knows, Cherri isn't just some bitch. She's my woman."

"Don't matter if she's your old lady. The brotherhood always comes first. You know that, man," said Throttle, one of the older members.

"You choosing a woman over the brothers makes you a mother-fuckin' traitor!" Banger yelled.

Silence descended over the room as all eyes were on Jax. He stood up, faced all the members, and said, "I know I let the club down. I put my feelings for Cherri before my loyalty and oath to the brotherhood, and I'm sorry for that. I won't make excuses. I'll own up to it and take whatever punishment you deem necessary for my transgression. But I gotta go, 'cause Cherri and her small daughter are missing. I gotta find 'em, and I hope you all get that. I'm positive McFahey's involved in the abduction, and I'm afraid he's gonna hurt the baby and do worse to my woman. You've all known me since I was a kid, hangin' 'round here when my dad was patched. What I did was wrong, but I'm asking for some time to find my woman, and then I'll come back and we can finish all this up. If you don't do it for me, do it for my dad, who was loyal to the brotherhood until his death." Jax sat down, crossed his arms, and waited for their decision.

Clearing his voice, Banger stood up and said, "Let's put it to the floor. Who votes Jax can go help his woman first before taking the consequences for his betrayal?"

As all the brothers mumbled and shouted their "Ayes," warmth spread through Jax. His club, his family always had his back; even after he betrayed them, they stood behind him. Regretting he hadn't gone to them in the first place, Jax vowed never to forsake the brotherhood again.

"Go help your woman and her kid. This can wait. If McFahey is involved in this shit, he's gotta pay," Banger said.

"Thanks, brothers." Jax nodded his chin at them. Looking at Chas and Axe, he asked, "Do you wanna help me?"

"Let's go," they said.

The three men left the meeting room on a quest to find Cherri and to safely bring her and her daughter back home.

CHAPTER TWENTY-EIGHT

O PENING THE DOORS of the Dream House, Jax perused the room for Peaches. Until he saw her with McFahey, he had no idea she even knew him let alone was involved with him. The way Peaches acted when she saw Jax in McFahey's office convinced him she was not just fuckin' the councilman, but was probably in deeper. He had no doubt Peaches knew where Cherri was, and he suspected half the shit she spewed to him about Cherri and McFahey was a bunch of lies.

Peaches was crazy in love with him, and that was what made her dangerous. He figured she'd do shit to get him back, but he never imagined she'd set off a chain of events that would hurt an innocent baby. She was some piece of work. Jax needed to find out if his suspicions were true and whether the bitch knew where his woman was.

Filling in Chas and Axe about what was up with Peaches, the two men scowled and Axe told Jax, "If the bitch is involved in this shit with Cherri's disappearance, we'll take care of her." Chas nodded in agreement.

The three men sauntered up to the bar and leaned against it. Holt promptly placed three bottles of Coors in front of them. Taking a long draw, Jax asked, "Is Peaches here?"

"Yeah, saw her go in the back a few minutes ago," Holt answered.

Turning toward Chas and Axe, Jax said, "I'm going in back. I'll meet you guys at Willow's shack in a few. Get PJ and Jerry; they like this kind of shit." Smiling cruelly, Jax brought his beer bottle to his lips and drained it. Throwing a curt nod to Holt, Jax walked toward the back of the strip bar.

When he went behind the curtains, he saw Peaches bent over, her ass on display, going through a box of props. Fighting the urge to kick her in the ass, Jax said softly, "Hey, Peaches, what's up?"

Whirling around, Peaches flashed a huge smile, her eyes sparkling. "Hi, Jax. I didn't think you'd be here. I'm just trying to find something different for my act." She paused before she approached him and put her hands on his chest. "You know, I really don't have anything with McFahey. He's been helping me out financially because I've been strapped for money. I borrowed some from him and went over there to make a payment. I'm not fucking him; I just said that 'cause he likes me to."

"Baby, I don't give a shit if you're fucking him or not. I came back to see if you wanna go for a ride on my bike, but I see you're busy."

"No, I'm not. Oh, Jax, I'd love to go for a ride. I love being your back warmer. Let me grab my sunglasses."

After Peaches came out of the dressing room, she and Jax went out back to the parking lot. Jax's Harley sat gleaming in the sun, and Peaches grasped Jax's arm and cooed, "I love spending time with you. I've missed you. Missed me?"

"Uh-huh," Jax breathed.

Settling her ass behind Jax, she wrapped her arms around his waist. Anger rose in him as she leaned her head against his shoulder. Pulling the choke, he turned the ignition and felt the Harley come alive under him. With a loud roar, the bike took off down the street, and Jax saw the road scurry beneath him as he rode toward Willow's shack.

When they arrived at their destination, Peaches jumped off the back and stretched her legs. The faint breeze rustled the gold and orange leaves of the surrounding trees as Jax killed the engine and walked toward the shack. Inside, it looked as though it hadn't been used in decades. Rotting floorboards and dusty furniture decorated the abode. The shack had been abandoned a long time back after the gold vein in the nearby mine had dried up. After that, the crumbling place was the only testament to the miners who worked to find their wealth.

As Jax placed his gloves on a nearby dusty table, Peaches circled her arms around him, kissing him on the neck. "We could've just gone to my place, honey. It'd be a lot cleaner." She smiled at him.

As he watched her, she giggled, drew back from him, and began to take off her red top. "I can't wait to fuck you, honey. It's been too long."

"Where the fuck is Cherri, bitch?" Jax asked in a dangerously calm voice.

With her top halfway up and her red lace bra showing, she stared incredulously at Jax. "What?"

"I *said*, where the fuck is Cherri, *bitch*?"

Around the darkened corners of the room, several shadows emerged. Four Insurgents stared at her, smirking.

"What the fuck is this?" she asked, her voice laced with panic.

"You fucked with me. You told me a bunch of lies about Cherri. You're a spiteful cunt. Tell me where my woman is. Now."

"I… I don't know what you're talkin' about, Jax. I thought we were gonna have a little fun. What is this shit? I don't know anything about Cherri." Peaches pulled her top down and backed up toward the entrance.

Taking two steps toward her, Jax grabbed Peaches by the shoulders, slamming her against the worn wood walls. They groaned as Peaches hit them full-force, a whoosh of breath escaping from her upon impact. Placing his hands around her damp neck, Jax yelled, "You gonna tell me where she is, or are you gonna die? I have no fuckin' problem squeezing the life outta your skank-ass body. You bitch! You been causing all kinds of trouble, spewing your shit."

"Please, Jax. Please stop," she rasped as she clawed at his hands.

"I'm not stoppin' shit 'til you tell me where my woman is. Cherri and her daughter are in trouble 'cause of you. You jealous slut!"

Peaches tried to push him away, but his hands were like a vise around her throat. Thrashing around, her nails scratched his chest as she struggled for breath. Chas jumped in, hands on Jax's arms, saying, "Looks like she wants to cooperate."

Jax reluctantly let go and Peaches bowled over, sucking air in and out of her lungs as she coughed.

"Where is she?" Jax approached her.

Plastering herself flat against the wall, she said hoarsely, "At the old Thompson house in the basement."

"How many are there watching her?"

Rubbing her neck, she said, "Last time I was there, a couple guys were. McFahey comes and goes."

"Is the baby there, too?"

"No, she's with McFahey's lawyer. He arranged a private adoption. Couple paid big money for the little monster."

"Who's the attorney?"

She shrugged, glaring at him. Jax pulled her close to him and snarled, "I have no fuckin' problem twisting your neck until it snaps. Tell me the name. Now."

She swallowed. The glints of rage in his eyes and the soreness around her neck told her and everyone in the room he'd make good on his threat. "Phil, or Bill… something like that. I think his last name is Coyne."

"Call Cara and get the address for this shyster's office," Jax said to Jerry then turned back to Peaches. "Did Cherri agree to go back to McFahey, or was that a lie?"

Eyes lowered, she whispered, "I had to get you back. I figured if you knew she was McFahey's whore, you'd be finished with her. I love you."

"You spiteful bitch! You better hope I find her and her daughter in time; otherwise, you'll be pushing up wildflowers in the woods around here."

Jerking his head at PJ and Axe, Jax walked toward the door. As Peaches started to follow him, Jerry grabbed her arm, dragging her back. "You're not going anywhere, bitch."

With trembling lips and chin, Peaches pleaded, "Jax, don't leave me here."

Turning around, Jax saw the sweat glistening on her forehead, and he chuckled. *She's scared. Now the bitch knows how Cherri feels.* "Problem is, you messed with Insurgents' property. You gotta be taught respect."

"Jax, don't leave me here!" she screamed as PJ and Jerry closed in tighter around her.

Laughing, Jax walked out with Chas and Axe behind him. Peaches' screams were drowned out by the roar of the Harleys as they blasted away from the old shack.

CHAPTER TWENTY-NINE

TRAPPED IN THE small room, Cherri didn't know if it was day or night or how long she'd been there. She'd lost all track of time. Grateful no one had come in since McFahey left, Cherri kept trying the door in the off-chance it was unlocked. No such luck. It seemed like hours had passed since her confrontation with McFahey. What the fuck was going on? Why did McFahey want her so badly? She found it hard to believe he couldn't find another woman who would gladly scratch his itch. Was he punishing her because she lied about the abortion? In all the time she had Paisley, she never attempted to contact him. He must've known she wanted to forget her life with him and forge her own life with her daughter.

Thinking of Paisley made her heart ache and the blood rush to her head. Sweet, innocent Paisley was the pawn in the councilman's sick game of revenge. Having her baby was the best thing she'd ever done in her life. Loving her daughter more than her own life, she pulled at her hair while slamming her fists down on the lumpy mattress. All she ever wanted to give her baby was a good, safe life. Cherri had been terrified living with her stepfather, and she swore she'd make sure Paisley never felt that way. Screaming aloud from the depths of her throat, her shrieks bounced off the walls of the barren room. She failed her daughter—she didn't keep her safe.

Not knowing where Paisley was had her stomach in tangles and knots. A couple of days before, she thought she had a chance of a happy life in Pinewood Springs. With Jax in her life, Paisley close to her, and her savings growing, she dared to feel hopeful and happy. But then shit hit the fan, just like it always did.

Wishing she could slip back in time, she knew she'd be honest with Jax about McFahey. The reason she held her life with the councilman secret was because she was afraid for her baby, but none of it mattered because, in the end, she couldn't keep Paisley safe. She'd kept all those secrets for nothing. *Oh, Paisey, where are you? Your mama loves you so much.* Rocking back and forth on the bed, Cherri tugged at her hair, moaning. She missed having Paisley in her arms, and she missed being in Jax's arms. Being with him was the only time in her young life when she felt safe. It was the only time she trusted a man with her thoughts, ideas, fears, and sexuality. When she was with Jax, she knew he had her back. Being so protective of Paisley, Cherri never brought her around men, but the day Jax spent with her and her daughter showed her his soft, caring side. She wanted to try a life with him and Paisley, but fate stepped in and crushed the fantasy.

A gurgling, gnawing pain stabbed against her, making her realize she hadn't eaten since the previous morning. Crossing her arms around her stomach, she squeezed it as if to stop the hunger pangs. Lowering her head, she continued to rock back and forth on the mattress.

Click. Cherri's head jerked up and whipped toward the door as the knob slowly turned. Holding her breath, she wrapped her arms tightly around her knees and brought them closer to her chest, as if to make herself appear smaller. With her chest tingling, she darted her eyes around the room in search of a place to hide. Finding nothing in the sparsely furnished room, she buried her face in her knees.

The door swung open and McFahey, in navy blue trousers and a mint green Polo shirt, came in, his cologne wafting around the room.

"Miss me, honey?" he said smoothly.

"Where's Paisley?" she croaked as she lifted her head up.

"She's doing fine, honey. Don't worry. I'm not going to hurt our little girl. She looks just like her beautiful mama."

"I don't believe you. I heard you. You were saying something about a couple and adoption. If you give away my baby, I'll kill you. I'll fuckin' kill you." Jumping off the bed, she rushed toward a surprised McFahey and punched him in the chest.

"Fuck, what's the matter with you, bitch?" he threw her back and, losing her balance, she fell on the bed. "Don't try that shit anymore or you'll never see your brat again."

"Why're you doing this? I've never caused you any problems."

"I don't like loose ends. Having the brat around and knowing how you love money doesn't make for a good combination. I don't need the threat of blackmail looming over me, especially since I've got my sights on bigger political platforms."

"I'd never blackmail you. Fuck, I never even looked you up. I wanted to disappear, so give me Paisley and I'll go. Please, give me my daughter." Her voice broke and her eyes glistened under the overhead light.

McFahey skimmed his eyes over her face, his head shaking. "I can't take a chance. You've lied to me before."

"I only lied because I wanted my baby. I didn't lie to hurt you or blackmail you. Don't you know me?"

"I thought I did, but Peaches said she overheard you say you wanted to blackmail me. And you *did* run out on me in Denver."

"Peaches? What the fuck does she know about any of this? She's a jealous bitch because she wanted Jax and he dumped her for me. She's getting back at me. I just want Paisley, and I promise I'll go far away and you'll never hear from me again. Please." Wringing her hands, her blue eyes pleaded with his hard ones.

"What the fuck do you bitches see in that asshole Jax, anyway? He came to my office, acting all macho and shit. I punched him out and sent him packing." McFahey puffed up his chest.

Yeah, I bet you did, you fuckin' asshole. More like Jax beat your puny ass. "Really? Wow."

"That's right. I showed him not to fool around with me. I may not be as tall or buff as him, but I can deliver a killer punch, if needed." Smiling, he smoothed his hair back and pulled up his slacks.

"Why did he come to your office?" Cherri wanted to engage him in conversation. If she could keep him talking, maybe he'd get more comfortable with her like he used to, and then he'd let his guard down. Then she would try and escape. She had to try—any attempt was better than nothing.

"He came looking for you. Man, he's got it bad for you. I can see why he's hooked. You're a good fuck, honey. I could never get enough of you, and when you left me, I was so lonely for you."

No, I don't want to steer the conversation toward sex. No. No. No. "I was surprised to see you in Pinewood Springs, you know?"

"No shit. I was surprised to see you, too. What do you have with Jax?"

"Nothing. He's just my boss. You know, I work for the Insurgents."

"Bullshit. A boss isn't going to give a shit about an employee like he does about you. I know you're his whore."

"We've gone out a few times. No big deal."

"He better stay out of my face. I didn't like his possessive attitude about you. Next time, I won't be so nice. Next time, I'll lay him out flat." He flexed his flaccid biceps.

Biting her tongue, Cherri nodded then eased off the bed, inching her way toward the door.

"Those bikers are all dumbasses. They think they're hot shit because they ride Harleys and wear leather, but they're nothing. You been slumming long enough, honey. I'm back now, so you don't need to be a biker whore." Stretching out his arm, he caught Cherri by her waist and yanked her back to him.

Squealing, she scratched at his arm, but he tightened his hold on her until she had trouble breathing. "Stop. Let me go. Please."

"Trying to get away from me again? Not going to work this time. I'm wise to you."

"I'm warning you, the Insurgents don't like anyone messin' with their property. They'll kill you."

Laughing, he leaned in, nuzzling his face in her hair. "Honey, I don't give a damn about the Insurgents. They can go to Hell, for all I care."

"Can't we be normal and go back to the way we used to be?" Cherri asked.

"I'd like that a lot, but the problem is I don't trust you one iota, honey." Kissing her on the forehead, McFahey backed her up until her knees bumped into the bed. Shoving her down, she fell on top of the mattress.

With a racing heart and clammy hands, Cherri stared into McFahey's lust-filled eyes. Whimpering, she scooted away until her back was flat against the wooden headboard.

"It's time for you to give me something real special, honey. If you're very good, I'll let you see your brat." Grabbing her hand in his, he placed it on his crotch. "See what you do to me. Fuck, I'm rock-hard. You're the only one who can get me this hard." He unbuckled his belt and unzipped his pants. His penis sprang out.

Cherri, white-faced and trembling, pulled her hand away then curled up in a ball.

"Come on, honey. You know you love it as much as I do. You know how to turn a man on. Come on; be a good girl and come to me."

Flinching at his touch, Cherri recoiled from him. Her skin prickled like a thousand crawling ants were on it, and she wanted to flee. As he came closer, Cherri gritted her teeth and with all her strength, she rammed her body into McFahey, toppling him over. As she jumped off the bed and ran, he grasped her hair, pulling it back toward him. With arms flailing and screaming in pain, Cherri twisted away from him and darted for the door.

"Fez, get in here!" McFahey yelled.

In an instant, a six-foot-five hulk with about two hundred and sixty pounds on him came barreling in.

"Grab the bitch and cuff her to the bed. I'm tired of her shit."

Grunting, the thug scooped Cherri up as if she were a feather, slammed her down on the bed with a resounding thump, and cuffed her arms and legs to each bed post, stretching her out spread-eagle. After he completed his task, he left as suddenly as he entered. With beads of perspiration dotting his brow, McFahey stroked his penis while he leered at Cherri. Even though she was fully dressed, Cherri's cheeks burned and she dropped her chin to her chest as a thickness formed in her throat. Closing her eyes, she willed herself to find her safe place—her meadow with the colorful wildflowers.

"Open your eyes," he demanded.

With eyelids fluttering open, tears trickled down her face. Baring his teeth under curled, thin lips, he squeezed her breasts, pinching her nipples roughly. Cherri cringed. As he pulled her top up, he tugged one of her breasts out of her bra. Shoving her nipple in his mouth, he sucked loud and hard. Closing her eyes again, Cherri focused on the meadow, the sunshine, the babbling creek off to—

His thick tongue forcing entrance in her mouth brought her back to the small, windowless room. *No! No!* Biting down hard on his tongue, she tasted the coppery tang of his blood in her mouth.

Jerking his head back, red drops falling on her white skin, he yelled, "Fuck! You bitch!" The sting across her face made dark spots appear in front of her eyes. "You fucking need to learn how to treat your man." Pulling down her jeans, he put his hand inside her lace panties and rubbed between her dry folds. The friction made her squirm as she tried to get him to stop hurting and touching her.

With his length in his hand, he put his weight on top of her.

"No! No! Don't. Stop it, you fuckin' pig!" Cherri screamed out while she twisted and turned against her restraints.

"Shut the fuck up. I'm just getting started. And honey, you know how I like it when you resist me. You're making me so horny." McFahey placed his penis near her entrance.

The door swung open and Cherri's body exploded with nerves. *The thug's come back. He's gonna rape me, too. I have to go away. I have to get away.* As a sheen of sweat broke out on her cheeks and forehead, the hair on the nape of her neck stiffened. Gritting her teeth and closing her eyes, she repeated, "I'm in my safe haven. I'm in the meadow with the beautiful flowers—"

Heaviness lifted from her stomach and chest as she heard a yelp then a deafening pop. She kept her eyes squeezed shut. *I am someplace else, in a lush meadow next to a clear, running brook. The sun is warm on my skin.* Deep, almost guttural whispers pricked her ears. *Wildflowers are all around me, and the breeze on my skin is cool as I lie on my back looking at the clouds in the blue sky.* All she heard was snorting and thrashing, then scraping as if something heavy were being dragged across the concrete floor. Pressing her eyes tighter, she forced herself to concentrate on her safe haven, her lush meadow with chirping birds.

The mattress sank a bit next to her. *Oh, my God. Someone is next to me. Fuck, why can't I stay in my meadow? I can't be here. I have to be there. I have to feel the sun on my skin, I have to get away. I have to—*

Large hands uncuffed her wrists and her ankles. A soft hand caressed her face as gentle lips kissed her bruised cheek. She sniffed, and instead of smelling wildflowers, she smelled earth, musk and motor oil. Lips brushing against her ear caused her skin to dimple.

Strong arms raised her up and she crashed into a wall of muscle. The smell and touch were so familiar. "Everything's all right, sweetness," a low, deep voice said.

As her heart leaped against her chest, her eyes flew open, wet streams marking her face. Greeting her were Jax's eyes, shining with love and tenderness. Sitting up, she moved her mouth over his and kissed him slow and deep then buried her face in his hard chest. With his arms wrapped around her, she felt safe and protected.

"How did you find me?" she asked in a low voice.

"It's a long story for another time. You okay? Did the fucker rape you?"

Shivering, Cherri said, "I'm okay now." Lowering her voice, she breathed in Jax's ear, "All bad things have been erased. From now on, I have a clean slate. Do you believe it?"

Tilting her chin up and running his thumb across her lip, he said, "I believe, sweet one." Brushing his lips across hers, he stroked her hair.

After kissing him, Cherri pulled away and said in a tear-filled voice,

"I don't know what he did with my baby. I think he gave her away to a couple. Please find Paisley. Please." A sob escaped from her throat.

"Sweet one, I've taken care of it. Your little one is safe. Paisley is at your home, waiting for you."

Gasping, her fingers touched her parted lips. "She's okay? Are you sure my baby's safe?"

Smiling, his eyes twinkling, he hugged her close. "Yeah, she's safe and she's waiting for you. Fuck, woman, you're the sweetest babe I've ever met."

Pulling away a bit, a flushed, beaming face stared at Jax before she kissed him hard on his delicious mouth. Warmth radiated throughout her body as she suddenly felt ultra-awake, like she was rejuvenated by adrenaline. "Thank you. Thank you. Thank you." She peppered his face with light, small kisses.

"You never have to thank me, Cherri. Come on; let's go home. You got someone waitin' for you." Jax helped her to her feet.

As Cherri left with Jax, she noticed red tracks across the concrete floor. Looking up at him with a quizzical look, he nodded, and the silent tale of McFahey's fall from grace was understood. They walked outside into the night. Above, the moon lingered in the sky like a shimmering white disc while the stars glittered like scattered space dust.

When they approached Jax's Harley, the chrome gleaming in the moonlight, Cherri turned to Jax and said, "Paisley and I owe you our lives." Tears welled in her eyes. "I did something I'm not proud of, something I've never done before. I stole money from Dream House, from the Insurgents. I was so scared and didn't know what to do. I was desperate and had to leave town. I wasn't thinking. I should've trusted you enough to let you know what was going on with me. But I didn't, and I stole the money. Even though I had every intention of paying it back, what I did was wrong, and I take full responsibility. I want to tell the MC what I did." Watching Jax's face for a reaction, she shivered.

Nodding, Jax drew her close to him. "You don't owe me shit. I don't want your life, sweetness; I want your love. I know about the money, and I took care of it. Let's not think about it now. You got a little one waiting for you. From now on, everything's gonna be good 'cause I'm always here to take care of you and Paisley." Bending down, his lips caught hers. "Let's go home," he said against her mouth.

Tucked behind Jax, Cherri looped her arms around his waist and placed her head on his shoulder. A fuzzy feeling colored her insides, and she knew she was where she was supposed to be. Smiling, she closed her eyes as the wind whipped her hair about her face.

CHAPTER THIRTY

CHERRI RUSHED UP the steps, two at a time, and burst through the front door. On the living room couch, Cara sat with Paisley, who was dressed in blue denim overalls and a red checkered shirt underneath. Her blonde hair held a blue and red bow, which practically covered half of her head. Paisley turned toward the noise and when she saw Cherri, her cornflower blue eyes lit up like a Christmas light, and her chubby arms and legs jerked and curled in excitement.

Crying, Cherri ran over and swooped her baby girl up from Cara's arms. Covering her plump cheeks with kisses, Cherri pressed Paisley close to her. The little girl chortled while grabbing her mother's hair in her tiny fists.

"I love you so much. Mama's with you, and you're safe," she whispered in her daughter's ear.

Jax wrapped his arms around Cherri and Paisley, holding them close to him. "I'm with you, and you're both safe," he breathed into Cherri's ear, his hot breath stroking her. For several minutes, they held each other, basking in the comfort and joy of being together again.

Paisley's pink mouth opened wide as she yawned then rubbed her eyes. Smiling, Cherri broke away from Jax, sat on the couch, and cradled Paisley in her arms. After fifteen minutes, Paisley was fast asleep.

"Why don't you let me hold her so you two can have some private time?" Cara asked.

Looking at Jax, Cherri saw arousal burn in his eyes. Nodding, she handed her daughter over to Cara, laced her fingers around Jax's, and headed upstairs.

When they entered her room, Jax tugged her in him with one hand

and caressed her hair with the other. Bowing his head, he burrowed his face in her hair. "Sweetie? Are you gonna be okay if I touch you?"

Nodding, she whispered, "Thanks for asking me. I want you to touch me. I want to erase the shit from the last day." Staring intently at Jax, she said, "I want you. Very badly."

Pressing her tighter to him, he rasped, "I want you, too. Fuck, I *need* you."

Lightly breaking away from his embrace, she said, "Let me take a quick shower. Make yourself comfortable. I'll be out in five."

After she finished her shower, she came into the room and gasped. A warm, yellow glow enveloped the room as all the candles she possessed flickered and danced, casting shadows on the walls. Jax lay on the bed, the pillows propped up, his sculpted body on full display. Her eyes ran over him, and shivers of desire coursed through her as she viewed his hard pecs, his steel stomach with the perfect V, his sexy biceps, and his thick, rigid dick. Sucking in her breath, she dropped the towel she had been using to dry her hair and walked toward him.

On her way over to him, she let the bath towel wrapped around her fall to the floor. Naked, she lay on top of him, gyrating her pelvis against his hard length, his breath hissing through his teeth as his hands slid down her back to grip her ass. Securing one of her firm globes in his hand, he kneaded it as he captured her mouth in his. She parted her lips gladly, allowing his tongue to delve into her minty lusciousness.

With her hands all over his skin, he released her mouth, allowing her to kiss her way along his jaw and down his neck until she landed on his nipple. Flicking her tongue across it, he moaned from deep in his throat, his hand squeezing her ass tightly. Propping herself up a bit, she rubbed her tits against his chest as she dipped her head and sucked his nipple noisily.

"Fuck that feels good, sweetness. You smell fresh, and your skin is so fuckin' soft. It feels like velvet against me. Love it."

"Mmm, I love the way you taste," she said between sucks.

Grabbing a fist of hair, he pulled her head back, forcing her shining blue eyes to look into his heated ones. "I can't wait to fill you up with my cock, but first I want to taste and lick your sweet, juicy pussy."

A thrill jolted her down to her core when he licked her lip then gently bit it. "Are you gonna do dirty things to me?" she said breathlessly.

"Hell, yeah. My tongue is gonna be nasty and dirty, and you'll be beggin' for more, sweet one."

Her tightening pussy lurched as his hand slid down between her legs, his fingers lightly pinching her nub. Arching her back, she ground her mound closer to his probing fingers.

A deep laugh rumbled from his chest. "You like that, sugar?"

"Oh, yeah."

Circling his arm around her waist, he flipped her over onto her back and spread her thighs wide. With his eyes lingering on her glistening mound, he groaned then, with one finger, he touched her wet, swollen pussy. Desperate whimpers escaped her when he stroked her slickness over and over. Writhing beneath him, Cherri called out in a ragged breath, "Jax, yes. That feels so good. Yes!"

Locking his gaze with hers, his long tongue dived in her folds, using smooth, steady, and slow rhythmic licks. "Fuck, I can't get enough of your taste." he said, pulling away for a moment, his chin shining with her wetness. "I could lick you up all night, sweetness. Love your fuckin' taste."

As he tapped his tongue on her clit, wild moans burst from her, and as she bucked under him, she dug her nails into his shoulders. Just as she was ready to explode, he slowly inserted two fingers in her, making her insides instantly clench around them. As he thrust deeper in her, he raised himself on his knees and roughly seized her mouth, his tongue mimicking the movements of his fingers in her pussy. Clasping his tongue with her mouth, Cherri sucked its hotness, relishing in the feeling of total surrender.

Taking his big cock in his hand, he ran it up and down her slit, coating it with her hot wetness. Pulling his tongue away from her mouth, he trailed it down her neck, past her collar bone, and between her breasts. Catching her look, he took his drenched dick and pressed it against her entrance. A strangled cry escaped from her throat as he slowly sank all the way in, her walls relaxing to accommodate his girth. Her body tingled with the fullness of him, and he lowered his mouth on her pink nipple, his teeth softly biting it. Withdrawing his dick, he pushed it back in, his balls snug against the curve of her ass.

"Fuck, I could stay buried in your sweet heat forever." Jax's hoarse voice skimmed over her.

When he withdrew again, she wrapped her legs around his waist, drawing him closer to her. Watching each other's faces, Jax gripped Cherri's hips as he thrust deeper inside her, filling her core with a hot fullness. Bending down, he palmed her breast, his mouth hungrily sucking her nipple and causing threads of pleasure to weave throughout her body. Gasping, she raised her head. "Kiss me," she grunted.

Putting his lips on hers, they kissed deeply as he pushed in her wet pussy. "You're so beautiful," he said against her mouth.

As he sunk his cock deeper in her, she cried out while she pressed her hips up to meet his thrusts. Slipping his hand between them, his fingers played with her clit and tightness seized all of her muscles. Smiling, he slowly put his digits in his mouth and licked them, then brushed her lips with his tongue. Pulling back, he spread her legs further apart, and the anticipation of what was coming made sweat beads form on her forehead, along her hairline.

"Sweet and deep, or rough and fast? You choose, sweetie, 'cause as long as I'm snug in your pussy, I'm good."

Licking her lips, her insides ready to shatter, she said, "Rough and fast."

Throwing his boyish grin at her, he leaned back and grasped her legs, spreading them wide, then he slammed into her, taking her breath away. Her back arched on the deep thrust, and as he rammed into her over and over, their bodies fell into a fast, rough rhythm of clenching and releasing, filling and withdrawing.

"I need you harder, sweetie. Can you take it?" His voice was thick with need.

"Give it to me." Her need was rising and she wanted him pumping hard inside her, taking her to the edge so she could jump off into a wave of ecstasy.

Leaning in to her, her legs spreading wider, he trailed his fingers up and down her thighs, her stomach, and around her breasts. The tremors of anticipation possessed her and her body jerked, desperate for release. As he rubbed her clit, her cries of pleasure seemed to turn him on, and she could see his smoldering desire in his dark, hazel eyes. With a hard kiss to her lips, he leaned back, got on his knees and plunged his cock so fast and hard in her that it made her insides burn. Before she could catch her breath, he sank his hardness in her again. Whimpering, her heated sex gripped him each time he entered her. His deep growls told her he liked what she was doing.

"Fuck, you're so good. Damn, I can't get enough of your sexiness."

He leaned in more, grinding himself against her, pushing deeper until there was nowhere to go. The more he plunged, the more she clenched until he grabbed her hips and fucked her relentlessly, hard and fast. The slippery sound of his dick slamming in her drenched pussy was in unison with the slap of his balls against her ass.

Sweat formed on her hot, tingly skin, and her insides clenched his steely length tighter and tighter until spasms crept in, squeezing him even more. Hearing a deep groan and a "Fuck," Cherri closed her eyes as her insides shattered into a million pieces of pleasure, touching on all her nerves and emotions. Crying out, she sagged deeper in the mattress.

Jax, with a couple more thrusts, stiffened then, throwing his head back, groaned from deep down as his warm seed spilled inside her. Relaxing, he slumped on top of her, his head buried in the crook of her neck, her legs loosely wrapped around his waist. With ragged breath, he said, "Was it good?"

Trembling, she nodded as she said, "I felt totally in tune with you. It was amazing."

Rolling over, he chuckled as he snuggled her in his arm, guiding her head to his chest. "Sweetness, we're meant to be together. We've been through some shit, and we didn't trust each other like we should have, but that's all over. From now on, it's you, me, and Paisley. Any problem with that?"

After a long pause, she kissed his chest, looked up and held his gaze. "No problem at all. It feels good to be home again."

"Fuck, yeah. Just remember to hold onto me. I can get you through whatever shit comes your way, and I can help you get through the shit from your past. We have each other, and that's what counts. Promise me you won't run away anymore. Promise me you'll tell me what's going on so we can deal with it together." He lowered his head and kissed her sweet and deep.

Smiling, Cherri whispered, "I promise. I will be with you until you tell me to leave."

Pushing the hair off her forehead, he said, "That long?"

They held each other as they drifted off to sleep.

AFTER AN HOUR, Cherri's growling stomach woke them up. Laughing, Jax placed his hand on her belly, massaged it lightly, and said, "Hungry?"

"Starving."

"I could go for some chow, too. It's too late to order anything, though."

Bolting up from bed, Cherri said, "I can make us something. I think I have eggs in the fridge. Let's go down and check." Naked, her butt danced as she hopped over to her suitcase and took out a terry robe and a pair of lace panties. Turning around, she spied Jax propped on one elbow, his eyes fixed on her, giving her a lazy smile.

"Come on; get your ass up. I'm so hungry," she said.

"Sweetness, I'm torn between eating and watching your fine ass move. You wear the tight robe real good. I'm getting fuckin' hard just lookin' at you. Come on over here." He held out his arm to her.

Shaking her head, she said, "Oh, no. I'm not going near you until I eat. If I come over there, we'll be another hour, at least."

"Just an hour?" he asked with raised eyebrows.

"Or more, stud. I need food—the kind you put in your stomach."

He got out of bed, bent down to get his jeans, and pulled them on. "You win, but after we eat, I'm keeping you up all night, sweetie." He swatted her ass as they walked out of the bedroom.

Coming down the stairs, Cherri saw Paisley sleeping in her cradle, her pink mouth forming a perfect "O," and Hawk and Cara necking on the couch. Clearing her voice to let them know she and Jax were there, Cherri walked over to Paisley. Bending over, she lightly ran her finger over her daughter's soft skin. She loved the way Paisley's skin felt like velvet and satin together. Each time she touched or looked at her daughter, her heart surged and thousands of happy jolts coursed throughout her body. Jax's arm around her waist, pulling her up a bit, reminded her she had come down in search of food.

"She's been sleeping like an angel for a couple of hours," Cara said.

"Thanks for watching her." Cherri smiled at her. She avoided Hawk's stare because he intimidated the hell out of her. He always had a scowl on his face except when he was with Cara. He looked intently at Cherri in that moment, almost like he was battling with a rage inside himself. Her ears pounded and her stomach lurched; what if he knew about her stealing the money?

"Sweetness, are you zoning out on me? Didn't you promise me some eggs?"

Glad to get away from Hawk and his brooding gaze, she went into the kitchen and opened the fridge. "Ah ha, there *are* eggs, and some ham, peppers, cheddar cheese, onions—fuck, we got a lot of good shit in here. Sit down. I make killer omelets."

"Cherri, we're going to take off," Cara said as she gathered her purse and sweater.

"You guys don't want an omelet?"

"No, thanks. We have to be on our way. I'm glad things worked out well for you."

Cherri went over to Cara and gave her a tight hug, whispering in her ear, "Thanks for saving my Paisley. I don't know what I would've done if I'd lost her. You don't know how grateful I am to you."

"No need to thank me. I'm glad you and your daughter are safe."

Jax came over and nodded to Cara. "Thanks for helping out my woman."

"You're welcome." Cara smiled.

Walking out the door, Hawk began to follow then turned to Jax, saying, "Be at the clubhouse tomorrow at noon. Things need to be decided." Pulling Jax toward him, Hawk gave him a hug then turned and followed Cara to his Harley.

Watching the couple kiss then mount Hawk's motorcycle, Cherri cocked her head sideways and asked, "What did Hawk mean about things have to be decided?"

Hawk's motorcycle roared when the ignition came on, shattering the quietness of the night. Making a U-turn, he and Cara rode off. Cherri closed the door. "You haven't answered me yet, Jax."

"Uh… it's no big deal."

"Hawk sounded kinda scary, like almost threatening. And he kept giving me the evil eye. What the fuck is going on? Tell me, and don't start that 'club business' shit, because I'm not gonna buy it."

Sighing loudly, Jax rubbed the side of his face. "The MC knows you took the money from Dream House. And—"

"Fuck. They know? I knew something was up by the way Hawk stared at me. He fuckin' hates me."

"No, he actually hates me more. *I* fucked up. I let the brothers down by covering for you. I replaced the money you took, but I didn't know how much you took, so I put back too much. One of the brothers saw me leave the clubhouse with the money. They're fuckin' pissed at me. That's cool, I get it, but what I hate the most is the looks of disappointment they keep givin' me, 'specially Hawk. Fuck, he's like my brother."

With a cracking voice and shimmering eyes, Cherri said in a low voice, "I caused you all kinds of trouble. What the fuck are you doing with me? I made you betray your club, your brothers. What's gonna happen? Are they gonna kick you out?"

Placing his arm around her small shoulder, he frowned. "I'll be honest, I don't fuckin' know. I hope they keep me in. I got some years with them, and my old man wore the patch since the club began. Fuck, that should count for something, you know? And don't put the blame on you. I fuckin' made the choice. I knew I shoulda gone to the club and told them what you did, but I made the choice to cover your ass. I gambled and lost. I owned up to it, and now I gotta take the consequences like a man."

"They're not gonna kill you, are they?"

Laughing, he pressed her head against him. "No, sweetness, they're not gonna kill me. Beat the shit outta me, probably, but not kill me. I'm not a fuckin' snitch."

"I'm scared. Are they gonna come after me? I mean, I'm the one who stole their money."

"Yeah, they usually would teach you a lesson, but since you're with me, you'll probably escape the Insurgents' wrath. Don't worry. It's gonna be okay. If they throw my ass out, I'll be feeling like total shit about it, but you know what? If I had to do it all over, I would still cover for you. You're in here, sweetness." With his thumb, he tapped on his heart, and tenderness misted his hazel eyes.

Looping her arm around his neck, Cherri lowered Jax's face toward hers and her mouth crashed against his. They kissed deeply. When Jax pulled back, he held her gaze, his eyes blazing with emotion. "Sweetness, I want you to be my old lady. I know you've had shit luck with men and you're afraid to love, but I fuckin' know you love me. I can tell by the way you kiss and fuck me."

Cherri, eyes brimming, buried her face in his neck. "I'll try and be what you want. I've never had a relationship with a man where I felt something other than disgust or friendship."

"I want you to be you. Fuck, woman, I'm willing to give us a chance.

I'll try like hell to be faithful to you. Cherri, I love you. I've never loved a woman before, so the whole damn thing is new for me. After tomorrow, when I find out where I stand with the Insurgents, we can get on with our lives. I wanna take care of you and Paisley. Fuck, I just love you, sweetie." Tilting her chin up, he bent down and captured her mouth, his tongue dancing with hers.

Tears rolled down her cheeks from the corner of her eyes. Cherri murmured, "I love you, Jax. I'm scared as hell because I've never loved a man before, but I wanna take a chance with you. All I know is when I'm with you, I feel protected, warm, and happy. I want this to work, for us and for Paisley."

Kissing her again, Jax held her so tightly she thought he'd squeeze all the air out of her, but she knew, deep in her soul, she had finally found what had been missing from her life. She finally got it right—the love of a good man. No more nightmares, no more cuts under her breast, no more worries. Her knight in leather, riding a Harley, had shown up for *her*, and she'd be damned if she was going to blow it.

Grinning at Jax, Cherri said, "You may change your mind after you taste my cooking. You know, I've never cooked for a man before."

"Sweetness, you could serve me horseshit, and I'd still love you. Now let me try one of your omelets so we can finish and I can show you how long I can fuck you." His eyes twinkled as a broad smile broke out over his face.

"One omelet, coming up." She swayed her hips as she walked into the kitchen. Picking up the frying pan, she turned on the burner then began cracking eggs, her panties damp from the thought of what was to come later in her bedroom with the love of her life.

CHAPTER THIRTY-ONE

J AX WALKED INTO the clubhouse a little bit before noon. Several of the brothers milled around, chugging beer and talking. Silence descended over the great room when Jax came in. Avoiding Jax's gaze, the brothers turned away, giving him the major chill. Grim-faced, Jax's stomach twisted in knots as he leaned against the bar and pretended he didn't give a damn. Ordering a Coors on tap, he gulped the cool, frothy beer while he checked out the room. Banger wasn't there, and neither was Hawk. Wanting to get this over with and go back to Cherri, he downed his Coors, wiped his mouth with the back of his hand, and went over to Chas.

"Hey, man, what gives?"

Chas worked his jaw a few seconds before answering. "Church is gonna start in a few."

From the corner of his eye, he saw brothers pointing at him and heard grumblings coming from voices he couldn't identify. "Fuck, never thought I'd see the day when a brother picks a bitch over the brother-hood," a brother in the corner said.

"Should kick his ass, take his colors, burn off his Insurgents tats, and kick his weak pussy ass out," another brother said.

"You feeling that way?" Jax asked Chas.

"Not sure how I'm feeling. Pretty pissed at how fucked up your decision was, but we go back a while, you know?" Chas stared straight ahead.

Blowing out a long breath, Jax said, "I know I fucked up. I'm here to take whatever it is you all throw at me, but bitchin' and talkin' shit about me isn't gonna change what happened." He looked around at the other brothers. They ignored his glances.

"Yeah, I know, but the brothers are fuckin' pissed at you and if your ass gets to stay in the club, it's gonna take a long time to gain back their trust. It's just the way it is." Chas finished his beer and placed the bottle on one of the tables near him and Jax.

" 'Spose so."

Before Chas could answer, Axe came into the great room and said, "Church. Now." He walked out of the room. Scraping metal on concrete and the shuffle of boots across the floor were the only sounds audible as the members made their way to the meeting room.

Inside the room, Banger sat at the head of the big wood table with Hawk to his right. It was hot from the heat of thirty members crowded in a space intended for twenty. Even though the air conditioning ran at full power and an oscillating fan blew blasts of cool air to various parts of the room, Jax sweated profusely. He was so damn nervous. He hoped the club would let him take the punishment for both him and Cherri. Thinking of what the club could do to his beautiful, sweet woman made his skin crawl.

Pounding a large gavel on the table, the noise quickly got the attention of all the men. Banger stood up and said in a loud, clear voice, "We've called emergency church to deal with a wayward brother. A brother who had our trust until he betrayed the brotherhood for some bitch he was fucking. I know we're all shocked, disappointed, and fuckin' mad. We gave this brother the title of Sergeant-At-Arms to show how we trusted our club's safety in his capable hands." Banger paused, took a long draw on his beer, then looked at each brother in the room except for Jax.

Jax hung his head.

"So, what are we gonna do with this brother? What the fuck do you all suggest?" Banger sat down and waited for the outburst of opinions from the club members.

"Throw his ass out!" several members yelled.

"Beat his ass and pull a train on his bitch," one of the older members said in a hard, cold voice.

Have Cherri pull a train with all the brothers? No fuckin' way. I'll kill anyone who fuckin' goes near her, let alone touches her.

After ten minutes of yelling, fist-banging, and cussing, Banger said, "We're gonna take a vote, but let's hear from the asshole." Boring a hole in him, Banger said, "What the fuck do you have to say for yourself?"

Jax stood up, threw his shoulders back, and his imposing figure broadcast the message *don't fuck with me.* He turned toward the faces he had known and loved since he was a kid, and said, "I'm not gonna make excuses for my actions. What I did was wrong. I know I shoulda come to Banger or Hawk and told 'em what the fuck Cherri did, but I didn't. I can't change that. I thought I could get to her before anyone found out the money was missing, then—"

"What the fuck you're sayin' isn't helpin' you, asshole! The fuckin' point here is not whether we woulda known or not known the money was missin'. The point is your loyalty was with the brotherhood, not with some cunt you've been fuckin' and wanting to protect. Your first order of protection is with the brotherhood, you piece of shit!" Throttle bent over the table, his finger pointing at Jax, red-faced as rage spewed from him. Several brothers whistled and clapped as he spoke.

Jax stood still, his arms crossed over his chest. Knowing his brothers were pissed made him humble. He honestly couldn't say he wouldn't be cheering Throttle on if the tables were turned and he sat in judgment of a brother who betrayed the club.

"Let's keep it down. We're all pissed, but we owe Jax something. Fuck, his old man was patched before most of us were born. Some of you, like Skeeter, Bear, Chuckles, and Dew—you all knew Jax's old man." Hawk narrowed his eyes as he looked at Jax.

"Sounds like you're standin' up for what he did, Hawk. You letting your feelings override your duties as vice president of the club?" Throttle threw Hawk a challenging stare, and it was not lost on Jax.

Before Hawk could respond, Jax said, "I know I did wrong. I let pussy and tits take over my head and made a shitty choice. I fucked up big-time on my judgment, but I didn't use Insurgents money—I used my own to replace the money Cherri took. You see Cherri as a bitch or whore I fuck, but she's not. She's my old lady. I'm asking you to remember all the times I had your backs, all the times I fought and killed for the club. I want you to remember my old man, and how I grew up with the Insurgents. Fuck, I don't know how to be anything else but an Insurgent. The club, the brotherhood, all of it is my identity—it's in my blood, but I'll take whatever you decide to give me."

The silence was so thick, a knife could cut through it. Standing up again, Banger wiped his hands on his faded jeans. "It's time we talk 'bout this and take a vote." Glancing at Jax with a hard, steely look, he said, "Get out. We'll call you when we've reached a decision."

Jax strode out of the room, giving an air of confidence even though his insides were lurching. In the great room, he plopped in one of the padded chairs, stretching his legs out in front of him. Taking out his phone, he glanced at it and saw there were four unread messages. He opened them up. They were all from Cherri:

Cherri: Hey, just checking to make sure you're ok. What's going on?

Cherri: You probably can't talk, but I wanted to make sure to tell you I love you.

Jax's lips twitched as he read the text. Smiling, he reread it a few times before he opened her other two.

Cherri: Now I'm getting a little nervous. Can you just text me anything so I know you're good?

Cherri: Jax, I'm scared. I'm so fucking scared. Text me. Are you ok?

Reading her last text, Jax heard the desperation in her mind. If he didn't respond, she'd be sitting all afternoon scared out of her wits, thinking of all the worst things possible.

Jax: It's ok. Just waiting to hear their decision. Worst case—I'm out of the club.

A few seconds later, Jax's screen blinked, telling him Cherri responded:

Cherri: *What's the best case?*

Jax: *My ass gets a beating.*

Cherri: *You call that good? What kind of men are your brothers?*

Jax: *Fucking good brothers—the best.*

Hawk's low, deep voice startled him. "Let's go. We've made our decision."

Jax: *Gotta go. They've voted. Later. Love you.*

As he entered the meeting room, all eyes were on him. Banger nodded to the chair to his left and watched as Jax sat down. "We've come to a unanimous decision. You said earlier that no harm was done, but a lot of harm has been done by your actions. You lost our trust. Since I've been in the club, no bitch—old lady or whore—ever came between brothers. Your woman stole from us, and under normal circumstances, she'd either be eating dirt or having to wear a burka to cover her acid scars. Since you've claimed her and she had a history with our departed brother, Gunner, you can choose to either take her punishment as well as yours, or just take yours, and we'll take care of her."

Without hesitation, Jax said, "I'll take the fall for her."

With pursed lips, Banger nodded and glanced at Hawk. Leveling his eyes at Jax, anger mixed with regret shimmered in his eyes as Jax met his gaze. Hawk said, "Your rank as Sergeant-At-Arms is stripped. We'll remove the patch from your jacket and cut. You're still in the club, even though you should be thrown out, but your past loyalty and your dad's history with the club saved your fuckin' pussy ass. Since you want to take your punishment and your woman's, you'll be taken out to the barn behind the compound for a double beat-down by all the members."

Hawk nodded to Axe who took out his switchblade, and in three swift moves, Jax's Sergeant-At-Arms patches were cut off.

Giving out a long sigh, Jax's chin dropped to his chest as he stared vacantly while his head felt like it was spinning. Shame colored his cheeks and shrouded him, and he didn't dare look at any of the brothers.

Several minutes later, Banger said, "Get your sorry ass outside." Jax stood up, still avoiding any eye contact with his brotherhood, and shuffled to the barn out back.

Inside, the building was quite large and sunlight filtered through the slats in the walls, making the shards look like swords. The brothers lined up in a row, fifteen on each side. A club beat-down cast the brothers in the role of fighters. The member who was to be beaten couldn't fight back. He could fend off blows by lifting up his arms to lessen them, but he couldn't throw a punch or do anything to fight back. It was a brutal form of punishment bestowed on brothers who fucked up, but still proved to be valuable enough to stay in the club.

Standing in the beginning of the line, Jax's mouth was dry and the sweat under his arms soaked his t-shirt. Banger gave the signal by lifting his arm and bringing it down, like the flagman at a car race. When Jax stepped in, one of the brothers landed a full-on punch on Jax's ear, and he immediately felt the warm trickle of blood oozing from it. As more punches landed on his face, blood started pooling in his mouth and spurting from his nose. Vicious punches, kicks, slams, and stomps assaulted his body. As the brothers beat the shit out of him, they cursed and screamed, "Fuckin' asshole!" or "Was her cunt worth it? Think your pussy ass can take more?"

As he neared the end of the line, Banger and Hawk each took their turn. Turning his bruised and battered face toward Hawk, he could barely see out of his swollen eyes. From his bleary vision, he saw Hawk's fist come smashing into his jaw. The force of it sent him on his knees, and he collapsed on the floor, facedown, dirt and splinters smashed against his lips and teeth. With his steel-toed boot, Banger kicked him hard in the side. The pain was excruciating and numbing, and he thought he heard a crack, but he wasn't sure. All he could see was dirt, and even it faded as he passed out.

Coming to, every inch of Jax ached, even his hair. Rubbing his hand under him, the coolness of the sheets soothed him. Figuring he must be in his room at the clubhouse, he tried to see out of his nearly swollen-shut eyes. Not much luck-all he saw were pinpricks of light and movement from dark silhouettes. He hurt something awful. From the other side of the room, he heard Hawk's voice.

"Call his woman to come here and take care of him. He's breathing funny, so call Doc Jenkins and tell him to hurry his ass. He needs to bandage up Jax, but that's all. We don't want him to have anything that'll knock him out."

"Sure thing," Chas said as he reached for his phone.

After Hawk left the room, Chas whispered in Jax's ear, "Fuck, man, you're in a bad way. I'm gonna call Cherri, then the doc. Fuck, I hope you think her ass was worth all this."

Fuck, yeah, she's worth it. Jax tried to vocalize his thoughts, but his split and bruised lips were swollen shut, and when he tried to break through the dried blood sealing them, the pain was too much. He didn't want Cherri to see him like this, but he couldn't tell anyone that, and even if he could, he knew the brotherhood wouldn't give a damn what he wanted at this point. For the next several years, he was going to have to work hard to get their trust back. *Fuck.*

A couple of hours later, Jax woke up to the coolness of a cloth on his forehead, and the soft, warm lips of his woman on his battered face. Wetness fell on his wounds as she loomed over him, and he hated that she was crying after seeing him like this. Every time he breathed, a sharp pain stabbed his sides, causing his head to pound harder. Knowing Cherri was there comforted him, and he let her soothe and take care of him as he drifted into oblivion.

Fighting back the bile in her throat, Cherri stared at Jax's broken and bloody body on the bed. Gently applying a cool cloth on his forehead, she took another washcloth and started cleaning the dried blood all over his bruised and cut face. As she did so, Jax moaned in his sleep. A burning heat flushed through her body as she ground her teeth, trying to stop the tears which kept escaping from her eyes. Horrified at the condition Jax was in, Cherri cleaned him up and bandaged his cuts, but from the way he was breathing, she knew he needed more than bandages and alcohol wipes.

As she listened to his labored breathing, her mouth went dry and her heart raced. *Where the fuck is the doctor? Fuck, Jax could die.*

Running out of Jax's room, she slammed head-on into Banger. Rubbing her head, she said, "Sorry... I didn't see you there." Recognizing the MC president, her eyes became cold and flinty as she stared at him. "Jax is beat-up bad and needs medical attention. I can't fuckin' believe what you did to one of your own. Fuck, it was barbaric. Where the hell is the doctor?"

Staring at her, his blue eyes cold and flat, Banger said, "There's one coming. Jax knew the consequences, and he took the beating for betraying the club and for your stealing ass." Leaning in close, Banger said in a menacing voice, "If you ever fuck the club again, no one, not even Jax, will be able to save your pretty ass. Count yourself real lucky on this one."

"Banger, I'm sorry about everything. I swear, I would've paid back every penny. I was just so desperate to get out of town. I didn't care about me, but I was terrified McFahey would take my daughter, and I'd never see her again. I didn't mean for any of this to happen. I feel so bad seeing Jax like he is. I fucked up, but I didn't do it for greed. I did it for the love of my daughter." Placing her hands over her face, she sniffled as her breath hitched.

"You did fuck up, but I can't say I don't understand *why* you did it. I got a daughter, too, and I'd kill for her, so I get what made you do it. Next time shit comes at you, you fuckin' take it up with the club, or Jax. Don't be making decisions against the club. Now that Jax has claimed you and you're his old lady, you owe the MC respect and loyalty. No more of this shit. If we can't trust you, then you'll have to take your ass outta here. Do you understand me?" Banger held her gaze until she looked down.

"Yes, of course. I'm not proud of what I did, and I'll never do anything ever again to make the club not trust me. I promise."

"You better damn well keep that promise 'cause if there's ever a next time, it won't turn out so well. You got my drift?" Banger's voice was low.

Nodding, Cherri said, "You'll always be able to trust me. Jax is suffering because of me. Can you please help him?"

"His wimp ass will be just fine. He's suffering 'cause he fucked up big-time. He knew what he was doing. Fuck, he grew up in this life— knows it like the back of his hand—and he fuckin' betrayed the club. Nah, his ass needs to hurt for a bit. A lot of the brothers think he got off easy."

"I just hate seeing him like this. I hate how he's in so much pain. He's really hurt, and I don't want something real bad to happen to him." Cherri's voice cracked as the tears escaped from the corner of her eyes.

Watching her tears run down, Banger's face softened a bit. "As I said, doc's already been called. He'll be here soon." Banger turned around and walked away, disappearing around the corner of the hallway.

Blinking rapidly, Cherri wiped her running nose with the palm of her hand. Rushing back into Jax's room, Cherri breathed easier when she saw him sitting up, even though he clenched his left side.

Sitting next to him on the bed, she moved the hair off his drenched forehead. "How do you feel?"

In a low, raspy voice, he said, "Like fuckin' shit. Damn, my left side is killing me. I think my ribs are cracked or broken." He grimaced when he shifted his weight.

Fighting back her tears, Cherri whispered, "Oh, baby, I'm so sorry for causing you all this pain. I fuck everything up."

Lifting himself up more, he yelled, "Ow, fuck!" then he settled down, streams of sweat running down his face. "I'm in pain 'cause I betrayed the club and got what I deserved. I made a bad choice, and the brothers were right in beating the shit outta me. Enough said. I'll heal, and our life will go on. Fuck, you're the best thing that's ever happened in my life. I love you." Grunting in pain as he leaned forward, he fell back against the headboard, exhausted from the effort.

Before she could say anything, a knock on the open door stopped her. Turning around, she saw a man in his fifties standing in the doorway. With a curt nod, he said, "I'm the doctor." Walking toward the bed, he motioned Cherri to move. She got up and let him examine Jax. "You want to stick around while I stitch and patch him up?" he asked as he threw a sideways glance at her.

"Stitch him up? Is he in a bad way? I mean, he looks horrible."

Opening up his medical bag and laying out his instruments, the doctor answered, "He'll live. He's got some cuts that need stitching, some bandages and ointment can handle the others, and from the sound of his breathing, he's got a few broken ribs, and possibly a bruised or collapsed lung."

Gasping, Cherri clutched her aching stomach to keep from vomiting.

"It sounds worse than it is. I'll get him on the path to recovery." Diverting his attention to Jax, the medicine man said, "You're going to be in a lot of pain for about two weeks, but you should heal okay. I was told not to give you anything for the pain."

"What? That's fuckin' crazy! You gotta give him some pain meds," Cherri yelled.

"Just doing what I was told. So, you want to stay and watch?"

Before Cherri answered, Jax said in a heavy voice, "Go on and get out, sugar. I'll be fine."

Going over to the other side of the bed, she leaned over and kissed him gently on the forehead then dropped her mouth to his ear. "I love you madly," she whispered as she squeezed his hand. She left the room quickly, not wanting Jax to see or hear her crying.

After going downstairs, she went into the great room. The moment she came into the room, a silence fell all around her, making her uncomfortable. "What the fuck are you doin' in here?" one of the members asked in a hard voice.

"Waiting for the doc to fix Jax," she said, defiance shining in her blue eyes.

Grumbling echoed around her, and she held up her hand to silence them. When they stopped bitching, she said, "What happened to Jax is club business, and I'm not here to take it apart. I *am* here to take my man home to nurse him as he heals. I don't give a fuck if you want me to or not. He's comin' home tonight, and I need a couple of you to help me get him in my car. Are there any volunteers?"

Looking at the stony-faced men, Cherri threw up her hands in exasperation. Deciding she'd have to manage on her own, she started walking toward the front door but before she reached it, Chas blocked her way. She met his look, with her chin tilted high in the air and her shoulders pushed back while a fluttery feeling consumed her chest. "You gonna fight me on this?" she said in a challenging voice.

"Nah, just gonna help you get him in the car," Chas said.

Axe stepped forward. "Let's go up and get him so we can haul his busted ass outta here."

As the two members made their way upstairs, two other brothers, PJ and Jerry, stood by the doorway, waiting for Jax to be brought down.

After about an hour, Chas and Axe came down, supporting Jax's weight with an arm around his waist. Stumbling, Jax cursed as each bump or misstep made his battered body ache. Watching him come toward her, Cherri thought he looked like Frankenstein with all the bandages and stitches. As the guys dragged him past her, she reached out and stroked his cheek. A tiny smile played on his stitched lip.

The four men helped get Jax in the car then followed Cherri home so they could help him upstairs into her room. After they had the patient settled in, they left the house. They never said one word to Jax or to Cherri.

he door behind them, Cherri sprinted upstairs to the bath-
з her emergency stash of Hydrocodone, she grabbed a glass
..ater, went into the bedroom, and gave the pills to Jax.

"I'm taking care of you, baby, and I'm not gonna let you suffer. You took the beatin', and that's enough. I'll stick with you until you're a hundred percent healed." Cradling his head in her lap, she stroked his hair until the pills took effect and he fell asleep.

CHAPTER THIRTY-TWO

One month later

THE WARM GLOW of colorful trees lit up the landscape of a quaint, residential neighborhood as Jax slowed his Harley down. Cherri, hands splayed across his chiseled stomach, took in the brick houses set back on manicured lawns lined with large elm and blue spruce trees. The ruffling wind scattered the bold red and orange leaves down the sidewalks. As Jax stopped in front of a two-story brick house with a massive porch, Cherri wondered who they were visiting. She'd never been to this part of Pinewood Springs. She knew the area—it was the nicer part of town, but she never had an occasion to go there. Looking at the house, she noticed it was set back from the street, and the front yard had a weeping willow tree on the left and a big shady elm tree on the right. Both trees were ablaze in a tapestry of vivid color.

Jax killed the ignition then hopped off the bike. Holding out his hand, Cherri grasped it and, while getting off the Harley, she asked, "What're we doin' here? You got business with some folks here?"

"Wanted to see how you like this house." His boyish grin melted her heart.

When they arrived at the front door, Jax put a key in the lock and the large wood and stained glass door swung open. Pulling Cherri inside, Jax closed the door behind them. A sweeping staircase showcased the large foyer and emphasized the tall ceilings. Tugging her along, they entered a large living room then a dining room before going into a beautifully rendered gourmet kitchen, which opened into a family room replete with a large stone fireplace. An office and a bathroom finished the first floor. The second floor had four bedrooms and three full

herri loved the feel of the house, a cozy ambiance
ivorite blanket. The finished basement with a
ge backyard complete with a playset finished off

..... do you think?" Jax asked.

"It's beautiful. I love it. It has a real homey feel. To me, it gives off good vibes."

"Would you like to live here?"

"Who wouldn't? Maybe someday. It's good to have dreams and goals."

Drawing her flush to him, Jax buried his head in her soft hair and said, "Sweetness, this *is* our house. I put an offer in a few days ago, and it was accepted. I wanted to surprise you." Cupping her chin in his hand, he bent down and kissed her full lips.

Cherri shuffled a couple of steps backward as her hands flew up to her cheeks and she squealed. "This is *ours*? I don't believe it. *Ours*?" Looking around incredulously, her skin tingled as a warm heat radiated through her body.

As the reality of the situation filled her, she crossed her arms around her chest, looked downward, and tried to hide the tears which had been welling in her eyes since Jax told her he bought the house *for them*.

"You okay, sugar? You cool with this?"

Not able to talk, she nodded while she wiped the tears from her face with her hand.

"Come over here." Jax's comforting arms wrapped her close to his, her head pillowing against his broad chest. Kissing the top of her head, he squeezed her closer to him. "I'm glad you're happy. You and Paisley deserve to be happy."

Softly, she said, "You don't think it's too big?"

"Fuck no, sweetness. I can't wait to give Paisley brothers and sisters. You want that, right?"

Overcome, she kissed his shoulder. "I want that very much," she whispered. "I love you so much."

"That's good, sugar, 'cause I'm nuts about you." Hugging he[r], his hand slip down to pat her ass. "You know, I've never been i[n] with a woman before, so this is all new to me."

Smiling, she looked up at him through shimmering eyes. "That's just fine, 'cause I've never loved a man before. I guess we're both new at this."

"Fuck, yeah. We'll just have to learn how to do this together. As long as we have each other's back, sweetness, we have nothing to worry about."

Looping her arm around his neck, she yanked his mouth close to hers, capturing his soft, sexy lips. Responding, he kissed her back, hot and deep and wet.

I'm where I was always meant to be.

Six weeks later

"THAT'S THE LAST of it," Jax said as he and Chas loaded his computer on the truck. Earlier, they had packed up the girls' things. Cherri, chasing Paisley around the yard, flashed Jax a big smile. *Damn, she's beautiful. I never get tired of looking at her. Fuck, she always makes my cock wake up.*

"You ready to roll?" Chas asked, interrupting Jax's thoughts.

"Yeah. Cherri, grab Paisley and let's go." Jax walked back into the clubhouse to make sure he didn't forget anything. Seeing Hawk and Banger, he came up to them and gripped their shoulders.

"You leavin' now?" Hawk asked.

"Yeah. When we get settled, we'll have a house party. Cherri's been planning it ever since we closed on the house. You know how women are."

"That I do." Hawk laughed.

"Be strange not having you 'round all the time. You been here since you were in high school," Banger said. "But it's time to be on your own with your own family."

"Yeah, I never thought I'd fall for a woman so hard," Jax said as he kneaded his neck.

"Fuck, tell me about it. I never thought of taking an old lady, and look at me, planning a wedding with Cara. It happens when you least expect it." Jerking Jax into a bear hug, Hawk said, "Take care of yourself. If you need anything, call me. We're all here for you."

Hugging him back, Jax said, "I know. Thanks, man."

"Your ass better be here for church tomorrow. And we got the rally next Saturday." Banger's face was tight, but his blue eyes twinkled.

"I'm moving in with my old lady, but fuck, the club is my family, too." He nodded at them then turned to leave. Looking over his shoulder, he said, "See you tomorrow."

Hawk and Banger tilted their chins as they brought their beers to their mouths.

Outside, the autumn breeze kneaded the patchwork of colored leaves as they shivered slightly. Fluffy fleece clouds drifted across the blue sky and the golden rays of the sun warmed the small group loading the truck. Tangy smokiness wafted in the air as the old ladies prepared the club's barbecue dinner.

"You coming back for food?" Chas asked.

"Nah, we'll catch it another time. We got a ton of shit to do." Jax slammed the truck's back door shut. Leaning in close to Chas, Axe, and Jerry, he said, "Fuck, I never figured I'd be the first to get hitched outta us." Throwing a glance at Chas, he said, "Now it's your turn, man."

With his hands up in the air, Chas laughed. "Fuck, no. I'm still reeling from my divorce with that bitch. Believe me; it's not in my plan. I like being single—easy pussy any time I want it with no strings attached. Fuck, it's the way to go."

"Ain't that the truth." Jerry chuckled.

Axe nodded while taking a hit on a joint.

Putting his arms around the three of them, Jax said in a low voice, "Everything work out okay with McFahey and that other shit?"

Jerry, grinning, said, "No worries, dude. Everything is cool. Me, Axe, PJ, Throttle, and Ruben took care of it. There won't be any bodies found. Ever. The fuckin' badges are stumped on McFahey's disappearance. It helped that he was such a fuckin' crook, 'cause they've dug up all kinds of shit on him. Everyone thinks he left 'cause shit was 'bout to hit the fan. It's fine by us." He threw his head back and let out a large belly laugh then, before Jax asked, he said, "Peaches had no one, so she won't be missed."

A satisfied smile spread across Jax's face. "Good. Okay, guess we're ready to head out. After we unload, we can christen the place with beer."

Clapping his hand on Jax's shoulder, Chas said, "Axe is gonna help you. I gotta go. Gotta pick up my son at the library. Brianna's supposed to do it, but she just texted me she's too busy. Bet she's fuckin' someone. What a shitty mom. Can't believe I ever *married* the bitch."

Shaking his head, Jax said, "Thanks for your help. I'll catch you later."

As they were ready to leave, the parking lot was filled with most of the brothers watching the young couple. Jax turned to everyone and said, "We're heading out, but wanted you to all know Cherri is officially an old lady. She's wearing my patch." He drew her close to him, his arm around the leather vest he gave her the previous night which bore the phrase, "Property of Jax."

Hoots and whistles rang out as Jax kissed her tenderly on her cheek. Blushing, she burrowed her face in the crook of his arm.

"Don't be shy, sugar. You're a part of me and my world."

Whispering in his ear, she said, "It's just they've seen me strip. It feels funny, that's all."

"That shit's in the past. It's done. You're happy, right?"

"Oh, yeah, babe. I'm very happy. I love you."

"Me, too," he breathed in her ear. "Let's get the fuck home so we can start adding to our family."

The End

Make sure you sign up for my newsletter so you can keep up with my new releases, special sales, free short stories, and other treats only available to newsletter readers. When you sign up, you will receive a FREE hot and steamy novella. Sign up at:

http://eepurl.com/bACCL1

Visit me on Facebook

facebook.com/Chiah-Wilder-1625397261063989

Check out my other books at my Author Page

amazon.com/author/chiahwilder

Thank you!

Thank you for reading my book. I hope you enjoyed the second book in the Insurgents MC series as much as I enjoyed writing Cherri and Jax's story. This rough motorcycle club has a lot more to say, so I hope you will look for the upcoming books in the series. Romance makes life so much more colorful, and a rough, sexy bad boy makes life a whole lot more interesting.

If you enjoyed the book, please consider leaving a review on Amazon. I read all of them and appreciate the time taken out of busy schedules to do that.

I love hearing from my fans, so if you have any comments or questions, please email me at chiahwilder@gmail.com or visit my facebook page.

To hear of **new releases**, **special sales**, **free short stories**, and **ARC opportunities**, please sign up for my **Newsletter** at http://eepurl.com/bACCL1.

A big thank you to my readers whose love of stories and words enables authors to continue weaving stories. Without the love of words, books wouldn't exist.

Happy Reading,

Chiah

CHAS'S FERVOR

Book 3 in the Insurgents MC Series

Available Now!

The first time Chas saw his son's teacher, he wanted her in his bed.

Chas, the hardened, tattooed member of the Insurgents Motorcycle Club, has sworn off women since his divorce left him bitter and jaded. The last thing he wants to do is settle down with another old lady.

His relationships now are easy and free—exactly the way he likes it.

Until he meets curvaceous Addie. The sexy redhead whose eyes set him on fire.

He has to have her between his sheets.

And he knows she wants him. Eyes don't lie.

Addie O'Leary has lusted after her student's dad ever since she saw him.

She has guarded her heart and her life for the last two years. Now Chas, the muscular, dirty-mouthed, rugged outlaw biker threatens to tear down all her barriers.

Always loving the bad boy, Chas is a dangerous badass with an attitude *and* an outlaw MC. His charming smile pulls at Addie's heart and his chiseled chest makes her body overheat.

Carrying around a deep, dark secret, Addie is afraid her past will destroy her future. Chas seems to be her only hope for redemption. Will he be able to intervene before it's too late?

Chas knows Addie is hiding something. He makes it his mission to find out what it is, and, once he does, he'll claim her as his woman.

Excerpt

CHAS'S FERVOR

PROLOGUE

LIZZIE QUINN WASHED her hands again, but no matter how hard she scrubbed, she couldn't get the blood off her fingers. Looking under the bright lights above her bathroom mirror, she saw streaks of it filling in the grooves and ridges of her skin. There was just so much blood.

Her husband lightly knocked on the door. "Lizzie, aren't you done in there yet? You've had the water running for the past hour."

"Go away, Ian." A stray strand of golden red hair flopped in her face, and she blew it away while she continued scrubbing. She'd never be able to get rid of the blood, or the horror of what had happened. Lizzie leaned over the chrome faucet and sobbed, her tears dripping into the sink below.

Lifting her head slowly, she stared at her reflection in the mirror: redness around her puffy, green eyes made her porcelain skin appear more translucent, and the dark circles under them made her look like a stand-in for a zombie movie.

How had a beautiful summer day morphed into such evilness? If only she'd stayed home instead of following Ian earlier that day. It'd been Lizzie's suspicions of him having an affair which had coaxed her out into the white sunlight, making her duck into alleyways, bushes, and storefronts to avoid detection.

When Ian had entered a large, two-story brick house in a genteel, suburban neighborhood, Lizzie figured her hunches had been right.

She'd stood before the bright red door, battling with whether she should go in or leave. She'd decided to go in and catch her cheating husband in the act. Lizzie had turned the doorknob then stepped into the marble foyer, frigid air from the air conditioner washing over her as she'd listened for sounds of betrayal. Nothing. The silence had been deafening.

Then she'd heard it—a loud *swoosh*, like the winter wind, followed by a gurgle somewhere to the right of her. Walking down the large entry, she'd entered the kitchen, and shock slapped her in the face: Ian calmly opened a large plastic bag, placing a bloodied hunting knife in it. Lizzie looked from Ian to a woman in her thirties who was crumpled on the hardwood floor as pools of red pulsed around her, soaking into her white cotton dress. The woman's eyes were dull and lifeless like two blue marbles, sucking Lizzie into the dark, sunken holes. And as much as she'd wanted to tear her gaze away from the lifelessness of them, Lizzie couldn't.

"What in the *fuck* are you doing here?"

Startled, she'd turned and caught Ian's icy stare. Shaking her head, she'd padded over to the collapsed woman and knelt down, taking the lifeless hand in hers—the skin still warm.

"What's going on here? We have to call 911." She'd glanced back at Ian, and his stone-cold indifference had frozen Lizzie to the spot.

"We're not calling anyone."

"But she's dead," she'd whispered.

"I know, that's the point." With precision, Ian had placed the wrapped knife in his briefcase, and Lizzie noticed he wore gloves.

Wide-eyed, she'd gasped. "You *wanted* to kill her? Why? Who is she?"

"I don't know. I'm not paid to get to know the targets, just to eliminate them. You shouldn't have come here. You've left all kinds of evidence." Snapping his briefcase shut, Ian had straightened his tie and walked toward the backdoor. "You've made a mess of things, Lizzie."

"I'm going to call the police." Dialing the number on her phone, she'd stopped when Ian rushed over.

By the way he'd gripped her arm, bruises would be inevitable. In a low, hard-edged voice, he'd said, "You won't call the police unless you want to be arrested. Your finger and footprints are all over the place. Your hands are covered in blood, as well as your clothes. Unless you want to spend the rest of your life in prison, you'll go home, clean up, and decide where you want to go for dinner tonight. Do you understand?"

With a fallen face, she'd nodded, numbness overtaking her.

"Good. I'll be home later. I'd give you a goodbye kiss, but I can't chance any contamination from you." At that, he'd left the house, closing the back door quietly.

After he'd gone, Lizzie had leaped up and rushed over to the kitchen sink to wash her hands. With trembling lips, her racing mind told her to go to the police, but Ian's words haunted her. He was right—her finger and footprints were everywhere. The only thing she could do was run. Run far and run fast.

ANOTHER KNOCK ON the door brought Lizzie back to the present.

"Open up now, we have to talk."

Dreading seeing him, she dried her hands and turned the doorknob. Ian stood just outside the door, a scowl on his lean, smooth face. As he grabbed her arm, she yanked it away and brushed past him, walking to the floor-to-ceiling windows which gave a beautiful view of the Chicago cityscape.

When he came behind her and put his arms on her shoulders, she shrugged them off.

"We need to talk," he said in a low voice.

"Do we?"

"Don't be like that. Why don't you get dressed in something nice and we can go out to La Petite Maison—your favorite restaurant. We can talk there. Does that sound good?" He placed his thin, cold lips on her neck, making her shudder. "I have a quick errand I have to run, but I'll be back in less than two hours. Be ready." A thin thread of danger weaved through his voice.

Nodding curtly, Lizzie leaned her head on the cool window and looked out at Lake Michigan. From the penthouse, the sunbathers, joggers, and sailboats looked like mere dots in a vast landscape painting.

Ian's heels clacked on the marble floors as he walked out. After she heard the front door close, she waited fifteen minutes, staring at the dots below, not daring to move. When he didn't return, she dashed to the closet and took out her suitcases. Lizzie threw only the necessities in them then pocketed the wad of cash Ian had in the wall safe. With suitcases, cash, purse, and keys, she left her penthouse condominium. Having no clue where she was going, she decided to grab a cab and take a train out of the city. She'd have to reinvent herself, but she didn't have any idea how to do that. The only two things she knew for certain were that she wasn't going to go to prison for something she didn't do, and she had to flee from Ian.

Ian, the man she loved and married two years before, for better or for worse, was a paid assassin, and blood money bought everything they owned—cars, the condo, her clothes, *everything*.

Looking out of the cab as the city streets whizzed by, she made a decision—Lizzie Quinn would disappear forever.

CHAPTER ONE

Two years later
Pinewood Springs, CO

LOOKING AT THE clock on the wall, Addie fumed as she saw the hands read five o'clock. The eight-year-old boy seated next to her at the reading table tried to act as though he didn't care that his mother was forty-five minutes late picking him up.

It had been a few weeks since Jack had joined the pilot reading group. Addie had liked him instantly. The young boy was so eager to learn and in just the short time he'd been in the program, he'd shown some marked improvements. Addie had five students in her after-school program at the library. As head librarian, she'd been able to put the program together, and if she could prove its success to the city board, she could obtain funding for future sessions.

Jack's big, brown eyes looked down at his hands as he rubbed them over and over. A slight tremble made his lower lip shake, and his dark brown bangs fell down past his forehead into his eyes. Picking up the phone, Addie called Jack's mother for the umpteenth time, and again, the call went straight to voicemail. Addie left a message much more curt than her previous ones on the mother's answering machine.

"I don't think my mom's coming," Jack mumbled as he looked down at his hands.

In a soft voice, Addie said, "Oh, I'm sure she just got tied up. She's probably rushing to get here, but in case she's running very late, I should call your father and see if he can pick you up instead."

A smile cracked over Jack's face. "Yeah, he'll come get me."

As she began to dial the number she had in Jack's file, a jangle of chains and the loud clack of footsteps on the linoleum floor made her look up from her task. Coming toward the reading table was a tall, lean, muscular man. Dark brown hair fell in long layers a little bit past his collar bone, and his black eyes shone like well-polished quartz. A strong jaw and high cheekbones were covered by his five o'clock shadow. His legs were powerful, every corded muscle emphasized by the tight denim covering them, and his fitted black t-shirt showed off a finely sculpted chest. He exuded confidence, power, and blatant sex. Staring at him, she was rendered speechless, and his commanding presence and sensual angles of his handsome face captivated her. After glancing briefly at her, he rushed over to Jack, bent down, and ran his hand through Jack's dark hair. Jack looked up at him, smiling, while tears brimmed in his eyes.

Crouching down, Chas put a large hand on his boy's shoulder, moving Jack closer to him.

"Hey, little buddy, what's wrong? Why're you all upset?"

"He thought his parents forgot about picking him up," Addie said as she stood up and crossed her arms over her ivory blouse.

Ignoring her, Chas hugged his son. Circling his small arms around his dad's neck, Jack hid his face.

"You know I'd never forget you, right, buddy? Your mom called me just fifteen minutes ago telling me to pick you up, that's all."

In a hitched voice, Jack asked, "Why didn't Mom come? She knew she was supposed to pick me up after the reading circle."

"At four-fifteen, forty-five minutes ago," Addie interjected as she went to the table and leaned against it.

"I'm aware of the time. I learned how to tell time when I was in grade school. I don't need you telling me what I already know." He threw her a sideways glare then focused his attention back on his son.

"Apparently, you weren't a very good learner," she muttered under her breath, but the way he stiffened his back led her to believe he had overheard her.

"Your mom had something unexpected come up. She called me, and here I am. You know one of us will always be around to pick you up, right?"

Jack nodded slowly.

"Okay, so all's good now, right?"

"Yeah. Am I going home on the hog?" Jack's eyes lit up, the fear in them gone since his dad was there.

"You bet."

Standing up, Chas turned to stare at Addie full-on, a look of surprise crossing over his face. Pushing back on his black engineer boots, his dark gaze moved up her body, lingering on her curvy hips—accentuated by her pencil skirt—then brazenly rested on her chest for several seconds before stopping on her rose-tinted cheeks. Heat flushed against her fair and lightly freckled skin, making it blush pink as he blatantly checked her out.

Flustered, she walked over to one of the bookcases and pretended to straighten a book. Regaining her composure, she turned around and looked him straight on. "Jack was scared not knowing when he'd be picked up. I phoned your wife several times and left many messages, but she never picked up."

Jutting out his jaw, he narrowed his eyes and said, "She's my ex, and I'm here now, so it's all good." Giving her the once-over again, he walked up to her, leaving barely a few inches between them. "What did you say your name was?"

Black eyes under perfectly shaped eyebrows bored into her. White teeth flashed when his lips curled into a smile. In his right ear, a silver Celtic cross earring dangled and swung when he moved his head. Trying to create some space between her and his imposing figure, she flattened her back against the rows of books behind her. A sliver of satisfaction gleamed in his eyes, as her discomfort was transparent.

Tilting her chin up in defiance, she looked at him pointedly and said, "Ms. O'Leary. Please, don't take any offense, it's just I worry about the kids and how they feel when parents are late, or when they don't know where their parents are. Jack was very scared he'd been forgotten."

"And you're the teacher?"

"I'm the librarian, but I engage in the after-school reading group your son is in. Since he's started, he's doing quite well."

"I'm the boy's father, Chas. Nice meeting you." Extending his hand, she grasped it and small electric currents tingled against her skin. Blinking, her green eyes locked onto his coal black ones, and for a moment the current connected them. As the heat rose up her neck, she pulled away, looking sideways as her embarrassment colored her face. *What is the matter with me? I'm acting like I've never seen a good-looking guy. Dammit.* Chiding herself for her absolute lack of professionalism, she glanced back to his face. He smirked, moved away from her, and went up to his son.

"Were you scared, buddy?"

"No, I knew it was okay." Jack grinned, exposing two front spaces from his recently lost teeth—it made his dad laugh.

Messing up the top of his son's hair, he winked and drew the kid close to him, giving him an extra hug. "That's my boy."

Watching this tall, mean-looking man display such overt affection to his son touched Addie. His good looks, badass attitude, and tats peeking out from under his t-shirt also touched her, but in a very different way. Drooling inwardly, she couldn't help but imagine what his large hands would feel like on her skin. Not believing how his mere presence could place her body in overdrive, she shook her head, trying to dispel thoughts of her student's father. How could she even think about his hands running over her, or his full lips kissing her in places she had never been kissed? *For God's sake, he's off-limits. Dunk your head in a fucking bucket of ice water, Addie. He's Jack's dad. You can't be doing this.*

"Why don't you meet me at the Harley, okay, champ? I'll be there in a few minutes. We can get dinner and ice cream before we head home."

"Oh, boy, Dad. That's great." A pink blush dusted his cheeks as his eyes shone. Looking at his teacher, he said, "I'll see you tomorrow afternoon, Ms. O'Leary." Scooping up his backpack, he dashed off.

"Wait, Jack, you forgot your book for tomorrow." Addie started after him when a strong arm pulled her back. Startled, she lost her footing and fell back against something hard and solid. Whirling around, she stared into the chiseled face of Jack's father. "Oh," was all she could muster.

"I'll take the book and give it to him. Does he have to read it for tomorrow?" he asked in a gravelly baritone.

"What? Oh, yeah… I mean no… I mean he has to read some of it." She turned away before he saw her cheeks flushing a bright red. She hated her fair skin because it revealed every emotion she was feeling.

A deep chuckle rose from the depths of his throat. "I didn't mean to make you nervous, but I like that you *are* bothered by me."

"You didn't make me nervous, nor am I *bothered* by you. I'm tired because I had to wait for an errant parent to pick up his son." With her back to him, she went over to the reading table to gather the strewn books she'd have to re-shelve before she left.

A large hand grasped her fleshy arm like a vise. "Don't ever fuckin' call me an errant parent again. What the shit do you know about me? Also, don't chew me out in front of my son again." Flashing eyes scanned her taut face. "And I don't give a shit if you *are* his teach. You wanna say something to me, say it when he's not around. You got that?"

His scorching hand on her skin unnerved her, and tiny shivers traveled from her stomach to her inner thighs. Mad at herself for her body's response, she jerked her arm out of his grasp and faced him. "Don't bully me. I'm not in the mood to debate your family situation. I felt sorry for Jack because he was so forlorn and didn't think anyone was going to pick him up. My anger for that is probably misdirected at you. Please, in the future, make sure either you or your wife is on time to pick up Jack."

"It's my ex, and apology accepted, teach."

"I've had a long day, and I have to straighten up before I close the library. It was nice meeting you."

There was a feral, predatory look in his eyes as he skimmed her body. He took her hand, shook it, and said, "It was nice meeting you." He leaned in close and whispered, "You look pretty when you're embarrassed." Then he winked at her and swaggered away.

With her hand still burning from where he touched it, she looked at his retreating back and noticed his leather jacket with *Insurgents* on the top and *Colorado* on the bottom, an emblem of a skull next to two smoking pistols in the middle. When he turned sideways to exit through the glass doors, she saw the diamond 1% er patch and a skull with the number 13 underneath. Throwing her a half-smile, he walked out of the library.

Addie watched him leave. She had no idea Jack's father was so gorgeous. She also didn't know he belonged to the Insurgents Motorcycle Club. A person couldn't live in Pinewood Springs and not know the Insurgents were an outlaw biker club who didn't mess around if someone got in their face. *Yeah, Jack's dad is a real badass, and from the minute he walked in, I was a bundle of nerves and excitement. What the fuck?*

Mad at herself for acting like a sixteen-year-old girl, Addie absent-mindedly touched the spot on her arm where Chas's hand had just been. The thrill that coursed through her body when he touched her left her craving for more. Never had she been so drawn to any one person as she was to Chas. Even though she knew she was entering the danger zone, she desired to see him again. *What's my problem? He's just a good-looking man with a helluva lot of sex appeal. A chick magnet, that's all.*

The loud rumble of an engine jerked her from her thoughts. When she gazed out the window, she saw Chas straddling a big-ass Harley, the streetlights bouncing off its chrome, and Jack snuggled behind him wearing a belt and helmet. The iron horse jumped forward then roared into the traffic. Leaning against the windowsill, Addie watched them until they disappeared. *I have to stay away from Jack's dad; otherwise, I'll be so screwed.*

She always went for the bad boys, and her poor parents had had their hands full when she was in high school. Trying to cure herself of the bad-boy-syndrome, she'd accepted Ian's invitation to dinner after she met him at a friend's party in her last year of college. Thinking he was the kind of guy she needed to take care of her, she was happy to tell her parents she had met a responsible man who was CEO of Minecorp—one of the largest gold companies in the world.

Shaking her head, she snorted at the irony of her life. Ian turned out to be way worse than a bad boy. A calculated killer who murdered for profit, Ian destroyed her life and put her on the run from the law and him.

It had been two years since she'd arrived in Pinewood Springs with a new name, profession, and life. Everything so far had been wonderful; she loved the small town of nine thousand people, and she adored her job and the kids she worked with. Life was peaceful for her, and she'd even begun to relax a bit and quit looking over her shoulder every time she heard a noise. Her life in Chicago seemed more and more like nothing but a bad nightmare as time passed.

The last thing she needed in her new life was a badass. Addie appreciated a handsome man with raw sex appeal, though, and it *had* been two years since she'd been with a man. As a matter of fact, Chas was the first man to have touched her since she fled from Ian. Even though Chas's contact with her body was most probably inadvertent, it seared right through her, reminding her how good it felt to have a man's touch.

As lonely as she had been over the past two years, she wasn't interested in being involved with another bad boy. She'd had her fill of them, and she was doing just fine without a man. Running the library and the pilot after-school reading program took up most of her time. She really liked the children, but her favorite—before she'd laid eyes on his sexy dad—was Jack. He was a good kid who struggled with his reading, but who never gave up—he was a bright, curious, and ambitious boy. Making a mental note to call his mother and ask her if Jack could set up one-on-one reading sessions two times a week, Addie went into her office to clean off her desk before she headed home....

Other Titles in the Series:

Hawk's Property: Insurgents Motorcycle Club Book 1
Chas's Fervor: Insurgents Motorcycle Club Book 3
Axe's Fall: Insurgents Motorcycle Club Book 4

CPSIA information can be obtained
at www.ICGtesting.com
Printed in the USA
LVOW07s0634210917
549528LV00015B/449/P